MW00982108

Liz Munro
April 5, 2012

Deadly Expectations

By Elizabeth Munro

The Chronicles of Anna
Book 1

Blue Swell Books
Nanaimo, B.C.
Canada

First Edition: February 2012
ISBN: 978-0-9878335-6-3

Visit www.elizabethmunro.ca

Chapter 1

"Anna? Where the hell are you?"

Alina. I was in trouble.

My sister was my only caller these days since Paul's last message to say he was moving on. It was barely a month since our brief intense string of occasional nights together; all but the last ending in sweat, exhaustion and staggeringly good moods.

I put a hand on my belly as I watched my late dinner turn in the microwave's yellow light. I was sure Paul left something behind that night or maybe one of the others. When didn't matter. Certainty waited in a little box in my backpack.

I didn't bother opening the microwave door when its bell went. Instead I sat at the table pulling the machine and the phone with me, nearly dropping them as my thumb found play.

"You know what day it is," her tone didn't lose any of its firmness as it came from the little speaker. "Call Dad. I already did. Don't screw it up again. I don't care how late—"

Stop.

Easy for her. Call him up from half way across the country to tell him she loved him and missed mother too. It was three hours later there so he wouldn't keep her on the phone. I had no excuse for avoiding him. Dad only lived three blocks away. She'd made it sound like she was lucky getting a position in Toronto's busiest emergency room. Truth was she was a brilliant doctor. All she had to say was 'put it over there' and they would have built a hospital around her.

I dialled. It was only nine and he'd still be up.

"John Creed."

"Dad? It's Anna."

"Hey, what's up kid?" He did a poor job of making it sound like a phone call from me wasn't a big deal.

"I …"

"Take your time, Sweetie."

I sighed as he waited.

"I want wontons Dad." They'd been Mom's favourite.

"That place up the road still in business?"

"Yeah," I answered. I was a regular there. He hadn't set foot in the door without her.

"Pick you up in ten?"

"'kay."

I gently put the phone down and dressed. My long blonde hair was still damp from the shower so I quickly put it up and pulled a knit hat over top to keep the heat in. At least it wasn't raining. It had been ten years earlier when Dad had taken his inconsolable daughters to the lone car at the far end of the hospital parking lot. In spite of the cold drops washing the tears from my face I remembered I could taste salt.

The street light at the end of my short empty driveway lit up the air I exhaled. It wasn't cold for the first week of October, but it was humid. I tipped my head back and blew a cloud straight up as I took a few steps watching it stretch and disappear behind me. When I looked forward again I saw the figure of my father on foot a block south just coming over the little rise in the road. I went to meet him.

"Something wrong with your truck?" I asked him as he gave me a quick awkward hug letting me go before I could get my hands out of my pockets to awkwardly hug him back.

"Mm mm. I only use it for work now."

We walked past my house, then a block over before getting on the road to the Chinese food place.

"It hasn't changed a bit," he commented as we got our seats. Like dinner in a jewel box Mom used to say. Gold and red lanterns hung everywhere, some waving their tassels as they caught the breeze from the ceiling fan. Dark carved wood and bold wallpaper decorated every surface. A candle in a plastic mesh covered red glass holder flickered in the middle of our table.

"Neither have you," I replied. "You look good."

That got a smile. He was still trim in spite of having an appetite like mine.

"You want a beer or something?"

I thought briefly about Paul and the lifestyle change I was nearly certain was coming. "I don't drink much these days."

"You're a good kid Anna."

"So are you Dad."

He and Mom were eighteen when Alina came along. Me less than a year later. She'd run a daycare to make ends meet while he got his

2

electrician's ticket. He was a smart hard working man and within a few years had a crew of a dozen and Mom stopped replacing kids as they left. He was forty-four now; closer in age to Paul than I was.

"I thought this would be harder you know," he said as he pushed his flat bottomed spoon around the fat wontons and singled out a piece of pork. "We spent as much here as the whole rest of the food bill. I'm glad you and Alina got her good looks. My Allison was such a pretty little thing. You were already taller than her when she passed … never expected you two to shoot up like weeds."

I nodded and wiped my cheek.

"Nearly caught up to you," I laughed. He was six foot one.

"In town long this time?"

"Mm mm," I shook my head, my mouth had a whole wonton in it. "Ride out tomorrow. A month, maybe six weeks. Got a couple of big magazine shoots booked in California. Then I'm going east through to Florida for another job."

"Still single?"

"Yeah Dad," I dropped my eyes as I felt my cheeks warm. "Boys can't catch me when all they see is my tailpipe disappearing into the sunset."

"Suppose not … sorry to pry."

"You're not," I sighed. "Some days I really need her. If I ever have kids I want to be just like her."

"I think we both know exactly how much that would please her, Sweetie."

When I looked up at him he was refolding his paper napkin before he wiped his eyes.

On the walk back I held his elbow. He didn't seem to mind and hugged me a little less awkwardly at my door. I locked up behind him as he started his quick walk home then I watched the headlines run past until exhaustion took hold and carefully walked around the discarded motorcycle gear I'd shed on my way to the shower a few hours earlier.

Sleep found me quickly, my legs shoved under the laundry pile I shared my bed with.

Chapter 2

I didn't expect to have my eyes open again until well past noon when I found myself looking up at the dark ceiling just as tired as when I'd closed them. There was nothing but the sound of my breathing for a minute and I felt myself drifting off.

A sudden thump drove out any sleepiness I had left.

"Damn it … bitch!"

3

The staccato rattle of my uncooperative door knob accentuated his swearing.

I modestly grabbed for a blanket then went for my dresser instead after realizing it would just wrap around my legs and trip me. Top drawer. Gun. Bottom drawer. Rounds. If I had a proper cabinet for the damn thing I'd have to go make coffee for my guest while he waited.

The next crash sounded like dishes then a heavy thud as my table went over. Fighting the urge to bolt to the bathroom to do something about the sudden looseness in my stomach I neared the kitchen to see the window was wide open. Table toppled over pinning a chair to the wall and broken glass on the floor.

"What the hell?" the angry voice said.

Another step and I could see a stranger struggling with the door. He was half a foot shorter than me, dirty blonde hair nearly down to his shoulders. When he turned in my direction I saw the sneer on his lips went up to his nose. The dent in his forehead matched the edge of the counter and blood ran freely down his face dripping on my floor.

The handgun went up, both hands, elbows locked. My instructor's words echoing in my ears as his phantom hand brushed my hip. "I'm not letting you leave until you hit *something*."

He froze for just a second as he took in the gun, then he charged a few steps at me waving his arms as he laughed. I fumbled with it, unable to find the fucking finger hole as he backed up and returned his attention to the knob. In a short second he had it open and was gone.

I pulled in a few weak breaths and shoved my feet in my nearby boots so I could cross the floor for the phone. My legs gave out as I backed up to the hall pushing 911. When I put the gun on the floor I noticed the trigger lock still in place. All I needed was a puddle to sit in to complete my pathetic picture.

Under the couch it went before I had to answer any questions about my lack of legal storage and the permit I likely needed for transporting it loaded from the bedroom to the kitchen.

I was weak, vulnerable, and completely alone.

It only took a few minutes to see the officers' flashlights light up the shed and trees in the backyard. The light gave me hope that what was beyond wasn't completely empty while the lingering adrenaline in my muscles bound me to the floor.

Sun exposed the little burglar's blood on my kitchen floor. My upstairs tenant Mrs. Desmond had been moving around for a while. As the coffee machine started to grumble and spit hot water into the basket I took the little box from the drugstore to the bathroom.

I had most of the night to think about exactly how late I was and realized I already was the last time I'd seen Paul. It didn't surprise me.

It just wasn't in my wiring to keep track. I'd never counted the days and hours as I worried about the repercussions of anything I'd done in the back seat of a car or the powder room at a friend's house like some of the girls in high school. Granted I was two years younger than my peers and had my mind on other things but there hadn't been anyone until Paul so I'd never gotten the hang of it along the way.

I picked up the test stick and looked at the two blue lines.

Then I double checked the instructions.

They said think about finding Paul because he never did anything to hurt you. Then figure out how you're going to pack a baby around on a motorcycle as you float from one place to another until you have nowhere to go and have to come home. Think about getting a car and a real job and how you're going to do it alone because you won't let anyone close enough to help. Think about it Anna.

The instructions were right.

Mrs. Desmond let herself in as I returned to the kitchen. She was armed with a plate of cookies as she stepped carefully over the spots on my floor.

"Good morning Mrs. Desmond," I told her as I kissed her cheek. "I'm so sorry you were disturbed last night."

The police had woken her despite my dire warning to leave her alone. She shook her head as she looked at the blood. "If he had gotten into my house he'd have been just as sorry."

"Yes," I said remembering her choice of words with the policeman.

I put the kettle on to make her tea as I started on a cookie and she started scrubbing up the mess at my front door. Something was missing from the sill; a small picture of Alina and me in a little frog shaped frame, our heads centred in his spotted back. I couldn't imagine the little bastard taking it.

We chatted for a while as I ate then she went back upstairs and I made a few phone calls to cancel the work I'd told my father I was going south to do. Every time I went in the bathroom the test was still there on the counter, reminding me I wasn't alone anymore.

As dinner time got closer the urge to run away became too much so I packed for a couple of days and gave my bike a once over before I hit the road again.

Chapter 3

I'd forgotten what day it was or I would have filled up somewhere else. My old friend Kenny appeared in front of me as I closed up the tank. Once a week he led his buddies out after work for a group ride

5

either up or down Vancouver Island.

"They finally open the gates of hell and let you out?" he asked.

I made a face. He needed a haircut and some sit-ups.

"They said to go find someplace worse and try and brighten it up so I came straight here to see you," I said sweetly.

"You're a bag," he muttered.

"Hey Roger," he called to his buddies. "The little lady said I'm still the best she's ever had."

Roger would remember me from high school.

"Not you Kenny, I was talking about your dad," I said as I pushed myself right up into him and stuck my nose in his ear, insincerely flattering him with a bit of heavy breathing. "The old man really knows what he's doing."

Roger laughed and so did the others. Kenny glared at me.

"You riding or what?" he asked.

"You know I'll do just about anything to see your fat ass from behind."

I heard snickering behind him.

"Good, 'cause that's were you'll be." He pointed over to three riders off to the side. The little one had his helmet on already. "Those three rode up from Victoria today. They found us online. You follow them."

I didn't care. I could fall off the end any time I wanted and nobody would notice plus I'd be far enough behind Kenny that I didn't have to look at his fat ass. When we got back the tunnel to the mainland would take me to the highway south. Maybe make my way down to California to find Paul. Maybe not; that felt too much like stalking by the pregnant ex.

The two hours or so north to Campbell River were uneventful. The rear end of our staggered procession was about what I expected and we'd almost split into two groups. Kenny and his friends up ahead then a big space in front of the men from Victoria dawdling along with me behind them. Although I appreciated the number on the speed limit signs we passed I would have forgiven them for pushing it just a little.

The drone of my engine helped me think. Nothing guiding my destiny but the movement of my body over the shapely racing bike beneath me. It was simple and taking up the rear I didn't risk running anyone off the road as my mind wandered.

I remembered the last time I'd ridden with Kenny's group. I hadn't made it back with them instead returning hours later alone and exhausted. In a heap of trouble from my father on the front porch waiting up for me at 4 am. Glad I wasn't drunk in the back of a police car again and just as mad as if I had been.

I was just a few months past my sixteenth birthday. Old enough

6

that at eighteen Kenny didn't see me as a kid anymore and only a few days earlier he'd decided to show me exactly how far from childhood he thought I was. In his excitement he'd humiliated himself. He begged me not to tell anyone then he called me the afternoon of our last ride together to make sure we were cool about what happened.

He came by my house to pick me up and I followed him to the same gas station tonight's ride started at. It was only the second time I'd ridden solo with them and the previous time he'd put me right behind him. Proud of his little prodigy. Before he'd always taken me double and treated me like his kid sister. That night was different.

No sooner had we arrived than he'd unzipped my jacket and picked me up by the backs of my thighs, my legs spread around him and heaved me up onto the back seat of his bike. He put his hands inside my jacket grabbing my hips and started pushing himself into me rocking it on the kickstand.

"Kenny!" I'd squealed as my cheeks burned.

"That's what she said a few days ago," Kenny said to his friends as he pushed his mouth onto mine.

"'I liked it so much better when I could ride you at the same time,' she said. She begged me to bring my bike in the garage ... we closed the door. You should have heard her as she showed me how much she liked to ride like this."

I tried to push myself away but I was perched on my butt and had nowhere to go other than backwards onto my head.

"Come on Anna," he said. "Tell them how you want to ride everything you can so you can be sure you have the best. I'll set you guys up with her ... she needs a lot of attention."

I felt hot tears on my cheeks. Other than the barely dirty girl talk I'd overheard between my sister Alina and her friends my only experience with boys was the few minutes of sloppy kissing Kenny laid on me before he'd climaxed in his underwear beside me on his parents' sofa a few days before. As he continued to shove me around I tried to push his face away and left three painful red welts down his cheek and neck before my nails found his shirt and I stopped taking up skin.

He pulled me off his bike and I got my feet underneath me just in time.

"If you want to ride me like that again you're going to have to work your way up to the front one guy at a time you dirty slut. When you've been through them all come to me and say 'please.'"

I nodded dumbly not understanding what happened. The laughter behind me burned through my skin and destroyed the shaky self esteem I'd recovered since losing my mother two years before. Roger and his brother were arguing about who would stand lookout while the other satisfied me in the shrubs behind the gas station.

Kenny slapped my butt and laughed as I put my helmet on. I stood still until he walked away then I started my motorcycle and took my place at the end of the line.

On the highway I fell back and screamed into my helmet letting disgrace claim me. I screamed until the pain in my throat equalled the pain I felt inside and I wanted nothing more than to tear my flesh off until there was nothing left but impenetrable bone. I knew I couldn't face them at the next gas station. Tension built in my spine as humiliation tuned to anger.

Suddenly I felt myself swerve over on the shoulder, panicking as I pushed the big nine hundred back into position. It was over so quick I wasn't so sure it had even happened until the adrenaline swept through my limbs upsetting me even more. Then again across the centre line just after a logging truck passed going the other way. My wish that I'd lost control just a few seconds sooner scared me. I wanted to get drunk. Drink hard and forget what happened. A strange absence of headwind sucked me down on the tank and tension filled my body right up into my helmet.

Recklessness took over as I thought about getting as far away from them as I could. I pulled into the oncoming lane, intentionally this time, and closed my eyes as I hammered the throttle down.

Then there was quiet. Just the idling of my bike as my eyes focused on the sun. No lower than it had been when I tried to pass Kenny's pack with my eyes closed. I shut the engine down as I looked around.

Port Hardy was six hours away from the last place I remembered and the odometer said I'd ridden every single kilometre to get there. Not a minute appeared to have passed but the muscles in my back and shoulders disagreed. They were describing each and every one to me. I filled up and hit every all night gas station I could for a top up for fear of running dry at the side of the road. I had no idea what had happened, but in the years since I'd experimented and found that I could take those magic short cuts on purpose. And frequently did.

This night I wouldn't. I needed time to think and get my head on straight. A day spent sleeping off the fatigue that followed a jump as I'd come to call them wouldn't give me any time to think at all.

After I filled my bike I got the key from the attendant and went around to the restroom. When I got out Kenny was waiting so I pushed the key at him on my way past. He took my hand, stopping me.

"Wait …"

Even though I didn't like him holding on I paused and held my tongue instead of ripping into him again.

"Why are you here?" he asked me.

I thought of pointing to the restroom door.

"Where?" I asked.

"Riding ... with us ... tonight. You haven't come out in years."

I shrugged. "Not sure really."

Kenny loosened his grip on my hand and slowly worked his fingers around into my palm.

"Something's different about you. Has there been someone?"

I didn't answer, I watched his face instead. It never bothered Kenny that I was a little taller. The thought of me with someone else however, did.

"Yeah," he answered for me. "Did he hurt you or something?"

"No Kenny," I said.

"Hm."

"Hey Kenny, saddle up." Roger leaned around the corner. "She not gonna shake it off for ya?"

"Piss off Roger," Kenny said, not taking his eyes off me then I watched Roger watch us for a few more seconds and leave.

"Look Anna ... we can keep being assholes," he said. "Remember when we were kids? We were good at looking out for each other. You kept me out of trouble and I did the same for you. We didn't keep score. I know that fell apart ... I've stopped keeping score about that too."

Kenny looked away briefly. When he looked back there was sadness in his eyes.

"I know I've let myself go ... losing the wife and kids was hard. But I ..."

He took a deep breath and tried again.

"I ...," he gave up.

"Think about it," he finished before he squeezed my hand and walked away.

I gave him a minute to get around the corner before I followed. Kenny stood with his buddies, back to me. The reflective pin-striping on his jacket caught light from somewhere and lit up. Roger opened his mouth to speak, stopping when Kenny slapped his shoulder. I gave Roger the finger and took the key in.

The return trip wasn't going to be like riding north. If I decided to bail on them I'd have to be obvious about it, passing everyone. Kenny led us out and after a few blocks we all got bunched up at a red light. When it turned green the first of the Victoria three stalled his ride and couldn't get it back in gear until we'd missed it. We inched up to the red and waited for him to get it going after another stall. I swore quietly in my helmet and thought about zipping around.

Kenny and the rest were out of sight by the time we got going. If any of them even noticed. The three in front of me didn't seem in any hurry to find the tail lights we had lost. I muttered something nasty and distracted myself thinking about Kenny's strange offer.

He'd be twenty-seven this year: marriage, two kids and a divorce that wrapped up a few years before. Now that he'd figured out it wasn't reasonable for me to be saving myself for him at twenty-four I was interesting again. Try as I might I couldn't find any reason for him to be interesting to me. In spite of my complete inexperience our first night together Paul and I figured out quickly how to rattle each others eyeballs loose. Sorry Kenny … baby's father has dibs.

As I finished that thought the rider ahead suddenly rolled off the throttle and swung into my path. I did the same, moving over to the centre line to avoid rear ending him. My horn whined a warning as he got back in position. Maybe he was fatigued; they'd been on the road an hour and a half longer because their ride started in Victoria. I reminded myself that I measured the length of a ride in days, not hours like these guys would. I gave him a little more room as we continued our limp south.

Now that Paul had moved on with someone else he wouldn't want me. I needed to tell him about the baby and give him some time to decide where he wanted to fit. I didn't expect him to dump her and marry me and set up house. I'd tell him that. I also didn't want him to hold back because Kenny was hanging around. Not that I would want Kenny even if I wasn't knocked up.

Next it was the rider two ahead, the other one in the shoulder side of the lane who dropped back sliding past the one who tried to hit me the first time. I swerved to the centre line just in time. He matched my speed and pushed in dangerously close to me. I had to choose between the car in the oncoming lane and braking. I put on the brakes.

Fuck this, I thought. After the car passed I snapped my wrist down to fly past them and pulled into the other lane as they did the same, the lead rider swinging out blocking my way. Then the other two pulled ahead next to him, keeping me from getting around. I slowed right down, dropping behind as they got back in position in front. Apprehension started its slow spread into my legs and arms. If these guys ran me off the road here I'd be lucky if anyone spotted me in the trees even in the daylight. They were coordinated, much better riders than they pretended to be. They'd separated me from the rest at the lights and made sure the leaders hadn't stopped for us to catch up before they started playing with me. At least they couldn't get their hands on me if the bikes were rolling.

There was no reason for these three guys to be herding the lone woman rider on the dark highway. Normal men wouldn't do that. If I stopped overreacting for a few minutes I'd figure it out and we'd all laugh about it later. I'd be through the tunnel and riding the highways in Washington State in a couple of hours.

After ten minutes I started to calm down. I convinced myself that they were from a lot farther away than Victoria, had no idea where they were, and didn't want me abandoning them. I also succeeded in disregarding how they tried to run me into a car.

I was still nervous. Anxious. Craving safety. The feelings I kept at bay reminded me of the fear I experienced the night I met Paul. After dinner we walked to my hotel room. Paul noticed the scrutiny of a kid in the parking lot. I'd written it off to the normal sort of getting checked out I'd become used to but Paul knew him. I worked under an assumed name and Paul worried about the damage if that got out.

He'd taken control. He held me around the corner from the parking lot, the tension in him soaked into me as he watched for the kid to leave. I'd let him look after me, welcomed it. I hadn't let myself need anyone since my mother died and now I needed Paul in control again. Covering me with his body until all the trouble had gone away.

I made up my mind to find him; decided that I badly needed him just as the lead bike went down. We were maybe doing sixty kilometres an hour and the sudden feel of gravel under my tires told me why he'd lost control. The other two bikes' brake lights came on at almost the same time as I started feathering my brakes to stop as hard as I could without skidding, suddenly grateful for knowing Kenny and spending so many hundreds of hours running the logging roads on dirt bikes with him.

The rider up front slid under his bike as the other two went down nearly on top of him. I still had enough control to get over by a wooden building. There was a shout, then another as my bike stopped and I crouched down behind it. My helmet came off quickly as did my pack so I could run faster when I decided which way to go. I could see a fight; more people than just the three other riders in the lights that pointed every which way.

I heard what I thought was a gunshot so I turned and ran maybe thirty feet before I found an alley. There was a scream.

"There! Down that way!" a man yelled so I bolted into the blackness. Someone was on my heels. He didn't slow down one bit as he hit and the ground flew up to meet me. His full weight came down, forcing the air from my lungs as my shoulder slid forward and my chest flexed. My scream added to the shouts.

A knife flashed briefly in the moonlight above then his crushing weight on me was gone. The sun was up and the screaming had stopped. I was alone on the cold ground between two wooden buildings. Daylight. The sun had replaced the moon. My right eye was swelling and as I looked up at the walls and sky above me I realized that somewhere after the bizarre ride and being chased I'd jumped. Slipped back in time to escape the falling blade.

The effort of moving narrowed my vision and took the colour from the sky. I thought again of Paul, needing him as the pain became too much and I passed out.

Paul

Chapter 4

There was pain in my head when I woke. And my ribs. Smooth sheets on my skin as I stretched my bare legs. The hunger and building irritability I felt told me I'd slept off the jump to avoid the knife. I could hear voices far away and assumed with great relief that I was safe in the hospital.

Until someone else's weight shifted on the bed. I held my breath as I woke completely; eyes alert beneath my closed lids.

The movement stopped and I felt gentle fingers on my cheek. Rough, hard working skin brushed mine as softly as a child's. Breathing, close to me. I tensed and opened my eyes.

"Jesus Christ," I gasped.

Familiar deep green eyes, dark hair that would go curly if he let it grow. His nose had taken a couple of rights. We were only ever the same height in bed otherwise he was a good five inches taller than my almost six feet. I remembered the taste of his lips the first time he slept with a woman when it was her first time just a couple of months ago …

"No," he smiled with amusement. "It's Paul."

"Why am I in the hospital?" I asked, now not entirely sure where I was. I caught a glimpse of the tip of his tongue before he moved a little closer to peer into my eyes.

"You're in my room," he said, his levity gone.

"You're in the hospital?" I noticed the IV in my hand but the dark panelling, heavy curtains and mismatched bedding screamed man room.

"You're in my house, in my room, in my bed."

I blinked. "I … where?"

"My house," he repeated. "Ray?"

"She's gonna kill me." I said. Whoever Paul's new woman was would when she found out I was in his bed. Now I'd gotten him in

15

trouble. That was the last thing I wanted. Suddenly I felt very helpless. "Damn it. I'm so sorry."

"Paul?" I turned as much as I could toward the new voice. He had short hair like Paul's, a little longer on top. Warm face. "Hey Kiddo. Good to see you awake. How are you feeling?"

He sounded nice but I turned back to Paul as I slipped a hand over my mouth to try and hide my panic. Paul studied me for a second; my eyes, my hand. "Sugar, what do you remember?"

I watched his face feeling myself pulled in. In spite of the awkward situation that was coming when his new girlfriend found out I was here I calmed, trusting that as long as he was near I was safe. That didn't mean I was going to tell him all of what I remembered.

"I got chased down an alley," I told him. "He took me down ... I passed out."

Something briefly showed on his face as he glanced at Ray so I tried to explain.

"The group I was riding with ... three of them separated me, tried to run me off the road. Suddenly we were on dirt and they went down. I kept control, pulled over and ran, there was fighting. I got chased."

"On the seventh ... I had dinner with my Dad the night before."

"That was two days ago," Paul said as he moved closer. "You don't remember us finding you? Ray popped your shoulder back in ..."

I shook my head.

"That's okay," Ray's voice said behind me. "You got a bump on the head. It seems to be just a bad concussion ... no signs of anything more serious."

"Who is that Paul ... you hear him too right?" I asked.

"Yes," he answered.

"I'm Doctor Jackson. Paul's been a pain in my side for years. Call me Ray."

"Hi Ray," I said as I tried to roll over and push myself closer to Paul. I only made it to my back groaning with pain as my mouth watered with nausea. "It's Anna."

"Are you finished refusing pain meds?" Ray asked.

The only thing that would make me pass on relief was the baby. I didn't know what was safe so I shook my head and pressed my lips shut. Paul sighed. He didn't seem very happy about it.

"I need to get to the bathroom," I said. Pain wasn't the only discomfort I had. They carefully got me up and walked me to the door next to the curtains at the other end of the big room. I grabbed the IV bag from Ray and shut the door behind me. It took a minute to get my vision back together from the effort of walking but there was no way I was getting help even if it was from a doctor and someone who was already familiar with the lay of the land.

16

I wore only my underwear and a huge blue and white plaid pyjama shirt. One eye was swollen and bruised but none of my teeth felt loose. My toiletry bag was on the shelf by the sink so I freshened up as best I could and brushed two days worth of sleep off my teeth.

By the time I lay back down I was clammy if not visibly shaking. I was shaking hard on the inside.

"Are you sure nothing for pain?" Paul asked. He pushed my hair back; some was stuck to my forehead.

I nodded. "It's not that bad."

"I'll be downstairs Paul," Ray said. "It appears I'm not needed." He actually sounded hurt.

"I know where to find you." Paul replied. He put his hand on Ray's back briefly and closed the door behind him. Then he lifted the blanket and carefully rolled me to my side before curling up behind, pushing my weakly protesting elbow aside. His fingers went on my hip, tips just reaching under the elastic of my panties as he slid his hand around to my stomach.

"Do you know you're pregnant?"

I nodded as I started to cry. He shouldn't be the one telling me. Paul's nose went to my neck, inhaling, tasting me with his sense of smell. "It's mine," he breathed.

"Yes," I whispered, pushing back into him, giving in quickly despite how much it hurt. I relaxed my shoulder as he pulled the oversized shirt down off it so he could nibble at my skin.

"Stop," I said, shaking my head clear. My hand had slipped between us and I pulled it back.

"Why?" Paul paused.

"You broke it off for someone else Paul," I said quietly. "Now we're in your bed. She's gonna kill me. You were so distracted that last morning, then you dumped me with a message you were moving on. I don't know the name for what we were but it was important enough to me that I'm having a hard time getting past it. I just needed to see you to tell you about the baby. You don't have to want me … there's room for you with your child. As much as you want."

"Oh Sugar …" he whispered as he covered my shoulder back up. "We need to talk. There isn't anyone else. There never was so relax. I'm sorry I left you with that."

I nodded even though that gave me more questions than answers. And anger.

"Ray has pain meds that are safe for you and the baby and I'm going to be sick if I have to watch you hurt any more. Trust me?"

"Yes," I answered and grimaced as I tried to take a deep breath. I trusted him as much as my sister and my father. Even more since I'd told Paul about my family but I'd never told them about him.

17

"Not really allergic to anything?" he asked for some reason emphasizing the word 'really.'

"I've never taken anything stronger than what you can buy at the grocery store."

"Okay, sit tight."

By the time Paul came back with Ray I'd recovered from the knife in my side I felt rolling over. Ray pulled the cap of a needle and shot something into the line. "Just a taste. As long as you have no trouble breathing I can give you more."

"Okay,"

"I'd like to check you out, if that's alright," Ray said. I watched Paul and he nodded.

"Alright Ray."

He started with a little flashlight in my eyes then his fingers reached for my bruised cheek and he paused. "I like my fucking eyes were they are if you don't mind."

"Oh shit," I felt my cheeks colour. "I didn't."

"You did," Ray said.

"I'll keep my hands to myself. I'm sorry."

Ray hesitated a little longer than necessary before he started pressing around the bruising then he moved on to my neck.

"I'm sorry," I said again. "This isn't the first time I've woken up with a headache and a black eye to hear that I wasn't nice."

"Didn't think so," Ray convincingly deadpanned. "You did it like a pro." He looked at Paul who was trying not to laugh. "But I've been thanked by bigger boys than you. What happened last time?"

He'd slid a hand under my back to feel around my shoulder. It felt a lot better than when I passed out in the alley.

"I woke up with my father standing in my bedroom door with the home number for a policeman I had to call with an apology. I guess I felt the need to descriptively … ouch … question his parentage after he was kind enough to pull me out of a fight at a house party and drive me home." Ray had his hand on my ribs.

"They didn't toss you in the tank?"

"Not when you're fifteen."

Ray shook his head as he put more medicine in the line for me. "I think this will help with the headache. Alright … tummy."

I pulled the shirt up and he started under my ribs and worked his way down. "Tender? No bleeding?"

I shook my head for both.

"No getting out of bed and no romance for at least a week please until we're sure the baby is in the clear. Yell for me if you even think there's a problem, okay Kiddo?"

"Whee," I said, not really sure if I was still on the mattress.

18

"Better Paul?" Ray asked. "You passed out when I fixed your shoulder so I took blood because my uncooperative patient couldn't tell me what's the matter any more. Paul sent one of the guys in to Redding to drop it off at Shasta for me. That's how we learned about the pregnancy … got the blood work back a little while ago."

"Uh huh." My head swam as the pain started to fade. "Thanks for being sneaky."

"You're welcome. When you come down Paul we need to talk about who's paying my bill."

Paul lay down on the blankets next to me after Ray left. I watched both of him circle each other for a moment until my eyes started to work together.

"You were pretty mad at me when we brought you in the other night," he said quietly. "You feel up to talking about it now?"

As long as I didn't have to explain how I'd gotten close enough to California from Canada for Paul to find me I'd talk about whatever he wanted. "What did I say?"

"You made what you said to Ray look impossibly polite."

I took a deep breath and thought about it.

"Sorry Paul, whatever I said you didn't deserve," I told him. "You had your reasons … you weren't trying to hurt me."

"And?"

"You dumped me with a five word message. You changed your number. I've felt more for you every day since then, not less. You could have said 'call me when you get in,' you could have said that the awesome hotel room romps didn't make up for when I hid under the desk. You were in it for the fun and you're too busy for some psycho who's turned into—."

Suddenly his mouth was on mine cutting me off. He dug his elbow in to the bed and pushed himself up beside me catching mine open and turning my building anger with him into desire. Desire as detached as the pain I was in so there was no way I could sink my fingers in to use it even if Ray hadn't told me to look after the baby first this week. He withdrew taking my bottom lip with him and I tried to follow until my ribs told me far enough.

"How do you do that? I'm trying to be mad and you make the room spin," I muttered as I closed my eyes waiting for it to stop. Paul laughed and dropped his head to the other pillow. Then he returned, hovering just in front of me. I didn't even try to focus.

"Sugar," he sighed and brushed my cheek with his. "I got a call in the middle of the night from my CO. I had fifteen minutes to shake four guys out of bed and get them packed in a truck. I was running down the road banging on cabin doors when I called to tell you I was shipping out. My phone's been working for a week since I got back. CO is cheap and

19

shuts them down when we're in the field."

"You said 'sorry Anna I'm moving on.' That's all you told me."

"Shit yeah," his nose found its way behind my ear. "I could have been gone for months. I thought that was a kinder way to leave you than nobody here knowing to call you if there was bad news. I was going to call you in a few days ... I needed some time to adjust to being back after ... being away."

I nodded and brought a hand up to wipe my eyes.

"I'm sorry Anna. I left you hurting and alone. I promise it won't happen again. If we decide we don't want each other we'll both know why okay?"

"Yeah, okay." Paul rested his head on my shoulder and I got a hand up to his face. He was too close to see clearly so I turned and kissed his forehead as my hand felt the stubbly line of his jaw. "I had a really bad night before I came here. I've never felt so alone."

"What happened, Sugar?"

I turned my head away feeling weak for failing to look after myself.

"I had a break in. The kid from the parking lot where we met was in my house."

"Is that why you had a gun?"

"I didn't ... wait ... I got it out from under the couch to put away while was packing. Must have been doing too many things at once and stuffed it in my bag. I don't know why I bought it ... can't hit a thing."

Paul laughed.

"Can Ray call my sister? Alina Creed ... she's in my phone. Talk doctor to her and say I had an accident? And Tony. Tell him to get Mrs. Desmond her groceries every week on my credit card. He'll know what she needs. Maybe slip her some smokes."

"Yeah, sleep now ... we'll keep an eye on you. You're safe here."

Chapter 5

"Anna, wake up Kiddo."

Someone was gently shaking my arm.

"Ray? Morning."

"Not yet. I need to take some blood from you if that's okay ... prenatal stuff. I'll drop it off in town. Did Paul tell you?" Ray asked.

"Guess he forgot." I realized I was alone in the bed. "Is he going with you?"

"No. He goes for a run early most days but he'll be back for breakfast. Anyway, if you give me the name of your doctor I'll make sure he gets a copy of the results."

"Okay, go ahead but I don't have a doctor."

"No doctor?"

"Haven't needed one since I was thirteen … I guess you're my doctor now."

I was glad I was lying down. The IV was one thing. Seeing my blood was something else entirely.

"Without doctor stuff from time to time I had no idea until now that I'm squeamish."

Ray took my arm. "Why don't you close your eyes and tell me about the last time you needed a doctor? I'll make it quick, I promise."

I took a deep breath and closed my eyes. "Kenny next door was teaching me to ride his big brother's dirt bike in the empty lot by our houses. He was two years older and we'd taken the bike without asking. I had Kenny on the back behind me. It was a huge two stroke 650, the wrong bike to be learning on anyway. It was working pretty well for a while but then he put his hand up my shirt and helped himself to a big old squeeze."

Ray was already pressing a cotton ball on me so I opened my eyes and kept going.

"I let go of the handle bars and swung my elbow around at him as hard as I could, got lucky and broke his collar bone. The bike went down and he broke his wrist. Other than some gravel in my skin I was okay but we did some damage to the dirt bike."

He was opening a small band aid. "You want a smiley face on it?"

"Sure," I smiled. He got out a pen.

"That the same Kenny you were talking about when you got here?" Ray asked.

"The same," I said as my mood soured.

Ray was quiet for a moment. "You didn't dump his bike too did you? Do you want to tell me about it?"

"Maybe another time, I've poked an old wound."

I thought about it. I hadn't replied very nicely.

"Sorry Ray. It's not your fault. Kenny was my best friend. When I was sixteen I went to his house for dinner. He said his parents were getting pizza or something. We'd trucked dirt bikes up Mount Benson and had been racing each other down the logging roads all afternoon. I was starving so I took him up on it.

"He'd started to think of himself as my boyfriend and I guess I should have put a stop to that sooner but I didn't. He started kissing me then he said he wanted me to make him a man. It sounded so corny I said yes. I couldn't believe guys actually said that shit. I don't know what I was thinking. Maybe I was feeling grown up at sixteen; maybe I just didn't care.

"Anyway he was finished before he got within a foot of me. He was so embarrassed. I mean you expect a short fuse like that at sixteen, but at eighteen you think he'd have had some self control. He cried. He begged me not to tell anyone and for another chance. I said sure Kenny but his parents were pulling in so we got dressed fast and I ran out the back.

"I didn't tell but Kenny did. The next time we got together with his friends he told them all Anna wanted was more and if any of them wanted to help him keep up with my needs he'd set it up. I'd been one of the guys until then. I thought they were my friends. I didn't ride with them again until the night I came here."

Then I gave him a small smile. "Mrs. Kenny gave him two kids before she took off with them to Nova Scotia. He's put on forty pounds now too. I feel strangely good about that."

I quickly covered my mouth as I yawned. Then I listened as words I didn't expect came out.

"Thanks for listening, big brother."

I closed my eyes but not before I saw Ray's mouth drop open with surprise. After a minute he turned off the lamp and left, my blood jingling in his pocket.

Chapter 6

I slept a bit after Ray left. Paul was in for a shower after his run then he disappeared downstairs for breakfast. I could smell bacon and coffee and hear the boisterous talk of more men than I could guess.

The last night I saw Paul before he left the message started out much like the others.

Food, sex, sleep.

I'd learned more about him since our first night together. He was ten years older and spent over a decade serving the US overseas. He couldn't tell me most of what he did other than to say his teams took care of things that needed to be done quietly. He said was still in touch with the men he served with and they helped each other out adjusting to life back stateside.

I'd woken from vivid nightmare, bolted into the headboard, fallen out of bed and crawled under the desk before Paul realized I was gone. He was usually the jumpy one at night. The noise I made woke him and he called to me sleepily from the warm blankets. When I didn't answer he turned the light on.

"What are you doing under there?"

I couldn't respond. He tried to pull me out I crossed my arms and backed in further. "You awake? Must have been a hell of a bad dream."

He sat next to me until I got up. I was chilled and at least had a chance of being coherent. He pulled me back to the bed and waited as I hesitated to get in. I couldn't lie on my side so I got in his.

"Are you in there now?"

I nodded, embarrassed.

"You move fast. You could have been on top of me before I had my eyes open."

I curled up closer. "You usually have your eyes open when I'm on top."

"True," he said and reached over to turn off the light. "Do you want to tell me about it? It won't be in your head any more if you let it out your mouth."

I shook my head.

"Are you sure? It can't hurt you," he encouraged.

He was right. I was still learning to put my stubbornness aside when it came to Paul.

"I was in a cabin. The man who brought me there came in while I slept. The fire had gotten low and the room was cooling off. I didn't know who it was at first.

"He said, "I know you're awake." And he pulled me out of bed.

""You stink of him," he said.

"He hit me a couple of times and let me drop to the floor." I reached up to rub my cheek. Even awake it still stung. My words ran on as I watched it replay.

"I don't understand why he was so mad. He kicked me on the ground over and over then he rolled me on my back and in the fire light I saw he had a beautiful dagger. The guard was like lace sparkling in the flames. He held it to my throat.

"Then he heard something outside. He picked me up with one hand and threw me on the bed. He turned me to face the door and said if I moved we would both die. Then he went to stand by the fire and pretended to clean his dagger.

"Another man came in, crouched low with a knife in his own hand. He didn't see me right away and when he did, he stopped.

"The man by the fire said. "You're too late."

"They stared at each other and the second man got down on his knees. He dropped his dagger and opened his collar. Then he lifted his chin and closed his eyes.

"The man who beat me walked slowly around behind him and grabbed him under the jaw. He watched my face as he cut his throat. His neck opened up. His blood shot out and ran. When he stopped breathing he let him fall.

"He said "Are you still with me, Catherine? I know you are. Maybe he'll have better luck next time."

"He cut my stomach open. I died before I could watch him leave."

23

My eyes were wide open in the dark.

"It's just a dream," Paul whispered. He held me tight like he was trying to hold me in the present.

"I can feel the blows Paul. If I walk over to the other side of the bed my feet will stick in the blood and I'll trip over his body. I can see it."

"Can you turn the light on so I can see something else? Please?"

He did. Then he pulled the blanket up to my chin.

"It's over Sugar. Just a bad dream. Try and sleep now."

I tried but all I could see inside my lids was the dead man on the floor.

In the morning Paul was quiet. I was still too shaken to notice how withdrawn he'd become. After a sullen breakfast downstairs he said goodbye in the room and went to his cab.

I didn't think he'd call again. His no commitments casual sex girl had turned into something that was work. Frightened. Hiding. Needy. I upset myself with my behaviour. It came out of nowhere and exposed a part of my character I worked hard to get by without. He was a different man when he said good-bye than he'd been when he greeted me at the door the night before.

I packed as fast as I could and fled. The drained body was still on the floor. Its dull eyes seemed to follow me wherever I went. I jumped home as soon as I was clear of the city and slept for eighteen hours.

A polite tap on the closed bedroom door snapped me out of my reverie. Paul or Ray would just come in.

"Miss Creedy?"

Creedy? I thought. "Anna?" I answered.

"No it's Denis ... Lieutenant Martin, I—"

There was a clatter of cutlery followed by an 'Ah shit.' He had food and a solid vocabulary. I liked him already. "I helped the Captain carry you in the other night. Are you hungry?"

I quickly made sure I was buttoned up and my legs were covered. "Bet your ass Denis."

The tallest man I'd ever seen pushed his way in. He had a huge grin on his face and a tray in his hands. He made Paul look like he'd have trouble reaching the top of the fridge.

"I knew it," he said as he put the tray down on the foot of the bed. "Any patient of Ray's is hungry." The tray held two plates heaped with steak, eggs, and fried potatoes. There were two cups of coffee and two bowls of Jell-O.

"Be right back," he said over his shoulder and thundered down the hall. He was back in a minute with fresh steak knives, two glasses and a carton of juice.

"Someone let on that I'm a sucker for orange Jell-O?" I asked.

Denis passed me a plate and slid the tray closer so I could dump cream in my coffee. "You won't be after you eat that. Ray is such a bad cook he took two terms of screwing up Jell-O in university. Nobody should have to eat it alone."

I quickly forgot about wondering how you could screw up Jell-O with the first bite of steak. "I think I'm in love Denis."

He laughed and dug in. "You won't tell Ray I fed you, will you?"

"He seems to be under enough stress already," I said wincing as I straightened up.

"Yeah, but it's endearing in a way. Oh and with the exception of the new words you taught him when you came in you've been a really good patient. It's going to his head. Most of us would rather bleed out than eat his Jell-O."

I got my arms around my ribs as my laughter turned into a moan of pain. "How many did you break?" Denis asked.

"Feels like all of them."

"Then you broke three. I've broke plenty; both my own and other peoples. Your bike is nice … you got a Canadian mechanic?"

"No," I paused as the spicy potatoes melted in my mouth. "My Dad taught me if you can't fix it you shouldn't drive it or live in it. Do it myself."

"Really? Not much to do around here though the Captain manages to keep us busy. Your bike is stashed in the shop," he pointed back through the bathroom, "and there's always things to fix. Your gun's in the lockup downstairs. I'll take you shooting when Ray lets you out."

He was interrupted by the sound of the fallen cutlery being pushed out of the way outside the door.

"Ray?" I whispered.

"Naw, he can sneak up on anything. One thing I'm glad of is I'm not smaller than Ray," he said as Paul came in catching me shoving the last of the steak in my mouth.

"What's going on Lieutenant?"

"He was starving her Paul," Denis started, eye roll emphasis on 'starving.' Paul cleared his throat suddenly looking bigger than Denis. "Lieutenant Jackson was starving her Captain Richards … I could hear her stomach rumbling all the way to my cabin."

Paul thought a moment then swiped a piece of potato from my plate before reloading my IV with painkiller and swapping the bag.

"I could too," he said as he left. "Visiting hours are over in ten Denis or I'm telling Ray you're constipated."

Denis gulped, his eyes wide. "You better get to the Jell-O Miss Creedy." He passed me one and took one for himself. He finished it in a few mouthfuls and I watched him breathe through his nose for a minute like he wasn't so sure it would stay put. "If you can't get it down or keep

25

it down then you're not well enough for real food but it's so damn bad. Down the hatch."

I took a spoonful and put it to my nose. It smelled fine so I put it in my mouth as Denis started to smile. I smooshed it around with my tongue as he nodded. "See?"

"It's lumpy," I said after I swallowed. "And chewy; otherwise it's not too bad."

Denis laughed as he got our plates together. "I'm sure you'll still feel that way after you eat the ten that are still in the fridge. I'll leave you be."

Chapter 7

"Why'd you do it?"

Paul was loud and for a moment I thought I heard the legs of the chair he was in hit the hardwood floor for emphasis. I'd spent much of the last five days as still as I could. Ray had taken out the IV when I finished the Jell-O and I had a bottle of pills instead. The curtains were closed and in the lamp light his green eyes were grey with anger. I slowly shook my head; I had no idea what he was talking about.

He held up a piece of paper. "You were pregnant before we met. Was it some drunken mistake you thought you could pin on me?"

"No Paul," I stammered as my doped up brain struggled. "I think it was Vancouver … torn in the trash Vancouver." There had been a torn condom in the garbage when I was packing to leave Vancouver two weeks after we met. Only the second time we'd been together.

Paul put a hand on his head and tipped it back; a gesture I hadn't seen before. "Twelve weeks … even out here in the bush we can read a calendar. Fuck Anna."

The number helped with the math and damn it he was right. I'd jumped a lot during the summer and could easily have lost that many days to my magic travel.

"Should I be flattered? Do you wish it was me?"

I got an arm underneath me and pushed up to sit. "There's only been you Paul," I tried to stay calm not knowing how I could talk my way clear. "You know that. The paper is wrong."

"Sure," he said sarcastically. "I thought it was wrong when I first found out so Ray redid it. Was it your high school sweetheart Kenny? You said when you got here that he wanted his shot."

"It wasn't Kenny," I answered wondering what else I'd gone off about during my blackout.

"Then who?"

"Paul Richards," I spat out.

26

He shook his head and looked away. Then he pursed his lips and shoved them up at his nose.

"You know, I think of myself as a gentleman. If you're woman enough to tell me the truth I'm man enough to back you up. The one thing that gets to me is lies."

"Paul Richards," I repeated.

"No Anna, not Paul Richards. Tell me it's not me, tell me who it was and promise me that he doesn't have a hope in hell with you otherwise I'll get out of his way."

"It was you Paul," I stuck my legs over the edge of the bed and quickly wiped tears from my eyes with the back of my hand.

His anger seemed to soften as he stood. "I know you have feelings for me. You want it to be me. But it isn't. Even when it's here in black and white you're sticking to the bullshit.

"I won't tolerate being lied to," he said raising his voice.

"And I won't stand for being called a liar," I shot back.

"There's only one person who can fix this and it's not me. I'm giving you a chance. Then we'll see if we have anything we can put together for your kid."

My arms reached around me and held tight so I could yell back. "I won't lie to you!"

"You already are!" he yelled then he stomped over to the closet and pulled out my backpack. "I'm getting a truck."

He threw it on the bed and stormed out.

I didn't touch it. Instead I pulled the curtains and stared out the window. Snow fell hard. The roof sloped away about eight feet and it was already at least six inches deep. It clung to the branches of the trees thirty feet away at the far side of the overgrown back yard. I rested my elbows on the high sill and my forehead on the glass and watched the little circle I made change size as I breathed.

He'd never believe the truth even if I told him. The truck roared up to the front of the house and I heard Paul stomp snow off his boots before he came in and up the stairs. I knew he could see me from the other end of the long hallway since he left the door open.

"You're going like that?" he asked. I wore one of his tees and a too big pair of pyjama pants Ray had scavenged for me. My breath hitched painfully in my chest and I sniffled. Paul disappeared into the bathroom and came out with a couple of tissues for me. I took them without looking at him as he leaned back against the window beside me.

"We never even got out the gate did we," he said. "I thought your secret could explain it but I guess it can't. I can live with the truth. I think there's more for us ahead. I can't live with the lie that I'm your baby's father."

I sat on the bed and looked at my fingers, trying to smooth out the

27

wrinkles they'd already made in the tissue. Paul didn't move. He shoved his hands in his pockets as he watched me.

"What secret?" I asked.

"You said a lot of things when we brought you in. Between swearing at me for cutting off your favourite leather jacket and trying to take Ray's eyes out you told me how you got here. We thought it was how hard you got hit on the head. I didn't pay much attention until something happened later.

"I don't think you've ever told anyone. Maybe you're afraid I'll think you're crazy but if you are then I'm right there with you." Paul took three quick steps toward me and dropped on his knees. The paper was half under the bed. He picked it up and turned it into a ball.

"Please Anna," he said desperately. He needed proof more powerful than the email with Ray's name on it from Shasta Medical. His hand went on my stomach.

"Please," he said again. "Don't let your stubbornness screw this up. It's more than just two adults here. I know in my heart he's mine. Tell me how I got you pregnant before I ever laid eyes on you."

"You didn't Paul," I whispered starting to bend. "Tell me what I don't remember." I hadn't asked anything about how he found me or my two missing days. I'd avoided it so I could avoid the discussion I couldn't get out of now.

"Trust me, Sugar … then you'll tell me?"

I nodded. So help me I would.

"Denis radioed when we were having dinner … said we had an intruder. He'd found something. Your motorcycle was there. I ordered a search. It was cold and if you'd wandered into the woods you'd be in trouble.

"I have a couple of big store sheds down the west road … you were hiding. You wouldn't let us get a collar on you or anything to move you. Said men were coming for you … attacked you. I finally had to phone you to stop you from going out but there was no answer. It didn't make any sense. You gave in and let us wrap you up and move you in here. You said it was too late to stop them."

Paul got up off the floor and sat beside me. "Then what?"

"You said you were riding by your home with a bunch of people. Three of them separated you and tried to run you into a car. You were scared … then you were on dirt and the other three crashed. You pulled over and ran when you saw a big fight. Ducked down an alley."

He looked away. "Someone ran you down hard from behind. You were in pain, saw a knife. Then he was gone and the sun was up.

"You said you were in the same place he attacked you but you went back in time to get away. It sounded all mixed up. You thought I was on Vancouver Island and had no idea where you really were.

28

"Ray finally let you off the board and you went after him for trying to give you morphine. I was pissed at him but he wouldn't without your permission. Mercifully you passed out while we relocated your shoulder."

Paul moved closer, putting his arm around me and I let my head rest on his shoulder.

"The road out front filled with the sound of motorcycles. I ran out … those fuckers who hurt you were back and I wanted my piece. I don't think I ever ran so fast, there was still dust in the air from their crash. Lieutenant Wells pointed one of them out to me running for it, they had the others."

I could hear his voice tighten as he went on and his other arm went around me. I tensed not knowing why.

"He ran between the sheds and I flattened him with every ounce I had. He screamed like a girl and I heard his head hit the ground, felt him flatten underneath me. I slammed my elbow in his face but he wasn't going anywhere … got my knife out … ready to make him pay for what he did to you. I started to drive it to his throat … and I was alone on the ground as my knife sunk into the dirt and your scent filled my nose."

His hand went up and wiped his eyes.

"The bikes were gone … the three who came with you were gone. You were gone. I ran back to the house and you were still passed out.

"It was me Sugar. I didn't listen. I'm the one who hurt you, I know it."

I took a deep breath and turned my head to look at him. "I remember the pain and the knife in the moonlight," I admitted. "I didn't see your face … then I was alone and the sun was up. I pushed myself behind the barrels and woke up here in your bed."

Paul let me go and moved away a bit.

"Are you afraid of me?" He sounded so small. His guilt rolled in to me in waves. I took his elbow as I turned to him carefully putting one knee to his side and swinging the other over. An involuntary gasp from the movement hurt my side more than the movement did. I straddled him, not too close and pulled his face to mine.

"You were protecting me," I told him.

"I tried to kill you."

"Would you ever lay a hand on me?" I asked and he shook his head. "Then how could you try to kill me? You were trying to protect me."

He met my eyes briefly and nodded, seeming to relax a bit.

"How did it happen?"

"It was Vancouver," I told him. "Two weeks after we met."

Disappointment spread over his face. After telling me his crazy story he obviously wanted to hear something other than what he'd heard already. "But more days have passed for me than for you. You saw some of those hours yourself. To you I didn't get hurt until after you and Ray treated me."

"How?" he asked again, whispering.

I leaned on Paul to rest a bit and wrapped my arms around his head. "When I left you to go home the day after we met I rode west. It didn't take long to decide I would jump home. That's what I call it. I waited for dark. I'm never sure where I'll wind up so it feels safer.

"Every season being out in the open gets harder. I can feel something up there, pressing on me. Agoraphobia is a fine thing for a nomad on a motorcycle.

"I knew I'd be just as exhausted if I jumped as if I rode straight through. At least I'd be spared the days of fear. I don't think I made a single trip anywhere last summer without jumping home."

Paul reached around my butt and pulled me close.

"When it got dark I started to set it up," I said as I straightened up so I could keep an eye on his reaction. He just listened and I was fine with that. "I picture where I want to be. I think it's emotional. I have to really want to be there. Pressure starts low in my back as I let desperation for the place take over. It climbs and as it gets into my shoulders I get pushed around."

His hands worked their way up my back as I talked and I felt my tension disappear, not build like I described. He wanted to believe me. I shifted my hips on him needing to be much closer than I was and he leaned back kissing my chin in response.

"Mm," my voice lowered. "It gets up in my helmet … doesn't matter how fast I'm going I get pushed down on the tank and the pressure gets up in my head."

Paul worked the knots from my neck as my mouth quit working. "Go on …," he breathed as he settled for holding me. He had to cool me off if he wanted to hear the rest of it.

"I … it gets so strong it hurts … I make sure I'm completely focused. Then I close my eyes and open up the throttle. I was sitting in the trees. The smell of pine and damp earth was right so I knew I was near home. It was the same day and time as when I started the jump but I was three thousand kilometres away. My phone rang … it was you."

"You said you were five minutes from home, up the hill by the city pound."

"I was. A car passing below lit up my bike in its headlights and I went home. Paul I had three days of gas receipts … days that hadn't happened yet. My passport was stamped at Peace Arch three days away. The odo showed the whole trip.

"The next day I fell asleep for a long time … eighteen, twenty-four hours sometimes. A long black sleep; nothing wakes me. I aged three days I don't remember. I know I did. Cuts heal, nails grow. My menstrual cycle speeds up. I could be a year older than my driver's license shows. I just don't know."

"Incredible," he said after a minute. "If I hadn't seen it ..."

"Something went wrong this time Paul. I've only ever gone to a place ... never to a person. And I jumped twice. Once to where you found me and the second time to stop you from doing something you'd never forgive yourself for doing."

Paul nosed me until he found my mouth and pushed his hands down the back of my loose bottoms to grab my bare skin.

"I never lied to you Paul ... did I say anything else?"

"You said you love Denis ..."

"He's adorable in a loud and rough kind of way," I laughed. Paul gave my butt a slap making me yelp in surprise.

"And Ray," Paul added.

"Mm," I answered. "He's so serious and mysterious ... ow."

Paul turned and pulled me down beside him so I rested on my good side. He reached behind me and folded the bedspread over top.

"You said you love me."

I paused as I felt the truth of his words.

"I didn't lie to you," I whispered putting my hand over my chest. "I think I did before you left me ... I couldn't let go. Maybe it was too soon to get so attached."

"I think its okay Sugar," he replied as he tucked my head into my favourite place under his chin. "We're having a baby. It's okay."

"Did you say you love me too?" I yawned settling in to sleep.

"Yes."

"I don't feel empty anymore Paul."

"Neither do I," he whispered. I closed my eyes and gave in to the pain pills for a while.

"Is she asleep?" Ray whispered. Paul nodded and I agreed. I was definitely asleep. "It's interesting. He'll get his long memory from you but what do you think he'll get from her? Your son could be unlike any who have come into the family."

Paul eased himself out of bed and I slept a little longer in silence. "You know that's a long way off Ray. Damian knows she's here now and the pregnancy is the only thing that grants her our protection. One way or another, he can't have her."

"You didn't always live by that Paul," Ray said. "I'm glad I don't have your job."

"Yeah, you never did like me sleeping with your sister."

Chapter 8

I stood on the street in front of my house looking north, facing the flames. Bright orange light washed everything, flames licked as far as I could see and in the distance they obscured what I couldn't. The heat stung my skin and I kept my eyes squinted in the hot dry wind.

This dream had been the same for years but this time was more. I'd been on the main floor, in Mrs. Desmond's part of the house. My back was to the explosion when it came. I had been in her bedroom doorway.

The roar of the plane filled my ears then everything shook as the ball of fire tried to crush my house and threw me on to the bed. The pain in my back was enormous. I could feel the burning and without thinking I rolled over to smother the flames. When I could stand I used something to knock as much of the broken glass as I could from the window frame and escaped to the outside, cutting myself up in the process.

My bike was on its side by the driveway, lying in the smouldering grass. That was disappointing. It had never been down before and it would stay down until I could get some help to stand it back up.

Everything stung in the heat of the inferno. My feet were cool and when I looked down I couldn't see them, my huge belly blocked my view. I put my hands on her. It's okay, I thought. It's okay. She booted my hand. She knew ... and she didn't like it. She wanted to get back to Paul.

"Anna? What are you doing outside?"

I peered into the flames and couldn't see anyone.

"Is somebody out there?" I called back.

"Anna, it's below freezing."

I still couldn't see anyone and my skin hurt from the heat.

"Who's out there?" I yelled at the fire.

"What? It's Paul. Get inside before you freeze."

I looked at my crumpled house. Not likely, I thought.

"Paul? I don't see you. Keep talking."

"What do you mean sleepwalking?" Paul asked but not to me. I hadn't said anything about sleepwalking. I waited for him to say more as I strained my eyes to see him.

"Well what do you want me to do?" he said

I started to panic. His voice came from under my neighbour's apple tree.

I yelled to him. "Paul, get behind me! The tree is going to come down any minute!"

"Anna wake up," he called back.

"Get behind me please, you'll be crushed." I could hear the alarm rising in my voice as I reached to him and felt the heat cut through to my finger bones. "Please, please, I'll burn if I get any closer. Hurry, there's no time."

"Okay, I'm coming," he said.

"Run Paul," I yelled into the inferno.

I heard his foot steps then his voice behind me. "Now what?"

Having Paul there I lost track of the rhythm of my dream. The tiny pops and gusts that marked the passage of time. Suddenly the branch came down with an enormous crack. I wasn't expecting it so I pulled myself around my baby as much as I could. A hand was on my back to steady me.

"Jesus! You're hot!" Paul exclaimed. His hand quickly disappeared. It was time for me to leave him behind.

"I'm sorry Paul, I have to go now. You can't follow me."

"What do you mean Anna, where do you have to go?" He demanded.

I turned as far as I could to his voice. "I have to go count the dead Paul. I'll be back soon …"

He gasped. "Oh my God Anna, your eyes …"

"Soon," I said, and started down the alley.

As I woke I became aware of the cold. After the fire it felt so very good. I sat with my eyes closed for a few minutes, letting my mind go blank and my body cool. Eventually I became aware of men's voices so I opened my eyes.

In the porch light I could make out Paul's front stairs and the snow covered road. There was a strange backpack in my lap. I remembered closing my eyes then the dream. I had no idea how I'd gotten out here. The cold was becoming more than a relief so I stood up with my bag and went in.

I sat on the stairs to get my boots off then I undid my coat. Apparently I'd done more than go outside for a nice cool sit down. I didn't recognize anything I was wearing. After putting the pack over my shoulder I headed down to the opening into the common room across from the kitchen and poked my head around the corner.

Paul's back was to me. He was talking on the phone to someone and sounded upset. Denis was near him checking a handgun and a couple of Paul's other men were looking at something on the desk. I stepped in the doorway and Denis looked up.

"Anna?" he said.

Paul fell silent and turned.

"Hi?" I replied.

"No, come back now," Paul said into the phone. "We found her."

He hung it up. The look on his face said it all. Something bad had happened.

"Anna, where have you been?" he demanded.

I gestured to the front door with my thumb. "Out on the porch for the last few minutes," I said slowly beginning to wonder what sort of trouble I was in. They were all armed. "Why?"

"We've been looking for you for hours."

I pulled my bottom lip between my teeth.

"I don't know what happened, Paul." I whispered then I bolted for his room.

Paul caught up to me quickly and stopped me half way up the stairs. He held me until I started to relax. I didn't realize how wound up I was.

"What's up with the guns?" I whispered.

"I couldn't be sure you wouldn't come back with company," he explained. "I'm sorry; you wouldn't have been expecting that. Come on, let's get you upstairs. Ray's going to want to give you a once over."

The stairs were much easier than I thought they would be and I had no trouble managing the bag. I wondered how much time my ribs really had to heal.

I went through the coat and gave the receipts to Paul. "When are these for?" I asked him and started in on the bag. It was packed to bursting with clothes. "I've been shopping ... I hate shopping."

"Seven days worth ... all stores in Toronto. There's a huge hotel bill," he said. "Did you get me anything?"

"Doesn't look like it," I said. "Can I have a drawer? I don't want to live out of this bag."

"Yes," he said. "You can have a drawer."

"Thanks."

Paul was quiet for a minute as I pulled the clothes out one piece at a time and started sorting them.

"We were eating lunch," he said. "We heard the front door open and close then out the window we see you on the road, no boots or coat. You were looking up at the sky and then watching the house.

"When I got out there I told you to come in, you were already starting to shiver. You wanted to know who I was. Ray said you were sleepwalking. You started on about a tree falling on me and insisted I come and stand behind you, so I did. All of a sudden you jumped a foot. You almost fell over so I put my hand on your back. You were so hot. Then you turned to me and said you had to go and count the dead.

"Anna, I saw the reflection of flames in your eyes ... it scared the hell out of me. You said you would be back soon. You took a couple of steps and froze then you just faded away. I've been worried sick. We searched for hours then you walk back in the front door like you were out there the whole time."

I sat down beside him.

34

"That's about what I remember, except this time you were in my dream … and the hours I spend in the fire."

"What do you mean this time?" he asked. "This happened before?"

"I've had the dream before. Over and over. A plane crashes near my house. For some reason it's my job to walk through the wreckage and account for all the dead. I have to make sure they're all there … it's really horrible.

"She was with me this time." I finished.

"Who?" Paul asked.

I put my hand on her.

"You know it's a girl?" He was surprised.

"Yes, this time I was really huge. She knew it would be okay. All she wanted was to get back to you."

"How do you know that?"

"I don't know Paul," I shrugged. "Just a dream."

I let him think a bit. He and Ray believed she was a boy but now I suggested a girl. I had the certainty of what I learned about her during my dream to keep doubt away and apparently a week to accept it.

"Can you help me get this shirt off?" I asked. "There's something stuck to my arm."

"I can't pass up a request like that," Paul said. "That must have taken a while."

Under a layer of plastic covering my arm was a full sleeve of tattooed angry red and orange flames.

I changed into a light green button up shirt and clean jeans and got back to unpacking the rest of the bag. Other than a lot of high end skin care products and a box of cigars at the bottom there wasn't much else. I pulled the bag out and dumped it on the bed.

"How much money did you spend?" he asked. "That stuff is pretty much unaffordable."

I picked the receipt out of the pile of bottles and jars and gave it to him.

"No idea." I piled my clothes on the chair. I didn't want to rearrange Paul's things; I felt like I had imposed enough.

"I can put these away tomorrow," I hinted. He had two dressers so hopefully one had space.

He pointed to the one by the bathroom. "The bottom of that one is empty if you want. All your clothes should fit in there."

Paul watched me move in without comment.

"Are you sure about this?" I asked him. "It feels sort of semi-permanent."

"Yes I'm sure. I won't regret giving it our best. I know my place probably isn't what you were expecting, but hopefully you'll stay for a while."

"Definitely. Besides," I joked, "I'm snowed in until spring and by then I'll be too big to fit behind the tank."

"I guess I get to keep you then," he agreed. I took the cosmetics into the bathroom and shoved the things I would use most onto the shelves behind the mirror and knelt to find room amongst the toilet paper and cleaners under the sink for the rest of it. When I stood I saw Paul in the mirror staring at me from behind, his elbow on the wall and his hand behind his head. His eyes dropped taking me in as I watched him.

He was so observant and withdrawn at the same time. Perhaps some familiar soldier mode he needed occasionally; purely defensive for both his body and his spirit. When I turned and approached he didn't move. His eyes said exactly what he wanted.

Our fight hours earlier felt distant to me. Even though I didn't remember the week emotionally I was aware of its passage. For him it would still be fresh as would Ray's hands off for two more days edict.

"Almost gone," I brushed the bruise on my cheek. As I got close I reached for the buttons on the shirt I'd just put on and slowly opened them all up. Then I unzipped the jeans and worked them down off my hips. Usually I bought things a little looser for comfort crouched over the back of my motorcycle. Once free I let them drop and kicked them aside. Panties came off as I stepped out of them then the shirt slipped from my shoulders and landed on top. Last my bra then I took my hair down and shook it loose. I could hear Paul's breathing change charging me inside.

My nose nuzzled the side of his throat for a moment then I tackled his shirt. One button at time, the heavy grey cotton slowly spread to reveal his worn undershirt beneath. I tugged the shirt up and free from his pants then lifted the undershirt to feel his stomach. He wasn't chiselled but he was lean and his abdomen was firm and warm under my fingers.

The man I believed to be a trained killer involuntarily tensed his muscles under my touch and my own stomach tightened in reply. He put his lips on mine and walked backward out of the bathroom as I followed his kiss to the bed.

Chapter 9

Dinner had been amazing. The smell of winter barbeque followed Ross and an empty platter in as we came down the stairs. After Ray took out the IV I'd been allowed down for meals and had met everyone. Paul, Lieutenant Ross Wells, Denis and Ray were the Officers. The rest were from what I could tell enlisted men.

36

After dinner I went up and got the cigars. "I don't know if these are any good, but they were in my bag."

Paul's eyes went wide with surprise. "Anna, these are really expensive … are you sure?"

"I won't smoke them and if they're expensive I'll have to take your word for it."

He opened the box and took one and passed it around the table. A couple of them lit up at the table and Ross shooed them out.

"I guess I'm pretty generous when I don't have to pay for the presents." I told Paul as we found a corner in the common room.

"Am I paying you back for these?" he asked.

"No, I won't be paying for any of the things I got."

He sulked for a moment. "Is someone else paying you back?"

I nudged him with my shoulder. "The credit card number on the receipts is mine, but the charges will never show up on my bill."

"Wait," he said. "You had a ten thousand dollar week in Toronto and you don't have to pay for it?"

"Long weekend?" Ray asked. He'd come in with short glasses of something for him and Paul and took over the armchair beside us. "No scotch for you Anna."

I made a face. Never did like the smell.

"She has seven days of receipts including six nights plus room service at a really expensive hotel." Paul explained.

"You told him?"

"He figured it out first," Paul said.

Ray must have talked Paul out of tossing me straight out on my ass so I offered a smile in thanks. "Technically, I'm off bed rest now."

"Yeah, I heard you," Ray said.

I felt my cheeks turn pink and looked away. I'd have to remember how good Ray's hearing was.

"Why don't you have to pay?" Paul asked again.

"Well, my cash is gone, spent … physically left behind; anything I picked up comes back. But I'm not going to be there tonight running up a hotel bill, or buying cigars in two days, or checking out in seven. I'm here … so I'm never actually there.

"Anyway, I'm keeping a shopping list in my pocket for next time in case there's anything you want me to get." Neither of them seemed particularly pleased with the idea of a next time.

"Smoke. I'll go earn my keep." I went to give Ross and the others some help with the cleanup. Then I grabbed my coat and boots and went to sit outside to get some fresh air. It took longer than I thought for Paul to come looking for me.

"Did you lose something?" I asked.

"No, I thought you went up to bed but you weren't there."

"Ah," I said. "So are the cigars any good? Maybe I got them so you could hand them out in the spring but I figured they'd be stale by then, so why wait."

He ruffled my hair. "I can get more."

"Already on my list," I said.

"Ray's looking for you."

I yawned and got up. "Can you distract him for me? He can find me tomorrow."

"Okay," he said. "Give me sixty seconds."

"Thanks, should I wait up for you?" I asked playfully.

"Unless you want to be woken up," he replied. "Sixty."

After I counted to sixty, I snuck upstairs. I'd pinched a Do Not Disturb sign from the hotel and I hung it on the doorknob. Maybe it would keep Ray out until morning. I was still warming the bed when I heard Paul laugh at the sign. The smell of cigar smoke came in with him.

Paul took off his knife and gun and put them on his night table. He also had a bullet proof vest under his heavy jacket.

"Do I need one of those?" I asked. I was beginning to wonder if I might need protection from whatever he was worried about.

"Mm," he said. The sound he made when he had to choose between lying and not answering.

"It was easy to be without you when I could just call you up and see you again. I could run around working or be here and you would always answer the phone and be there with me no strings attached. But when you disappeared today …" he trailed off, dropping down on the bed with his back to me.

I crawled up behind him and put my arms around his waist and my head on his shoulder. He was warm on my bare skin in the cool air of his room.

"I spent a month needing you back in my life," I whispered into his back. "I don't care the time or the place, as long as there's going to be an again … I just need to be smothered in you … again … and again."

He turned around, wrapped an arm around me and dragged me up to the pillows. I was already helping him undress as we dug our way under the covers.

Paul got up a few hours later.

"What?" I asked.

"I have a shift on watch. You'll still be asleep when I get back."

"Mmf," I said. "I don't have to like that, do I?"

"No Sugar, you don't."

"'kay," I said. "Look after yourself."

After he left I went to the bathroom. When I looked in the mirror the woman was there, looking at me from my own bathroom back home.

Paul's mirror went all the way down to the sink so I could see that she was different from me ... that was something new. She had always appeared as I did. Except she spoke to me like a mean big sister. Her stomach was big and flames covered both her arms.

So, everything's fine now?

What do you mean?

Sex. Everything's working below the waist so it's all right with the world?

That's crude.

All Paul's parts are working fine too?

Do I have to answer that?

No, but don't you find his place a little weird?

I hadn't thought about it.

You have ... he's getting suspicious.

I'm trying to not cause problems.

You're forgetting what they said ... they're protecting your daughter, not you.

I dreamed that, I told her.

Didn't and you know it ... when did you turn your instincts off girl? She turned her head slightly listening to something behind her. *Oh I know. It was when you met him. You told me to fuck off in the restaurant bathroom and took him straight to your bed to spend your virginity underneath him.*

My nostrils flared with anger but she reacted faster slamming her hands on the glass. I felt it in my hips resting on the sink and I leaned forward, nose to nose with my evil reflection.

They watched you disappear at lunch and smoked your cigars from the future like nothing happened while all that went through your mind is you're getting laid again.

I had no answer, she was right. I hated that.

She startled and raised a defensive hand to her face. *You're going to fuck everything up!* I was surprised to see a tear break through her heartless veneer. *And if you need a reminder I highly recommend you take a look at what's stashed under the tarp behind the small garage.*

You need to jump. Jump and find help. There are things he can't tell you that you have to find out on your own. Things he won't tell you either.

Like what? As usual you're thin on the details.

I won't spoil the ending. Jump. Find help. Take Paul to his father.

How do I do that?

You'll figure it out.

You were wrong last time.

Then I was looking at my real self in the mirror.

"Maybe next time you show up you could be a little more helpful," I muttered.

I turned off the light and blind in the dark, headed toward the bed and bounced off a wall.

"Who's there?" I panicked and as I tried to duck back into the bathroom I backed into the door jam before I found the corner by the sink.

"Who were you talking to Anna?"

"Paul?" I asked.

"Who were you talking to?" Paul asked again.

Don't lie, I told myself. You won't be able to keep things straight. "Myself. You could actually hear me?"

He didn't say anything.

"Could you hear her too? I thought it was all in my head."

"Hear who Anna? Who were you talking to?"

"The woman in the mirror," I whispered.

The light came on and I had to blink in the brightness that had made me blind in the dark. Paul put out his hand.

"You sounded angry," he said softly. "I thought you were mad with me for going out. You got a concussion not that long ago. Ray said to watch for any odd behaviour from you for the next little bit ... just in case."

My hand shook as I took his and I stepped out of my corner. I was still naked and Paul towering over me in his boots with his gun was intimidating and reassuring at the same time.

My voice shook. "You really startled me good."

"Come on, you're shivering. I came back for another layer and I heard you. It sounded like you were fighting with someone. You can tell me about it in the morning when you warm up. I'm running late," he said. "Sorry for startling you."

Then he kissed me again and disappeared out the door.

Tension rolled down my body leaving me momentarily numb. I woke disoriented. I had fallen asleep on my sore ribs and pain quickly had me wide awake. Paul was facing me, eyes closed, so after carefully making it over to my good side I backed myself into his lap and tried to go back to sleep. His arm curled around me and he relaxed with a big sigh. He was cold from the outside.

"I woke you up."

"No," I said. "I did that to myself. I fell asleep on my sore side. It's better now."

"Ray's worried your concussion was worse than we thought. I'm worried too."

I was surprised. "Why?"

"You were arguing with someone in the mirror last night," he said. "Not normal."

I sighed. "Is there anything about me being here that has been normal? Anyway that woman has been around for years, not just last night. She tries to keep me out of trouble ... I put up with her ... she can be sort of mean sometimes."

"How?"

"Well, the night we met she wanted me to run the other way. She thought I would be some sort of prize for you, that you would ruin things for me."

He thought a moment. "Like Kenny?"

"Ray ..." I muttered. "Yes, like Kenny. What did he tell you?"

"Everything," he said. "I guess it helps me understand you more."

I didn't say anything. Fresh humiliation filled me. I put a hand on my face to try and hide from it.

"Short fuse?" he asked. "Do girls really talk like that?"

"I guess I picked it up from Alina and her friends." I told him. "I finished high school and left home at sixteen to ride around the southern States alone. She seemed to know when I was headed for trouble. The last time I saw her I told her to beat it and went back to join you for dinner. I hadn't seen her since."

"Mm, what did she want last night?" he asked.

I thought about it.

"She said that just because everything is working from the waist down again doesn't mean we can dodge any decisions we have to make."

"Wise woman," he said.

If you only knew half of what she said, I thought.

"I suppose, but anyone who is going to demand to know if your parts are working right is crossing the line."

Paul laughed then he yawned.

"Breakfast is in a couple of hours, let's get some sleep."

I could smell cigar smoke on my pillow and closed my eyes. Slowly Paul warmed up against me. Maybe he was doing the same thing ... lying awake thinking that I was asleep or lying awake knowing that I was pretending.

Chapter 10

I'd found the only quiet place in Paul's house was the far end of the kitchen table when all the hustle of dinner was gone. With the light out and a warm mug of something I could put my feet up on the sill of the big window and look down the road that led past the cabins to the gate or on nights like this watch snow fall in the porch light. After

41

spending my first few rough days stuck in Paul's room it wasn't my first choice of places to go if I wasn't tired.

Paul and I had a couple of armless chairs and a blanket on our legs to fend off the draft from the old window. The heat from the wood stove in the common room called it a draw with the cold from the window about half way down the table so the blanket was necessary.

I heard something in the hall as Paul took a breath to speak and I quickly put my fingers on his lips to stop him.

"Captain?" A voice from the kitchen door. Paul went to whisper with him for a few minutes then he came back to me.

"I have a few men who just got in … wasn't expecting them for a couple of days and I need to get them settled. I'll be back in a while."

I tried to hide a yawn. "Are you bringing them here? Do you want me to get out of sight for a while?"

"Yes, late dinner, they've been travelling most of the day … and not unless you want to."

It was only about twenty minutes before I could hear Paul and the newcomers stomping the snow off their boots on the porch. I'd hoped to make myself scarce before they showed up and meet them in the morning. I stopped at the other side of the foyer, about ten feet from the door.

"Ah, I'm glad you're still here." Paul said to me as they hung their coats. He introduced the first two and sent them along to the kitchen. The third was a younger blonde version of Paul.

"Anna. I'd like you to meet my second in command. Lieutenant Richards."

"Joshua," he said to me. "Paul says I'm going to be an uncle. Congratulations to you both."

Uncle … that explained why he looked so much like Paul. I looked at Paul over Joshua's shoulder. He was trying to keep his grin under control. I put out my hand for him and he shook it. "Nice to meet you, Joshua … and thank you," I said. "Come on, there's a stack of chicken in the fridge."

After only a couple of steps Joshua whispered to Paul. "Score big brother. You finally tied down one of those models you've been chasing."

The last thing I wanted was to end up with that label or stereotype. I stopped dead and spun on my heel, put my hands behind my back and stared Joshua down until his grin fell. I tilted my head and looked at Paul again over his shoulder. He was struggling to keep a straight face. I turned my attention back to Joshua.

"Lieutenant Richards … let's try this again." I said and held out my hand. He reached out slowly and took it.

"Lieutenant-Commander Creed, Canadian Forces." I pronounced

42

it lef-tenant then I paused. Joshua was starting to lose a bit of the cold air pinkness from his cheeks. I let go of his hand and made a fist, putting it in my palm. "If I hear any more trash like that come past your lips we're going to go behind the house to compare service records. You won't piss right for a month ... clear?"

"Clear. Yes Ma'am," he stammered.

"Very well," I said and stepped out of his way gesturing to the kitchen.

After he was past me Paul whispered. "Isn't it against the law to impersonate a naval officer?"

Joshua stopped.

"Only if you're wearing the uniform ... I think." I whispered back as we burst out laughing.

Joshua turned around.

"I like her," he said and headed off to the kitchen.

Paul was still laughing quietly.

"About time I met your brother," I told him.

"He was called out a while ago ... he'll spend a week or so here then spend some time with our folks before he comes back."

I thought a moment. "Do your folks know about me ... that they'll be grandparents?"

"Does your father?" Paul countered.

"I don't know if my father would shoot you or be relieved that my wandering days could be over."

"Mine would be in the relieved category ... you have no idea how often my mother uses the words "nice woman" and "grandchildren" with Joshua and me."

After everyone had gotten dinner the two men went to the cabin Paul assigned them I cleaned up the kitchen while Joshua and Paul went to the common room. Paul got out the scotch and two of the remaining cigars.

While I unloaded the dishwashers I heard bits and pieces of their conversation. Shop talk, their family. A lot of laughter. Joshua's laugh was just as loud as Paul's and I was quite certain I wouldn't get much rest until Paul came to bed. I wiped down the counters and the table I turned off the light and went to sit back down and watch the snow.

"She's gone upstairs?" Joshua asked after a while.

"Must have," Paul answered.

Joshua laughed. "Lucky bastard, you told mom?"

"That I'm a lucky bastard?"

"No, that you finally found a nice woman with poor eyesight."

There was more laughter. I laughed quietly; Paul wasn't hard on the eyes at all.

"Hm ... you know mom's all but given up on you. I get the

43

grandchildren talk ten times worse than you do. If you were a good big brother you'd tell her and get the heat off me for a while."

"I haven't known her all that long. I met her at one of the rallies in the summer, spent the night in her hotel. My God Josh, she makes an old man like me wish he was ten years younger.

"We spent a few nights together before I called it off. She's got so much ahead of her. I didn't think it was fair for her to have one one-night stand after another with a man who'd never be any more than a ghost in her life."

Paul hadn't told me that. Maybe that was part of it. The part he would tell his brother.

"Then a couple of weeks ago she rides down here to find me. Tells me she's pregnant. She thought I'd met someone else and only came down to open the door with the kid. She never left. I spent a month regretting saying good-bye. Now I can't imagine a day without her. And I'm going to be a father. Someone is smiling on me."

"Whoever it is send them my way." Joshua said. "You let her in Paul … to this house. Your life here. You never did that with anyone else. And she didn't run the other way."

"No, she didn't," Paul laughed quietly. "She said she loves me."

"Someone has to ask you before it goes too far. Do you feel the same way or are you just trying to do the right thing 'cause maybe you should have kept it in your pants?"

There was silence for a few seconds.

"I know what you're saying Josh. Even between the nights we spent together she was on my mind. I stopped putting my line out. Knowing I'd see her again was distracting. I'm a better man for having her.

"Yeah, I feel the same way."

Joshua didn't say anything as I heard more scotch slosh into their glasses. I closed my eyes and put my feet up on the window sill, crossing my arms and turning slightly in my chair so I could rest my head. Paul's house felt like home more than any place I'd known since losing my mother and hearing Paul tell someone else about me made me sure I belonged here with him.

"She said when she got here that she'd quit work, wasn't going back for a while. I did the same. I don't want a night without her. I can listen to her breathe, my bed's warm when I get in at three in the morning. I can fall asleep sober and know if the bad dreams come I won't wake up alone … but I haven't had any since she got here."

Paul paused.

"Anna thinks it's a girl. I don't think she cares where we are, as long as I'm there with her."

"You know when mom finds out she'll be on the first flight here to help you pick out a ring and she'll already have the tent booked for immediate family and five hundred of her closest friends for the reception."

"Yeah …" Paul said.

"And there will be nothing you can do about it."

"Uh huh."

"Well, I like her Paul. When she looks at you you're the only other person in the room. Lucky bastard."

They were still talking when I fell asleep. Joshua was complaining that he'd never meet anyone in the compound or living with his parents. His mother pointing at every woman she saw and asking 'what about her?' Paul suggested he stop living with his parents.

Paul found me later and brought me up stairs. The bed was cold but we were both warm. His lips tasted of scotch and he pushed the hair off my forehead as I wrapped my leg over him.

Chapter 11

I struggled to reconcile what Paul told his brother and his conversation with Ray when we all thought I was asleep. He and Ray had talked like they were family and our child would be part of that but Ray wasn't related to him, Joshua was, and Paul hadn't told him how I'd gotten here or even mentioned the man named Damian.

Then there was the woman in the mirror. She'd always been right in her mean way.

I found some things in the shop I could fix up quickly and a couple of bigger projects including an older four-fifty dirt bike. It would get me out if I needed it or to help if the woman in the mirror had her way.

Ray was able to pick up most of the parts I needed on his next supply run so I kept busy making the four-fifty my main project. Days in the shop and nights with Paul. He spent time in the shop with me in addition to whatever else he had to do running the camp. He went out for watch most nights and his cold skin woke me.

The woman in the mirror had succeeded in getting under my skin. After days of not thinking about the tarp behind the shed it was now all I could think about. I quietly worked on my lunch smiling appropriately at Paul when he gave me a little elbow but never really pulling myself free of her words.

Stashed under the tarp. Like a delicious forbidden treasure; secret and hidden. I was by nature observant and cautious which served me in good stead when my wanderings found me alone in rough places. Also shamelessly curious when I got the idea that someone might be keeping something good from me, a trait I shared with my sister.

Ray or Denis sometimes cluttered up the shop with their less and more helpful presences respectively but today Ray was in the middle of something and Denis and Paul were both on watch. Today was ideal. By the time Paul got the heaters fired back up for me my eyes were itchy with the need to see what they'd hidden.

I took a bit of time doing a few things that didn't require a lot of attention; changed the oil on my bike and reconnected some fluid lines on the four-fifty. Once I was certain I'd be alone for a while I took a quick look up the road then went down the passage between the garages. She'd said the small one so I looked behind it. There were several tarps there over various things. Also a small garbage dumpster and some trash cans.

The first couple of tarps yielded little including a pile of folded tarps. I was careful to just peek, only lifting up the edges. The only thing more satisfying than having my curiosity rewarded was if it also went undiscovered.

The last one was the size of a large piece of luggage and had a couple of bungee cords hooked around it like the others to keep it in place. It covered a large plastic tote and after a bit of hesitation disturbed the tarp enough to get the top off.

"Jesusfuckinchrist!" I exclaimed as I scrambled backward before I found a spot in the snow several feet away and hastily wiped my face on my sleeves and tried to rub my hand clean on my jeans.

It wasn't the colour that bothered me really or the non-existent smell my brain tried to imagine in compensation for its frozen absence. Or even the way the fingers were partly clenched. It was the first seriously dead person I'd ever seen but that wasn't it either. I stared mesmerised even though it was out of sight behind the plastic side of the tub only a tiny bit aware of my body heat melting the snow I sat in so it soaked through my pants.

"Anna?" It was Ray's voice from inside the big garage. "Anna?"

I heard him trudge over the footprints I'd left in the snow no longer caring if I got caught.

"Are you okay?" Ray asked. I shook my head. "Hurt?"

I pointed at the tote.

"Shit," Ray sighed under his breath as he tried to pull me to my feet. I wrapped my arms around my legs refusing. I wasn't leaving without an explanation. Ray took out his radio instead of trying again. "Victor Whiskey."

"Whiskey Victor," Paul's voice replied after a minute.

"Ten twenty-five Station Two," Ray said. God, I wondered if he was going to take me to the house in the back seat of a car.

"Copy Victor, Whiskey out."

"Come on Kiddo," Ray tried.

46

I shook my head. Ray squatted down in front of me to block my view so I stared through him. Our stalemate continued until Paul arrived.

"She okay?" he asked with concern at seeing Ray kneeling over me.

"Tote."

"Ah fuck," Paul said. "Sugar, I need you to get up and come with me."

I looked up at Paul as I slowly clued in. As I took in the man in charge who made the decision to put the dead man in the box anger and queasiness vied for my attention. My hands came up as I stood and took a step back from both of them.

"Why?" I demanded mentally digging in to challenge him.

"Because I'm asking," he said. Your tone wasn't asking at all, I thought. I glanced between them at the tote. The jacket and helmet stuffed in with him I recognized.

"He tried to run me into a car."

Paul's face started to twist into a menacing grimace as one hand absently dropped to his knife and the other took my elbow. Only his voice was calm. "Then I don't want you near him." Knuckles whitened around the handle. I had no doubt the death grip on the hilt wasn't meant for me, the hand on my elbow remained relaxed.

I stuck my chin up at him mostly in defiance but also to help keep lunch down. "Why is he with the garbage?" I hissed through my teeth.

He looked incredulous. Shaking his head he let go of the knife, furiously stabbing his finger at the dead man for emphasis. "He tried to put my girl and my baby through a windshield! He is garbage!" Paul was turning a colour you could only get by mixing red with blue. "Then he brought a gun to my house and tried to shoot one of my men."

I started to nod in understanding. This was nothing but petty punishment that wasn't hurting the dead man at all. I shook free of him.

"What's on his hand?" I demanded.

He looked over then back at me.

"The shiny round thing?" That was what upset me so much. He shook his head.

"He stopped being garbage when he died Paul," I said quietly as I tried to calm us both down. The madder I got the closer I got to throwing up on him. Paul crossed his arms and looked away.

"Somewhere there is someone just like me who's thinking about him every day. You can just bet she wasn't on a motorcycle on the highway with me. She had no idea where he was or what he was doing."

I glanced at Ray a few feet away and stepped closer to Paul.

"You dumped me so I wouldn't be that woman," I whispered trying to speak as privately as I could. "Now you're fucking over someone else's wife. Nice work garbage man. You're being an asshole."

47

I staggered off shivering in my wet jeans and shaking with nausea making it half way down the alley before lunch landed in the snow. A hand rested on my back and I recognized Ray's legs. When I finally stood I held my head high and walked away back to the house. Paul hadn't turned up by the time I'd warmed in the shower and pulled on one of his tees. His room was cold so I added his robe and after considering getting in bed and pulling the blankets over my head I pulled the big comforter into the closet with me putting it over my head as I broke down. The mean bitch had lured me into finding a body.

I was still sniffling in my cocoon when Paul finally came in. The door opened and he took a few steps and I heard him sigh. His boots got louder as he approached the closet then the door folded open a little more and I heard him climb in. My feet cooled a bit as he lifted the blanket.

"Sugar?" he said softly.

"Yeah, it's me," I answered as his hand took my ankle and moved up my calf.

"You sure made short work of calling me out."

I pulled my foot back. "Thank you."

"He's former military … a traitor and deserter. He's wanted," Paul explained. "My CO ran his ID. Married."

"He'll take care of him no questions asked."

I nodded, letting my feet creep closer to Paul and lifted the blanket offering him room underneath.

"Thank you Paul. It would kill me to be her if you were in the box."

Paul dug in head first under the blanket and pushed me down on top of his pile of shoes. "I'm sorry for making you cry."

I shrugged. "You're not an asshole."

"I was," he chuckled. "I hope I'm not now."

Paul's head found mine in spite of the enormous blanket and the bottoms of his clothes weighing down on it. He untied the robe and reached around to grab my butt and turn me to face him.

"Are we sleeping in here?"

"Yes," I answered. Even so angry with him I could put my size eight right up his ass his arms were the first place I wanted to be when I was upset. "Alina and I used to do it all the time."

"Sleep in my closet?"

"Yes," I laughed feeling forgiveness as my nose felt his Adam's apple. Paul's free hand felt my little tummy. I had to admit it was getting firm already. Then he started to make his way up my shirt. "Going for second in the closet Captain?"

"Something like that Commander."

"Lef-tenant Commander," I corrected as his broad hand perfectly covered what he found.

"There's no effin Lieutenant," he replied. "Mm," he added as I softly got my teeth around a chunk of his neck and dragged them along.

"You will be if you keep that up." She'd sent me to look, I found, then I slipped right back under his spell.

Chapter 12

A soft kiss on my forehead lightened my sleep then a hand rested at the side of my face.

"Paul?" I mumbled. "Look after yourself."

I waited to hear him tell me he loved me but he was completely still. My lids fluttered open and blue light from his alarm clock explained I was alone. I must have nodded off before he was even out the door.

I was also damp with cozy warm sweat. The cold spell had eased and now there were too many blankets on the bed. As I pushed off the bedding and sat I heard voices downstairs. Paul's for sure. He didn't sound happy about something although I couldn't hear precisely what.

My glass yielded a scant mouthful as I tipped it back. I groaned. That meant I had to go downstairs for a drink. Nothing taller than a coffee mug would fit in the bathroom sink. I preferred kitchen water anyway even though it came from the same place.

Paul's robe was still mashed on top of his shoes so I hastily turned it right side out and opened the door. Light came up the stairs at the far end of the hall and showed me the way was clear.

Part way down I was able to make Paul out. "We all just got back. Don't you have a team who's a little fresher?" He sounded aggravated. I needed to get past the common room and quickly.

"Captain," Joshua's calmer and much like Paul's voice said. "We haven't even unpacked … and it's an easy job."

"Gentlemen," an unfamiliar voice spoke sharply. "I don't recall assignments being a negotiation."

Didn't like the sound of any of them shipping out, especially Paul. A chill started to fill my cheeks and work its way down making me shiver by the time I got to the bottom of the stairs. I checked to make sure the robe was properly shut and tried to get by the door with a hand covering my eyes so whatever was going on could happen in privacy but they fell silent.

"Anna? Everything okay?"

I dropped my hand and stopped, holding up the glass. "I'm so sorry to interrupt. It won't fit in the sink." There was an older man I didn't know beside Paul. Old school brush cut and his clothes were so unwrinkled and tidy he was most likely military.

"Sorry," I repeated. "I'll just be a sec."

"Who's the new recruit?" The older man asked.

Paul sighed and held out his hand to me so I approached a step or two but the man was already headed for me with Paul right behind him. I could imagine the tangle my hair was in from crawling around with it wet under the blanket earlier.

"Colonel Iverson, this is my girl ... Anna Creed. Sig is my Commanding Officer."

I held out my hand to the Colonel as he glanced at my stomach. I felt like he noticed the baby even though there was no way he could in the big robe.

"Miss Creed, please call me Sig." He kissed my knuckles and took another step closer to kiss my cheek. My nose tickled terribly and I nearly knocked him in the chin stifling a pair of sneezes inside my elbow.

"Bless you," he said generously.

"No, wow, excuse me, those came out of nowhere."

"Lef-tenant Commander Creed," Joshua whispered from his chair and from the corner of my eye I could see him grab Denis in a brotherly headlock, silencing a laugh.

"Lef-tenant Commander?" the Colonel asked.

I looked pleadingly at Paul who had his hand over his face.

"*Restigouche*," Denis blurted out when he got his mouth free of Joshua's armpit. Ray booted him in the thigh.

"*HMCS Restigouche* was decommissioned nearly two decades ago Lieutenant Martin," Sig said.

"Just Anna, please."

The Colonel nodded, apparently resisting the urge to turn and look at the quiet scuffle behind him.

"How long are you staying?" he asked me.

My lips turned in to an O and I looked at Paul.

"As long as she wants," Paul got an arm around me and started to steer me to the kitchen. "Excuse us Sir."

"I have a bit of business Sugar," he whispered. "Then I'll be up."

Paul took my glass and ran the water for a minute. "I don't think I can get out of this," he said quietly. "It's a quick and relatively safe job ... maybe two weeks."

I looked down feeling my lips try to curl and trigger tears. Paul got his arms around me. "Sshhh," he whispered as he held my head to his shoulder. "Easy, easy. I don't want you going home alone. Will you stay here? Denis is on my team. Josh and Ray will be here. They'll look after you."

If I wanted Paul this was what I got for free. Part of the package. "Or maybe you want to go stay with Alina?"

"Here," I mumbled.

50

"Okay," he nodded. "I think I'd like to come home to you."

I turned my head up to him and moistened my lips and was rewarded with the kiss I was inviting.

"Really?"

"Absolutely really," he answered as Joshua barged in right up behind Paul bumping him into me.

"I win big brother," Joshua said. "My boys are up."

"Josh ...," Paul started to complain.

"Colonel seems to think you're needed more here right now. Hey, can I borrow your babysitting job magazines? It's gonna get lonely ..."

Paul rolled his eyes.

"That's unsanitary Josh," I whispered as I wiped my eyes on a big sleeve. "Get your own."

Chapter 13

After another week of shivering over engines and bikes in the workshop I found myself falling asleep on Paul's shoulder. He shooed me upstairs and I slipped under the cold blankets, barely remembering pulling them over me. I dreamed of Catherine again, at home with her father before she moved to the cabin where she died. The year was 1777.

I woke outside my sister's apartment. At least I felt awake even though I knew there was no way I could be there.

I recognized the door; cream with gold numbers. 1502. I could still make out the little nick in the paint by the knob where Alina had missed with her key. We had taken a taxi back to her apartment completely smashed when I visited a year earlier. No idea why I was here ... or needed to be here. No idea of the time either.

I took a chance and knocked. As I decided she wasn't home the peep hole lit up then darkened as she looked out. She fussed with the deadbolt then opened up as fast as she could.

"Anna? My God, what are you doing here?"

She grabbed my hands and pulled me in then threw her arms around me. I hugged her back. It felt really good to see her. She was stunning in a snug little blue dress with matching pumps.

"I just got in," sort of the truth, "and you're on the way to my hotel. Thought I would take a chance ... last minute job. I jumped on it so I had an excuse to see you."

"You're back at work already?" she demanded. "That Doctor Jackson said you broke your ribs and dislocated your shoulder!"

"I did."

"Was he cute?"

"Alina!"

She sighed. "Well that was what … six weeks ago at least? I guess you have to go back to work eventually."

Six weeks. My stomach tensed. I only remembered three weeks at Paul's.

"Alina? Is everything okay?"

A man? I mouthed to her.

She nodded and seemed to cringe a bit.

"Yes." She called back. Then to me, "I'm sorry, I tried to call and tell you but your machine is full."

"With messages from you," I told her.

She grinned and held up her hand flat above her head. *He's tall.* She mouthed then she quickly looked back behind her to the living room then held her hand flat down by her knee and nodded. *Everywhere*, she mouthed.

"Alina!" I whispered. God I missed her.

"If I'd known I would have called first. I'm not sure how long I'll be in town and I want to spend some time with you."

A man appeared around the corner and slipped his arm around her middle. As she'd said he was taller than her even in the four inch heels. The sleeves on his expensive dress shirt were rolled up and he'd loosened his tie. His nose went into her hair and he inhaled as his hand dropped and slipped out of sight behind her. He laughed as her back straightened and her cheeks started to colour.

"Damian …," she whispered. "I want you to meet my sister Anna."

"Major Howard," he said as he pulled his eyes off her and turned his attention to me. I took his hand and found myself ever so briefly wondering how his nose would feel in my hair.

"Anna Creed," I replied.

"Damian," he said as he let me go.

"Major …," Alina laughed again. "My Damian is in the US Army."

So is my Paul, I thought.

"I'm sorry," she yawned. "I just came off six early shifts. Day of rest tomorrow."

"Dinner then?" Damian suggested. "Why don't you two meet up for lunch and girl stuff then dinner, my treat."

Alina smiled.

"Please Sweetie?" she asked. She knew that I knew exactly what she was asking for and how small a chance there was of me agreeing without some sort of sisterly blackmail: shopping, salon and a formal dining room.

"Okay Alina," I replied surprised by how quickly I'd conceded. And that it wasn't for her. It was because it was what Damian wanted.

"I'll call you in the morning."

"Yes!" She was beyond happy with our date. She kissed my cheek and we said goodbye.

"Wait a sec. I'll see you to your taxi."

Damian disappeared and came back with a jacket on. In the elevator he told me how worried Alina had been since my accident and he thanked me for coming to see her. He could see already that her mood was lightening. She hadn't said anything, he told me, but she had been thinking about me a lot. I blinked away a sudden image of Damian and me up against the elevator wall, my finger on the stop elevator button.

As we spoke I absently tried to look through the small purse I had under my coat but his presence had me completely distracted. I wasn't hearing the words of our conversation at all, just impressions of the subject.

Once outside I took his elbow and we walked down to the next block, something about a taxi faster on the busier road. Suddenly he grabbed me by the throat and carried me down the alley. His rage was terrifying; his strength. He pushed me up off the ground by my neck so my feet were dangling and I grabbed his arm to hold myself up.

I was still making sense of what was going on as he leaned in close, furious.

"I wasn't going to come after you myself this time," he seethed. "I have Alina. But having you here is just too tempting."

He started to squeeze. I tried to kick at him but he pushed himself up against me. My foot banged against the metal garbage bin beside us. He smelled me then he squeezed harder.

"Tell me bitch, did you spread you legs for him that first night, or did you make him wait to fill you with his son?"

His hard breathing filled my ears. I started to see spots as my arms weakened, my hands kept slipping off his jacket as I struggled. He groaned and pushed himself against me even harder. He panted with arousal, his breath fragrant with wine and garlic.

My vision narrowed; head tilted to the sky. I could see the apartment lights above me, fading slowly into the blackness that covered nearly everything around it. Then his weight shifted and he held something long and shiny up where I could see it.

"Remember this Catherine? Filthy bitch," he growled. "You were mine."

Slowly he lowered his hand and twisted the point of the knife against my skin like a corkscrew. One arm dropped, then the other. I was too weak to swat the knife away. Desperation rose. Fear. Pain. The tip popped through then more skin stretched and tore. Then he dropped his wrist and angled the point up to my heart.

I closed my eyes and thought desperately; *Paul.*

The pressure of Damian's body on mine was gone. My feet hit the ground and I fell. My ears roared with life and every bit of air I got in only gave me the energy to cough harder.

There was wood floor beneath me, not pavement. Part of me could hear voices in the distance. I had to move before he found me. I opened my eyes.

I was on the floor in Paul's room.

I coughed again. And again.

I tried to call for help and only wheezed so I started kicking the dresser. The voices downstairs quieted. I could hear boots in the hall and the door burst open.

Paul was first in, then several more. I stopped kicking when I saw him.

"Paul," I coughed again and pulled in a few more breaths. I realized I was holding my hand tightly over where Damian's knife had been in me.

"Anna?' He was so worried. "Where's the blood from?"

"Paul," I held out my bloody hand to him. "Ray."

Paul looked back at the others and one ran out to get Ray.

I put his hand on the hole in my stomach and covered it with mine as another burst of coughing hit me. He felt my blood seep through his fingers on its way to warm my hand.

"Ray!" he yelled. He pulled my hand away and pushed my shirt back to expose the wound then he grabbed a wad of the fabric and pressed it on the hole.

"How long was I gone Paul?" I whispered.

"Sshhh," he said.

"I've been stuck in Toronto for three weeks. Couldn't get back," I wheezed.

He looked at me. "You went up to bed an hour ago … three weeks?"

Ray ran in. He looked under the piece of my dress that Paul held on my stomach and then at my neck.

"I don't think it's very deep. Look at her neck bruising up," he said. "Get her on the bed."

The one who ran off to get Ray brought in the red bags. As they put me on the bed Paul sent the others out. "Sweep the compound," he told them.

"Damian tried to kill me. He has my sister," I whispered, now connecting Alina's boyfriend with the man they had spoken of when I thought I was sleeping. Then I started coughing again.

Paul looked at Ray. He shrugged and started an IV.

"I have to clean that out and stitch you up. You'll be out for a bit."

"Don't worry if you can't wake me," I said. But I was already slipping under.

Chapter 14

Morning sun came in past the open curtain. Ray's back was to me so I closed my eyes and thought about the pieces I'd gathered since I last slept in Paul's bed. Ray and Paul's talk of Damian, my dreams of Catherine and Damian's attack calling me the same name. Why would Damian be satisfied with Alina instead of me?

The woman in the mirror was right; there were things they weren't telling me. They were the only ones who could help me fit the pieces together; even then I would have to find help. They may have thought they could protect me but the previous night had changed everything. I stretched my arms up over the blankets and sighed with dismay. My left was now just as colourful as the right; flames licking all the way up from my wrist and disappearing under my sleeve.

"One night or two Ray?"

He turned around and came over.

"Just one Kiddo," he said. "How you feeling?"

I lost my smile. "Like I've been strangled. I don't think I had very much time left when I got out of there."

He sighed. "The wound to your stomach wasn't deep or near the baby, it was messy though. I'm sorry there's not much I could do to make it look pretty."

"It's okay Ray. He twisted the knife as he eased it in." I felt anger in my face as I talked about it.

"You want to tell me about it?" he asked quietly.

I nodded. "But I'm not reliving it twice ... I'll tell you and Paul at the same time."

"Okay," Ray said. "He's finishing up a watch ... should be back soon."

I closed my eyes and waited. When Paul joined us he came over and kissed me and rested his hand on my stomach. It seemed to make him happy.

"I thought I might lose you both." He said quietly and pulled the chair up so he could sit close. "Sorry I had to leave for a bit."

"'Sokay," I said. "I feel the black sleep coming. I want to tell you what happened before it hits."

"Okay Sugar," he said, "then rest."

"You said I was only gone an hour ... I came up to bed and I think I was asleep before my head hit the pillow. I want to tell you about the dream first because I think that's what made me disappear. I dreamed about Catherine again."

"Not the nightmare …" Paul said.

"This was better … it helps me understand the other one. After you left that morning I could still see the body on the floor. I could smell the blood. His dead eyes followed me around the room as I threw my things together and ran out. I thought my reaction scared you off."

I felt tears in my eyes but I ignored them.

"I was sixteen and had been keeping house for my father and five brothers since I was eight. My brothers had gone to fight the British at Saratoga in '77. He felt that sixteen was old to marry off and when a man arrived with a letter of introduction from his mother … my father's cousin … he moved quickly. Giving me to the man to marry would keep his money in the family. I was angry and afraid, but I knew there was nothing for me there. I wasn't worth anything to him unmarried.

"He took me to the church first thing in the morning to meet my husband. I knew what was expected of me on my wedding night and I was scared but as soon as I saw him my fear went away. I couldn't take my eyes off him. I could hardly wait for him to take me away."

I closed my eyes. I couldn't look at Paul while trying to ignore the feelings I was reliving.

"We rode all day and it was nearly dark when we arrived at a small cabin. He took me straight inside and ignored my need for him. He could have had me but he beat me and raped me instead. In the morning he said he would be gone for many months and his brothers would look after me bringing me food and firewood. He said if I ran off he would find me and kill me.

"One of his brothers came every few days with food. They just dropped it at the door and rode off. One stayed. He shared my bed that first night and every night when he came to my cabin. I loved him. It was like I had always loved him."

I watched Paul. There was no expression on his face as he listened.

"Then he stopped coming and I found myself sick with his child. I'd seen enough children come to know that there was no way I could pass off my lover's newborn son as my absent husband's a year after my marriage. I could only hope he would return and take me away. I waited months and he did return; the same night my husband did."

"After my husband killed him, he cut our son from my stomach before he let me die."

Paul's eyes were tight and he looked away. I paused for a moment to pull myself together. My dreams of Catherine were intense and so hard to separate myself from.

"Then two nights ago I found myself at Alina's door. I didn't know how I got there or what time it was … I took a chance and knocked. She had a man there so I didn't stay long.

"It was so good to see her. I know every little naughty thing she's going to say before it even comes out of her mouth. Anyway, she had the next day off so I promised to call so we could get together. She said my accident was six weeks earlier ... I was scared I was stuck there. I had no idea how to get back. I'd been there three weeks already.

"Her boyfriend Damian walked me down to the taxi."

Ray's eyes opened wider for a quick moment but Paul remained impassive. My voice fell to a whisper and I suddenly felt like the air was going out of the room. I began to doubt my ability to go through it again even if it was just with words.

"He took me down the block, I could only follow. I wanted to go where he said. Suddenly he was dragging me down the alley then up against the wall by my neck. My feet were off the ground and I had to hold on to his arm just to breathe.

"He said that he hadn't planned on coming after me himself this time since he had Alina, but it was just too tempting to have me there. Then he pressed himself into me and started to squeeze my throat. I could feel ... it was turning him on ... he liked it."

I closed my eyes and turned my head away. I could feel my lips curling with disgust.

"I was getting weak and things were going dark ... I was losing. Then he held up a knife. He said remember this Catherine? He said I was a filthy bitch. He said that I belonged to him. I could feel my skin pop and tear but little else. My last thought was of you Paul, of coming home to you.

"Then his weight was gone, the wall was gone. I was alone. When I opened my eyes I was in here."

I turned to look at Paul. He wasn't looking at anything, but he was angry. Very angry.

"Damian has my sister. Help me put the pieces together."

He didn't say anything for a few minutes as his colour went back to normal. Ray was still white.

"Catherine is just a dream Anna ... your sister's boyfriend is a nut." He said slowly like he was trying to believe it himself.

"Really," I said. Then I repeated part of the conversation he had with Ray when they thought I was asleep. "Damian knows she's here now. The pregnancy is the only thing that grants her our protection. What's your job Paul, who's Ray's sister?"

"Please think about it," I whispered as the black sleep took me.

Chapter 15

The only work I had left to do on the bike was reconnecting clutch

57

line and adding fluids so I turned on the lights and setup the heater. I opened the big doors to get the bike out just as Paul was walking up.

"What are you working on up here?" he asked.

"Just going to see if the four-fifty will start ... I think I have all its parts in order."

I pulled the choke on the bike and put my leg over. Then I started stomping the kick start. It started the second try so I held the throttle open to keep it going.

"Nice."

"Are you worried I can't protect you here?" Paul asked. "Your gun is gone from the armoury."

"No," I gave him a small smile. "It's not here I'm worried about."

"You think you're going to disappear again?"

"I hope I'm not." I eased off the throttle and left it running on the choke. Then I undid the knot in my hair and grabbed my helmet from the wall.

"It'll be all over if someone takes it from you," Paul said.

I countered. "It'll definitely be all over if I don't have it at all. I can't count on disappearing home."

"You really think of this place as home?" He asked.

I slipped my cold hands inside his coat. "Yes ... where ever you are, we are home."

He thought about it. I put the choke the rest of the way in and the bike kept running just fine.

"I'm wearing the only pair of pants I can do up." I said. "And I'm not sleeping when I'm by myself. Wake me up when you go on watch."

"I'm going to run it through its gears," I said as I passed him my gun.

Then I kissed him, put on the helmet and rode out of the shop. It made it to third just fine as I passed the house and I kept the speed down as I approached the warehouses at the other end of the road. Tires were better than I thought.

Heading back up I hit the throttle hard and pushed it through all the gears. I bent my knees and elbows as I approached the bump in the road and shot up a few feet and flew nearly fifteen. Paul watched with amusement as I ran it around in donuts spitting snow out everywhere before I took off down the hill again. After the jump I opened it up again and tried to guess my speed. I figured I was able to do better than the bare minimum to jump. If I had to get out of here, I could.

"I would say it's cured." I said. "You want to take it for a spin? That bump just down the road is awesome."

"Maybe another time," he said and turned up the volume on his two-way radio.

"... me Paul? Get her off that thing. Do you have any idea how

58

... " Then he turned it down.

"Yikes," I said. "I think the fresh air has made me hungry anyway."

"I'm assigning someone to you when you're out."

"Like a babysitter?" I wasn't too pleased and didn't make any effort to hide it from my voice.

"I was hoping you wouldn't feel that way," he said.

"That's a lot of trouble for you to go to for some bad dreams and a nut in Toronto."

He stopped.

"When you got back this last time I thought I might lose you both." He put his hand up under my coat to feel my stomach. "Please indulge me ... she's worth it and I'm not taking any chances."

"Okay," I agreed. "I can't promise I won't be any trouble."

The sun had moved so shade covered the road and its warmth was quickly disappearing.

"So what about the rest of it?" I asked.

Paul frowned.

"Who is Damian?"

He didn't say anything.

"I can do a better job of staying out of trouble if I have an idea what's going on. You're all armed; so something's up. After what happened three weeks from now I think I have a good idea how he feels about me."

He was silent.

"Is the babysitter for my protection," I demanded, "or to keep me from sneaking around behind the shed?"

"Both," he said.

Something above got my attention. I turned my head up and scanned the blue sky. There was nothing to see but I could feel it. Pressure. Dread. Like the air had become thick with something I didn't want in my lungs.

"Can you feel it?" I asked Paul. I wrinkled my nose; I could smell it.

He looked up. "Feel what?"

Each inhalation was like breathing syrup. "We have to get inside ... something's coming ... can't you feel it? Pressing on us?" My lips were starting to tingle.

"No ... Maybe you overdid it ..." He didn't sound convinced. "You're turning white. Come on."

"Wait ..." I turned slowly until my back was to him. Suddenly I felt myself flying toward the darkness I knew was off in the distance, hidden by the trees. My pounding heart seemed to knock what little air I had out of my lungs. When I held my hand up to point toward the cabins

Paul's men lived in it trembled.

"From that way," I whispered.

"South?" Paul asked. "Inside. Now." He said firmly and took my elbow to pull me along. I couldn't take my eyes off the sky. I was so angry that I was helpless again. Helpless to fight. Helpless to run. I felt like some crazy balloon he was pulling along through the snow.

"A week ... days ... at least one man," I whispered.

I wasn't breathing any better when he handed me off to Ray.

"She's having trouble breathing," Paul told him as he pulled off my coat.

I watched the colourless sky until the door closed behind me. Paul went ahead to the pantry to put my confiscated gun away and Ray took me down to the room at the end of the hall.

"You're shaking Anna," Ray said. "What's going on?"

"I f ... feel silly now. It was so strong outside." My mouth was still a little clumsy with what was left of the numbness. "I couldn't breath, the air was so thick. It felt like the sky was coming down on me."

I held my hands out, they still shook. Ray took my wrist and held it still for a moment.

"Your heart's racing," he observed. "Sweating? Dizziness?"

I nodded.

"Okay Kiddo. Let's lie you down for a while until it goes away." Ray helped me with my boots and I put my head down.

"Do you remember what you were thinking about before this started?" he asked.

I managed a deep breath. "I was asking Paul about Damian. He wouldn't say anything," I told him. "I can't help Alina if I'm falling apart like this ..."

"Anna, your body is reacting to the stress and anger you're feeling about the assault," Ray said. "It can't tell that it's not real, so it's trying to protect you. Acute episodes like this don't last too long, but your body could keep trying to cope for a while ... a couple of weeks sometimes."

Ray patted my arm. He stopped Paul at the door and pushed him out. I held my breath to listen.

"Symptoms of acute stress," Ray said. "She could struggle with it for a few days or weeks."

"She's as tough as she is stubborn Ray," Paul said. "But everything's turned upside down for her now."

Ray sighed. "I know. She's holding up surprisingly well."

"She said she saw something in the South ... danger, someone coming." Paul said. "I'm inclined to believe her ... I can't disregard it at any rate. We're overdue for guests from the east."

Then they were whispering.

"Okay. You and Denis. Two trucks. Get your supply list ready." Paul told him. They whispered a while longer before they came in. I felt a lot calmer but the dizziness had been replaced by heaviness and nausea.

"You look more like your old self," he smiled quietly. "Ray says this isn't unusual considering what you went through."

"Yeah," I said. I was enjoying the gentle rocking as his hand moved on my back and as long as I kept taking deep breaths it didn't make the nausea any worse.

Ray checked my pulse again. "That's more like what I want to see. You're safe to sit up now if you want."

The dizziness didn't return but the nausea started to build.

"I think I need a minute or two," I said as the nausea began to head for the point of no return. "Excuse me."

I ran out and up to Paul's room where I quickly undressed and pulled the bandage off my stomach. I threw up in the shower. The bathroom door was open and I was looking down at Ray's handiwork on my stomach when I noticed Paul watching me from the end of the bed.

"It's almost pretty," I said. "It looks like the sun."

"No Anna. It looks like an eye."

I tilted my head sideways to look at it in the mirror then looked straight down at it again. "Yeah, you're right ... but from up here it looks like the sun."

"Are you sure you feel a little better now?" he asked. "I heard you get sick."

I did. I nodded. I couldn't see the smudges now. Maybe they'd stopped moving. Maybe it was stress. I went over and sat with him on the bed.

"Adrenaline I think. I feel like I'm running on anger right now," I said. "So we have some time before dinner?"

"You do," he said. "I have time before watch then I won't have to leave you tonight. Did you have something planned?"

"I missed you," I told him. I took his face in my hands and started to kiss him. "And I need you all to myself for a while."

"I missed you too." He said and pulled me over with him but I hesitated and braced my arm keeping myself up. Then my knees came in and my arms around them.

"Hey ...," Paul said softly as he let go but he didn't move away. "You're scared."

I shook my head and wiped my eyes.

"Are you sure you still want to touch me after he marked me up?"

"Awe," he said, "that doesn't change a thing. I love you, Sugar. I never thought I would be lucky enough to have such a strong partner in my life ... I never thought that the way I live would ever give me a chance to be a father. Now I have both."

61

"Partner," I murmured and rewarded him with a smile. "That sounds almost long term …"

He traced the flames on my arm. I closed my eyes and felt my skin shiver under his fingers as I relaxed and beat him to the mattress.

Chapter 16

"Anna," Paul's hand gently rubbed my shoulder.

"Come on, get up."

"Watch?" I asked. He said he wouldn't have to leave.

"No, get dressed … we're going to Reno. You said you need some things and Denis and Ray are going anyway. Can you pack for a couple of days? You can sleep on the way." He was half dressed already.

"Okay," I mumbled.

Ray and Denis were already downstairs having coffee. When Paul came into the kitchen I noticed his gun was missing. I put my hands on his hips as he came to sit down with his mug and pointed it out. He held open the sides of his loose jacket and had one under each arm.

"Jesus Paul," I said. "We going to rob a bank?"

He shrugged. "We're all licensed to carry."

"That's not what I was worried about. I'm not licensed to drive so someone is going to have to wait in the get away car with me."

Paul tried to be serious. "Sorry guys, no banks this trip."

I leaned over and nudged him with my shoulder. The elbow in the ribs he had coming wasn't a good idea with the gun there.

"Cowboys …" I muttered.

I hesitated at the door. Nothing seemed wrong. The black smudges to the south appeared to be gone. Maybe it was just the memory of them playing back in my mind that made me feel like they were still there.

Paul put his hand on my back.

"Ready?" he asked. "Need a minute?"

"No," I told him. "It's …" Nothing, I thought as I stopped again on the porch, turning my head slightly listening to something far off. My brow furrowed with frustration and I turned my head to try my other ear.

I gasped. I'd been looking where they were last and had looked right past them. Paul got his arms around me as I gently pulled his head down.

"Two groups, closer now, smaller one in front. Not due south … more south-east."

He straightened up and looked.

"I don't like feeling like this," I told him. "Can we go now?"

Paul helped me up into the truck in front. I hadn't paid much attention to them when we first left the house but now I noticed that they couldn't be much more conspicuous. Two almost identical black heavy duty four door trucks. Long boxes in the back, canopies with dark glass. I didn't get a look at the front or back and I wouldn't be surprised if they had sequentially numbered government plates.

We drove past the cabins to what I guessed was the gate. This was the furthest I'd been out of my small new world in weeks. Ross appeared out of nowhere and into the truck's lights. Paul stopped and rolled down the window to talk to him.

"We might have two groups coming from the south-east," he told him. "Smaller one in the lead. No firm time yet. I'll let you know right away if plans become any firmer."

Ross nodded. "Good luck Paul."

"Good luck Ross," Paul replied.

They looked at each other for a moment, then Paul rolled up his window and we drove on. I didn't ask what was going on. First I wanted to give him an opportunity to explain himself. My half crazy ramblings were an odd scenario to base a drill on.

"You're not saying anything," he said eventually.

"I guess not. I was waiting for you."

He sighed. "There are two reasons I wanted to get you out of the compound for a few days. You're not yourself since the attack. I hope a change of scenery might distract you for a while."

He seemed to be looking for the right words for his other reason. "There are so many things about you that I can't explain. Things I can't question because I've seen them with my own eyes so when you say that someone's coming I have to consider that you're right in which case I don't want you anywhere near the compound."

He was quiet for a minute. "Anna, I need to ask you something."

"You want to know if he's with them," I told him. I'd considered that.

"Yes. Ray said I shouldn't ask. He said if you're imagining things it might encourage any reckless behaviour. I know I can look after you either way … but if it's real then I can look after you better."

I held my fist up with my thumb out and moved it like I was rubbing it on something tiny in front of me.

"They look like little smudges off in the distance. When I first felt them yesterday it was like I was rushing toward them. I couldn't even turn away. I was going straight for them. They were moving fast too … toward me."

I still held my hand up, picturing them in my mind. "Today it was like the memory was teasing me. I thought … hoped I'd been imagining them and they were gone. It startled me when I realized that they were closer.

"But if you want to know if Damian is with them I have to say no."

"Are you sure?" Paul asked.

"No," I said. "In three weeks he'll say he wasn't going to come after me himself. So I can guess he's not one of them now. Then again I don't know if I can believe anything he told me. How well do you know him?"

"I first knew him by reputation," Paul started. "He ran a team like mine. He was of course, very good. But there were rumours about him. That he took far too many risks. Maybe he was a little unstable.

"We shipped out with his team on a big assignment. It was Damian's show but I had my orders. We suspected he had his own agenda. I had to keep an eye on him. He turned his back on us. Some civilians died. And some of my men before we stopped him. He disappeared. Killed a couple of my men once we were back stateside. We were making plans to move everyone north to where we are now but it was still a ways off.

"Are you sure you want to hear this?" Paul asked me.

I looked at him and nodded.

"A few years ago I had a little place near San Diego. I didn't live there alone. Ray's sister lived with me. She didn't like the travel much or the women I was around when I was away but it was good otherwise.

"I'd just got in from a couple of magazine jobs out east when Ray called. He looked out for her when I was away. She had no idea. He said there were a couple of men around, watching the place. He thought they were there for me. I met him nearby and we caught up with them. We dumped them in the hills. When we went through their car we found they were there for her. Not me.

"By killing her he could hurt both Ray and me. I had to let her go … Ray agreed. He knew how much it would hurt her, but he could encourage her to get out of the country to start over. She had a lot of options … job offers she'd been turning down to stay with me.

"I sat in my car the rest of the night drinking. The sun was well up when I staggered in. I was all bruised up from the fight. Their blood was on my clothes. I don't remember much of what I said to her, but Ray said I was pretty thorough. The gist of it was I had picked someone up at the bar and gone home with her. Got caught and got in a fight with her husband. I said I struck out with the women on my road trip and needed a little something to get me through being stuck with her. I passed out on the couch and she was gone when I woke up.

"I loved her, Anna. I'd bought a ring and had made plans to give it to her but she never would have come north with me."

He was quiet for a while. I could sense that he wasn't done so I watched the road disappear under the truck for a while.

64

"I thought I could walk away from you too," Paul said. "I almost had. We'd only been together a few times. It should have been easier. When you turned up I wanted to send you on your way as fast as I could … until I found out that you're pregnant. You were tied to me then … and there was no way Damian would let you go. I couldn't simply break it off to make him lose interest in you.

"The first few days you were here I realized how much I had shut off inside. You were already filling holes in my life I forgot I had." He looked over at me. "Please tell me what you're thinking."

"What was her name?" I asked quietly. If I was going to be jealous anyways I might as well get the full experience out of the way.

"Catherine."

I felt numb.

"Damian has changed. Like I said, there's a lot about you that I don't understand … I don't know if your dreams about the other Catherine are a coincidence or something else. Maybe he thinks you're Ray's sister in a way."

"Please," he asked. "Tell me the rest of what you're thinking. I feel like I've left myself wide open to being misunderstood. Please just start."

"That's the man who has my sister."

"Yes," Paul said.

Everything else needed to be put away; all I could picture was Alina in her little blue dress. Dangling by her throat while her stocking feet thrashed uselessly inches above her fallen shoes.

I could get to Toronto but then what? There was nothing I could tell her that would convince her of what I already knew. If she didn't love Damian now she would soon. I was outmatched even if I saw him coming. It was hopeless. Maybe I would just knock her over the head and put her in the trunk of a car. Or lure her down here with some crazy story … tell her I was getting married and I wanted her to be here. I sighed. She would send my father here to knock me on the head and drive me home in the trunk of his car.

"Anna?" Paul asked. "What are you thinking?"

"I can go get her," I told him.

He put a hand on his face and rubbed his eyes like he was getting a headache.

"My answer to that is no. Anyone ever tell you that you're completely reckless?"

"Nobody ever had to," I told him. "I'd haul her away from there a hundred times even if she hated me forever after only the first."

Paul laughed softly into his palm. He was still holding it over his face. Then he held his arm out too me.

"Come here," he said.

I moved over to the middle seat. He put his arm around me and pulled me in to kiss him.

"So what's your plan then?" he said kindly.

"Loan me a truck."

"Imagine that she feels as much for him as you feel for me. Do you think she could ever talk you into leaving me?"

"No," I told him. Defeat shading my voice. "Not in a million years."

"We have a couple of weeks at least. Give me some time to come up with something. Okay?" He asked.

"Yeah," I said weakly. I hoped it was too dark for him to notice the tears on my cheeks.

"In the meantime, don't do anything rash. It just makes it harder to look after you," he said.

"I don't like being sidelined Paul," I said. "Even when you're right that there's more going on than I can look after myself."

"I know," he said. "But I need you to look after our baby. And let me look after everything else. It's what I do best."

Andre

Chapter 17

We stopped in Redding to fill the trucks. Denis came with me
around to the restroom in the rear while he took a smoke break. They
were still pumping gas when we got back. I hated to think how much
that cost. I could fill up my bike for under twenty and would be halfway
to Reno by the time they were done. Once we were back on the road I
curled up on the front seat with my head on Paul's thigh. He grabbed a
blanket from the back seat for me.

I closed my eyes and thought about sleeping but the movement of
the truck was too unfamiliar to relax. I decided I should tell him what I
thought about his story while it was still fresh and not leave him
worrying.

"Paul?" I said.

"How come you're not asleep?" he asked.

I put my hand on his knee and gave it a squeeze.

"I had more to say … I asked her name to get some time to put my
thoughts together and got side tracked worrying about Alina."

"Oh." I squeezed his leg again.

"I'm surprised how jealous I am of her," I told him. "You gave up
so much to keep her safe. I'm grateful to be the one that was able to help
you get some of it back."

I thought a while longer. "Would you still have killed those men if
you knew before they were after Catherine and not you?"

He didn't say anything for a bit.

"I don't want you to think of me like that," Paul said. "It's such a
small part of the things I've done in my life. It's absolutely critical that I
can but it's not who I am."

"I know that," I said gently. "But you didn't answer my question."

"Yes," he said simply.

69

I rolled over to my back to look up at him. "Hearing you say yes doesn't make me love you any less. I feel safer, especially since I know first hand who I'm up against."

"Have you ever thought of yourself as generous?" Paul asked.

"It's always been all about me," I told him. Honestly I thought.

"You find a way to turn what caused you to feel jealousy into something to be grateful for. I never thought that anyone would feel safety in the things I've done, but you do it without hesitation. You don't dismiss the bad things you feel at all. Your generosity makes you open to seeking ways to balance them out."

"I'll have to let that sink in I guess."

"You make me happy," he said eventually.

I rolled back on my side and reached my hand further over his knee until my finger nails could hook around his inseam then I gently traced my fingers back and forth a bit, slowly feeling the bumps of the stitches. Then I watched my fingertips draw little circles on his leg in front of me for a while.

Paul sighed deeply. "I really want you right now."

"Does this seat go back any more?" I asked. I'd been thinking the same thing.

"Yes ... but now?"

"You brought it up," I said, working my boots off my feet. "We can find a side road."

He looked back at the tint darkened headlights of the other truck in the mirror and shook his head. "It'll have to wait."

I knelt on the seat and started to pull up his shirt. "Come on, you watch the road ... I'll do the work. We'll be quick," I breathed behind his ear.

I was reaching for his belt.

"Anna ..."

"This was your idea, don't back out on me now," I told him. "Be reckless with Anna."

"Shit," he said and reached down to let the seat back.

Chapter 18

When I woke up Paul was standing in the open door of the truck with Denis and Ray. I sat up to find us in a parking lot facing a restaurant. I got my boots on and pulled the blanket tighter around my shoulders before I slid over behind the wheel next to Paul. He leaned back toward me and I rested my head on his shoulder.

"You should have let me drive," I told him.

"Sure ... you can't drive," he said.

70

"I never said I can't. I just never bothered to take the road test and I can get it started for you in less than a minute if you lose the key."

They laughed.

"You'll find a use for my misspent youth yet."

"Probably. Hungry?" Paul asked.

Paul's phone interrupted breakfast so he went outside to take it. I took advantage of the open end of the booth to go to the restroom. He wasn't back when I returned.

"Misspent youth?" Ray asked.

"I took orders," I told him. "I got caught on my last job. Because I was fifteen and they thought I was put up to it they released me to my father but I'd been taking one or two a week for over a year."

"One or two what?" Denis asked.

"Cars, motorcycles, trucks … we knew where pretty much everything unprotected was. People can be pretty stupid. It's like they want you to take their car."

"The Captain know you were a petty crook?" Denis asked.

"Yeah. We met when he caught me trying to lift his wallet," I winked at him.

Paul took his seat. I hadn't noticed him come back in. He was distracted and had a hard time looking at me. Denis saw his mood and dropped the subject.

"Did something happen back at your place?" I asked.

"No," he said and patted my knee before he went back to brooding.

I leaned closer. "Do we need to talk?"

He shook his head, not looking up from the half full cup of cold coffee he was holding. On the way out Paul put his arm around me and pulled me aside. "Do you mind riding with Denis? I have to talk to Ray."

"No, I don't mind," I told him. He eyed my crossed arms and realized I wasn't happy about it. "I don't mind riding with Denis but I hoped we were past hiding problems from me."

He smiled and shook his head. "Nothing like that, okay?"

"Okay," I sighed and uncrossed my arms and reached them up over his shoulders to hug him. I didn't like reaching around under the guns he was carrying.

"There's no trouble," he whispered.

He helped me up into the truck and we pulled out behind Paul and Ray.

"Where are we going?" I asked Denis.

"To see Willy."

"Willy?"

"Willy's Toy Store," Denis grinned.

71

It sounded like some adult shop. I wasn't going to ask any more questions.

Willy's Toy Store turned out to be a gun shop. Paul was out of his truck and over to my door as soon as we'd parked. He seemed to be in a better mood after half an hour with Ray. Denis was already ringing the buzzer so we could be let in past the big barred windows by the time I had my feet on the ground. I left my coat in the truck. It looked like Denis might have us here a while.

The door clicked and Denis went in first. As we followed him in Paul whispered, "don't mind Willy, he's a little … old fashioned."

That didn't worry me. I could play along with old fashioned. Denis and Ray had already disappeared and Paul took me up to the big glass counter.

"Just a minute Richards, I can't seem to find my glasses."

"You knew we were coming, you could have had them ready," Paul called back then whispered to me. "Bet he's checking you out in the camera."

I looked up at the camera in the corner above the opening to the back room and gave it my most endearing smile. Paul and the voice in the back room chuckled at the same time then Willy came out. He in his sixties, still had all his black hair; oiled back like he hadn't changed the style since his teens.

"So is this Missus Richards?" Willy asked. He had his hand out and I took it. If he was going to make a quick jab at Paul I didn't see any harm in jabbing back.

"It's Miss Creed," I told him still wearing my sweet smile. "You must be Mister Willy."

Paul sounded like he was quietly trying not to choke on something. Denis had less tact and started roaring from the other end of the store. I let my smile falter a bit.

"Awe, she's a sweet one Richards," he told Paul. "Willy's my first name, Miss Creed."

I acted embarrassed. "I'm so sorry, Willy. You called Paul by his last name so I thought that was yours." I leaned uncomfortably close to him.

"You must call me Anna," I insisted in a soft voice as he finally stopped holding my hand.

Willy cackled and disappeared into the back room. "If I was ten years younger you wouldn't stand a chance with her Richards. I got yer stuff ready here."

Paul shook his head and gave my butt a gentle smack. "You're shameless. Why don't you go make sure Denis doesn't put anything in his pockets before Willy makes a pass at you? I'll get you when we're ready."

"For what?" I asked.

"Hopefully he has something you can't miss with. We can shoot downstairs."

"You can't fix hopeless." I told him as I made my way to where Denis' laughter had come from.

Denis and Ray were going through the crossbows. Ray seemed to have control of himself but there were still tears in Denis' eyes as he mimicked my higher voice.

"You must be Mister Willy," he set himself off laughing again.

I sighed and shook my head. When I looked back at Paul he was going through some hand guns. They had been talking quietly for quite a while. Suddenly in a louder voice Willy said, "Back in my day Richards when a man knocked a woman up he bought her a ring, not a gun."

I put my hand on my mouth to try and hide my smile. Neither one of them looked up. Denis was starting to giggle again and Ray gave him a not so gentle slap in the back of the head.

"You know what I like best about you Willy?" Paul asked.

"What's that Richards?"

"It's your complete inability to control the volume of your voice."

Willy laughed. "That's what my fifth wife always used to say."

It wasn't much longer until Ray elbowed me. I'd been leaning on the wall next to him with my eyes closed, trying to pick up the smudges again.

"Wake up Kiddo, Paul wants you," he said.

I looked over and he was waiting at the door to the back room so I followed him downstairs. Willy already had Paul's choices out. Paul shot first neatly hitting everything. He seemed satisfied so he reloaded and Willy ran out fresh targets. As I expected I couldn't hit a damn thing.

"Wimmins got no business with a gun Richards," Willy said. "I told you that already."

Paul shook his head. "She's one of my best with a rifle Willy. But she can't hit shit with a handgun." I remembered the hopeless small arms lesson Denis had given me two weeks earlier before I showed him up with the rifles. He'd scribbled Lt-Cdr Creedy on my exemplary targets and taped them up in the underground range.

Willy ignored him. "They wants a weapon as sharp as their tongues ..."

I was facing Willy, listening to him talk and he lobbed a big double edged hunting knife toward my right side. The throw was sloppy and it tumbled in the air. Paul grabbed for me to pull me out of the way as I reached across my body with my left hand avoiding his fingers and cleanly picking the handle out of the air. With a quick flip of my wrist I had it up on the back of my hand perfectly balancing it on the big

73

knuckle.

"Jesus Willy, you have to stop doing that," Paul said.

I looked over at Paul, then back at the knife. I gave it a gentle spin with my other hand and watched it move around in a perfect circle before it came to a stop. Willy was laughing.

"Tole you Richards. She's a knife fighter."

"Where did you learn that?" Paul asked me.

"No idea," I told him and sent the knife in another circle. Then I dropped my hand as I flipped it over and caught the handle. I put it down on the table with the guns.

"Can I keep it?" I whispered to Paul.

"Sure, but you have to do something for me first." He was reloading the guns. "I want you to try left handed."

I looked at him for a moment then I picked one up with my left. "This feels really weird. Can you check my grip? It doesn't feel right."

Paul made some adjustments. It didn't feel any better. He watched over my shoulder as I aimed and ran every round through the centre of the target.

"That's my girl," he pulled the ear protection back a bit so I could hear. "Now the others."

I did just as well with them all.

"Problem solved Lefty," Paul laughed.

Chapter 19

After lunch we split up for a while. Ray took Denis to pick up some of the things on his list and Paul and I went to the mall so I could get clothes. I found a maternity shop with a tall section so I figured I could get everything I needed to get me through.

"Are you okay here for a bit?" Paul asked. "I'm going to go get you a phone."

"There's nothing wrong with mine," I said.

"Other than it's in your name with a Vancouver Island number. I can get you one that will be harder to trace back to where you are."

It made sense.

"Okay," I told him. "I guess I can't get into any trouble surrounded by fat mannequins."

I didn't like to shop but I had learned how from Alina. Once I found my size I had several bags full and was waiting out front on a bench for Paul within twenty minutes. I had the clothes I wore in packed up as well and was wearing some of the things I had just bought. I was much more comfortable. I had on a long sleeved top and a sleeveless jacket zipped up to my chin to hide the bruises that were starting to turn brown. Paul came and sat on the other end of the bench with me facing the other way.

"Did you get lost?" I asked him.

He jumped.

"Geez, I didn't recognize you," he said. Then he looked at the bags. "I was going to pay for that. It's sort of my fault you need it."

I stood and picked up the bags.

"Wow." Paul said. "Maybe it's because you're not crammed into your old clothes but you suddenly look a lot bigger."

I scowled in reply. He came around and put his arms around me.

"You look great," he whispered.

"Perfect answer," I said. "And you're right. I was way too uncomfortable in my regular clothes. I still need some shoes. I'm not stomping around the house in boots for the next five months."

"Is that all we have left to go?" His eyes seemed to be glazing over.

"Yes," I took his elbow and started to pull. "Shoes."

Shoes didn't take long either and we put it all in the back of the truck. Paul handed me a phone.

"It has a Baltimore number," he said. "I put me, Ray, and Denis in there and the house phone. You should memorize them all then delete them."

"Thanks," I said and put it in my pocket.

"I figured shopping would take you all afternoon … we're meeting up at the hotel for dinner in a few hours. What do you want to do now?"

"I never get to be a passenger. It's nice to look around," I told him. Paul drove toward the sun for a while. It warmed up quickly in the truck so I took off my jacket.

"I called my CO last night to let him know what was going on," he said. "I have to let him know when we're expecting trouble. We hadn't seen any action from Damian in a while. I told him that he's targeting you and may have men moving on the compound."

"Paul …" I said. "I could be imagining it."

"I know. I told him my information was incomplete and unverified and he agreed that we shouldn't take any chances. I told him that you're pregnant with my child and a few of us took you from the compound until we're sure that the danger is past.

"Anyway when he called back this morning he said he's concerned that Ray's combat experience may not be up to a maternity case. He wants you to check in with an obstetrician."

"Ray's doing fine," I was starting to panic a bit. "And how am I going to explain any more accelerations of my pregnancy to another doctor?"

"Please Anna, try and understand the other side of this. You're living on what is for all intents and purposes a government funded military base. There are liability concerns ... if you're under our protection we need to make sure that you're safe and that we don't fail to keep the baby healthy. That's why Ray had to go with me this morning ... to call in. We figured you'd feel that way. He told the Colonel that everything is going smoothly and other than a couple of routine tests he can't provide at the compound he can manage your care just fine as long as there are no complications."

"Three cheers for Ray," I said glumly. "So what does he have lined up for me?"

"Just an ultrasound tomorrow."

"You're going to be there with me?" I hadn't known any doctors other than Ray and Alina and I didn't trust anyone else.

"Of course," Paul said. He took my hand and kissed it.

"I suspect he had more to say about me sneaking across the border."

"Yeah, your file says to turn you away at the border for spending too much time here again this year, but he doesn't work at the border crossing so he'll overlook that for now. Once the trouble blows over you'll have to go back for a while or decide if you want to stay permanently."

Stress rose Paul's voice. His grip on the wheel tightened; his knuckles standing out white against his skin. Then I noticed that a gas station we passed looked familiar and it dawned on me that we'd passed it already. Paul had been circling but then he took us in a new direction, into a little strip mall and stopped in front of one of those quickie wedding places I'd only ever heard about.

"He said that he would only have to call in a small favour to let you stay here permanently if we were married." He just sat there. I slid over to him and put the truck in park and turned off the key. Then I took one of his stiff hands off the steering wheel and held it in both of mine.

"Paul," I said softly. "Are you scared I'll say yes or scared I'll say no?"

He didn't answer.

"Paul?" I tried again.

He sighed. "Both I guess. I'm sorry. Do you need some time to think about it?"

"No," I answered. "I don't need to think about it at all."

"Okay," he paused. "Will you marry me?"

I put my hand behind his neck and kissed him.

"Not because we have to," I told him. "There's nothing they can do to keep me from coming and going. The easiest promise I could ever keep is to love you forever, Paul," I paused. "Yes ... I will marry you."

He put his arms around me. "I can love you forever too Anna. I want you to be my wife."

After a minute he put his hand to his face and rubbed his eyes then let me go.

"So I guess we need a license?" I asked. "Where do we go for that in Reno?"

"You mean you want to do it today?"

"I thought that was why you brought me here … sign says they're open late. I can be Mrs. Richards before dinner."

Paul laughed. "Okay."

It took less than an hour to get our license and we stopped at the first jewellery store we came to for wedding bands. Paul wanted to get me an engagement ring. I would have been fine without one but it was important to him so I agreed as long as it was sturdy. He picked one with a big square stone in it and heavy claws. He proposed again right there in the store and put it on me. We didn't hurry back to the mall. We had everything we needed.

We were in and out in less than twenty minutes. Getting married didn't feel sudden or reckless at all. It was the right thing to do for so many reasons. I sat in the middle seat with my head on Paul's shoulder holding his hand and tried to count them in the truck on the way to dinner but I kept coming up with more … or maybe counting the same ones twice.

Ray and Denis were just sitting down in the hotel restaurant when we pulled in. Paul ran in and got our key. I could see Denis point out his ring then they both stood and shook his hand. Paul pointed to the truck and then gestured for them to stay put.

"They don't miss much, Mrs. Richards," he said when he helped me down from the truck. We had driven around to our room.

"Good for them, Mr. Richards," I replied.

We got all my clothes and our luggage from the back of the truck and took them up to our room. Paul threw everything in the door and picked me up to carry me in. We were both laughing. It seemed an odd tradition for a hotel room. Then he kicked the door shut with his foot and carried me straight to the bed.

We made it back downstairs before Ray and Denis left.

"Creedy!" Denis said much too loudly when we got to the table and got up and hugged me. Ray did too only he didn't haul me up off my feet.

"Why didn't you tell us before?" Denis wanted to know as we were sitting down. "Now I'll have to sneak him out for his stag later."

I squeezed Paul's hand under the table. "I didn't think a stag would be quite your style Denis … or Paul's for that matter. You're all such gentlemen around me."

I glanced at Paul. His mouth was entertaining a little grin. Ray elbowed Denis and shook his head at him. *No.* But Denis started in anyway.

"Nobody ever told you about us out on leave? The Captain was the worst of us ... I could keep you up all night without telling you the same story twice ... there was this time he found these two girls at the casino—"

The waitress interrupted with four menus, not two.

"We were waiting for you," Ray explained. I was glad the restaurant wasn't well lit. My cheeks darkened a bit.

Denis ordered another pitcher of beer even though he and Ray still had a half pitcher on the table and refilled Ray's and his own glass and poured for Paul.

"So, you said two girls Denis?" I asked. I squeezed Paul's hand under the table again.

"Oh yeah," Denis said after he swallowed. I'd caught him with his glass at his lips. Ray elbowed him again. "Next thing we know the three of them had disappeared ... by the time we found them he had them both in the back of the truck—"

"Wait a sec," I interrupted him. "How many did you get?"

"What?"

"Did you pick anyone up that night?" I asked him. Paul was trying to hide his grin, Ray wasn't.

"Well, no," Denis admitted. "But we could have found the truck in the parking lot with our eyes closed they were making so much noise—."

"Sorry Denis. I'm a little confused," I interrupted again. "Instead of taking the opportunity to learn from your Captain's shining example you decided to go find him instead?"

"Well, yes ... but—"

I put a puzzled expression on my face. "Wouldn't it have been more fun to take someone out to the truck yourself?"

Denis frowned. "It's still a good story."

"I'm sure it is ... but maybe you should save it for another time."

Ray and Paul were both laughing at him. Denis shrugged and went back to his beer.

"Never seen him shut down so fast before," Paul whispered to me. "Thank you."

"Two?" I whispered back.

Paul turned his attention to Ray and changed the subject.

Chapter 20

Denis was in rough shape at breakfast the next day. Ray didn't look so bad but he didn't look so good either. Paul had sent them out 'on him' after dinner to keep them out of the adjoining room for a while. Unfortunately by the time Ray dragged Denis in we had the door between the rooms open and the noise woke us up. Ray was telling Denis that maybe if he hadn't had so much to drink at the pool table then maybe all his money wouldn't have wound up in Ray's pocket.

Paul and Ray had no trouble getting breakfast down while Denis stuck to drinking black coffee with his eyes closed and Ray said I had to skip breakfast.

"Empty stomach for an ultrasound?" I asked him.

"Well, no ... I was able to arrange a few more things after lunch yesterday," Ray said.

I frowned at my untouched cutlery. "I'd rather have breakfast."

"Could be worse," Paul said. "You could feel like Denis."

Denis stomach made a nasty sound. "'scuse me," he said and hurried off to the bathroom.

"I'm not riding with him," I said.

Paul shook his head. "We'll leave him here with a truck."

"We need to get going anyway," Ray said. "I have to redo all the paperwork now you're on Paul's medical with a different last name."

I didn't feel bad for Ray at all. He wasn't the one who was going to be run through tests all morning. The only one I was interested in was the ultrasound anyway. I knew that he and Paul were humouring me that the baby was a girl and I wanted to put them in their place about it.

At the hospital I waited almost an hour for them to even get started while Ray cleaned up the paperwork and another two after that spent in one waiting room after another before I saw him again. He had two glasses of water for me.

"Down the hatch," he said. "And you can't use the bathroom until after the ultrasound."

"I don't think the vampires are done with me yet," I whispered to him. They had given me a bottle of disgusting orange pop to drink and had been sticking me every half hour since. "When is it?"

"About an hour and the vampires are almost done."

"How's Paul doing?" I asked.

"Bored. He's asleep downstairs."

"Lucky," I said. "Thanks for coming to find me. I haven't been in a place like this since my mother got sick."

"You're doing fine, Kiddo," he put his hand on my arm. "We'll go get lunch soon, okay? I have to wake Paul up and get him back to sleep in another waiting room," he winked and disappeared out the door.

The nurse came to poke me one more time and then I still had to wait almost half an hour for Ray. By then my eyes were floating and I was too uncomfortable to sit.

"Ready?" he asked.

"I think we need to hurry," I muttered. I was already starting to feel cold sweat coming through my pores.

Ray laughed. "All ready for you, come on. Paul's waiting."

After three long hallways and two elevator trips we found Paul. He looked as relieved to see me as I felt uncomfortable. As he hugged me I wiggled my toes in my shoes to distract myself. He noticed my fidgeting.

"You okay?" he asked.

I rubbed my arm where the nurses had kept taking blood. "The getting pregnant part was a lot more fun," I whispered to him. He smiled and kissed the top of my head.

"Dr. Jackson, Mrs. Richards ... come on in now," someone called us. I took Paul's hand and we all piled into the little room.

"I'm going to get all my pictures then show you around," she explained. Ray stood beside her and watched but she kept the display pointed away from us. I reached for Paul's hand and kissed it then he kissed mine. The pictures seemed to take forever. I thought the full bladder was unbearable enough before she started pressing on it so I tried to relax and concentrated on just getting through the next few minutes.

"Alright, ready for the tour," she said as she turned the screen to us. Now I had to crane my neck around to see it. I held on tighter to Paul's hand. Moving had broken my concentration and I had to focus on my breathing again to push away the discomfort.

She showed us her profile first. "Looks like mom's nose," she said. Then she showed us her hands and feet and her heart. Those were obvious. She also pointed out her kidneys and other things that I couldn't really make out.

Then she asked "do you want to know what it is?"

"A girl," I answered right away.

I heard Paul chuckle quietly. "We haven't had a girl born in my family as long as anyone can remember."

Then I noticed the little smirk on Ray's face.

"Better go buy some pink paint, Dad," she said. "I'll print you a picture to take home."

Paul's amazed laughter filled the little room.

Chapter 21

Our fourth night in Reno I dreamed of Alina. Everything had been peaceful at the compound while we were away so we were heading back in the morning.

I was dead on the ground at Damian's feet watching helplessly as hers kicked; her shoes fell landing in my blood. She was strong and kicked hard. What little air she could get whistled through her tightening windpipe. One of her heels was bloody from banging against something sharp behind her.

Damian's heavy breathing started to win. After another minute I couldn't hear her anymore. Blood ran down her legs and mixed with mine. Her feet kicked more and more slowly. Eventually one was limp. She pulled the toes back on the other. Her bloody foot trembled briefly. Then again, and was still. The weight of her body in the little blue dress falling on me startled me awake.

"Alina!" I gasped, sitting up.

"What?" Paul mumbled. I stayed sitting, breathing hard. He propped himself up on one elbow and put his hand on my chest.

"Lie back down," he said. "Bad dream."

Soft sounds reached my ears. As my breathing quieted I figured out what it was. "Do you hear her crying?" I whispered.

"No," he lay back down.

I listened. We'd been leaving the door open to Ray and Denis' adjoining room at night. Paul felt it was safer and at least we could all sleep. Anyone trying to get in would wake everyone up.

"It's coming from the other room," I whispered. "I think it's her."

"What?" Paul was awake now.

"The woman in the mirror," I got out of bed and tip toed to the open door.

"Anna, come back here."

"No."

I paused at the door to the other room and looked toward their bathroom. He came up behind me and put a hand on my shoulder.

"Do you see the light from the bathroom?" I asked him. It moved like how the light from a TV moves with the action on the screen.

"No I ... what the hell?" Paul sounded tired.

"The crying; it's coming from in there."

"I don't hear it," he said. "But the light is wrong."

I stepped through toward it. I didn't care if Paul followed or not because I had to know why she was crying.

The sound grew stronger as I stepped in. Soft, exhausted sobs. She was very pregnant; her white t-shirt stretched snugly over her belly. One arm tight around her ribs holding the elbow of the hand that covered her mouth.

"Anna ..." I whispered to my mismatched reflection and put my hands on the glass. The light was on in the bathroom she was in. Its glow lit up Ray and Denis' things on the counter.

"Oh Jesus," Paul said.

I looked over at him. He held the door frame with both hands, gaping at the mirror.

"Captain?" Denis whispered over the sound of their blankets moving as they got quickly out of bed.

I looked back at the mirror and touched her face with my hand.

"Where is she?" Paul whispered. He could see that the bathroom in the mirror wasn't the same one we were standing in.

"It's my tenant's bathroom ... she doesn't know we're here."

She wiped her eyes on her sleeve and turned her back on us to blow her nose. The light went out and as she walked away I heard the low rumble of a descending plane. I put my fists on the glass.

"Run to the bedroom run to the bedroom run to the bedroom ..." I chanted. The roar became deafening; the glass vibrated under my hands.

Suddenly both bathrooms exploded with hot orange light; the other one with fire. I heard her scream. Paul grabbed me from behind to pull me back and I fought hard to stay near the glass.

"No!" I yelled at him.

I struggled to keep my hands on the mirror as its companion in the other bathroom shattered into orange pieces. They fell away in chunks leaving black spaces in the fire until it was gone and I stood trembling in Paul's arms.

"Get the light Ray," he said quietly.

The mirror was intact. Paul held on to me tightly.

"I thought the dream would make me disappear," I told him.

"You're not dreaming," he said. "We all saw it."

I shook my head. "The dream that woke me ... I was dead at Damian's feet. He killed Alina, dropped her body on me ... it woke me up. Then I heard her crying. You saw all that?"

"Yes. Come on," he led me back to our room.

I sat in the small hotel armchair, sticking one knee out and pulling the other up to my chest.

"I never thought it was going to be real," I told him. "She always knows things ... things that come true. She lies to me sometimes to get me to do the right thing. But I just saw it happen to me ... her ... I'm going to be there when the airliner comes down by my house."

Paul knelt down beside my chair. He put his hands on my shoulders and gently shook me until I looked at him.

"Did she say anything?" he asked.

I shook my head. "Just crying ... something terrible must have happened. But I don't understand why she would be there. That's Mrs. Desmond's suite upstairs. Nothing would get me to go back there now that the plane is really coming. It must have made sense to go anyway ... I know at least that she'll survive the crash.

"I just thought she was all in my mind. But when I saw her a few weeks ago she had flames on both arms ... I still had just one. She was in my bathroom at my house then but this time she was upstairs. It's not what I saw in the mirror that scares me. I've seen her and the plane come down many times. It's the dream about Alina that bothers me."

Paul thought for a moment.

"Do you want to call her? I think you should reassure yourself that she's fine."

I sighed and smiled weakly.

"Yes. If she was on shift last night she'll still be up."

Then I frowned. "What if he's there?"

"Just end the call nicely. Remember he hasn't met you yet and we don't want to cause a problem for your sister."

I got my phone. A man did answer. I pulled Paul over to listen.

"Alina?" I asked.

"No," the man's voice laughed. "You missed her by an hour. She's gone into work. It's Damian."

I was glad I was sitting because I was suddenly weak. Paul held his breath beside me; what I could make out of his expression was unreadable.

"I'm sorry," I managed. "I can try her again another time."

"Is this Anna?" he asked. "You sound just like her."

"Yes ... I just wanted to let her know I'm up and around now. I'll try her again in a few days. Can you give her the message?"

"Sure," he said.

I said thanks and hung up then I gave the phone to Paul. I didn't feel any better. All I knew was that Damian said she was okay.

"We know where he is ... can't we just go get him?" I asked.

"It's not that easy," Paul explained. "We can't just go run an operation like that in another country."

"That's bullshit Paul," I hissed.

He sighed. "It's not that simple. My CO is aware of your sister. He's working on it."

"I'm sorry. I know you're doing all you can ... maybe some fresh air will help," I put my hands behind his head and pulled him close to kiss him before I stood up. "I thought I left my anger at home. I didn't mean to take anything out on you. Maybe I should have lied about who I am."

"He knew already," Paul said. "That would have been suspicious. You did the right thing."

I stuffed my shoes on and pulled my coat over my pyjamas.

"Denis?" I called. "You going out for a smoke?"

"Yeah Anna, just a sec."

Denis and I went out to the little table and chairs outside the door. I sank back in my chair and listened to him smoke. Breathing in and out. Picking out the gentle crackling sounds of the bits of tobacco igniting.

Focusing on it was relaxing but the blackness that had returned to my mood wasn't so easy to push back.

Absently I reached for the pack and took one. I grabbed his metal lighter and opened my eyes just enough to make sure that the flame touched the end of the cigarette. I pulled the smoke down deep in my lungs as I welcomed my old lover.

He slid the cigarette pack and the lighter off the table and I heard them go in his pocket. Then he left.

Asshole, I thought.

Always stingy with the fags. He'd go complain that I stole it … have it put in my file. Screw with my chances for promotion. I didn't care. The army had me exactly where they wanted me doing exactly what I did best.

Killing.

How many was it yesterday? Fifteen? We'd pushed our way up the hill through the bush and I took them down until I ran out of enemy. It bothered me that I'd lost count. I took another drag and retraced my steps acting out my movements as I relived each kill in my mind, counting them up.

What are you doing?

I put my finger to my lips to tell him to be quiet. The goddamn Lieutenant. He'd get promoted faster if he'd just back off and let me do my job. I paused for another pull on my cigarette and kept counting. He cleared his throat and I ignored him.

Twenty-one, I smiled to myself.

What are you doing with the cigarette, Andre?

I put a hand on my knife. "If you can show me another man here who even came close to taking out twenty-one of those sons-of-bitches like I did yesterday then you can complain about me bumming a fag from someone who has more of them than he knows what to do with. I think I deserve one before you send me back up that fucking hill."

What?

"It's my numbers that got you promoted … maybe think about backing off."

It wasn't like me to be so blatantly insubordinate, especially in front of the others but the man had to know he hadn't done it all by himself.

Look at me.

I tilted my glasses up at him as I kept my eyes closed. Sod off.

Look at me, he demanded. The Lieutenant voice. I couldn't ignore it so I raised my chin and opened my eyes.

"You're not the Lieutenant," I said. The man in front of me wasn't the Lieutenant … neither were the two next to him.

"What?" he said. Maybe all the gunfire had affected his hearing.

"Anna, what are you talking about?"

I blinked and stared up at him.

"Paul?" I asked.

"Yes. Paul."

Impatient.

"Why did you call me Andre?" I asked.

"I didn't. Why are you smoking?"

Ludicrous, I thought. "I don't smoke."

He took the nearly burned out cigarette from my hand and put it in the ashtray. Then I noticed the taste in my mouth. "That's disgusting Denis. You should quit."

"You still need to pack up Lieutenant Martin?" Paul said. It wasn't a question.

"Yes Sir," Denis disappeared. Ray stayed outside with us. I ran my tongue around the inside of my mouth. I'd never tasted anything so bad ... or so good.

"How long has Denis been helping you sneak cigarettes?" Paul asked. He looked just as mad at me as Ray did.

My mouth dropped open. "Never!" I exclaimed. "I have no idea how it got there. I thought I dreamed it."

"If one of my men talked to me like you did a few minutes ago I'd drop him," Paul said quietly.

I laughed. My eyes unfocused as I started to slip back into the dream.

"That's just what the Lieutenant did," I put my hand to my jaw and it popped loudly as I opened my mouth. "Then he sent us back up. I got my twenty-one again before I ran into someone better ... never made it back down."

I was still laughing. "Smug little SOB, didn't have enough of us left to clean out the latrine after that."

My hand moved to my throat and I gagged as the air from my lungs rushed out a hole in my neck. For a few seconds I could feel my blood spilling down between my breasts and into my lap. My fingers scrambled to hold my neck shut as I shook my head and tried to pull myself out of it. Their looks of anger had changed to concern but I kept going.

"Another South Pacific island; I don't remember the name. They pointed me where they wanted me to go; I put my knife in everything I could get my hands on." Sigh. Smile. "I really liked my job. I didn't like that Lieutenant though."

"Anna," Paul said sharply.

I turned my head up to look at him.

"Come inside now."

The taste in my mouth tried to pull me back in so I grabbed what I was going to wear and went straight to the sink to scrub my mouth out. With the taste gone I realized how much I had wanted another cigarette. No wonder Paul was pissed; thinking that his pregnant wife had started smoking.

I expected Paul to come in to voice his displeasure privately but he hadn't yet so I started to undress for the shower. I could make out Ray talking with him out in the room. I was dried off and dressed by the time he knocked and let himself in.

He stood there for a minute. "Are you okay?" he finally asked.

I gave him a stiff smile. "Aren't you tired of asking that?"

"I'm not. Ray thinks that was some kind of lucid dream ..." he said.

"... or psychotic episode," I finished. "It was so vivid ... I feel like I have the last few hours of someone else's life in my head." I stepped close to him and lowered my voice. I didn't know how far it would travel.

"I don't need another evaluation from Ray. The only thing Denis did wrong was leave his pack of cigarettes on the table," I told him. "Andre helped himself."

"Andre?" Paul said. I nodded. "Denis isn't in any trouble. He came and got me ... he said you helped yourself. We came out and you're smoking away acting out some kind of knife fight."

I laughed quietly remembering it. "Yeah ... Andre was enjoying himself. He'd lost count the day before and was going through them one by one to figure out how many he had killed."

"How many what?" Paul asked.

"Japanese. I ... Andre wanted out. He called out the Lieutenant to provoke him. Maybe he could find his way into a military prison or find someone good enough to end his service. He liked what he did too much and there was nothing for me ... him back home. He got what he hoped for that day."

"So the Lieutenant straightened him out?"

I nodded. "Andre just stood there and took it. Didn't feel it. The Lieutenant got a couple of good shots in and finally knocked him out. He wouldn't have had a chance if I'd ... Andre fought back. When the sun finally came up Andre was the first one he sent up the hill. Never came down."

I looked at him seriously. "Tell Denis if I ever do that again to just leave the cigarettes on the table and get you like he did before ... Andre would have been quite happy to stick him for going to the Lieutenant and probably would have if he'd tried to stop him from taking one."

He frowned. "Maybe we should wait on you carrying your gun ..."

"Not Andre's style," I shook my head. "Too impersonal. Too

quick. He was just as deadly with a gun but he never used one. It's fading Paul. I feel … distance from it now. It's funny. Andre was a lefty, frowned on back then but he did it anyway. And that Lieutenant reminded me of that man with my sister. Can't put my finger on why."

"You're not sleeping much … you're probably trying to dream when you're awake."

I didn't realize that he had noticed. Mostly I just tried to lie still at night. "How could you tell?"

"You don't move around as much as you used to. And you're getting circles under your eyes," he let me go and ran his thumb along under my eye. "You could ask Ray if there's anything he can give you to help so you can get caught up on your rest."

I looked up at him, brushing the tip of my nose along his chin. "I've never slept well in pyjamas … I'll sleep better when I can wear less at home."

"Debatable," Paul whispered in my ear, flirting back. "I'm considering keeping you away a while longer. I can send Ray and Denis back and we can move on somewhere else for a while."

"That's your call," I told him. "I'm not the one ultimately responsible for you and your men."

I thought a moment longer. "Did you see how big she was? The baby is close for her. I know I'll get through the next few months. I'm not afraid to go home," I told him. "At least there I'll have a weapon and a chance. Here … I'm just a target."

Paul struggled for a minute with his decision.

"Okay," he said. "We'll go back. You promise you'll carry your gun always. And please let me do my job … you'll need to take any precautions I tell you to take."

"I won't let you down Paul. We'll be okay," I promised.

Chapter 22

It was almost a week after we returned from Reno. I'd given up trying to stay awake and stopped worrying about disappearing. I figured that my two trips to Toronto had been to learn about the danger we faced from Damian. Without running into Damian I wouldn't have known Alina was in trouble.

We'd emptied the other rooms on the top floor of Paul's house in preparation for turning it into an apartment and I'd been making holes in the walls to find out what sort of nightmare waited inside them. All those rooms were warm. Paul's was the only cold one so I figured it was just a blocked duct or something easy to sort out. We'd been in the warehouse going through his old tools to see what was up to the job and what we would still need.

My back was to Paul as he put the warehouse keys in his pocket when something got my attention from up the hill. It was a man, dark like a shadow. The closest smudge I'd seen a week before. My breath froze in my throat as I turned.

I forced out Paul's name as a bright red light filled my eye. He reacted and several things happened far too quickly for me to have caused any of them. He stepped between me and the source of the light. I only knew that because it went out. Then he grabbed the front of my coat with both hands and sprung toward the corner of the warehouse.

He managed a few steps before something hit him hard in the back. He stumbled and pushed me behind the building but he was off balance. His head hit the corner of the warehouse with a loud crack and he dropped nowhere near making it around the corner with me. Luckily he sent me spinning so I was rolling when I hit the ground avoiding a hard landing. I scurried to the side of the warehouse as soon as I knew which way was up and knelt down low on the ground.

Paul was on his stomach his head turned towards me. Blood ran from a gash on his temple and dripped into the snow. The red light shone on his shoulders. It kept reaching trying to touch his head but the ground was uneven so it kept jumping from his shoulder to the snow a few feet beyond. The light tried a few more times then went off.

I turned my head toward the man on the hill. Even with the building in between us I could easily pick up his location. He was waiting for me to do something stupid like run to Paul. Paul's eyes blinked a couple of times and looked around for me.

"Keep still," I told him. "He can't get a shot at your head the way you're laying."

Paul looked at me. He still wasn't all there. The only blood dripped from his face; none was visible around the hole in his jacket. I watched his eyes staring back at me then I froze.

I didn't see Paul any more. I saw Catherine's lover lying in a pool of blood. His dead glassy eyes watched me the same way. I knew with infallible certainty as my husband lay immobile on the ground before me in a sniper's sights that I'd watched the same man die two hundred years before. I knew what Ray had meant by Paul's long memory from that pain laced conversation I overheard weeks before. I knew if I did nothing it would happen again.

Paul tried to move so I put all the anger I could muster into my voice. He had to follow my orders while he was in no shape to give them.

"Stay down Paul," I barked at him. "The man on the hill has his gun on you."

The smudge watched.

Waiting.

I pulled out my gun.

"Can't hit … too far," Paul gasped.

"Noisemaker."

I pointed my gun to the sky and squeezed off two rounds then two more. The look of panic faded from Paul's face as he understood. The smudge sat up, getting my attention. He was going to move. Now that I'd alerted the others he was going to have to move fast. I didn't have much time.

Once he was on his feet I jumped to Paul's side, my gun tracking his position.

"Anna, get back," he tried to snap at me.

"No … I can see him. Now that everyone knows there's a problem he's finding a new position to get a better shot."

My right hand undid the snap on Paul's belt and took his knife. "What are you doing … wait."

"No time," I said. "He's going to kill you and six others including me before the rest get him … somehow I know."

Paul was trying to shake his head.

With all the authority I could pull off I growled at him. "You stay down or so help me I'll knock you out so you do. I've watched you die once already. It's not happening again." The man on the hill looked back at us, almost in position. He'd moved so fast; he thought he could get me first then Paul. I put my gun down and gently brushed the blood from his forehead then I hurried back behind the building.

"Don't move," I growled again. I could feel the anger in my face. "I'll be back in a minute then we'll talk about keeping things from Anna."

"No, no, no …" Paul struggled. It didn't matter. I would sort out the man on the hill before he could get a round off. I moved Paul's knife to my left hand. The man on the hill was prone, putting his rifle to his shoulder.

"I love you," I told Paul and disappeared.

I re-appeared already bringing Paul's knife down in both hands, my feet planted on either side of the man on the hill. I didn't hesitate. Just as his finger went to the trigger the knife sunk deep into the fold between his shoulder and his neck. The force I put behind it pushed him down into the snow sending the muzzle up. The rifle discharged; the bullet exploding into a nearby tree.

Anger clouded my vision and a void of indifference filled me. I'd saved my family. Paul, me, and our baby. I had no other choice. None at all.

The man took his hands off his rifle and tried to grab the knife. That didn't worry me. I used all my weight to drive it in and there was no way he was getting it out. I put my boot on his head and held him down; I didn't really want to see his face.

The man was bleeding out quickly; he'd stopped pushing up on my foot so I took his sidearm. I popped out the clip and made sure the chamber was clear before I put both in my pocket. Then I took his rifle and unloaded it as well. He'd stopped moving so I put my hand on his back. He exhaled once and was still. I relaxed and stepped off him.

I quickly patted him down and found another handgun under his arm so I pushed his coat up on that side to get it. A river of blood flooded out into the snow. While I waited for it to stop I looked back at Paul. He'd seen me and I noticed someone peeking around from the warehouse.

"It's okay," I called down. "There was just one."

Nobody moved. I carefully fished the other hand gun out of the shoulder holster avoiding the blood and yelled again while I was unloading it.

"I got him, you can come out now."

When it was in my other pocket I moved to the man's head and put my foot on it. It took some wiggling but I finally got Paul's knife out. There were two men with Paul and two on their way to me so I slung the man's rifle over my shoulder and with the still dripping knife in my hand I walked past them down the hill.

Ross and the other man with Paul had him sitting by the time I got there. I knelt beside him. There was pain on his face now that the glassy look was gone. I put the rifle down on the ground beside him.

"He shot you with this," I told him.

Then I pulled out the man's hand guns and the clips. I put my own gun back in its holster under my arm.

"What were you thinking? I told you to stay back." Paul demanded.

Ross quickly checked all three weapons.

"They're secure," he said.

"He was half a second from sending a round through your head," I whispered in his ear. Ross and the other man were busy briefing the others who'd arrived. "This was the small lead group I told you about before we left for Reno. He would have killed seven including our baby before he was stopped. If you think I was out of line by defending us when you were incapacitated we can discuss that privately."

He set his jaw and looked at me. "No, I guess not."

"I don't know where the others are. I didn't see him until he had his sight on me. I'll keep looking."

Paul looked down at his bloody knife. "You used my knife?"

"I put my gun down to wipe the blood from your face … I must have left it," I shrugged and looked away as I started to get angry again. I backed up and leaned against the wall to let Ray work. Paul's knife was still in my hand and I crossed my arms and pulled my knees up as far as I could to hide it close across my stomach. I wasn't giving it up.

Most of the men had been sent out to check the compound by the time the men who went up the hill after me came back to report to Paul. "She just about took his head off. We tracked him back about a hundred yards over the hill to his camp. Looks like he was ready to dig in there for a long time."

I didn't remember it like that. From the corner of my eye I saw Paul look over at me. I didn't look back. Instead I got up and walked up the hill to the house then right toward the south end of the compound. They could look for me for a while; the danger was past for now. I needed to try and find the others who were coming for us.

The south road was deserted so I went forty or so feet into the trees and sat down against a sturdy trunk. I pictured myself moving away to the south, searching as I went. I searched for a while until I got sleepy and dozed off. I woke cold … and certain of where the last two men could be stopped.

Paul waited in the open front door for me when I got back to the house. I stopped for a moment to look at him. Then I smiled, tears of relief started to run down my face. Relief showed on his face too and something else. Anger at me maybe, for what I couldn't guess.

"Hi," I said as I got close to him.

"Where were you?" he asked as he put his arms around me. I held him with one arm. One still held the knife. I rested my head on him and breathed him in. He was warm and alive.

"I fell asleep just south of the compound. That jump drained me. I was looking for the second group."

"Upstairs," he told me.

Paul stiffly sat on the bed. A line of fresh stitches disappeared up into his hairline. I left the door open a bit so I could hear if anyone came up and stood with my arms crossed guarding him.

"You went after them by yourself?"

"I didn't," I told him. "I was trying to see them like when I saw them before."

He frowned. "Can I have my knife back now?"

"Not until the danger is past. It's not over yet."

"And you're going after them?" he demanded, crushing handfuls of bedspread.

"No, I ..."

"Haven't we risked enough for one day?"

I crossed my arms tighter. "You can be as mad at me as you want but that doesn't change what happened today. He almost got us both."

"And you know this?" he asked. "How?"

"Yes ... and I'm figuring that out."

We stared at each other for a few seconds.

"How about we talk about you keeping things from me?" I asked.

"What things? I told you everything you asked about."

I nodded. "But then you didn't really ..."

"The funny thing is I'm not even mad at you for keeping it from me. I was earlier but not now because I wouldn't have believed it. It was when I saw you on the ground looking up at me half conscious. Barely seeing me. I knew who you were. And who I was. Why our first night together felt like I was reconnecting with an old lover, not finding a new one.

"You felt it then too," I said quietly. He stared back.

"You don't have to say anything. You were Catherine's lover years and years ago. You thought I was dead so you gave up. I watched him kill you." I took a step closer, my arms relaxed.

"He said you were too late. He was right. I wouldn't have survived the beating. Now I know what Ray meant when he said our son

95

would get your long memory … will our daughter have that too? You remembered me from that long ago … it just took me a while to figure it out.

"I was Andre too. I didn't know you then. But I knew Damian," I could feel my temper start to rise. "He was that asshole Lieutenant chicken shit coward. Hardly ever got his hands dirty. Like now. Sitting back indulging himself with my sister. Sending his men after us in his place. Men like him … men like you. I think I can see them when they come because they remember too.

"How many of your men are like you. Ray for sure, probably a lot of the others … and the man I killed. I have a feeling that I broke whatever tied him to his long memory. He'll come back, but he won't remember."

I moved closer to him. My arms had fallen to my sides. I turned my wrist slowly, impatience tapping the dirty blade on my leg.

"Aren't you going to say something?" I demanded as I moved my arms away from my body.

It was then Ray got me from behind. Paul's eyes had stayed on me the whole time never betraying his presence. He held me so I couldn't move my arms; they stuck out from my sides. His leg between mine leaning me back just enough that I couldn't leverage my own off balance weight.

"Let go of the knife Anna," Ray said quietly into my ear.

"No," I told him. "You're going to have to take it."

He shifted his weight just a bit and the nerve in my arm pinched painfully. I sucked air in between my teeth as my arm went numb and the knife started to slip from my fingers. There was no way he was going to come between me and protecting Paul. I disappeared and reappeared at his side for a fraction of a second to hold the handle of his gun then I disappeared with it and reappeared behind him holding it to his back.

I waited for the knife to hit the ground.

"Ray …" I said quietly. "Don't move until I tell you too."

Paul's eyes were wide.

"If you turn to grab it I'll be on the other side of the room before you even get half way around." He didn't know that wasn't true. Three jumps had completely drained me.

"Anna," Ray said as he raised his arms. "Please put it down. You've been through a lot and you're not yourself."

"Are you sure? Is my voice shaking? How about my hands?" I asked him as I held his gun steady.

"Trouble breathing?" I pulled in a deep breath through my nose.

"No," Ray said.

"So you're questioning my mental state because I saved seven lives today?'"

"You killed a man."

"No. I saved my husband, myself and my baby and four of the men. I'm thinking very, very clearly. Don't compromise my ability to do that ever again."

"Okay Anna," Ray said going along with me; waiting for me to make a mistake. I watched him closely. Listened for sounds in the hall. I'd taken things up a notch and the next person to walk in wouldn't be so gentle with me.

"Paul," I said not taking my eyes off Ray. "You know that frozen pond a couple of hundred yards south of the compound?"

"Yes."

"Just after twenty-one hundred tonight the last group will arrive there. Two men. Heavily armoured. Heavily armed. They'll split up and circle the compound, setting up positions for a turkey shoot tomorrow. If you ambush them there the only loss of life will be theirs. You have to take them at the pond. There's not a lot of time."

"I'm not leaving the house," I said. "Three jumps today and I can't pull off the control I need to be of any use at all. It's not the distance that tires me so much. It's the precision and without immediate danger to myself or to Paul I wouldn't go anywhere.

"I'm starting to understand it ... getting stronger," I was having a hard time with my words. I took two steps back and bent my elbow, pointing his gun at the ceiling.

"Take your gun," I said softly, my voice fading with exhaustion.

He turned slowly and took it. My knees started to go and Ray steadied me. Paul pushed himself up and came to help. They moved me to the bed and got my boots and coat off. I looked down at the dried blood on my hands.

"I'm okay," I told them after half a minute. I took clean clothes from the dresser and went to the shower. I wasn't getting in our bed covered in another man's blood. I washed up as best I could with one arm and came out. Ray was waiting and I heard Paul speaking quickly to someone as he walked away down the hall. His knife was gone from the floor where it had fallen.

"How long will it take for my arm to work again Ray?"

"Not much longer," he said. "I don't believe you feel as good as you say you do Anna."

"Neither better or worse." I shrugged. "I bet you were behind me for a while. I'm not upset about it. I wouldn't have let me around him either. I just reacted ... I wouldn't have hurt you. I know you're protecting him too."

Ray nodded. "If we thought you were going to hurt him he wouldn't have gone upstairs alone with you. We just wanted you to put the knife down."

"He's getting ready to go to the pond?"

"Yes," Ray said. "You're not stopping him."

"No, I'm not. I can't distract him now."

I thought a moment.

"Ray ... you need to go too," I told him as the outcome of the confrontation to come found a place in my mind. "Tell Paul that just because I said none of them will die doesn't mean nobody will get hurt. Those men ... won't stop, won't retreat. Don't drop your guard for a second. They'll need you before it's over. Get your stuff and hurry."

He thought about it.

"Go," I squeezed his hand. "I'll be good."

"I'll know if you're not."

"I'm sure you will."

I waited upstairs for a few minutes after everything went quiet downstairs. It was half past eight. I was close to sleep and I would do everything I could to stay awake until Paul returned. I got a blanket from the laundry room and made hot chocolate. Snow came down hard outside the dark kitchen window. The drink kept me busy. I didn't taste it.

Shortly after nine the smudges neared the pond. Pulling my blanket up and around my shoulders I let myself out the front door. Paul had left two guards behind on the porch. I stood for a moment watching the south.

"Mrs. Richards," the one named Jones said. "The Captain wants you to stay here until he gets back."

"I am staying here. I thought I might be able to hear something from outside," then I took a seat next to them. "It's starting."

I didn't think I could hear anything given the distance and heavily falling snow, but the soft pops of gunfire made it to us. One smudge faded right away, flickered a few times and disappeared. The other headed quickly west into the trees then doubled back east unseen. The man could see Paul's men moving in on where he entered the forest and he kept going east to find a new position behind them. Panic rose in me.

"Jones, can you talk to the Captain?"

"Private channel," he pointed to his earpiece.

"Tell him the remaining target went east, they're going in the wrong direction."

Jones looked at me, yeah right.

"Tell him I said it, he'll decide what to do with it ... you need to hurry. I'm not asking."

Jones sighed and shook his head. He adjusted the radio on his belt.

"November Whiskey," a pause. "Romeo reports the remaining

target has moved east of your position. Over."

Romeo? I wondered how long I'd been tagged with that.

"He copied."

The pops stopped a few seconds later. We waited.

And waited.

There was more gunfire from the south. He'd hit someone ... he didn't know how they'd refocused so quickly on his position. Then a small explosion as the smudge evaporated into the air like a popped balloon.

Then silence. I'd become so used to their weight on me that it was a shock when it lifted.

"It's over," I said as Paul's voice came from the radio.

"Jones, we need medical evac to the south pad and get Spanks down here with a stretcher and all the B positive he can carry." Both men burst into the house and Spanks was out the door with the stretcher under his arm and a small pack on his back in seconds, running full speed south to the pond. Through the open door I heard Jones give the location for the helicopter.

Eventually I heard over the radio that Ray had the wounded man stable. He'd lost a lot of blood and would need surgery. I pulled my feet up beside me under my blanket, turned sideways in my chair and closed my eyes finally giving in to sleep.

Chapter 23

Paul's weight moving the bed woke me enough to roll to my back and put my arm under his neck. He put his head on my shoulder and his hand on my belly.

"There was a time today when I thought I would never get to do this again," he said.

I gently ran my fingers across where I had wiped his blood away earlier. "You saved me first, remember. If you hadn't thrown me clear things would have ended very differently."

"Yeah ... listen Anna," he said. "About me remembering you ... it's true. We've known each other a very long time. You never remembered before.

"When you had that first dream about Catherine, I knew something was different this time. You'd never seen how we died before ... you'd only ever had good dreams about us. We've been together twice since then ... I don't know why you remembered that time."

"I think I do," I told him. "My first dream of her was that weekend after Sturgis. I was pregnant then. We just didn't know it yet. That's why I dreamed of Catherine. She was pregnant too."

"Perhaps," Paul said. "It's not common for one of us to father a child because it only happens with a woman who has a trace of our ability to remember. When we do it's a son who joins the … family. It's not the same for the women. You could have a child with a regular guy.

"Most of who I am now comes from this life: my appearance, my name, personality. We're usually tall, heal fast … don't always live very long. I guess we take bigger risks because we know there's another shot at things around the corner."

He slid his arm around me and squeezed me before he put it back.

"The same for you," he said. "You're very different from how I remember Catherine's personality. I don't understand how so much of Andre can be in you. I've never seen you pull so much of who you were before into who you are now. It's rare to live as the other gender."

"Much of Andre's personality faded when Ray got the knife from me," I told Paul. "I just have memories again … I'm back to just being Anna."

"My father could explain what's happened to you. We haven't found him in a long time. It's frustrating running the show without him."

I remembered the woman in the mirror telling me to take Paul to his father. I tried to imagine the dual meaning family would have for someone like Paul then my eyes went wide with understanding.

"Ray is my brother, isn't he?" I asked.

Paul nodded on my shoulder. "But don't ask me to explain how that works. If my father ever told me I wasn't paying attention. I tended to ignore him when he tried. He didn't seem to make much sense."

"Like Joshua is your brother?"

"Joshua is my brother like Alina is your sister. He's not like me … we have the same biological parents. My father has been my father for a very long time. Maybe father is the wrong word … I don't know how else to describe it."

"What about Ray's … other sister? Same thing?"

"Yes," Paul said.

"Why you would have wanted to send me away when I got here … if we have been together so much," I said.

Paul was quiet for a long time.

"I didn't think I could go through losing you again," he whispered. "Damian knew we were together. The men who came here with you were his and two got away. The little blonde one isn't like us … he uses them. Makes them think if they're loyal he'll make them like us but they're expendable. And invisible to the few of us who can pick them up like you seem to.

"We served with Damian and his men. Put up with each other for a while. Now that you're with me he doesn't have polite disinterest in us any more. He'll play to eliminate us all again.

"Nearly all the men here right now are family for which I'm very grateful. Trust, loyalty and obedience. They define us and the codes we live by. They explain why you accept that we accept what you can do. Their loyalty to me binds them to protect you. Josh's team and the other I have in the field right now aren't family and that keeps things thankfully simple.

"I tried to convince myself we didn't matter, that I'd walked away from you like Ray's sister. That wasn't right. I didn't give us enough credit. I underestimated your courage," he laughed a bit then. "You're as committed to protecting me as I am to protecting you. That's surprised me. You wouldn't let me go ... you found me just by wishing for me."

We lay still for a while, holding on to what we almost lost. I started to doze again when I felt a burst of butterflies under Paul's hand. I put my hand on top of his. My fingers found his ring and I started to gently trace its curve back and forth over his finger. The butterflies started again then it felt like a small pop.

"Did you feel that?" I whispered.

"Mm hm," he answered sleepily.

"That was her Paul," I put my hand back up to his face.

"Really?" he was wide awake; absolutely still. We waited a while but didn't feel her move again. Paul pulled me over toward him. He ran his hand down my back to my thigh and pulled it up over his.

"Anna," he breathed in my ear. "Can you help me forget what happened today ... for a while?"

And for a while I forgot too.

Chapter 24

Paul was in uniform when he woke me up.

"Hey," he said. "Come down for breakfast. Colonel Iverson flew back with Ray a while ago. He brought immigration paperwork for you and has been debriefing us regarding what happened yesterday."

That worried me. "How are we going to explain how I snuck up on a sniper so fast? Or how I knew about the others?"

"I don't think how you got him will be important and he knows I don't talk about my sources. He's more concerned that you're able to do your part to keep things quiet. He needs to satisfy himself that you're not a security risk. Three more dead ex-marines on my land could look pretty bad if it's not handled properly."

"If he finds out how I did it I'm going to spend the rest of my life in some hospital somewhere. Do I tell the truth, lie, or pretend I don't remember?"

"It won't come to that, okay? He'd never believe it anyway," Paul said. "Come on, I need you to join us."

I wished that the black sleep had taken me already. At least I could avoid this. He was half way out the door.

"Paul?" I said. He stopped and turned to me. "You look cute."

He winked and disappeared down the hall.

I decided on black pants with a stretchy tummy and my snug black long sleeved t-shirt. I was giving some thought to what Iverson might want and I figured if his main concern was that I could tell a big lie with a straight face then I might as well play the part. I put my hair up and got the rest of the blood out from under my nails before I put my gun on, gently circling my shoulders until the leather shoulder holster felt right. Paul carried his so I would too. Besides, he told me I had to keep it with me and hadn't said it was okay to do otherwise. I hoped the pregnant lady with a gun image would be contradictory enough that he would buy into whatever I told him just to make sense of me. I put the phone Paul got me in my back pocket and followed him downstairs.

From the foyer the small talk at the table was quieter than usual. Not the conversation of two dozen men but far fewer. I stepped around the corner into the kitchen looking down and pretending to be smoothing out the front of my shirt like I had been in a great hurry. My hope was to catch everyone off guard.

"Apologies gentlemen," I said. "I hope you weren't all waiting for me to get started."

Fortunately they weren't. I caught a couple of them mid-mouthful. It was a smaller group than I had expected. Just the officers: Ray, Denis, Ross and Paul and the Colonel of course.

They all stood when I came in. I thought that was funny. They had never done that before and I kept my good behaviour face on. Paul came around the table to take my elbow as the Colonel approached.

"Mrs. Richards," he took my hand and tilted his head at Paul. "This cranky old man hasn't scared you off yet?"

"No Sir," I smiled. "I think he's stuck with me."

"Well, congratulations on your growing family. Please join us."

I nodded. Paul took me to the seat next to him and pushed my chair in for me. The others finally sat down when he did. They all looked somewhat uncomfortable in uniform and I would have to be careful not to think too much of it if I was going to keep from giggling. I had no idea who cooked, but my breakfast was served so I ate. Small bites, remembered to use my knife. I noticed the others had table manners, unlike the usual chow time behaviour I had gotten used to.

It wasn't long before the Colonel wanted to include me in the small talk.

"So Mrs. Richards how did you and Paul meet?" he asked.

I finished the bite in my mouth. "We were both shooting the customs down at Daytona last spring. For him it was work. I was on another assignment but I have a ... quiet and substantial financial stake in a couple of the shops represented there so I went to the competition too," I paused. Daytona was a fib ... it was actually early July. "I don't get to say hello to my builders very often; usually just at the shows so I shoot the customs whenever I can."

"How did they do?" he asked.

"Both my shops placed. It was a good week for them," he could check that out if he wanted to. Then I smiled at Paul. "I was reloading in an alley out of the sun when he swooped in to my shady corner to do the same thing. Saved me from my dried up lunch."

"How so?" he asked. For some reason the man didn't want me to eat.

"A simple gift of water," I beamed at Paul and went back to my breakfast.

"Do you ride too?" he was asking now.

"Almost everywhere during riding season ..." and my phone rang. "I'm sorry, I grabbed it without thinking."

I pulled it out of my pocket to silence it then I showed it to Paul. Unknown number.

"Alina?" Paul asked.

"She doesn't hide her number ... I bet its Damian with a health check."

"You don't have to take it."

"I'm not afraid of him," I said. And I wasn't. Andre didn't fear him so I wouldn't either.

"Keep him on the line as long as you can," he was already running to the common room. "I'm going to call in for a trace."

I took a deep breath and popped the phone open.

"Allan Creed Photography," I sang into it. The fake name I worked under. I could hear breathing but nobody spoke.

"Allan Creed Photography," I repeated. The Colonel listened closely.

"Put in your quarter love," I said sweetly.

"Anna," Damian's voice said. He wasn't fooled.

"This is Rachel with the answering service sir."

I tried to speak somewhat slowly to drag the call out, but not too slowly.

"Damn it," Damian said. "Stop the bullshit."

"I'm sorry," I said. "This is Anna, who am I speaking with?"

I heard him breathing into the phone. He was angry. Paul came in and gave the Colonel a thumbs up and quietly stuck a microphone to the back of my phone.

103

"Hello?" I asked again.

"It's Damian," he said.

"Damian ..." I paused then replied brightly. "Alina's friend?"

The microphone connected to a small tape recorder. Paul had plugged an earpiece into it and put it in his ear. He had given the cordless from the common room to Ross.

"Yes," he hissed into the phone.

"Did you give her my message?" I asked.

"No ... I called to talk about your friend," he said.

"Who?" I sounded bewildered.

"Richards ..." he hissed into the phone again. I looked over at Paul and tapped my wrist. He motioned for me to keep going.

"You mean Paul?" I asked.

"Bitch," he muttered. "I think he's had a problem." Damian laughed coldly.

I let Andre's insubordinate tone seep into my voice. "Yeah ... no ... he didn't mention anything this morning ..."

"Bitch," he said again. Then there was just angry breathing on the phone again.

"Did you lose something?" I asked. I looked at Paul again. Keep going.

"Or someone?" I finished.

"Maybe that little fellow you sent by to borrow a cup of sugar?" I would pretend for now that we didn't know about the others. Damian knew nothing about his men. He was starving for information.

"He hit one of the men ... right in the vest." I put on my best nine-hundred number voice hoping to hold his interest.

"Then he just sat there. I'd gone up the hill before he shot ... he hadn't seen me. I got up behind him." I said, my voice getting huskier. "Idiot had his headphones on. Blasting out some techno dance shit. I had a knife.

"I got so close," I breathed into the phone. "I stood over him and wrapped both my hands around it."

"Mmm," I almost moaned into the phone. "He shot a tree when I drove it in hard up to the hilt. He was weak. His hands tried to pull on it but they were so slippery with his own blood he couldn't hold on."

I laughed.

"I put one foot on his head to hold him still ... to see if I could secure his weapons before he bled out. He wasn't a gentleman," I breathed into the phone again. "He finished before I did."

Damian went off swearing at the top of his lungs; raw fury blasting me over the phone. Paul winced and I held the phone as far from my ear as I could.

"Ross," I mouthed.

"It's traced into Canada. They're getting started," Ross whispered.

"Keep going," Paul whispered. "Try and get control of him."

I had an idea, or Andre did.

"Lieutenant Nielsen!" I bellowed into the phone.

Damian shut up. Paul and the Colonel looked confused.

"Listen … Rex," I took the insubordinate tone back on. "I don't think that's all you lost yesterday."

"Bitch," Damian hollered again and went back to panting into the phone.

"That may be … but I'm not your bitch," I said coldly.

Ross was talking quietly into the phone.

"Twenty seconds to complete trace," he whispered.

I can do that. I thought.

"It's a sad story … there's a small pond … just south frozen over this time of year. But it's been mild, too mild to go on the ice.

"Mmm, are you listening Damian? Watch found a big hole in the ice late last night. At first we thought one of ours fell in … so we panicked. Got all hands down there … we pulled them out."

"Bitch, bitch," Damian was muttering into the phone.

I kept going with a random question in a ditzy voice. "That stuff you sent them with … was it … like … expensive?"

"What?"

"Some of it was shiny so I bet it was expensive."

Ross gave the thumbs up. They had a location.

"You're an idiot Damian. Weighing them down like that and sending them out on thin ice. Incompetent. They didn't stand a chance. You just give me a call anytime you need a reality check. Cheers." I finished sweetly and hung up.

"Sorry about anything I said," I told them. "He didn't believe a word of it but I got him so mad he couldn't stop listening … I'm really starting to dislike him."

Paul put his hand on my shoulder and shook his head.

"We've never completed a domestic trace on him, much less an international one. Good job."

"How do you get away with an international trace?" I asked.

Paul shrugged. "Can't say."

"Fair enough," I answered. "Why do I feel like I just put an even bigger target on myself?"

"Who is Lieutenant Rex Nielsen?" the Colonel asked.

Andre's Lieutenant, I thought.

"No idea, Colonel," I said. "Damian is so arrogant. Getting his name wrong was a good way to get his attention back."

I got up and put my plate in the microwave to warm up my cold food.

Denis whispered to Ray. "Sure glad she's on our side."

"Amen," the Colonel whispered back. Then to me, "Mrs. Richards, you were able get close enough from behind to attack him?"

"No sir," I said, "I had taken the Captain's knife. I'd have my own but a belt is getting a little awkward these days. I had a clean throw from about thirty feet. It had to hit hard." Andre could throw further and I had no doubt I could pull it off.

The Colonel blinked. "Thirty feet … through the trees?"

"Yes sir," then I dropped my eyes and let my voice go cold. "I don't miss."

"With what Paul says about your shooting I don't doubt that's true."

I put my plate on the table and sat back down to finish my breakfast.

"So, where did you learn these skills Mrs. Richards?" the Colonel asked. "From what I've learned about you, you don't have any military training, yet you are quite comfortable with the lifestyle that my men have chosen here and if you were one of my men it's arguable that you would be one of my best."

Paul kept his eyes down on his empty plate. I leaned back in my chair and thought for a moment.

"Respectfully, perhaps the Colonel is concerned that Mrs. Richards might not appreciate how important it could be to be able to sincerely share another version of what happened here yesterday … should the need arise."

"Perhaps," the Colonel said. "Why don't you tell me something about yourself that I wouldn't find in my security check on you? Then perhaps I can be satisfied to give you enough of a security clearance to allow you to know what you did yesterday."

Okay, I thought. I guess this is where he wants to hear me lie.

"I have a pretty good idea what you found on me. I own my house and I'm well enough off to be able to swing a modest retirement at twenty-four. That I left home at sixteen and for the past eight years I've made a lot of undocumented border crossings. Returning to the US when I haven't left. That sort of thing. Bet you unsealed my criminal record."

Paul's eyes widened. He didn't know.

"That was for my last job. I was released to my father in exchange for a guilty plea because the Crown thought the older boys I hung with put me up to it, but the truth was we had been stealing one or two very nice vehicles a week for a year and a half. They were shipped overseas. I was fifteen. The record stuck, but it was sealed because of my age."

I sunk back in my chair and frowned.

"I spent a lot of time with a shrink after my mother died. I was anti-social, acting out. He diagnosed me with some odd personality

106

problems. Including an inability to empathize or feel remorse if I hurt someone. These men," I gestured around the table, "are far more troubled that I killed someone yesterday than I will ever be. I believe whatever comes out of my mouth. Most … medical truth aids don't work on me. I'm very intelligent … I finished high school at sixteen in spite of the nights I was out stealing cars. I'm extremely manipulative. But you heard that when I talked to Damian. I have very little regard for my personal safety. The Captain can tell you that.

"I guess I got flagged somewhere for my … traits … and was quietly recruited at eighteen by the Canadian government to take on some challenging work that most of the real soldiers wouldn't have the stomach for. The shrink's records disappeared a long time ago. You won't find them."

I stood. Andre had helped me take Paul's knife again without him even knowing. Andre's knife work was going to help me sell my story. I balanced it by the handle on my fingertips. Paul's hand went slowly down to his scabbard. He shot me a look but didn't say anything. I started bouncing the knife in the air. It would go almost up to the ceiling before I balanced it again. As I continued I caught it in my palm and flipped it over to the back of my hand to balance it like I had at Willy's. I spun it on my knuckle and watched it like it was something beautiful.

"I work under several names. You might know a couple of them. I have valid ID as the wife of all the men I pretend to be. Passports as good as yours. Nobody suspects a woman …" I let my voice trail off.

I launched the knife up in the air again, meaning to get the back of my hand under the point, between my knuckles and break its fall slowly. I got it between the knuckles fine but I didn't slow its fall quickly enough. It sunk in a good quarter inch into my hand.

"Whoops," I said quietly. I licked my lips as blood began to drip from my hand. Andre only did that one with gloves on I remembered and I giggled.

"Jesus Anna …" Paul said.

I went back to bouncing it by the handle. "I don't … feel any pain from a knife wound," I said distractedly as I watched the pretty knife. Then I pulled up my shirt to show the eye on my stomach.

"Damian gave this to me a couple of weeks ago," I shook my head as I let my shirt drop.

"Nothing," I said. "Felt nothing."

I put Paul's knife on the counter and wrapped my hand in a clean towel. Blood dripped off my elbow. I was surprised how little my hand hurt. Andre would be impressed with how sharp Paul kept his knife.

"Mrs. Richards can't tell you anything interesting that she has done in the past six years any more than Captain Richards could ever tell me what he's done in the past fourteen." I sat back down. "I thought I had moved on from all that. I was rather insubordinate and a bit of a danger to anyone unlucky enough to be assigned with me. My leaving was mutual. I didn't get off on the work any more.

"But I guess here I am," I peeked under the towel, looking as fascinated with what was underneath as I had with the spinning knife. Blood was still welling up. "Mrs. Richards certainly appreciates a good cover story."

"Ray ... do you have a minute?" I said sweetly. "Can you excuse us a minute or two gentlemen?"

There were looks of shock on all the faces around the table. I had no idea what Paul was thinking. He hadn't known about my record.

"Uh, yeah Anna," I got up and went down to the first aid room. Ray followed. I'd left quite a mess for Paul to clean up with the Colonel.

Ray looked at the wound and shook his head.

"Do you think he bought it?" I whispered.

"Anna, we all bought it. I think Paul believes he married Mrs. Hyde."

"I thought the Colonel wanted to know if I could pull off whatever cover story there might be," I said. "Ouch, that's really starting to hurt."

"He did ... but I think your knife act might have sold it as the truth."

Ray froze my hand and stitched it up. Then he wiped the blood off and wrapped it.

"The black sleep is hitting me soon Ray, I need to get to bed. Any idea how long it will take to wrap things up with the Colonel?"

Paul came in then to answer my question.

"The Colonel is going down to brief the cleanup crew, they just got here ... you got your security clearance," he shook his head. "He's going to make a couple of phone calls to see if your story is true. He left the paperwork behind ... .but a criminal record Anna?"

"It's sealed ... could be for jaywalking for all he knows. It's for exactly what I said it's for and I don't think he could get it open. I had to be honest just in case he had seen the file. You knew I got in some trouble."

Paul sighed. "And who is Rex Nielsen?"

"Andre's Lieutenant."

"You didn't." Paul said he rubbed his hands on his face. "You're ageing me."

"I did," I told him. "I want Damian to know exactly who he is dealing with. This isn't ending his way. I have to keep his focus on me ... to keep it off my sister."

Ray looked at Paul, puzzled.

"I'll fill you in later," Paul said.

"Damian's in Toronto?" I asked.

"Yes."

"I could have told you that. Hopefully as long as he's mad at me …" I wished now I wasn't going to sleep for a while. "I can't wait much longer to get him away from Alina. I have to get to bed now unless someone wants to pack me upstairs. I think I've run out of time. See you in a couple of days."

Paul followed me upstairs. I quickly stripped and put on pyjamas. He stayed with me until I fell asleep. It didn't take long.

Chapter 25

I didn't remember anything, other than a dream. A dream I was with my daughter. She was all grown up … living in Paul's house with a nice young man who loved her deeply. I was going to be a grandmother. We sat on the porch together in the shade. She wore a purple summer dress with a high waist, comfortable and roomy. She expected her baby soon. I was still in my pyjamas. She didn't seem to find that at all odd. Neither did I.

The baby's father is like my father … he'll be like both of them.
Like me? I asked her.

No. You're not like any of us at all, she smiled at me. *Not this time.*

I didn't understand.

I want to show you something. Wait here a moment.

She came out with a small handbag then she took my hand and led me down the stairs.

The house is the only part of this place I kept up, she told me as we walked south past the cabins. I looked at them as we passed. The paths to them were overgrown. Some were leaning, their windows broken when the glass refused to bend with the passing years. Their siding faded to match the forest that had protected them and now welcomed the land back.

Uncle Joshua kept the land in trust for me until I turned eighteen, she explained. *He and his wife raised me after Camille got sick and died. Ron didn't live much past her. They had always been so much in love …*

I didn't want to think about what that meant. Not at all. Just past the last cabin the road took a sharp right to the gate. A well worn foot path continued on straight into the forest. I looked around as she towed me through the trees but I couldn't spot the one I had slept against the day Damian's men came.

After a few minutes the smell of the forest changed. Grass and flowers. Sunlight welcomed us to the pond. We crossed the flowered meadow until we reached the edge of the water and then followed that to the far side. I had only seen the pond through the eyes of the third man who had come for us. Through the dark, frozen over in the heavily falling snow. It was hard to believe this was the same place but it was. Unmistakably.

Twenty feet up the bank at the south side of the pond was a fenced off square. The fence was metal, wrought iron, a small gate in the centre of the side that faced the pond. She let us in. The markers were weathering already, but the names were clear. She sat us on a small bench facing them.

Yes, she said in answer to my questioning look. *This is how you are here with me now. You're here alone ... I don't know where my father is. Camille always said he was at Arlington but I've been there and he isn't. I don't think they found him.*

Uncle Ray put you here. You passed away in the house just after I was born. You showed up here alone ... dying ... he had to take me from you as your heart stopped. At least with a marker for my father it feels like we're still together.

She wept quietly. Her grief had long past, leaving only sadness.

Let's sit by the water for a while, she wiped her eyes and smiled at me. *Uncle Ray said you would come. Not for very long ... but to expect you before the baby comes. That was years ago. I've had a lot of time to think about what I wanted to do with the small amount of time we would have.*

At the side of the pond she put her hand on my stomach.

That's me in there, she said.

Yes.

Sit, she gestured to the ground and carefully lowered herself down in front of me then she dug around in the bag and passed me a hairbrush.

Please mother. I took the brush and ran it through her hair. Her dark hair was part way in between my waves and Paul's curls. Closer to mine. The dark brown was all Paul. The curls smoothed out as the brush went through and then sprung back as I brought it back up for another pass. Her face tilted up to the sun. The smile on her lips reminded me of my mother and Alina. She sighed.

Your turn. I got up and sat in front of her. She started at the ends, working out the sleepy tangles. The tips of the bristles were soft as they moved over my skin.

Uncle Ray said that you're unique. Nothing like they had ever seen. He told me how you can travel, about the soldier you remember who helped you with what you were meant to do.

Somehow I have my father's gift ... to remember. As strong as his. Uncle Ray helped me understand. But I don't know if you will keep yours. We'll find you again but you could just be the way my father remembered you before. I could just be your friend. You may never know me as your daughter.

She sniffled and the brush paused as she wiped her eyes.

This could be the only time we have.

She picked some of the little purple flowers around us and put them in my hair. They were the same colour as her dress. She lay down in the grass then and I lay down to face her. Paul's green eyes sparkled at me from under my own familiar lids.

You went away for a while, after you and my father were married. To find out what your gifts meant. It was hard on him. Very hard.

Uncle Ray said you went to stop my father-in-law. She paused as my face showed my surprise. *My husband ... the man you know as Damian is his biological father. You had to stop him. He had divided the family ... caused us so much pain over the long years.*

You can't let my father interfere with the work before you. He will try. He loves you so much, she said. *You told Ray that's what cost you your lives before you passed. He'll forgive whatever you have to do to keep him away.*

If you do it alone ... we might all see spring here together, she smiled at me and put her hand on my face, like her father did, running her thumb over my cheek bone.

I will. I told her. I will.

We fell asleep on the shore of the pond together, warm in the afternoon sun, listening to each other breathe in the sweet air.

Chapter 26

I woke up from my dream alone in Paul's room, determined to get the help the woman in the mirror told me to get. Paul said I'd found him just by wishing. Maybe I could find the answers I needed the same way.

I showered and dressed. Part way downstairs to fill the big empty space in my stomach I heard a woman's voice and Paul's voice saying 'Mom.' I stopped in my tracks. Paul's parents were here ... they knew nothing about me. I had to talk to Paul before I went down so I crept back upstairs and slammed one of the doors in the hallway. Then I went to sit on the bed to wait for him. It wasn't long before he came up.

"Welcome back Sugar," he said. I stood to hug him.

"Hi Paul," I smiled back. "How long was I asleep?"

"Four days ... you got yourself to the bathroom but it was like we weren't here," he swayed gently back and forth holding me and kissed my head. "I knew you'd wake up eventually but it was a long wait. I missed you."

"I missed you too."

111

I noticed he had taken his weapons off. "We get the all clear or is there another reason you're under dressed?"

He sighed. "My parents came up to surprise Josh and me ... Ray and I had to stash them behind the sofa. I make excuses if they call ahead ... usually doing something I can't tell them about. Regardless, I had it coming. I've gotten used to keeping most of everything I do from them. I don't always remember when there are things I do need to tell them."

I looked down at what I was wearing. Plain dark colours. Gun. I hadn't realized how much I'd been dressing like Paul and his men until I needed to think about meeting his parents. I'd picked up a couple of more feminine things in Reno; I wasn't sure why at the time but I was glad now that I did. I put my gun in a drawer and changed into white pants and a dark pink short sleeved shirt. It had a low neck with a wide ruffled collar and a tie in the back to adjust the size of the front. Then I ran the brush through my hair one last time.

"There," I said. "Presentable?"

"Beautiful as always," he said. "I haven't told them about you and Mom hasn't noticed my ring. Guess it's fair to surprise them back."

His mother and father were speaking with Ray when we got downstairs. They stopped when we came in unsure what to make of me. His mother looked at my face, my stomach, the rings on my hand I hadn't hidden, at Paul and then back to me. She was quick. But she didn't say anything.

"This is my Anna," Paul said. "My parents, Ron and Camille."

I knew the names from my dream. They might spend the last few years of their lives raising the child that was still inside me.

"Your Anna?" She looked at Paul. "Would it have killed you to pick up the phone to tell me you have an Anna?"

"No Mom," Paul said and I imagined his feet shuffling behind me. His father shook his head behind her, the poorly hidden smile on his face in stark contrast to her well hidden one, if she had one at all.

"Anna," she said. "I hope my son's inability to call his parents doesn't reflect badly on him. He's a good boy."

I reached back to hold Paul's hand. "Yes he is," I agreed.

"So are you the woman who is going to settle him down?" she asked. Right to the point. I got the impression that as much as she wanted her boys married off she still had final say. "You've known each other long?"

"He's been my competition for the past couple of years. We've known each other professionally for a while ... and started spending more time together this past spring."

"I see," she pursed her lips just I'd seen Paul do as she turned her intimidating stare to him. "Anything else you haven't told us?"

112

I squeezed his hand. He looked up at the ceiling and sighed. "We eloped in Reno two weeks ago," he said. "And we're expecting."

She squealed, charging with her arms out and hugged me pulling me away from Paul her firm demeanour gone. She was almost as tall as me. His father was almost as tall as his him. I could see where Paul and Joshua got the tall genes from. "We are so happy! I thought my boys would be bachelors for the rest of their lives. Do you have a sister you could introduce to my poor Joshua?"

"I do, but you would never get her away from the hospital she doctors at in Toronto. But maybe if Joshua wanted to move I could arrange something …"

"Ah, I'll get to work on that right away," she said. "My Ronald is a doctor too. It would be wonderful to have another one in the family. I wish I had a daughter I could marry off to Ray …"

She was going on to Paul's father now. "Do you think they'd mind if I sneak off to the kitchen?" I whispered to Paul.

"Go ahead if you don't mind her following you."

In the kitchen I found plenty to warm up in the fridge. Paul was right. She was right behind me, chatting away.

I yawned as she paused for air. "I'd probably sleep better at night if I didn't sleep half the day too. I guess it will get worse before it gets better. Still have half way to go."

"Half way … my goodness. You know we still have a bunch of Paul and Joshua's old toys and things. Are you going to find out what it is?" she asked.

I nodded. My mouth was full.

"We have," I told her.

"What?" she asked and moved to the edge of her seat.

"You'll have to ask Paul," I told her. "I'm fine with telling but I don't know how he feels about it. He might want to surprise everyone."

"Paul," she called as she hurried out of the kitchen to get her way and I could hear her exclaiming in the common room.

"A girl! My goodness! She's the last woman to marry in to the Richards line!"

She went on for the next two hours. All about my family, Paul's family. She was disappointed that we weren't moving closer but they could spend a lot more time here in a few years when Ronald retired.

As she went on I became distracted. She would raise my daughter if I couldn't stop Paul from helping me with whatever I had to do in the next few months. Hurting Paul would be terrible but I had to believe whatever it was I faced was coming whether I got ready for it or not. I planned to go that night. I would jump the four-fifty I'd fixed up and would hopefully find what I needed.

After his parents left I went back to the kitchen for more food.

Ray and Paul joined me. Paul had brought up a cold six pack from downstairs and they each had a bottle.

"My dad says that's the first real peace he's gotten this whole trip," Paul said. "You're brave for taking on my mother for that long."

I shrugged. "If you just let her talk she seems to entertain herself. How did they get past the gate?"

Paul smiled. "Everyone here knows what my parents look like. Gate radios in … everyone hides."

"I hope Camille doesn't find out about that," I told him.

"Me too."

"Paul," I asked. "Are you sure I was up there the whole time? I had such a vivid dream and I slept so long, I wonder if I disappeared somewhere for a while … maybe it was just a dream. I don't feel any bigger."

"What did you dream about?" Paul asked.

"Our daughter. She lived here with a young man. They were expecting a baby … she was way bigger than I am. She was beautiful Paul. She looked like me with your dark hair and green eyes. It was late spring and we walked down to the pond to the south … tall grass and wildflowers. It smelled so good. I was only there for a few hours, but it made her happy."

Suddenly I felt the butterflies in my belly again. Ray had been up getting a second round for himself and Paul and stopped when he noticed the look on my face.

"Anna … Are you okay?" he asked.

I pointed at my stomach.

Moving, I mouthed.

Paul came around and sat by me and put his hand on her. We waited a minute.

"She stopped," I was disappointed. Paul stuck his nose behind my ear and kissed me.

"Moving?" Ray asked.

I nodded. "We first felt it the night the men came."

"That sounds about right."

"Ray, did you need to check me out? I'm going to lie down for a while before I hit the fridge again."

He looked at his second bottle of beer. "You're off the hook … the doctor's impaired."

"Fine with me," I punched his arm on the way by. "I'll be back down when I hear dinner."

Paul's room was cold. I decided I would try and fix the heat so I went to one of the other rooms down the hall that we had moved some tools into, took a big flat-headed screwdriver. I pulled the front off the old metal register.

114

The cause of the heat problem was obvious. Someone had jammed a big wad of fabric down into the duct. When I grabbed it something sharp bit into my palm through the cloth. I pulled my hand back for a moment then carefully grasped it in a different place and pulled it out. Hot air immediately started to pour into the room. It was strange how little dust there was considering how ancient the ball of cloth looked.

I opened it up. It was a long lacy shirt of some kind … covered in dark brown stains. I paused in excitement when I saw what was wrapped in it. Craving to test the weight of it in my hand and needing to run the other way at the same time. Shining in the lamp light was the gold handled knife that had killed Catherine and her lover. I was certain. The delicate gold guard around the handle, the narrow double edged blade. I held up in my shaking hand and looked at my palm. Just a small dent from the point. A small drop of blood on my skin.

This knife knew me.

I balanced it in my left hand then I laughed. It was a good knife. I stuffed the old shirt back in the duct and replaced the cover not wanting to give away that I'd found it. The knife went into the bottom of my pack beside my dresser then I put the screwdriver in my drawer. I wouldn't have much time to pack and get to the bike later and it was coming with me.

I decided to strip the bed and put clean sheets on it before I lay down. They had been on there a week so I pulled the blankets and quilt off and tossed them on the chair. Then the pillow cases and the top sheet. I stopped and looked at the bottom sheet; there was something there.

They were clusters of little purple flowers. There were more in the shower. I had gone to see her. Not for long, but I had gone. I opened one of my drawers and pushed the clothes aside to put the flowers there for now. I didn't know where else to hide them.

I took out a notepad and pen from a pocket on my pack and wrote Paul a letter. I hid that in my drawer then I put what I would wear on the top of one drawer and what I would stuff in my bag on top of the other. I made sure I knew where everything I would need from the bathroom was so I could get it quickly.

This would be our last night together for a while so I went to find Paul. I wasn't going to miss another minute of it. He was asleep on the sofa so I got out the paperwork the Colonel had left for me and started on it. I had it done by the time dinner was ready.

"Come on cowboy, time for grub," I told Paul as I nudged his knee with mine. "Let's eat."

He blinked up at me. I took his hands and helped him up.

"How are your ribs feeling?" I asked.

"Just stiff now," he yawned quietly.

"I hope you have some energy left for me," I whispered to him. "I already did all that paperwork for the Colonel so if you fall asleep I'll have nothing to do."

He yawned again. "Maybe there's still some coffee on."

There wasn't. With the food in him he seemed to perk up. As usual I helped cleanup after dinner and Paul got the first night watch out the door. Ray and Paul were whispering about something when I came in to the common room to join them. They had retrieved their weapons from behind the sofa and looked pretty tired.

"I won't ask how little sleep you got the last four days," I told them. "You should know better than to try and stay up as long as I can sleep."

Ray shrugged.

"The sky wouldn't have fallen. You both look wiped."

Paul yawned. I laughed quietly.

"You're more than a little distracted tonight," he said. "And you haven't talked about Alina all day."

"I did … I offered her to your mother for Joshua," I winked at him.

"That's not what I meant," he said. "You're not still thinking of going after her, are you?"

I was glad I didn't have to add lying to Paul to running out on him.

"No … I think that man is sufficiently angry to come after me here. I just don't like risking everyone … I might not see him coming next time."

"Anna," Paul hesitated. "I guess your clearance covers this. We have standing orders to deal with Damian and his men. However we can. Here we have the home field advantage … it's what we want."

"Yeah," I responded. It wasn't what I wanted but I didn't want him coming for me anywhere. My eyes closed as I tried to relax. "Andre would love a few minutes with him alone if I get the chance. He owes him. Big," I told them. Paul sighed loudly. I could hear the low growl in his throat.

"Just saying. And he really likes your knife," I told them.

"Anna," Paul said. "You're not going Andre on us again, are you?"

"No," I smiled at him. "Just Anna in here is crowded enough. I'm sorry. I guess that big sleep left me a little out of sorts."

"Okay, warn me please if he comes back? Too much of him in you would be … concerning."

"Sure Paul," I told him. "No Andre."

"I think I'm going to turn in," Ray said. "Three hours of Camille with a beer chaser has tired me out."

"Seconded," Paul yawned.

I shook my head. I had her on me most of their visit and I wasn't worn out like they were. Next watch change would be soon. The change after that Paul would go out. Then I would.

Paul's room was colder than it was before dinner. I huddled in to him to try and keep the bed itself from freezing me until it warmed up.

"We're going to have heat in here when we're done, right?" I asked him. If I didn't warm up soon my teeth would be chattering.

"Mm hm," he said. He was working his way down my neck with his lips.

"Some of that paperwork from the Colonel is for you. I got the rest done."

"Okay," he mumbled.

Then he stopped. "Are you stalling?"

"No," I said and curled myself in closer.

He lifted his head up and looked at me in the lamp light.

"This doesn't hurt you, does it? Or her?" he asked, concerned.

"Not at all … we can go until you're in danger of being crushed by me," I smiled to him.

"I don't notice the cold in here any more. You're like a little furnace."

"Okay then Paul," I laughed. "Stop stalling."

He laughed too. We had missed each other a lot.

Chapter 27

The knock on Paul's door came too soon. I didn't want to go out in the cold; I just wanted to wait to warm him up when he got back. He dressed quietly and kissed me goodbye.

"I love you," I told him. "Forever."

"I love you too Anna," he said and kissed me again.

Then he was gone.

I quietly pulled on the clothes I had put aside and put on my gun. The knife was still in my pack so I grabbed my things from the bathroom and stuffed them in. Then my clothes. I took my wallet, passport, phone and charger. The front door closed.

The letter for Paul went on top of his dresser, along with the flowers I found in the bed.

Nobody was around on the dark main floor. I didn't expect anyone. I watched him go quickly down the road until he was out of sight. I tried not to cry, but tears came anyway. I took the garage key from its hook above the desk and got out as fast as I could. The wind started to nudge me from behind as soon as I got to the bottom of the stairs. Steadily pushing me, stronger gusts hurrying me up. Pressure was building in my spine already. That was good. I probably wouldn't get away with this if I had to turn around at the warehouse and head back up for a second run. The bike would have woken the whole camp by then. I stumbled as the gusts pushed me harder. The cold cut through my clothes and blew my hair in my face.

I quickly opened the door to the garage and started the bike in the dark. It kicked to life right away so I held the throttle open for a few seconds until it would run on just the choke. The helmet and gloves were where I remembered and I found them easily in the bit of moonlight that came in the windows in the overhead door.

"Anna."

Shit.

Ray's voice.

"What's up Ray?" I asked. I gently cranked the throttle on the bike to see if it would rev up smoothly and pushed the choke in a bit.

"Paul thought you might go after your sister."

"Really?" I replied. "I'm not. Can you get the big door for me?"

"No," he said. "I'm going to get Paul for you."

"Please don't do that."

I opened big overhead door just enough to get under it on the bike hopefully not letting too much sound out. The bike would need more time.

"Why not?" he asked. "You're not going after Damian alone."

"I'm not going after Damian," I told him. I walked up to Ray and a big push almost knocked me into him. "It's the gusts of wind that push me when I jump. The pressure is building in me … it will take me away whether I take the bike with me or not. If I take the bike I have a better chance of jumping home. How did you know I was here?"

"Paul asked me to stay in the house while he's on watch … you just about ran me over in the dark getting the key."

Another gust pushed me into him.

"Sorry … can't you feel it? How come it's not pushing you?"

"I just feel the breeze in the door."

I stood for a minute, listening to the bike, hoping he would let me leave.

"Ray … while I slept I did disappear. I spent a few hours with my daughter. She told me that Paul's family raised her … she has her father's long memory. You helped her understand. She said my gifts are for something big … I have to get help to find out."

I pushed the choke in the rest of the way as I was pushed into the bike.

"She said someone tried to help me … they made a mistake and I lost Paul. I showed up here, dying, you had to cut her from me as I slipped away. You buried me by the pond … she showed me." Tears started to fall down my face again.

"She never knew me. She'll find me again, but I'll never get a chance to be her mother. Paul will find me again, but I won't remember him. She called you Uncle … unless I can find out how to do things right I have less than twenty weeks left to be your sister. Then I go back to being your best friend's girl."

The next gust nearly pushed me over the bike. I exhaled hard as it punched me. "That's really starting to hurt," I gasped then I straightened up and held him. He held me tight.

"Please big brother … let me go. I can't keep it from sending me much longer. Do your best to look after him … he's going to hurt over this."

The pressure was painful. I'd never let it get so bad.

"Anna … he won't understand," Ray said.

"I've left him a letter. That's the best I can do. I'll be back as soon as I can." I held the back of my neck and moaned with pain.

"Please, I'll call him up here. You can explain …"

"Ray, I have to go now. It's too painful … I can't hold on."

I went back to the bike and quickly put on the helmet and gloves and got on it. I put it in gear and rode past him. He didn't move. I hadn't counted on the dark and luckily with the clear sky and the moonlight I could make out where I had to go. I quickly got it up to speed and flew over the bump in the road. The pressure behind me was enormous. I focused, opened the throttle up and closed my eyes.

I thought, *help*.

My Dearest Paul,

The hardest thing I have ever had to do is to hurt you now. I'm so sorry. I can only imagine what I'm putting you through.

When I slept I disappeared and went to see our daughter. She put these flowers in my hair down by the pond. She said those few hours I was with her would be the only time she would ever get to see her mother. She never knew you either. I need to fix that. She said this trip I have to make was hard on you.

My gifts are more than you can help me understand. Loaned to me for a task I can't explain yet. She said something got screwed up and she lost us both. I lived long enough for Ray to save her.

Wait for me. I can't stand to be away from you a moment longer than I have to.

When I get back I'll take you to your father.

I love you forever
Anna

Chapter 28

I was hot. Damn hot. A layer of sweat filled my coat and ran down my neck after escaping my helmet. Bright daylight and miles and miles of open horizon faced me. Nothing but blue sky and waist high corn everywhere I looked.

The hot breeze started to take the moisture from me as I stuffed the coat into my pack. Before I stood I pulled out my phone and opened it up. The face lit and the little words *No Signal* in the corner ruined my plans to phone home. I turned it off and put it away.

After a minute's indecision I kicked the bike to life. Help wasn't going to find me standing here so I rode a ways down the dirt road past the rows and rows of corn. After only a few miles I came to a metal mailbox. The name Pilot was painted on it, along with a bunch of familiar purple flowers. The driveway that it marked disappeared into green stalks.

I decided to look further down the road; I could always turn around if I didn't find anything. After another ten or so miles there was another mailbox. From a distance it looked a lot like the first and as I approached I saw why. It also said Pilot and had purple flowers painted on it. The driveway disappeared into the corn. I reached around to the side pocket on my pack, pulled out the pen and tossed it on the ground beside the mailbox.

After another ten miles I spotted another mailbox. Pilot and purple flowers. My pen on the ground next to it. I hopped off the bike and retrieved it, returning it to my pack. I looked back down the dirt road then ahead again.

I put the bike in gear and turned onto the long driveway into the corn. The stalks grew taller as I went, after a mile they were over my head. The driveway turned and I emerged in front of a low farmhouse. Its deep porch stretched across the front and from what I could see went around the sides.

The roof of a large faded barn stuck up over one end of the house but otherwise there were only buildings. No cars, tractors, trucks. It was so quiet that the idle of the engine offended me. I turned off the bike where the cornfield ended and pushed it to the house.

When I neared the stairs up to the porch I put it down on the kickstand. I hoped it wasn't deserted. It was the only place I could get to from the road. As I took off my helmet something moved in the shade covered chair on the porch. He'd been so still I hadn't noticed him and by the time my head was uncovered he was standing.

I put the helmet on the seat of the bike and took off the pack. My back was soaked with sweat and the hot breeze couldn't keep up with the moisture springing from my skin.

"You didn't come to shoot me miss, did you?" he asked, tilting his head to the side. He was just a kid; curly red hair and all of twelve years old. Dressed like I remembered my grandparents in my father's family albums.

"No sir. I forgot I had that out," I quickly took it off and found room for it in my pack. He seemed satisfied it was out of sight.

"I don't get visitors," he said. "This place is very ... private. Where did you come from?"

"California sir," I told him. I was twice his age but I felt so small compared to his huge presence just a few stairs away.

"That's not what I consider a place," he said. "When did you leave California?"

"In the middle of the night sir," I told him.

He shook his head and waited. I didn't understand what he was getting at.

"You have somehow managed to travel here to me, but you don't understand where you came from," he asked like he was speaking to a child.

"I'm sorry ... I'm looking for help."

"By the sounds of things you surely need it miss," he said. A little more condescending than necessary.

"Yes sir," I acknowledged and waited.

He sighed. "Where you came from has a place and point in time. That is what I asked for."

I nodded. "California. Mid-November ... the year two thousand and ten."

"That is a long way," he said. "Have you ever travelled so far before?"

I was starting to understand. "Usually only a few days and a couple of thousand miles."

"Usually?" he waited.

I thought about the dreamlike trip to see my daughter and tried to guess her age.

"I recently travelled twenty-five years." I told him.

He nodded. "Well done. And how long did you stay before you had to come back?"

"Just a few hours sir."

"Well. You have travelled twice that to see me here. I would guess you have only half that amount of time and you spent the first half hour driving past my mailbox." He gestured to a chair on the porch so I went to it. He waited for me to sit and he sat next to me.

"I am Pilot," he told me. "I know you. What name do you use

now?"

"It's Anna, sir," I told him.

"Anna," he said. "You are my son's sister."

It took a moment. "You're Ray's ... father?" I asked.

Again condescending. "You will run out of time if you continue to be so slow. Perhaps you should ponder what I tell you later?"

"Yes sir," I agreed.

"I see you have brought my nephew's child to see me," he stated.

"Yes ... our daughter." I would have to try and keep the strange family tree somewhat straight. No doubt it was very important that I understand it ... at some point.

"Daughter ..." he laughed. He threw his head back nearly tipping his chair. "Yes, a daughter ... who has the gifts of a son."

"My, my Anna ... you have broken a lot of rules ..." he sobered.

"Yes sir," I paused. "That must be for a reason ... I think that is the help I have come for."

"Indeed," Pilot said. "Don't ask any more idiotic questions. You must understand the family first. What is the daughter's father's name?"

"Paul," I told him.

"Paul's father is my brother ... Paul is one of your mates," he told me. I opened my mouth and closed it before the question came out. He nodded approvingly. I hoped the answer was coming. "My other brother ... he is your other mate. Do you know who that might be?"

I shook my head.

"He hunts you ... he competes with Paul for you ..." Pilot prompted.

"Damian," I said. "Damian is his name."

"Good job miss," he said. "There were originally three brothers; Damian, me, and Paul's father. He exists in your time."

"Damian believes that he is a god among those who aren't like us. He seeks to control them ... to create an army of gods such as himself. Do you have any idea how our family grows?"

I shook my head. He sighed.

"We have sons ... with women who have a very weak tie through their long lives. Imagine there is a chain connecting your Paul from one life through the next ... for most people it is not a chain. It's like a row of feathers; too easily blown away by the passage of time. The women in the family; theirs is like a thread. It exists, but it is weak and cannot pull along the memories of a chain."

I nodded. What he said paralleled what Paul had told me about remembering Catherine.

"I won't bore you with the whole family tree. Suffice it to say that your brother was my first son. Paul was my brother's first son."

"Paul's sister is also mated to Damian ... and to your brother."

"Alina ..." I sighed. To Ray, I finished in my head.

"Yes. Men like us and women like you don't just come from the family ... they just happen sometimes too. Don't make the wrong assumption that we are all related. You have had a confrontation with one of us ... yes?" he asked.

"Damian," I said.

"No that is later ... another one," he told me.

I just nodded; he was talking about the man on the hill.

"You took his life." Pilot paused. "Who is the man with the knife who helped you?

"Andre." I told him.

"Another broken rule," he waved his hands like he was dismissing the thought. "Do you understand that death by a knife in your hand breaks the chain for someone like me? Permanently?"

What I had suspected and told Paul while I was ranting at him in our room was true.

"Just feathers," I whispered.

"Good. Perhaps you can bring us peace." He thought a moment. "My brother you know as Damian must be stopped. He has taught our men that it is better to kill their women than to let them have a child with another mate. That is how Damian hopes to build his army; only sons loyal to him. That is not how things must be. Your Paul ... has been fighting back with Damian's rules. He barely remembers when things were different.

"He has killed you to stop you from having Damian's child before ..."

I looked at the ground. Nagging seeds of the memory of past betrayals from Paul started to form in my mind. The wind picked up a bit. A nice breeze made it through my hair to my scalp and cooled my head. More graced my hot skin through the slats of the chair. As I watched Pilot my hair blew into my face. His didn't move.

"I believe my visit with you is ending soon," I told him.

"Yes miss. It is," he said. "You will have until the birth of your daughter to bring peace to the family. Do you understand that?"

"Yes," I told him. I had until then to cut Damian's line free from him. I stood to get ready to leave. The seat of my pants was damp with sweat and the breeze felt good.

"He will come to you ... for your child. You can count on that. You need not seek him out."

I shivered in the heat.

"Damian's child must also survive," he paused to make sure I understood. "He is already mated to your daughter. The peace will not last without him. Their child is ... important."

The thought of Damian's son and my daughter wasn't a surprise. I stepped over the bike and kicked the engine to life.

"Perhaps she could send someone away," he muttered to himself.

I stepped off the bike and kept a hand on the handle bars. I braced my feet a bit as the gusts got stronger.

He looked off to the side, speaking quietly. "I stay here ... out of what the family has fallen in to. Perhaps I'm a coward ... sending you to try and fix what I can't."

He took my hand in both of his and kissed my cheek. It was smooth ... not the hand of a farmer.

"Thank you Pilot," I told him.

He nodded. "You will return to Paul where he needs you the most ... you travelled so far. You must have a strong place to focus on or you'll be way off."

Chapter 29

Snow stung my neck and hands. As I became aware of my sweaty clothes freezing to me the bike sputtered and died in the shock of the cold. I quickly yanked off my pack and pulled out my coat. The cold sweat in it let the winter wind pass right through. I zipped it up anyway and pulled on the gloves then I tried to start the bike again but I couldn't coax the engine to turn over no matter what I tried. That was bad. I had no idea where I was, it was night and I was leaking body heat faster than I could make it.

I went to the other side of the bike and crouched down out of the wind as best I could then I pulled off my helmet and pulled on my hood. At least the hood wasn't damp. I pulled off a glove and got out the cell phone and turned it on. The display flashed as it started up. I shivered as it played its little jingle.

January.

It had synced up with the phone company and updated itself. Now it told me it was January. What was a couple of hours for me was two months for Paul. I felt sick. I had no idea what would be going through his mind now with me being gone so long.

I dialled his number and put it to my ear. It rang a few times and the voice mail picked up. I tried again. Straight to voice mail this time. No Paul.

"Paul, its Anna ... I need you. Call me, please?" I begged into the little microphone.

I was shivering now. So I tried Ray. He answered after a few rings.

"Ray ... its Anna," I shouted over the wind.

"Anna? My God," he said. "Where are you?"

125

"I don't know Ray. I can't reach Paul. I was only gone a couple of hours but the phone says it's January."

"It is January, Anna," he said. "Paul is gone. He took a truck a week ago and left."

"Damn … Ray, I'm at the side of a two lane highway somewhere in a snow storm. The bike died. I can't jump home. I'm going to freeze here. My clothes are wet."

My teeth were chattering. I wedged the phone into my hood between my ear and shoulder and stuck my frozen hand in my pocket.

"I can try and trace you … get you picked up. Stay on the phone, okay?" I nodded even though he couldn't see me.

"Okay?" he repeated.

"Yes," my voice shook.

I stayed down behind the bike and waited. Hopefully it wouldn't take long to find me.

Ray came back to the phone. "They couldn't find which tower you're connecting to … some technical problem, they're trying again. Hang in there."

"'kay."

The second trace seemed like it was taking longer than the first. My legs were cramping up and I had to sit on the frozen ground. I huddled close to the bike but the wind had long since taken all the heat from it. It didn't give that much cover anyway.

A flash of light down the highway caught my eye. I watched where it came from and saw it again. A vehicle was coming up the rolling road, its lights popping up at the tops of the rises.

"Ray … there's a car coming. I'm going to flag it down."

"Be careful Anna; stay on the phone with me …"

I stood up and started waving. The wind took my hood off. I didn't bother to try and pull it back up; I needed both hands in the air. The roar of the engine got closer and closer then its lights found me. It wasn't slowing down.

"Stop … please," I yelled.

It passed me.

"Ray …" Then the brakes jammed on and it skidded to a stop half sideways on the road a couple of hundred feet away. "It stopped."

"Stay on the phone," Ray said.

I waited … nothing happened. The truck didn't move and the driver didn't get out so I started walking toward it.

"It's just sitting there Ray," I told him. "I'm walking over to it."

"Careful," Ray warned.

The cold was so intense I felt like my joints were freezing up. I stopped after only fifteen or so steps. The driver's side was toward me and I saw the door open. The rear floodlights came on and someone got

126

out. I was suddenly scared and wanted to go back and hide behind the bike. He started walking toward me. I was in the middle of the lane so I took a few steps to the shoulder.

"It won't start," I yelled though the wind to the silhouette of the man in the lights. No idea if he heard me. The cell phone beeped as the call dropped. I looked down. No signal. I closed it and put it in my pocket. The shivering grew worse and worse as he approached.

He was only fifty feet from me now. I took a few steps closer. He started to run … I took a few steps and started to run the other way. I'd left my gun behind with the bike.

"Wait," he called. The wind took most of his voice. I kept going. I was almost to the bike holding the weight of my stomach still with one hand as I hurried.

"Wait!" the man called through the wind as he got closer. I got my glove off and shoved my hand in for my gun. I had it out of the holster and the bag in a couple of seconds.

I held it in both hands, safety off, pointed up but ready to go. The wind blew my snow filled hair into my face and all I could make out was his shape. I straightened up.

"Anna!" he shouted.

I froze. Then I put the safety back on and pointed the gun at the ground. Paul had put his hands up when the gun came out but now he lowered them. He walked a dozen steps toward me and stopped a few feet away. It was definitely Paul, even in the darkness with the light behind I knew.

"Paul …" I said. I took the last two steps toward him and looked up at his face. He put his arms around me as I reached around him. One around my back and the other holding my head to his shoulder. He pressed his face into my hair.

"You smell like summer."

"Yes," I said as I shivered. Even in the cold I could still smell it in my hair.

"I'm sorry," I told him. "I'm so sorry."

"Sshhh," he said. "Later."

He would speak his peace. I knew I had that coming. Our daughter said he would forgive me, but that didn't mean that I wouldn't have to work for it.

"Can we get it in the truck?" I asked, gesturing to the bike.

Paul let me go and went over to the bike and got my bag.

"No," he said and kicked it hard; over into the ditch. "I don't want to see it ever again."

Fair enough, I thought. It felt like such a long walk to the truck. The sideways snow had been sticking to my clothes making me even colder. I ducked my head down toward him to try and keep the wind off.

"It's so damn cold," I chattered. He squeezed me with his arm. Next to the truck at least I was mostly out of the wind. My ankles were still getting blown but the rest of me suddenly seemed a lot warmer.

Paul opened up the passenger door. The truck was full of garbage. He scooped out all the food wrappers and bottles onto the road and helped me in then he went around to the other doors and did the same. The wind pushed most of it off the road. He'd left the engine running so I had already turned up the heat and was trying to strip off my wet clothes in front of it when he got in.

"Get up … don't sit on that," he said. I looked behind me and I'd almost sat on his gun. The letter I left him was crumpled underneath it. Paul put his gun away under his coat and put his hand on my shoulder to push me back down. He put the letter in his pocket. I was having trouble untying my boots so he helped and then gave me a hand getting the rest of the wet things off. He threw them in the back.

"Your clothes are all damp. No wonder you're frozen," his voice was strained, stiff.

I nodded. I wasn't going to try to get him to temper what he was going to say to me by making him feel bad for me now. There was a change of dry clothes in my bag so I took them out. It seemed to take forever for my skin to be dry enough for me to be able to pull them on.

"You're not any bigger," he said.

"No," I agreed.

Paul put the truck in gear and drove. Eventually I warmed up in front of the vents so I turned down the heater and slid over to the passenger seat. The falling snow seemed a lot less wintery from inside out of the wind.

"I called you when I turned up back there," I told him. "You didn't answer."

He picked his phone up off the floor. It was in two pieces. He tossed it in the back seat.

"I left you a message. I got through to Ray … he was trying to find me when you stopped but the phone lost signal."

My phone rang from the back seat.

"Give it to me," Paul said.

I knelt on the seat to pull the phone from the pocket of my damp coat. I gave it to Paul.

"Ray," he said when he opened it. I could hear Ray talking but couldn't make out what he was saying.

"No, you called her," then, "yes."

He sighed. "Yes."

He was silent for a while. I had never seen his dark mood this bad before.

"How did you know where I would be?" he asked.

I just said "where you needed me the most."

He laughed; a humourless barking laugh.

"Why was your gun on the seat Paul?"

He stared straight ahead.

"You didn't think I was coming back … decided to take a short cut to finding me again?" I asked.

I waited.

"It was in my mouth for the last time when I saw you on the road," his toneless voice told me.

I put my hand over my mouth and looked out my window.

"My fault," I said eventually.

"Damn right." He said angrily.

I slept for a while and woke up cold again. Paul was filling up the truck.

"Do you want to see him now or go home for a while first?" I asked him when we pulled out again.

"Who?"

"Your father … I think I have enough left to do it now. You'll have to let me drive."

He laughed.

"Your call," I told him. "I have no idea where we are. You know how long it will take to drive home. I can have us there in a few minutes."

"You know where my father is?" Disbelief.

"I won't know until we get there. I want to go home … we can go see him when you're ready."

He shook his head.

"Let me try and set it up … if that works I'll have to drive," I told him. "Home? Once I start we'll have to go …"

"Whatever," he said.

I closed my eyes and thought about jumping the truck. I would have to drive and I wanted to hold on to Paul … the last thing he needed was for me to leave him on the road somewhere. I thought about us at home … maybe he had been working on the upstairs. Our room. The pond. The truck seemed to drift a bit in its lane.

I kept my eyes closed and asked. "Is the road icy?"

"No," he said.

"Can you feel the truck move?"

"Yes."

"Good," I told him.

I continued to concentrate on the jump. The truck was moving more.

"Shit," Paul said as he pushed the truck back into its lane. "Are you doing that?"

"Yes," I said. "Floor the gas ... I need to know how much pickup this thing has."

He sighed impatiently but he did. It pressed me back into the seat. I probably should have checked that first but the truck had enough punch to do it. Less pickup meant more pressure for me. After a few more side gusts a big one hit from behind and the canopy door rattled so loud we could hear it. I unbuckled and slid over to him.

"Time to let me drive," I told him. Another gust slammed us from behind. The pressure was building in me fast. He didn't move.

"The pressure hurts Paul," I rubbed the back of my neck. "You need to move now."

He sighed and started to slow down, but the wind pushed us again and wouldn't let us.

"Have to do it on the fly ... no stopping now," I put a hand on the wheel and stood up a bit. "Slide out underneath me."

I bumped my head on the window as the truck recoiled from being hit again.

"Hurry," he finally gave in and moved. I sat down and quickly put my foot on the gas. "Now hold on to me and close your eyes."

"This is nuts," he said.

"Close them ... you'll feel like shit after if you don't."

That was true. I had done it once with my eyes open and threw up for hours after. I was glad I had remembered. He sighed and put his arms around me, one of his hands on the back of my neck. I held the wheel with my left hand and put my other hand around him.

"Ready?" I glanced over at him. His eyes were closed when I looked. Another gust pushed us into our seats.

"Yes."

I focused on home. Concentrated. Pictured us back there again. The pressure in my back peaked and I closed my eyes and matted the accelerator.

The truck leaped hard; I thought, *home.*

Chapter 30

I stood in the cold again. My hand on Paul's back. He was leaned over throwing up in the snow. When I looked around I saw we were beside the barrels where he had found me.

"You kept your eyes open, didn't you?" I asked.

He heaved in reply.

"Let's get inside, come on. We'll find the truck later."

I took him by the elbow and led him out from the alley and up to the house. The truck was nowhere near us but once we were close enough to see the house I spotted it parked in front. Someone was on the porch looking at it. Paul had to stop several times to throw up more before I thought I could make out who it was.

"Ray?" I called.

He looked over and came to meet us. He had to step back as Paul involuntarily threw up at his feet. As he gave me a quick hug I lifted my chin and kissed his cheek. "What's the matter Paul?"

"He didn't close his eyes for the jump," I told Ray. "He might be throwing up for hours. Funny ... no missed time. I don't feel like we've been driving for days. I guess I'm learning."

Paul heaved again.

"I'll be okay Ray," Paul managed. "I didn't think she could do it ... I wanted to make sure she didn't drive us off the road."

Ray helped him inside while I got our things out of the truck. When I got in Ray had left Paul at the kitchen sink while he went to get him a bucket. He also came back with a shot for him.

"Gravol Paul," he told him.

We got his jacket off and his sleeve up then we took him to the common room and he lay down on the couch with his bucket on the floor. Within half an hour the heaving had stopped and the shot Ray had given him had him asleep. We sat silently watching him for a while until my stomach rumbled so I went to the kitchen to see what I could find. It felt like breakfast time for me even though the clock said it was after eleven. I was taking care of the dishwashers when the front door opened.

"Captain's back?" Denis' voice.

"Yeah," Ray said. "Anna brought him in."

"Anna's here?" he asked.

I stepped around the corner.

"Hey Denis," he came over and hugged me.

"Where have you been?" Denis asked.

Ray looked at me to hear my answer too. I pressed my lips together and shook my head then I took my seat next to Paul. I ignored the watch change and the stares and the questions about the Captain until it was just the three of us again.

"He looks bad Ray."

"Yes," he agreed.

Paul looked thin, exhausted. He hadn't cut his hair since I left and the curls went every which way. The last week's beard had grey in it around his chin. In the truck I'd been avoiding the expression on his face but sleeping now he seemed so peaceful.

"So this is what it's like for you two watching me sleep?"

"Something like this," Ray said.

"You should turn in. I'll stay."

He didn't get up and eventually I fell asleep in the chair.

The murmur of their quiet voices woke me. My eyes popped open to see Ray watching me. I glanced at Paul, he was watching me too but they had both stopped talking. I couldn't look at Paul for more than that brief half second. I knew the expression I would see if I looked back. The black hopelessness I had put him through tightening every muscle in him. The anger in his eyes. I had pushed him to the very edge. I put my hands in my lap and looked at them instead.

"Did you find what you were looking for Anna?" Ray asked.

God I hope so, I thought.

"I found a lot," I finally said.

Ray waited for me to look up at him.

"Do you think it was worth it?" he asked, quickly glancing at Paul.

God I hope so, I answered to myself again. I risked a quick look at Paul. His expression hadn't changed.

"I need to see his father," I told them. "I'm not going alone."

That sat with them for a while.

Finally Ray asked. "You can find his father?"

"I found yours," I answered quietly. Paul finally moved; his head at least. He and Ray looked at each other. Nobody said anything for a long time.

"Am I sleeping down here?"

Neither spoke.

I went to the laundry for clean sheets, took my bag, and headed upstairs. If our room was in as rough shape as Paul the bed would need them. As I climbed the stairs I noticed that something was different. The hall light was on and parts of the walls were missing. The top floor hadn't been demolished. It had been assaulted. As I peered through the huge holes in the walls I could see empty whiskey and beer bottles. I understood how Paul had spent much of the past two months.

The door at the end was closed and when I opened it the air was as cold as it had been when I had left. I couldn't find either lamp in the dark either on the tables or the floor so I made my way to the bathroom and turned on the light there. With the bathroom door open there was enough light to see that the bed was just a pile of sheets and blankets. The same sheets I had put on what seemed like only hours earlier. I pulled everything off and put the clean sheets on. The blankets all smelled so I heaped them up with the sheets.

The dresser my things were in was tipped over on the floor. I stood it up. Fortunately none of the drawers were broken. The screwdriver I'd put in my drawer was still there so I pulled off the front of the register and tucked the old shirt in with the dirty bedding. Warm air came in.

I hauled all the dirty things downstairs and got clean blankets, tucked a spare roll of toilet paper under my arm and got a glass of water from the kitchen before I returned to our room. Paul and Ray stopped talking when I walked past and sat silently until I left.

The room warmed up quickly. Some of the blankets would have to go … probably long before morning but at least I would be warm if Paul decided to stay on the couch. Now that we were home Paul and I hadn't spoken to each other … only to Ray as if the other wasn't there. I had to break through that first if I was going to have a chance at patching things back together.

It seemed like a very long time before I heard his boots come down the hall making no effort to be quiet. He went straight to the shower. The toilet seat slammed up loudly and eventually the medicine cabinet slammed shut. When he came out he pulled the blankets back and dropped down hard on the bed laying down with his back to me.

"Paul …" I started quietly after a few minutes of silence.

He didn't answer so I put my fingertips on his back. He didn't pull away though his muscles stiffened under my touch.

"I'm really here," I whispered.

When he started to relax I traced around his shoulder blades, then up and down the middle of his back. He tensed up again but I kept going, pressing more firmly as he relaxed. His breathing slowed, deepened, his weight shifting slightly as more of him was drained of tension. My hand pressed finding little knots and gently working them out. He clung to the hurt I had caused like a shield to protect himself from any more.

"It won't mean that you're not still furious with me," I whispered at his back. "Or that you trust me again. It won't mean that you didn't spend the last two months in hell wondering if I was alive or dead. It won't mean that what I did didn't push you to the very edge. It won't get me out of hearing every angry word I have coming to me or the guilt and hard work to make things right again."

I kept working his back but he didn't say anything.

"It won't mean that you've forgiven me," I said quietly. "Maybe I don't deserve to ever feel you close to me again Paul … but you're not the one who's in the wrong here and that's not what you deserve.

"No strings …

"I don't believe there was a single night you didn't need me here in your bed with you," I told him. "If I'm wrong just say so. I'll move to the room downstairs and won't torment you like this again until you want me back."

He said nothing so I quietly rolled over and sat on the edge of the bed. I felt around with my feet for my clothes and found my pants.

"Would it have been better if I told you before I left? Started a big fight … you never would have let me go. I blew it before I was even out the door."

133

I got my pants on and found my shirt.

"I'm not running Paul, or leaving. I'm just going downstairs. If you say that my being here now just hurts you more I won't let the door hit me in the ass on my way out. You'll know where to find me.

"I love you forever," I reminded him. "It's our future I'm trying to protect. He said I was made to bring peace to a family I didn't even know I had and no, it doesn't seem worth it at all."

I got up and made my way toward the door. Paul blocked me so I looked up at him in the dark and waited. He tentatively put his hand up on my heart then slid it up my neck to my face, letting his fingers curl around into my hair as his thumb moved over my cheek.

"I have never been as angry with anything as I am right now with what you did," he told me, his nose brushing my forehead. "I don't even have the words for what I'm feeling. Maybe in a few days … a week. I need time to cool down." His lips were on my forehead, then my nose. "If I didn't still love you completely I wouldn't have spent the last week trying to find the nerve to pull the trigger." My ear, my neck. "No strings Anna … just come back to bed."

Paul woke me up later, climbing back into bed. The curtain was open a bit and the sun was up. He'd undressed and was pulling me in close again. I put my arms around him to pull him to me then I put a hand on his face. The beard was gone. When I reached up to his hair it was back as I remembered it … most of the curls were gone. I put my fingertips on his chin.

"Did I give you the greys?" I asked.

"Yes," he laughed a bit. More like the easy warm laugh I loved so much.

"Where do you get your hair cut around here?"

"Ross … now sshhh."

Chapter 31

My fingertips traced the loose ring I put on Paul's finger. Lunch was starting downstairs and I wasn't in a hurry to go. After what I put Paul through for the past two months I wasn't looking forward to facing the unvoiced judgement of his men.

"I fixed the heat in here," I told him.

"I noticed," Paul answered. "What was wrong with it?"

"It was blocked … you didn't do that?"

"No. It just didn't work this year," he said. "You keep me warm enough … I didn't bother to look into it."

"Who else would have put it there?" I asked him.

134

"Put what there?"

I showed him my palm. It still had the small triangular puncture in it. "I stabbed myself on it when I pulled it out the night before I left. I kept it and put the shirt back in. I thought you put it there and I didn't think you would want me to keep it so I put the shirt back so you wouldn't know I found it."

His dark mood had flashed briefly on his face before he pushed it back. I took the knife from my bag and lay it on the bed.

"It killed Catherine," I told him. "It was wrapped in an old dirty shirt of some kind. It's downstairs now with the sheets I took off last night.

"It's mine now … it's complicated but I need to keep it," I told him. "Did you … have any trouble from Damian while I was gone?"

"No."

My mind wandered to the kitchen and I shivered as I traced past the seats by the window.

"I know why … one of the men at the table isn't yours. He knew I was gone … maybe he blocked the heat. Thought you would find it … or I might and blame you."

Paul went for his clothes.

"Let's go Paul." I was getting dressed too. "I'm not sure which one he is … just that he's at the table now."

I put on my gun and headed for the door.

"No … you stay here," his arm around my waist stopping me.

I lifted my chin to face him. "Do you think he has any chance of moving even a couple of inches on me before I have his own knife at his throat? That's not why he's here anyway. We can't tip him off …"

He stared at me; the coldness returning to his eyes.

"Paul … I know it's your job to protect me right now … and I'm not making it easy."

He took a few deep breaths to settle down. His arms tightened around me and he didn't speak until his hold on me softened.

"Remember the night we met when I told you the truth would never hurt me?" he asked.

The shame I felt was crushing. I looked away.

"I remember," I told him.

"Be straight with me Anna. Are you going after Damian?"

I didn't hesitate. "Yes."

He winced.

"Why?" he asked slowly. He didn't want to know.

"Death by a knife in my hand will break him … or anyone like him. He won't remember any more. It's what I was made for."

I stepped in closer to him to avoid the dark stare. "I was made to want to finish him. Even pregnant I'm faster and better skilled than he

135

is. And when it's over those things about me will go away. I'll need you again for all the things you expect your wife to need you for, not just most of them." I sighed. "If you want me to stay up here can you bring me up something to eat? Or do you want me to come down and try and figure out who it is?"

He thought; pushing back anger at the past to deal with the present.

He decided. "Come down … but stay close to me, okay?"

"Okay Paul."

He put his arm around my waist and pulled me in tight as we went down the hall. Part way down the stairs he grabbed the railing and rubbed his eyes.

"Suddenly I felt like my eyes fell down into my feet," he explained.

I laughed quietly. "I thought I did all the work. That's my one hour warning that the black sleep is coming. Eat fast and get back to bed; you can't fight it when it hits."

"Okay," he yawned.

The sudden silence in the room said everything. I took a quick look around the table and all eyes were on us. Paul pulled me closer and loudly cleared his throat, almost growling. He sat me next to Ray and filled up two plates for us. I gave him a quick smile as he sat but his eyes were already scanning the faces around the table. I whispered in his ear.

"I can be less obvious about it …"

He nodded.

I started with the end of the table by the window, letting my mind just float lightly among them. I chewed absently waiting for something to come to me. Nothing. Just the sense that he was at that end of the table. I realized that I had been looking for what I had seen before in the other three. The smudges. This one wasn't like Paul, or Damian. I wasn't sure what to look for now other than maybe a weak version of Damian's flavour I had tasted so strongly in the first three. Or maybe even smelled but that wasn't it either. It was like I used some sense organ between my nose and the roof of my mouth. Paul nudged me with his knee under the table. I sighed; nothing yet.

I decided to target them one at a time to see what might make one of them stand out. After spending some time lingering in a few of them I got to Rice. There was something different about him. I couldn't put my finger on it. He just didn't quite fit. I moved along through the others. I was almost done eating by the time I had finished going through that end of the table.

BUTTON!

I jumped in my chair. Paul tensed next to me so I tried to stay relaxed and dismissed the distraction. My focus went right back to Rice

136

but I kept my head down and tried to keep eating. More like pushing the last of my food around looking like I was still eating. Rice stared up toward the ceiling, withdrawn from what was going on around him.

BUTTON!

It hit me again and it wasn't just the word ... it was the overwhelming and sickening sudden violence that I felt with it. Like an explosion of massive and overpowering rage. Maybe it was an experience he'd had. Some horrible event he'd lived through in his past that he kept finding himself in like I seemed to exist in the carnage of the plane crash. Paul was watching me. I looked back, my mouth trying to open in bewilderment. The cold quick obliteration I pulled from Rice started to sicken me and I felt myself starting to go white. I was going to throw up.

I took a few sips of water and focused on Paul. As I tried to pull myself together he started to droop. "Upstairs," I got my hands on him.

"Ray," I said quietly. "I need help ... get him out of here."

He looked and saw Paul going over. The distraction was enough for me to push Rice back out of my mind.

"Denis ..." Ray said. The room started to go quiet again as the others noticed what was going on. We got him up and out of the kitchen while his legs still worked.

"What's the matter with him?" Denis asked.

"Get him up to bed," I told them quietly. They each took a side and we started for the stairs.

"Anna ..." Paul mumbled. "Brief the officers if you found anything."

"Yes Paul ... bed."

We got him half way up when his legs quit working and they had to haul him the rest of the way. I had no idea how the three of them fit up the stairs at the same time. The stairs weren't exactly wide and the three men weren't exactly narrow. They got him up to the bed. We got his boots and pants off and covered him up.

"Is Joshua here?"

Ray shook his head. "He went to Paul's parents place before Christmas. We're overcrowded ... nobody in the field right now."

I nodded, understanding. That meant there were men here who weren't family.

Like Rice.

"Denis, can you get Ross up here please? Paul needs me to brief you on something."

"Okay Anna, he's on watch. I'll send out a replacement," he said then he left.

"I didn't think it would hit him, Ray. He sure went down fast. I usually get an hours warning ... he went down in half that time," I

137

thought about it. "I don't think it's going to hit me at all."

I knelt down and put my hand on Paul's face.

"The jump was too quick, too strong. I'd already travelled a very long way … twice. I think I used him for the jump home and drained him like a battery to recharge. If there's anything more I can do to hurt him can you tell me Ray so I can get it all over with?"

He put his hand on my shoulder. "He'll be fine in a day or two, right? He really needs the sleep anyway."

"Yeah, I guess," I stood up.

"Ray, has he told you not to talk to me about the family?"

"Not directly," Ray said. We heard Denis and Ross coming up the hall.

"I don't think it matters. They've seen me do enough weird things and just have to listen."

I turned my back to the door and stood facing Ray with my arms crossed. There was a knock and they came in.

"Ray," Ross said. "What's going on? What happened to Paul?"

I looked up at Ray and nodded.

"He's out of commission for a while," Ray said. "Maybe a day or two. Something's going on he wanted Anna to fill us in on."

"Is he drunk again?" Ross asked. "Just wake him up."

"No," I answered as I turned around. "And you can't wake him. I don't know who runs things without Paul or Joshua. I don't really care, but you don't even have a drunken Captain for a day or two to prop up in front of the men.

"The Captain believes we have a security problem … he wanted me to try and figure out who the problem is and to tell you if I found out."

Ross frowned. He appeared to be the one in charge now. "How would you know?"

I looked at Ray. He nodded.

"You've seen the things I can do Ross. I don't know what he's told you. I could see the first three of Damian's men coming … because they're loyal to Damian and they're like us. We have one who is not loyal to us or to Damian. I don't know why he's here yet … maybe leaking information."

"Who?"

"I'm suspicious Ross but far from sure," I told him. "How much do you know about Rice?"

"Rice?" Ross thought. "He's been with us about a year. Never been a problem."

"I saw a massive sudden loss of life … violent … quick. And a word. Button. Like on a shirt … no more like on a pair of pants. Maybe just something he's been through. Like I said, a suspicion. I'll let you

138

know if I see anything else. Whoever it is isn't going to move on us anytime soon … I'm not even sure if anyone is targeted for harm."

"It's not much to go on," Ross grumbled.

"I know. I don't like pointing fingers … I'm going to watch over Paul until he wakes up. Maybe someone can spell me for a while tonight when the house is empty so I can get some sleep."

"Sure Anna," Denis said. "I'll stay now."

I shook my head. "Remember the man on the hill?" I asked. "Do you really think anyone is getting past me?"

Denis looked a little uncomfortable. "No."

"Can you bring me a two-way radio? Otherwise I'll be here until dinner." After they left I moved the big chair to the end of the bed and put Damian's knife in the dresser.

Ross brought me up a radio. "I have the other one on this channel right now. I'll tell you if I'm handing it off. Press the call button if you need to speak to me and I'll come here. Don't speak over the radio, the channel isn't secure. Denis will come up after first night watch goes out … we'll each pull a couple of hours. Ray's coming up last."

"Thanks Ross," I told him.

"We've spent a lot of time looking after him over the past two months," Ross said pointedly. "He's compromised without you."

"I know," I said. I felt my eyebrows press together.

He stared at me for a moment. "Sorry … I didn't mean for it to come out like that. We've looked out for each other for a long time. I know he would have done the same for any of us."

I nodded and he left. After I cleaned up the bathroom I got all the empties together. Both the bedroom lamps were in the room down the hall that most of the empties had been in. The ceiling light wouldn't turn on with the switch so Paul must have taken them in to see what he was doing. I took them back to our bedroom and set them back up.

All the bending over had my back sore and there was still no sign that I was going to have the black sleep too so I went and sat in the chair. I closed my eyes and tried to think about Rice; to try and learn a little more but it was too easy to nap so I stood up and crossed my arms to try again. Without knowing where he was I had no hope of picking up anything new so I expanded my focus searching for smudges or anything else that shouldn't be there but still nothing.

I had no idea how they did it, watching over me, I would be silly with boredom in no time. Maybe we could move Paul to the shop and I could keep busy fixing things in the cold. I giggled at that. Tuck him in on the workbench.

"Anna?" It was Ray.

I left my eyes closed. "As usual I didn't hear you come in. I guess I make a pretty poor watch dog."

139

"I'll say. I wanted to check you both. I don't know what he was living on this past week but it probably wasn't good."

I opened my eyes and sat down. "The truck was full of garbage when he picked me up. Drive through wrappers and liquor bottles."

Ray nodded. He went over to Paul and pinched under his eyes and the backs of his hands.

"He's dehydrated. I'm going to give him some fluids."

"Ray," I laughed. "Sometimes I think you're not happy unless you get to give someone a balloon."

"Do want one too?" he offered.

"No, not really," I tried to be serious.

"Paul said you didn't look any bigger but if you don't mind I want to measure you and see for myself."

"I found him a couple of hours after I left you in the shop Ray … like I told you on the phone."

"Nevertheless," he said. "I'll be right back."

He set Paul up and I got up stiffly for him to measure me.

"Right where you were two months ago Kiddo," he said. "Are you sure you're not needing a big sleep?"

"Yes. You know, I made him hold on to me for the jump … I was worried I would leave him at the side of the road. But everything in the truck made it so that wasn't necessary. Maybe it's because I was in contact with him that it happened. The jump was so strong … could be his energy is more powerful than mine. Hopefully he won't have to sleep as long to recharge."

"We'll find out," Ray said.

"Ray, is Rice going to be at dinner?"

"I can check, why?"

"What I picked up was so sickening and violent. If Paul hadn't started to go down taking my attention I would have thrown up on him."

Ray was thoughtful. Then he tilted his head at Paul. "He would want you to find out as much as you can. I'll have Denis stay with him while you come down. Stick with me, okay? I know what's going on with you and can help if you need it."

"How do you and Paul do it?" I asked. "I'm so bored I could tie my own shoes together just to amuse myself trying to walk. Maybe I'll entertain myself with knife tricks for a while."

Ray shook his head. "Just radio when you need me to sew something back on. I'll send Denis up when dinner is ready."

I'd only wasted half the time from lunch to dinner. I thought about taking a pry bar to the walls but my back was sore enough and if the men thought Paul was drunk at the table I didn't need to reinforce that by making a bunch more noise up here. The second half of the afternoon passed incredibly slowly.

Ray was right; Paul would want me to keep working to find out what was going on with Rice or whoever it was. I didn't have to like it. I'd had my fill of what was going on in Rice's head. At lunch I'd probed deeply. Rice was like turning on the TV when the sound was cranked. The message was lost in the volume.

Paul's family had three lines. I had met the heads of two of them and since Paul was the first son in his line he was as close to the head as I was going to get until I found his father. Whether it was memory, our history or something else I was loyal to Paul. I understood from Pilot there were times I had been loyal to Damian instead. I wondered if Ray ever knew about Alina. Damian found her this time. And did he ever have a sister? There were so many questions I wanted to ask Pilot. He said we weren't all related so there could be other women like Alina and me.

I realized I'd been able to pick out Damian's men from their smell and Damian had smelled Paul in Catherine and me … maybe because we were both pregnant with Paul's child. At dinner I would distract myself from Rice for a while by seeing if I could find anything similar between Ray and Pilot. Then if Rice didn't overwhelm me again I could look at him further.

Denis and Ray finally came upstairs.

"Still have all your fingers?"

I shrugged. "It's no fun without an audience and I promised Paul I'd stop taking his knife without asking …"

Ray laughed. "For the better then."

"Thanks for sitting with him," I gave Denis the radio. "I'm sorry for what I put everyone through. I know you asked last night where I was but the truth is I don't really know."

Denis stepped over and squeezed me. "I can't say it wasn't tough, but he never gave up on you."

Yes he did, I thought, or I wouldn't be here now.

"Do they think he's drunk again?" I whispered to Ray in the hall.

He nodded. "We decided to let them think that. They've seen it before and it's easier for them to accept than the truth or anything else we could come up with."

"They must think I'm horrible," I sighed.

"Nobody held a bottle to his mouth Anna. Come on."

There were two seats at the table for us. The conversation quieted this time when I came in but I ignored them and Ray sent me to sit and brought me a plate. Rice was there so I kept my thoughts to myself.

I'd planned to try and recognize Pilot in Ray. Pilot had kissed my cheek, hopefully close enough for me to be able to remember his smell. I leaned a little closer to Ray for a moment and took a small breath in through my nose and mouth. I wasn't going to kiss Ray at the table.

141

At first all I could smell and taste was dinner so I finished my mouthful and washed it down with a bit of water then I tried to compare again with the little space just under my nose trying not to think about smell and taste at all. My eyes closed for a minute before I felt them roll up in my head and I laughed as they opened back up.

Ray gave me a little elbow.

"Almost identical ... whatever it is. I don't know what to call it."

"Identical what?" he whispered back.

"Exactly ..." I whispered back. "You remind me very much of the man I found."

He blinked a couple of times and got an expression on his face I couldn't read and went back to his dinner. Maybe I shouldn't have said anything.

I let my new sense wander lightly around and found a couple more that were similar. Then I leaned close to Ray to whisper again.

"There are a couple at the table that are very similar to you ... are they yours or your father's?"

Ray looked at me then gave me a funny shy smile before he turned away.

"I'm sorry. Did I say something awkward?" I whispered again.

He shook his head and wouldn't look at me. "We don't think of them like that when they're grown up."

"Sorry," I said again. I still had a lot to learn about this family. Instead of letting it go however I kept looking and picked up a few that were similar to Paul.

I couldn't help whispering to him again. "The ones similar to Paul ... are they mine too?"

This time Ray started to turn pink as he leaned toward me and whispered back right into my ear. "You'll have to ask him ... I'm not having this talk with my sister."

I continued to poke around the table. Almost half of the ones I could pick up weren't like Paul or Ray at all, or each other, the rest had nothing I could read. Like Rice. I hadn't picked up anything from him and dinner was almost over so I let my thoughts wander down to his end of the table and stay there. He was talking to Jones, laughing. Very different from the glassy stare I had seen at lunch. Eventually the laughter settled as he looked at the table. I felt his mind start to wander and I pulled back.

Rice continued to wool gather, his gaze becoming more and more distant as the men started to leave the table. Rice seemed aware enough to keep turning into a self absorbed statue from attracting attention but to me his mind was very obviously elsewhere.

Then I noticed it; very subtle. At first I thought that someone had left something on the stove but when I looked over at it all the lights were off. It was a sweet scorched smell that seemed to come up around me growing stronger. My nose wrinkled. It was hot and seemed to burn the little hairs inside as I inhaled so I breathed through my mouth. Rice smiled beneath his thousand-yard stare.

BUTTON!

The brutal quick deaths hit me. Not as strong as at lunch but after the gradual invasion of the smell it still took me by surprise. Ray looked over at me. I tried to ignore him and focused on not being connected to Rice but the smell had also doubled. I gagged so I picked up my napkin and held it over my mouth.

Ray's hand was on my elbow as I coughed. My eyes stung and I closed them. I could still hear people leaving the table. Why couldn't anyone else smell it? I forced my watering eyes open.

Rice was on his feet now, same expression on his face. He bumped into Jones and mumbled something appropriate. Jones nodded and kept going, Rice wandering along behind.

Ray reached his arm around behind me as I continued to struggle. "Anna, can you talk?" he asked.

Maybe he thought I had some food stuck somewhere it shouldn't be. I nodded and tried to answer but I couldn't. As I closed my eyes I looked down and saw what the smell was.

BUTTON!

It had hit my legs. What was left of them was scorched and black. Chunks of deep red and pink between the crisp charred patches. A shattered piece of bone stuck out from the end of the shorter thigh. There was blackened blood all over the chair.

"Oh God Ray ... my legs," I managed as quietly as I could.

"What's wrong with your legs?" he asked.

"Blown off," I wheezed. My stomach was trying to heave now. "I'm going to be sick."

"There's nothing wrong with your legs," he whispered. "Don't look. On your feet."

He was right. When he helped me up they worked just fine. Ray guided me down to the half bathroom by the laundry and took me in. Fortunately nobody was in there. I knelt on the floor and Ray closed the door behind us as I lost my dinner. I still had my napkin in my hand and when I was done I leaned back against the wall and wiped my mouth. I kept my eyes closed as the smell faded. Even though I could feel the cold floor under my legs I didn't want to look.

"Anna?" he asked.

"Okay now I think," I told him. When I took the napkin off my face the smell was gone. "I'm going to pass on breakfast tomorrow. Are you sure my legs are okay?"

"Yes," he said. "They always were."

143

"They didn't look that way to me," I opened my eyes and looked down. They were fine so I put my hand on my left thigh about two thirds of the way up. "The bone was sticking out of the shorter one here. All the flesh was burnt and chewed. The smell made me gag until I got sick but it's gone now."

I sighed. "I guess Denis should come down now. Can you help me up?"

Ray kept his arm around me as we went upstairs so Denis could get some dinner. Ross was just coming in from watch and Ray told him to come up when he was finished briefing his relief.

"Bring your plate up Denis," Ray told him. "Ross will be up in a few minutes."

Denis disappeared down the hall. Ray had me fill them in on what happened at dinner when they came back.

"The strange part was the look on his face," I told them. "The little smile as if he was thinking about something he really liked."

I shook my head. "I don't know. Maybe he was remembering something nice and I was picking up someone else."

Ross started. "I put a call in—"

I interrupted him. "Ross ... I don't want to know, please? I'll come down for the next meal he's not going to be there for and see if it happens again but otherwise I'd prefer to avoid him for now. If nobody's downstairs you could go down there or find somewhere else. I'm fine up here until Denis is back in a few hours."

After they left I sat back down and waited, brooding about what I had seen at lunch and dinner. Eventually Paul rolled over again and I had to go over and untangle his IV line before it either came out of his arm or off the wall. Shortly after that Ray came up and replaced the bag on it and slowed the drip. He also brought me up something to eat. I wasn't hungry but I ate some. Rice had killed my appetite. Ray took my plate and I was alone again.

Paul sat up suddenly.

"Paul?" I asked but his eyes weren't looking at anything in particular. He put his feet on the floor so I ran over and got his IV bag off the wall before he could go anywhere and followed him to the bathroom then back to bed. I guessed all the fluids Ray had given him were doing what they were supposed to. I covered him back up and turned off the lamp by his head and turned the other one on instead. The clock said half past eleven so I didn't have much longer to wait.

"Rolled over again?" Ray asked when he and Denis came in.

"No, he got up to pee. If he sits up you have a couple of seconds to grab the IV bag and follow him to the bathroom. He won't take it with him," I told them.

"Got it," Denis said. "Get some sleep Anna; you've been

watching him all day."

"Thanks for helping out guys," I told them. "Thank Ross too please in case I sleep through. Hopefully he'll be up tomorrow."

I put my gun on my table and kicked off my boots. Then I took one of the spare blankets I had tossed off the night before and lay down on the covers underneath it facing Paul. I started to think about seeing who Denis might be related to but fell asleep before I could finish the thought.

Chapter 32

"… the only time she left you was for dinner. It didn't go so well for her. I don't think I'll be able to talk her into it again," Ray's voice said. My mind was awake but my body was still asleep. I wanted to turn over to see Paul but I couldn't move.

I heard Paul sigh. "I don't think she liked the reaction we got at lunch. She isn't that bothered by what they think about her but she'd worry about what they think of me."

He was right. I had a fair idea what they thought of me and I could really care less. I was more interested in keeping things right with Paul. I'd weakened him in the eyes of his men. No doubt of that. If I left again he would have to know. I would have to find a way to make it his decision to let me go either by agreeing or ending it. She said he would forgive me. I had to trust in that.

"Paul," Ray said, "She was … reading the relations in the family at dinner."

"She was what?" Paul exclaimed then lowered his voice. "My father can do that a bit, a couple of the others, but nobody we found this time. How do you know she was doing it?"

"She was asking me questions about them," Ray said.

"I'm really sorry Ray." I could hear the regret in his voice. "She wouldn't know not to talk about it with you. Every other time she's been a child … she's part grown up this time and I keep getting surprised by it."

"At least she was discrete," Ray said. "I think she was trying to distract herself from Rice. It didn't take her long to pick out the ones she was interested in. It pleased her like she had a new toy or something. I finally told her I wasn't having that talk with my sister and she seemed to get it. At least she stopped the running commentary."

"Are you sure nobody else heard?"

"Yes," Ray said. "She was careful."

I felt Paul's hand on my shoulder.

"Did she say anything about where she was?" I could hear the darkness creeping into his voice, just a bit, and I desperately wanted to wake up and speak but I still couldn't move.

"Denis asked her where she had been when you were passed out on the couch after she brought you back. She refused to answer. Then last night she apologized. She said that she didn't really know where she had been. You'll have to ask her … maybe she's waiting for a chance to talk to you about it.

"I measured her yesterday. She's still about twenty weeks pregnant. When she phoned from the road she was surprised that it's January … she said she had only been gone a couple of hours. I would agree. But then why didn't she come back the same night?"

"She said she knew to find me where I needed her most," Paul said heavily. I heard his gun move on the table. "I had given up on her, Ray. My connection to her … she didn't feel dead, but it wasn't alive either. I was about to pull the plug when I passed her at the side of the road.

"I thought I was imagining her but I put the gun down and stopped. It took a minute looking back but I could make her out walking toward me in the tail lights even in the snow. Her hair smelled like summer and when I got her in the truck her clothes were damp with sweat. The cold wind was sucking the heat from her. She wouldn't have lasted long."

Wake up wake up wake up! I shouted in my head and was able to stretch my fingers under the blanket.

"Paul?" I managed to whisper. I felt his weight shift on the bed as he leaned toward me.

"Hey," Paul said softly. "You're awake."

"I've been awake for a while … I just couldn't move."

"Oh." He sounded like he'd been caught doing something he shouldn't.

"I didn't hear anything I didn't know already," I told him and clumsily rolled over. He was sitting up in the bed. Ray was in the chair.

"Okay," he said but he wasn't convinced.

"Morning Ray," I said.

"Morning Kiddo," he answered.

"You want to know where I was … I was with the person I said I was," I told them quietly. "Maybe an hour or two. I wasted a lot of time just finding the place when I got there. It was so hot … dirt roads and corn everywhere. By the time I was aware the jump was over there was sweat running out of the helmet into my coat. I was soaked … I must have been standing there for a while. I stuffed the coat in my bag so it didn't get a chance to dry. I don't think that would have helped anyway. My clothes were still damp when I left.

"I don't know where I was. I know I travelled twenty-five years forward to see our daughter and he said I travelled twice that to see him.

146

Backward I suppose judging by the way he was dressed. He was condescending and a little mean. Treated me like a kid even though he was a lot younger than me but I put up with it. He tried to explain how he measures travel but I don't think I really understood it. There's location and time and maybe something else I'm missing but I'm not sure what it could be. He said I couldn't stay long because it was so far.

"He told me what I was made for, about the family, how it grows. He told me what's wrong with it now and how it used to be. That it needs to be that way again. He said I had broken a lot of rules. The worst being giving you a daughter who already has the gifts of a son … but she's important to healing the family just the way she is.

"By the time I left he seemed sorry. I think he made me the way I am. He said he was a coward for sending me off to do something he wouldn't do himself. He said to go to you when you needed me the most … I don't think I would have made it back without that to focus on.

"If you hadn't given up on me yet Paul, you would still be waiting," I told him. "I'm so sorry. When I left I expected I would come back about the same time like with all the other trips … the missed time would all be for me, not you."

Paul put his hand on my cheek but he didn't say anything.

"Can I trust that man?" I asked. Just because Pilot confirmed some things that Paul already told me didn't mean I should trust him too.

Ray shrugged.

"I don't know," Paul said. I could hear the shadows of his anger with me in his voice again. "Did he tell you anything else?"

"Nothing consequential," I told him. "If you want me to tell you later why I left I will but it doesn't change the path before me now and I've already told you what that is."

I waited until his fingers started to stroke my cheek.

"Did he tell you about Rice?"

"Some. Denis and Ross will be up in a bit to brief me."

"Do I have to stick around for that?"

"I would appreciate it if you did," Paul said.

I sighed. Then I told him what the others already knew to save time.

"I don't trust my judgement Paul. Other than a couple of bad trips there's nothing I can put my finger on at all. Maybe Ray was right. I've just been through too much. What if I react to Rice, to some danger that's not really there and I hurt him? What if it's all in my head?"

I got up and put my gun on. I could hear Ross and Denis at the bottom of the stairs. "I'm skipping breakfast and going for some fresh air instead."

"Anna, just wait a minute. Please?" Paul asked.

I sighed and waited. Paul came and put his arms around me.

147

"Please wait," he whispered again. I could feel him start to relax as I slipped my arms around him.

When Ross and Denis came in he only loosened his grip. It was another reminder of how much I had damaged his trust in me.

Ross's briefing started with a recap of the watches. Nothing happened except someone had the flu so Ray quarantined him and they had to pull a replacement. Turned out quarantine was downstairs.

"Does he really have to have the flu in the house the pregnant woman lives in?" I wanted to know. Ray decided he didn't.

Ross went on about the watches anyway. I yawned as my attention drifted. The next thing I new I realized that Ross was an independent as I had come to think of them. Unrelated to any of the others. I hadn't meant to probe but nobody seemed to notice. Denis on the other hand was very similar to Paul. I decided to try and remove the things that were similar and see what was left so I turned slightly so I was facing Paul hoping Ray wouldn't notice what I was doing.

Another yawn came so I covered my mouth but I left my finger tips just under my nose.

Gradually Paul faded from what was left under my fingers. My eyes were closed again and I could feel them trying to roll up as my brain worked beneath them.

"Anna!" Ray whispered sharply.

Ross paused. Paul looked at me so I yawned again.

"Sorry. I'm still tired," I said but I kept brushing my fingers on my upper lip.

Ross started talking again; nobody shipping out, nobody shipping in, supply run done while Paul was away …

When I saw what was left it didn't surprise me at all. It was why I could keep him in line and still get along with him. It was why Reno felt more like a family trip than anything else. I had spent four days with my husband, my brother, and my son. Denis had been mine. Mine and Paul's.

I felt a little grin on my face and a bit of laughter starting but I pressed my lips together and put my hand down.

"Stop it!" Ray hissed at me. I didn't look up to see what Paul thought. He knew damn well what I was doing as much as Ray did. Ross stopped again, puzzled.

"What?" I said. Then I sneezed into my elbow. And I sneezed again. "Excuse me." The sneezing continued and I hid in the bathroom until it stopped. They were starting to talk about Rice when I got out.

"Anna, anything to add about Rice?" Paul asked.

I shook my head. "Nothing more than what I said this morning."

"So where are we at now Ross?" Paul asked.

Ross hesitated and looked at me.

"Sorry Paul. This is where I leave or kick you all out. I don't want to be here for it."

"She threw us all out last night," Ross explained.

Paul sighed.

"Ray, can I have the radio please? I'll step out for a bit. If you need me for anything let me know and I'll come back." I tipped my head up and kissed Paul. "I won't be far."

The road south was empty so I walked down to the bend and then straight into the trees. The branches had kept the ground somewhat clear of snow and I had no trouble keeping my path straight.

The pond was frozen over still. New snow and the uneven ground hid any evidence of what had happened when Paul and his men went to stop the last two of Damian's men. I stayed away from the edge; the slope down to the ice. I wasn't in the mood to slip down the hill and to try the ice out for myself. I could see where my daughter and I sat at the shore and I made my way to where Ray had put me. A tree protected much of the ground from the snow so I sat down there to look out at the pond. It was strange to think I might spend eternity here.

"Whiskey Romeo," Paul's voice crackled out from the radio.

"Romeo Whiskey," I answered.

"What's your twenty Romeo?" he asked.

I remembered Ross saying that it wasn't secure so I replied. "Where she took me."

"Copy, Whiskey out." Paul said. He understood.

As I waited something behind me got my attention. It was like Damian's smudges but weak, like a memory. It was the third one; the one that disappeared with the explosion I'd heard from the house. Maybe they hadn't found all of him. Curiosity got the better of me and I got up and walked toward the source of the memory tugging at me. It wasn't far, maybe thirty feet in, away from the clearing but the ground seemed rougher, the snow deeper, and it felt like it took a long time to get to the spot where he died.

The little space under my nose told me that the man was definitely very similar to Damian. Not just loyal to him as I had thought before. I started to remove Damian from what I picked up about the man.

"Anna?" Paul was calling me. I realized the ground had been clear where I entered the trees so he wouldn't have been able to see where I went.

"Over here," I called back and kept removing Damian from under my nose. I could hear Paul stomping through the snow until he came around and stopped in front of me.

"Hmm," I said and looked up at him. The man was mine; so twisted up with Damian's darkness that I didn't like what was left behind.

149

"What are you doing out here?" he asked as I started to sneeze again. Maybe there was something left behind from what I was doing that my body was trying to remove. Maybe it was all in my head.

"I've never been here before … I wanted to see the pond before I get put here forever. Then this got my attention."

Paul rubbed his palm on his face. "How did you find it?"

"Given what happened to him," I shrugged. "There was no way they could have found all the pieces. Once I was down here I picked it up like I did when they were coming. There was enough left behind for that."

He stepped closer.

"You shouldn't be here," he said softly. Then he shuddered. "I don't even want to be here."

"There's nothing to fear here. Ray told you what I was doing at dinner."

"Yes," he agreed.

"I was doing the same thing here … I get the feeling it's something deeply personal and I embarrassed Ray last night," I said. "I won't even apologize to him again if that's going to make it even worse."

Paul looked uncomfortable. "Just don't bring it up with him again unless he does first, okay?"

I nodded. "It's instinctive. I don't realize I've done it until it's done. Maybe it's defensive. So I know who is safe to be around and who's not. I won't talk about it again unless I find someone who's a problem."

"You said your father can do it a bit … can he also see who their mother was?"

Paul looked away like Ray had at dinner.

"I won't say any more … will you at least fill me in on what etiquette I stepped all over and give me the heads up if there's any other way I can make a fool of myself?"

"Yes," Paul took my arm to take me back to the pond but I stayed put.

"Was Rice with you that night?" I asked.

Paul nodded.

"Did he blow this man up?"

"No, but he was the first to get to him after," Paul said.

"Legs?" I asked. "Like I saw last night?"

"No. Let's go."

"Damn … I thought I might have it solved." I said. "I'm done here."

I thought since the man was mine then maybe I was seeing it through Rice. Like an amplifier of what was left here. But the death I saw through Rice was more than one person and I was no further along than at dinner the night before.

We made our way back out to the clearing, to where our markers would be one day. Paul took my hand and stopped, looking out toward the pond.

"I knew you were up to something," he told me. His voice was quiet, flat, like the emptiness I'd left him with inside. "Ray said he would come up to the house. He would watch you. I can't let you go after that man alone, no matter how capable you think you are. I got through my whole watch … not a word from him. He was there when I got back he didn't say anything. I went upstairs and you were gone. Just your letter waiting for me.

"I thought you had disappeared right out from our room. I ran down and told him you were gone … I asked if he'd heard anything. He said he followed you to the garage … he let you go. You took a bike and disappeared on it."

I could hear anger coming now. He'd been trying to control it but he was losing.

"I lost it with him. I hit him, hard. He stayed up and fought back." His fingers tightened around my hand as more of the anger came back.

"Ray tried to explain that you should be back soon … that you probably wouldn't be long … but you shouldn't have gone in the first place. I went upstairs to wait for you. You never came back." As pain replaced the anger his hand started to relax around mine and I could feel the circulation returning to my finger tips.

"I drank a lot. It seemed to help. It was weeks before I could look at Ray without wanting to smash him again …" I waited for him to continue.

"Finally I sobered up enough for a while to apologize to him. He was as mad at me for putting you in a position of having to run off as I was at him for letting you go. He blamed me. He told me what you said to him when you left … he held out a lot more hope than I did that you were coming back.

"I thought you were dead. It was hopeless. It would be quicker to start over on the other side with you than it would be to live out my life waiting. The small part of me that still believed you were okay was losing. I took the truck and drove until that part was gone.

"You know what happened then."

I nodded, even though he wasn't looking at me. Tears chilled my cheeks as the winter air cooled them.

"You knew for a while that you would have to go, didn't you," he said.

"Yes," I whispered back.

"You didn't think that I might have understood … might have

supported you?"

"You still wouldn't have found me again until you had given up … does it really matter now?"

He let go of my hand and turned to me. He put his fingers under my chin and tipped my face up to his. In the daylight I noticed the fine barely pink scar running along his brow bone into his eyebrow. It must have been from their fight. He was loud, but not as loud as he could have been. "The reasons you don't trust me matter more than ever now."

"Paul … I … no, I don't mistrust you."

He looked away, shaking his head. He didn't believe me.

"There are a lot of things I can live without … a lot of things I don't trust." I watched his face even though he looked away from me. Then I put my hand on his cheek and pulled him to face me. "You are not one of them."

"Why did you keep it from me then?" he demanded. He was so angry.

"Paul … I was so confused when I got here. I heard you and Ray talking … you were only protecting the baby. I didn't understand how you could separate the two of us. You would have to protect us both. But I thought I could be a problem to you too. I started making plans to leave on my own if I had to.

"I'd been independent for a long time … I lost that. Being able to choose to stay was important to me because it will be a cold day in hell before I ever let you go again."

His cold stare softened a bit, but not by much.

"The night you heard me talking in the mirror. She can be so mean. She's told me terrible things to keep me out of trouble. She told me you only want the baby. That you were keeping things … things you would never tell me. She said I would have to jump and get help but she didn't say what she meant. When I got back, she said, I should take you to your father. I didn't want to believe what she had to say … but I knew then that eventually I would have to get help. And I knew that I would be back with you after. That made it a little bearable but I hoped that there was some other way.

"Since then I figured a lot out myself. You told me I was right. About us … I know you'll always look after me.

"It was when our daughter brought me here and told me what happened to us I realized that there were things I needed to know that you couldn't tell me. That I'm something new … nothing any of you had seen before and I could only save us by finding someone who knows what I am.

"I knew you would want me to let him go, to be safe. But how many more times can you live to see him kill me and your child?"

Something I didn't recognize flashed on his face for a moment.

Anguish? Guilt? I had no idea.

"How many more times can you kill me to keep me from having his?" I whispered.

He put his shaking hands on his face and turned his back to me.

"Yes Paul ... I know about that," I told him gently. "I also know it never used to be that way. Damian changed the rules. When he's gone the infighting will stop. I'm not going to be the prize breeding stock in some twisted capture the flag game any more. Catherine remembered what kind of lover he was ... we've chosen you."

Paul was trying to keep his shoulders still. I put a hand on his back and he took a deep breath.

"You've become a father with me before," I told him. "Do you remember?" I wasn't going to tell him about the man in the woods.

He took a moment to pull himself together. "No."

"Yes," I said. "Someone here ... I read us both in him."

"Really?" he asked.

"He won't be our last. I'm going to make sure of that," I told him. Then I pulled on his shoulder and turned him to me. There were still tears on his cheeks and he quickly wiped them off. His anger was gone.

"He will come for me. I can count on that. We have the same deadline. I won't be able to finish him after she's born. When he comes ... I'll need to ask you to step back and let me do my job. Give me a chance."

He put his arms around me and held me close. I had to turn a little sideways now to hold him.

"I'm just grateful to have you back now," he said. "I love you Anna. I missed you more than you will ever know."

"I love you too Paul. I'm so sorry I made such a mess of things."

"I know you are," he told me. "Don't leave me alone in the dark like that again."

"Not again," I promised.

We walked back to the house and spent the rest of the morning in our room sleeping, talking, and making up.

Chapter 33

"Lunch," Paul said. He wasn't inviting me; we'd noticed the sounds in the kitchen. "I know you don't want to but it's important they start seeing me back in one piece. And you with me."

I pressed my face back into the little corner where his neck met his shoulder and sighed. I put my lips there to try and change the subject. "This is one of my favourite parts of you ..." Then I reached around him and pulled myself in tight at his side, wrapping myself around him. He let me have my way for a while.

"Ray and I will walk you out if you start to feel unwell again," he said, but he was close to giving in. "Damn you're persistent," he laughed as he rolled to face me, putting some space between us.

"Only as much as I have to be … you're not always easy," I laughed back. "Why doesn't someone just say something to him when he starts to gap out? Ask him what's on his mind?"

"I can do that," Paul said.

"And we have a trip to plan."

"I thought you were kidding about that Anna. He's not here this time. He would be here if he was."

"I wouldn't kid about your father … that man … said he exists in our time," I told him. "I'm sure I can find him. If I miss I can sleep it off then we'll come home or try again. I can take you and anything or anyone else you want to fit in the truck."

He thought about it. "How long can we stay?"

"Weeks I think. That last trip to Toronto was three and I didn't come back because I ran out of time like this last one."

"Okay, soon. Anna … will you tell me who the son is? The man you mentioned at the pond?"

I hesitated. "I don't want to run over any more taboos."

"It's okay because I asked you … and we're not talking about someone else's relations," he reassured me.

"You probably already suspect … it made perfect sense to me when I read it," I told him. "I think he's your favourite … I know he's mine … besides you and Ray of course."

Paul closed his eyes and thought. Then he smiled. "Of course … you're the only one who can manage Denis better than I can. Now that I know I can feel that connection to him too."

"You're not going to tell him are you?" I asked. "I don't want to embarrass him."

"I don't know if it's okay for you to tell him or not," Paul sighed. "Another question for my father, he knows all those rules. I can't see where the mother would ever have been aware before to even bring it up. But I know I can. Can he talk to you about it if he wants to?"

"Of course," I said. "My idea of family is probably very different from yours … I don't know what sort of attachment you have. To me being a mother is a deep honour. A gift that I'll spend my life working to be worthy of. He might get more than he bargains for knowing who I am."

Paul kissed my forehead. "No, your idea of family is not so different at all."

"Thank you," I said. "Paul, what did you tell your parents?"

"Joshua told them I shipped out for a while and you went to stay

154

with your sister." Paul looked sad. "He just went ahead and did it … I was mostly oblivious to what day it was. You missed your birthday too."

I put my arm around him and moved in closer, this time just to be close. "I'm so sorry about that … I just keep finding more things I screwed up."

He hugged me back. "Having you here in my bed again makes up for a lot of the things we missed."

I tucked my head in under his chin. "I think it's time we headed downstairs. It's sounding noisy down there."

"Mmm, you're right," Paul said. "I'll look after you down there."

"If I startle in my seat or start to cough it's time for me to leave the table, okay? Or if I do anything else weird. I'm really worried I'll over react and hurt someone."

"I know."

Downstairs smelled almost overwhelmingly of pine cleaner. I guessed that Ray moved his sick soldier somewhere else and disinfected everything. From the bottom of the stairs I could see the door to the first aid room was open and the bed was made. Ray was just going in.

"Paul … I think I asked too much of someone back in November and I need to smooth things over."

"I think you're right … I'll save seats for you two."

"Thanks," I said and went down the hall to face Ray.

I couldn't see him through the partly opened door. He was behind it where the supplies were so I knocked and called his name.

"Yeah Anna, come on in."

I had my arms gently crossed with nervousness and was absently rubbing my elbow when I stepped around the door and out of sight from the hallway. He noticed and came right over taking my arm.

"What happened?" he asked.

"Oh, I didn't realize I was doing that." I gently took my arm back. "Do you have a few minutes? I need to talk to you about something I did."

He stiffened and started to look uncomfortable so I shook my head. "Something I did quite a while ago."

"Okay," he said, looking at my arm like he would rather be dealing with an injury.

He stood close so I studied his face. I could make out the faint pink scar under his eye and another little one running up into his bottom lip. I cautiously reached up and ran my finger along the one on his cheekbone. He looked away but he didn't stop me. Then I touched the one on his lip.

"When I asked you to let me go I had no idea what I was asking of you," I said quietly. "Or that you would stand up for me with Paul … that it would test your friendship. I'm grateful and surprised and truly very sorry. It was short sighted of me and inconsiderate. I understand if I have to work to earn your respect back … to undo hurting you. You've been nothing but gracious toward me since I got back and I don't feel that I've earned it. I just wanted you to know that I'm thankful for having you and deeply sorry."

He looked back at me and put his hands on my shoulders.

"Anna," he said. "You don't have to apologize."

"I already did and I'm not taking it back. I can't promise that I'm going to stay out of trouble but I will always appreciate you and come out okay."

"Okay Kiddo," he said. "I've never been able to do anything for you like this … you've always been just Paul's. I'm enjoying knowing you … don't move"

He went quietly to the door and peered down the hall then he closed it. When he came back he stood behind me and put his hands back on my shoulders.

"Don't turn," he whispered. "It's easier for me like this."

"Okay Ray," I said and I waited.

"Was he … really my father?" he asked.

"I believe he is," I told him. His fingers squeezed my shoulders briefly and relaxed.

"Most of us gave up on our mates a long time ago. Damian made it so hard. Paul didn't give up though. I saw what he went through with you every time. He changed … became cold about it like Damian. But after Catherine something was different about him. He started to love you again … like he used to a long time ago but he was losing the strength to keep going the way that he had been. Like so many of us had already he was close to giving up.

"He found you this time … quite by accident. Usually we find our mates when we're young … twenty is late. He assumed that he wouldn't find you this time … it happens … so we went away overseas to serve. Improve our skills, experience new things. You're so much younger than him this time. You would have been much too young when he was twenty. He had his own life instead of running off to be with you like if he had found you at nineteen. I think he tried to let you go but you came to him here and he realized he couldn't. He's not like Damian any more. He just needs to be with you."

"I know that now, Ray."

He opened the door and we went down to the kitchen.

"Sit," Ray told me. "I'll get yours."

I ran my fingers over Paul's shoulders on the way past to my seat and joined him. He raised his eyebrows questioningly at me; I just smiled and nodded back. Ray put my plate down and I thanked him. He started talking with Denis and Ross about something. Officer talk probably. I ignored everyone and tried to imagine it was just Paul and I.

It seemed to work for a while. Rice was chatting with Jones again so I focused on Paul and pretended that the other end of the kitchen didn't exist at all until my eyes got tired and started to sting. Just a bit. I rubbed them with my palm. It felt good until I stopped and then the stinging got worse. Could be all the pine cleaner in the air was irritating me so I blinked a few times but that didn't help. I was having trouble keeping them open. Then my nose started to itch until I sneezed into my napkin.

"You okay?" Paul and Ray seemed to ask at the same time.

"Got something in my eyes, maybe all the cleaner," I said but I was starting to smell something burning, like an electrical fire. Not the sweet cooked flesh stench from dinner. "Do you smell something burning?"

"No," Paul said.

When I managed to get my eyes open everything was hazy and it was starting to get warmer. The itch was moving into my throat. Clearing it didn't help and I sneezed again. Then I coughed. I had no idea what Rice was doing. I couldn't keep my eyes open long enough to focus and the kitchen was too smoky for me to make out anything that far away anyhow.

"Ray ..." Paul whispered.

"Got her," Ray said and helped me up. I couldn't see where I was going. I tried to hold my breath but I still coughed a bit.

As we were in the hallway I could hear Paul say. "Penny for your thoughts, Rice." Then he said again. "Rice?"

Ray started to lead me to the bathroom again but I pulled him the other way.

"Fresh air," I managed and he took me through the foyer and out the door.

"What the hell," I coughed and kept going down the stairs and out onto the road. Then up toward the garage. We were half way there before the air started to clear.

"How could you see in there?" I asked Ray. "The smoke was so thick I couldn't make out the other end of the table."

"There was no smoke Anna," he said.

"And it was a different smell from last night," I told him. "The smoke was thick ... like there was a fire ... electrical." I smelled the sleeve of my shirt and it was in the fabric but not in the air any more. Then I took Ray's arm and smelled the sleeve of his shirt.

"It's in your clothes too."

Ray smelled his sleeve and looked puzzled. "Nobody else seemed to notice."

"At least I kept my lunch down. Thank you for helping me out of there. Between the smoke and my eyes burning I couldn't see a thing. It's gone now." I shrugged. "Do you think there's something wrong with me?"

Ray put his hand on my arm. "Nothing physical," he said. "But like you suggested maybe you've just been through too much in too short a time. Do you want to stay out a while longer?"

"No … I think I'll go upstairs and wash the smoke off. I'll come down when everyone's gone and get some more lunch. I didn't eat much more than half."

We walked slowly back to the house. The air stayed clear. It was clear indoors too.

"Ray, could you please tell Paul I'm upstairs? I think he worries now when he can't find me. He doesn't need that."

Ray nodded and went to find Paul in the kitchen. I went up and got in the shower. Paul still wasn't upstairs when I got out so I put on clean clothes and lay down to nap a bit. I was sleeping when he came in. He had curled himself up around behind me with his chin on my shoulder and his hand on my stomach. I reached up and put my hand on his face. I could still smell the smoke on him.

"Did Ray tell you what happened?" I asked him.

I could feel him nod behind me. "I don't know what to tell you. Rice apologized for not hearing me the first time and then went back to talking with Jones. Those two seem to get along pretty well."

Paul brushed the hair from my face then he put his hand back on my stomach. "He'll be on watch during dinner if you want to come down. Hopefully it won't happen again."

"Okay." I lifted my head so he could put his arm under it. "You're right. I guess Mrs. Richards has responsibilities here now. If I look weak it makes you look weak too. I'll suck it up."

Paul laughed quietly. "I don't think you realize what they think of you. They know what you did to that man, saw your targets downstairs. And a strange version of what you said to the Colonel got out somehow … I'm not too pleased about that but there's nothing I can do about it now. Half of them think you shipped out on some crazy Canadian covert mission, pregnant and all. You don't have anything to prove."

I giggled at that. "Well, if having a Canadian commando for a wife helps you lead then let them think it. Or I can put scented candles in the downstairs bathroom and arrange flowers for the dinner table and haul you off to romantic movies in Redding on Tuesdays too but I'll really hate it."

"Some of that might be good for them," Paul agreed so I gave him a gentle elbow.

"Have you thought about our trip?" I asked him. "We should go soon. I can't keep running from the table in front of everyone."

"I was thinking the same thing ... tomorrow?"

"Night would be best ... less traffic," I agreed. "Decide if you want to bring anyone or if it will be just us. Tell them to pack for a week or so and for warm weather too just in case. They'll need their ID ... cell phones off, cash only. We don't want Damian tracing us anywhere electronically ... or getting attention for being in two places at once. And maybe camping gear. I can't promise we won't wind up stuck in a cornfield until I recharge."

"You seem to have it all planned. But I thought all the electronic purchases are free?"

I laughed a bit. "This isn't my first barbeque. After the last trip I can't promise we'll go forward. I don't know how backward works but we need to be careful until we find out."

"I guess so. I'll bring Ray and Denis again ... then it will look like we're actually going somewhere else with sufficient people to look after you like before."

"Paul ... think about what you want to tell me about him so I know what I'm focusing on, okay? I don't want to wind up at Ron and Camille's for the weekend."

"That would make my mother happy," Paul said. "But I see your point. I'll have Ross leak that you're having complications and Ray wants you in the hospital for a while. If Damian does have someone here then that's a reasonable cover story."

"Okay," I agreed, but nothing had made me think that Rice or anyone else in the camp was Damian's.

"You should skip dinner if you're supposed to be having problems. I'll make sure Denis and Ray are packed and ready to go like before." He gently rubbed my belly then until it tickled and I started to giggle again. Paul sighed and relaxed against me.

"I really missed that sound. Try and get some more sleep ... we'll be up early. I need to get everything ready and I'll bring you up dinner soon. Actually, I'll bring you up a radio first in case you need me. Ray will be in and out of here pretending to look after you."

"'kay Paul," I said and closed my eyes, but I was already planning on the when part of the jump. All I needed was a strong focus from Paul for the where.

Chapter 34

I didn't sleep but I was so relaxed it didn't matter. So much stress was gone that I could lay on the bed with my mind empty. Now I could do something for Paul and make up the lost pregnancy time all at once. I knew Damian was coming but there was no sense in worrying about that

159

until it happened.

My peace didn't last long however. Paul's hands were full with the two-way radio and a couple of larger bags for us to pack and he was all Captain when he came back up.

"The Colonel's come early … his helicopter will be here in twenty."

I sat up and noticed what he was wearing.

"Do you need me to do anything while you change?" The last time Colonel Iverson had come Paul and the other officers had to be in uniform.

"No," he shook his head for emphasis as he tossed the bags over by our dressers and put the radio for me on my night table. "When the pilot radioed ahead he said it's unofficial … so he's not really here. He thinks I'm going to try and dodge him again."

"Okay … should I stay up here?"

"The Colonel requests the officers and Mrs. Richards. I need you downstairs waiting as soon as you can get there."

Maybe the Colonel checked out the story I'd told. Maybe it wasn't big enough or I'd gotten Paul in some kind of trouble by skipping out on him. My absence left the compound without its leadership. If they'd tried to cover up for Paul we could all be in trouble. That could be why he wanted the officers. We would find out soon enough.

When I got downstairs Ray, Denis, and Ross were already there. We still had ten minutes to wait so I went to the kitchen to get a drink and poked in the fridge for a bite to eat. The smoke that had filled the room at lunch was gone. I went down to the big south window but only needed to get within a couple of feet of it to smell smoke in the curtains. Then I went to the small window over the sink on the west wall. I had to put my nose right to those ones to smell it. The smoke was so much stronger near where Rice had been sitting.

"Anna?" Ray called me. "I can hear the helicopter."

I quickly finished my drink and put the glass in the dishwasher. Nobody had run them after lunch so I decided to turn them on after the Colonel left so we didn't have to listen to the two of them chew on the dishes through his visit. Ray and the others stood up so I didn't sit down. It still took a few minutes for Paul and the Colonel to arrive.

When they came in the Colonel had his hand on Paul's shoulder. He let him go and came straight to me and took my hand. I couldn't tell from Paul's demeanour what might be going on.

"Mrs. Richards …" he leaned toward me and kissed my cheek. As he did my nose tickled. There was something about him that was familiar. Very familiar, but difficult to place. "I'm glad to see you back."

"Hello Colonel," I replied as he stepped back and moved on to greet the others then he stood next to Paul.

"Lieutenant-Commander Richards," he said taking on an intimidating air of rank. Lef-tennant. I wondered what he was fishing for.

"Yes Sir," I replied indifferently. He could tell me what he was after. I wasn't giving away anything that might get us in any more trouble.

"You left my best Captain in a bad way for two months."

"Yes Sir," I said neither agreeing nor disagreeing with what he said even though I agreed.

"I have an ear in the gossip here. I spent a considerable amount of resources tracking you and you appear to have disappeared completely."

"Yes Sir," I said neutrally. I was distracted. The Colonel was family ... I just couldn't place whose. When I tried to focus to know for sure it disappeared. It was like looking at something faint in the dark. I could see it off to the side but as soon as I looked right at it, it was gone.

"My contacts in Canada have no knowledge of you ... and I have very good contacts."

I was glad Paul was behind him. He looked quite uncomfortable with where the Colonel might be going. I knew he was going nowhere. Maybe he just wanted to see how far I would stick to my story.

"I'm aware of protocol, Sir," I said. Disinterested again. I kept my face still and looked at Paul for a few seconds. He gently shook his head. He wanted me to come up with something other than the commando gossip.

"You found him after he went AWOL and got him back in here without alerting the front gate."

I had enough. It was one thing to privately call me a liar or to give me his personal opinion of the damage my trip left in its wake. It was something completely different to hurt Paul for what I'd done to him by going after me in front of the officers. That was none of his business. I also wanted to talk to him alone.

"Can I speak with you privately please Colonel?" I asked.

He held his palm out, arm pointing down the hall to the medical room. I nodded and walked that way as the Colonel followed behind. When we got inside he closed the door behind us then turned and stared at me. I stared back. After a minute neither of us spoke so I started.

"They don't know, do they?" I asked.

"That you may or may not be Canadian Special Forces?"

"No," I paused. "They don't know that you're family."

He sighed heavily through his nose and stared at the floor for a minute.

"No ... but I'm not really."

I tilted my head to the side. "I suspect you're some relation of mine."

"You shouldn't be able to tell that. I'm aware of Pilot's plan for you. He's been working on it for a long time. Did you get my present?"

I thought about it. I suspected Rice had hidden the knife in Paul's room. There was something in him similar to the Colonel. Something illusive. I took a guess.

"Yes … Rice has been troublesome to me since I found it."

"Indeed," Iverson said, "there has been some interest in him from the officers here in the past couple of days. That's part of the reason for my visit. Rice will be leaving with me today."

That was a relief. Not that I disliked him. I just preferred to be able to finish a meal without hiding in my room.

"I will expect that you respect our privacy with the men here," he said simply.

I zipped my thumb and first finger past my lips.

He nodded. "Can you tell me what troubled you?"

I quickly explained what happened. The Colonel looked concerned about what I said.

"I wasn't looking for it … the first time I was looking for which of the men wasn't loyal to Paul … the other two times I was trying to block it. It was too strong and Ray had to pull me from the room. I can still smell it in the kitchen curtains."

"I apologize for him," Iverson said, "he should know better. But there's never been anyone here who could pick it up. He's young."

I shrugged. So was I.

"Do you know what it means? The things I saw?"

The Colonel shook his head. "It won't mean anything to him either … he won't know what he projected; not even that he did it. Even if I told him the images would be meaningless."

"Are there others like him here?" I asked but he ignored my question.

"Anna, don't fail in your task. It's more important than you can possibly understand."

I knew that but I didn't really care. My own reasons it was important meant far more to me than anything else: keeping my sister from Damian, keeping him away from me. Making sure that my daughter didn't spend her long life mated to a man loyal to him.

"Damian Howard is insane, by our standards," he said as he came closer. "For many lives a past personality has dominated … controlled him. Time usually cures it but in his case it keeps getting stronger. A … permanent solution is all we have. That solution is you."

He took my face in his hands and kissed me.

"Godspeed Anna," he whispered as he held his hands on my cheeks and rested his forehead on mine. He stepped back and gave me a weak smile.

"Can you send your husband in please?"

"Yes Sig," I told him and walked out.

I didn't have to try hard to look like my meeting with the Colonel went well. I wouldn't miss Rice's intrusions into my senses and was strangely reassured by my conversation with Sig.

"He wants to see you," I told Paul when I got back into the common room. Paul didn't acknowledge what I said other than by walking back the way I came.

"How much shit did you get in?" Denis whispered to me.

"Who, me?" I batted my eyes at him. Denis laughed.

Paul was only gone a couple of minutes before they came out.

"Rice is leaving with me," Iverson announced. "No explanation will be offered."

Then he said goodbye quickly to the others before coming to me. He just shook my hand without commenting.

"Captain, with me."

With that he disappeared out the front door with Paul.

I turned the dishwashers on and went back upstairs to lie down. Paul came up about half an hour later.

"Can I ask what you said to the Colonel?" he asked.

"I just apologized for any problems I caused, refused to tell him where I had been, and invited him to chew me out privately next time I inconvenience him," I replied. I wasn't going to comment on Rice or ask Paul if the Colonel had told him anything.

"He's not usually like that," Paul told me.

"No biggie … I was nice about it. I wasn't going to tell him to piss off in front of all of you any more than I was going to take that from him in front of you."

"He would appreciate your directness," Paul said then he got to packing. "Are you going to ask me about Rice?"

"No. If there was anything I should know that you could tell me you would."

"Yeah."

It didn't take long for him to have his bag ready then he made sure I didn't need anything and went back downstairs.

Ray was in and slept in the chair for a while. He'd been up a lot during the past couple of days with the sick man and Paul sleeping off the jump. While everyone ate downstairs I got my bag packed and made sure that I had everything I told the others they would need. I put Damian's knife in one of the end pouches of the bag.

Paul brought up my dinner and the paperwork for the Colonel and worked on it while I ate.

"I think we'll be back in time for Ray to check me in for whatever he's pretending is wrong with me now and see the Colonel," I told him.

Now that I knew there was a time component to my destination I planned on testing that out. I had eight weeks to make up so I would aim at least that far back. Ray knocked and Paul called him in.

"Can I have the chair Paul?" he yawned and closed his eyes as soon as he sat down.

"What the hell is he doing?" Paul whispered after a minute.

"Checking on me I think," I whispered back. "I don't think he's slept much."

"This isn't a flop house," he grumbled. "Can you send him to his cabin in an hour? I have to get everyone sorted out for while we're away." Then he yawned. "I thought I slept it off."

"You won't sleep right for a while," I told him. "Give it a week or so."

"I have the next watch since we're leaving, so I'll be back in a few hours. Radio me if you need anything … I'm monitoring that channel. Okay?"

"Will do."

He kissed me goodbye and left, closing the door gently behind him. I tried to stay awake for an hour but I wound up falling asleep. Paul was back from watch and sending Ray on his way when I woke up again and the next thing I knew it was time to go.

Denis was watching me closely when we got downstairs. Ray and Paul didn't seem to notice but I did. I wondered if Paul had spoken to him about me but I wasn't going to bring it up to him. He would have to come to me and did while I was heaving my bag up over the high tailgate into the back of the truck. He grabbed it and lowered it in before it could crash down into the box.

"So how did you figure it out? I've been wondering for about as long as I can remember," Denis asked me.

"What?" I asked.

"Me," he said.

I felt a little awkward. "Are you sure you want to talk about it?" He nodded.

"I'm sorry, I didn't mean to pry … I figured it out yesterday morning at the briefing. Ray knew I was doing it. That's what he was telling me to stop doing … I didn't know it was bad manners. I hope I didn't insult you."

"You didn't," he said quietly and looked back at Paul and Ray. They were talking on the porch out of earshot. "I like you both very much. I'm lucky to know … most of us don't. But how did you figure it out?"

I glanced up the stairs and leaned toward him. Then I pointed to the little spot under my nose. "I have no idea how it works … but I put you and Paul both here and took away everything that was the same …

164

what was left was me."

Denis was trying hard to keep a serious face. "Now that Paul told me I can feel it. I know you're right." But then he started to give in to a very Anna-like case of the giggles. "But seriously … you put us up your nose?" He was laughing as he walked away so I made a quick snowball and pegged him hard in the back. He kept laughing as I caught Paul smiling at us.

It took over an hour to get to roads that were clear enough to go as fast as we needed. Paul had already warned Ray and Denis to keep their eyes shut and turn off their phones. They both looked nervous. I was too. Hopefully I could pull it off.

"Roads should be good from here on Anna," Paul said quietly. "If you're ready to start."

I was in the front with him and closed my eyes and concentrated on where we were going. First the time. I was aiming for the end of October; a few weeks after I had arrived at Paul's. The truck started to wander a bit from the small side gusts as I locked that in.

"Tell me about your father Paul," I said quietly.

He started to tell me about how the men would be drawn to his father. How without him they had found less than half of the family this time and how his father was in charge of everyone … the patriarch. But it wasn't working for me. Maybe he didn't want to say what he needed to in front of the others so I slid over and whispered into his ear.

"That's not going to work," I told him. "Those are the things you've been doing. Tell me the biggest reason why you need him now … with things the way they are. Not how things should have worked out. It has to be strong Paul … or we'll wind up at your mother's. Whisper it to me … they won't hear."

He was quiet for a few minutes. Then he said, "I need his help to raise our daughter."

"How?" I whispered to him.

"It's not just the regular parenting for us … there's a lot more to it. She'll need to understand her tie through her lives. This is the first she'll carry with her and she'll start to feel its attachment as she gets older." He rubbed the centre of his chest. "We feel it here … without proper guidance and understanding it won't be secured. It'll weaken. I'll find her a few times but eventually it'll become detached and she won't remember me at all. She'll be lost. For us it's a real death."

He kept his eyes on the road and didn't even glance at me. I knelt on the seat with my ear to his lips so his voice was barely a whisper.

"I don't remember how to teach her. I need to feel through my connection to her that it's been done right," he sounded so sad. "If what you said comes to pass then I won't be here to do it at all. That's why I brought Ray and Denis. They need to know, to help her if I'm not there.

165

It's just been so long since anyone has needed to do it that nobody remembers except my father. I need to find him so he can teach me again. When we find him next time it will be too late … her line will be set and if it was set wrong we'll lose her."

I kissed his cheek. "I thought it was scary enough for me to be raising a daughter without my mother. Thank you Paul, that's what I needed."

I sat back down I refocused on the time we would be going to. Made sure that was still set. I thought about what Paul had told me. His desperate need to find the one person he trusted with our daughter's future. The person who could give him peace of mind.

"Both hands on the wheel Paul," I said as the pressure grew then the truck was pushed hard over the centre line.

"Shit," he said. I smiled to myself as I felt Ray grab the seat behind me to hold on.

"Rushing that part only makes it worse," I said.

Another gust pushed the truck sideways as there was more pressure. After a half minute we were hit from behind.

"Better," he said.

I continued to refine my focus. We were hit harder and something shifted and fell over in the back of the truck. It was pretty full of gear and people so I let the pressure build far past the point it had when I brought Paul home.

"Okay. Time to swap." I took the wheel and Paul quickly moved out of the way as I sat down. We got hit again and he was almost pulled off his seat by the recoil.

"Eyes closed?" I asked.

Paul turned and looked back at Ray and Denis. Then he faced forward. "Yes."

I double checked my focus and made sure I had dismissed everything else from my mind then I closed my eyes and floored it. The truck jumped forward hard as we disappeared.

Chapter 35

Rain punished the roof overhead; clusters of hundreds of huge drops beat down in waves. The wind had to be strong to drive the rain like that.

"Paul?" I asked quietly.

"Right here," he said behind me and knocked something over as he turned around.

"Ray? Denis?"

"Here," they answered.

"Let's find out where we are," Paul said.

I turned around in the dark to see if there was anything I could make out. I could see a street light through the garage door window. The utility lines led toward us to the left and the familiar little tags from the cable company dangled from their silver box. That was disappointing. I rubbed my eyes with fatigue. They would have to wait for me to sleep this one off before we tried again. I didn't have the energy to do another now without draining someone else and I wasn't willing to do that.

"I'm sorry Paul. We're in my garage," I told him and he patted my shoulder. "Don't move ... it's a death trap. Let me get the light."

I made my way to the far end.

"Crap," I said as I banged my shin on something and knocked it over. "Who left that there?" Suddenly three flashlights were on me.

"Thanks," I said, wondering where the lights were before I had hobbled myself then I turned on the light. It was just as I remembered it. Every surface, walls and work benches, was covered in parts and tools. I had four motorcycles in pieces on the floor and no clear path past any of them.

"This is a mess Anna," Paul said.

I gave him a sideways shrug. "I usually spend the winter in here … I haven't been around to deal with the junk that piled up during the summer. We need to find the truck." I took the spare house key off its hook and opened the door to the outside. Cold wind and heavy rain immediately blasted me as I stepped out.

"Hope you can swim," I told them.

"Yuck," Denis said as he left the dry garage.

"No. It's fantastic," I disagreed. To me this was winter. The weather was always doing something other than the cold and white at Paul's. That was nice but I could watch the weather do this for days without worrying about my ears freezing off.

"I don't have the keys for the truck, do any of you?" They didn't. "It won't be more than a few blocks away, but with the keys inside it'll be gone by morning."

The three of them looked half drowned already. I hadn't felt the rain in a long time so I didn't mind at all. When I got out to the street the truck was only a block away so Denis ran to get it. Paul had zipped his jacket all the way up and stuffed his hands in his pockets.

"Does it rain like this a lot?"

"It's a rainforest," I laughed. "Ten months a year."

Denis backed the truck in and Ray started pulling things out.

"You two have to sleep on the living room floor … sorry. My spare room is full," I could see the sleeping bags in the truck. That was good. I didn't have anything like that they could use. Then I led them around back and opened up my door.

I stepped in cautiously, sniffing the air. It didn't smell bad but it didn't smell good either. I turned on the light so nobody tripped on the clutter.

"I hope you didn't marry me for my house keeping," I told Paul.

"If I did it would be over," he laughed.

"Living room is through to the left, bathroom down the hall on the right … first door. My room is on the left."

They started bringing stuff in.

"What happened to the hall carpet Anna? It's black," Ray asked.

"No other way to get bikes in and out of the spare room," I told him like he should know that already. Then I threw the dirty dishes from before I left into the dishwasher, gave it a cookie, and turned it on. Smell number one out of the way.

"Anna," Paul called from down the hallway. "When was the last time you made your bed or is this the laundry table?"

"Both," I called back. "Try and keep it down. If we wake up Mrs. Desmond we'll be whipped."

Then I went into the living room and turned it on to channel two for the listings. They went out to the truck for another load so I waited until they came back in. "Paul? Come here a second."

When he came in I pointed to the TV. "We have some time here at least before we need to get back."

He stopped dead and tipped his head to the side as he read it. "Nine pm October thirtieth? I need a minute."

Ray and Denis gaped at the TV beside him. When I realized they weren't going to move for a bit I put on CNN.

"Ray you and Denis can set yourselves up in here. Carpet is clean … it's just the hall that's trashed. I'll go deal with the bed Paul."

"Denis, do you have everything?" I asked him. I wanted to close the door.

"One more trip," he said.

I took the spare sheets from the closet before I pulled everything off the bed. The laundry went onto the floor. I gave the washer two scoops of soap before I turned it on. Smell number two dealt with. Then I turned on the dryer for twenty to get the wrinkles out of whatever was in it.

"You really live like this?" Paul asked from the bathroom door. I squeezed past him and started putting the bed together.

"No. I was home maybe a couple of days a month." I pointed to the heap of clothes on the floor. "I have dirty clothes at the bottom of the pile from nineteen sixty-two."

He shuddered.

"I'll get it caught up. Just don't open the fridge. I'll deal with that and get food for a couple of days tomorrow morning."

"Anna … how is it October?"

"It's right where I was aiming for. I'm getting better at it. Pilot gave me the idea that there's a time component in the jump. I figured I would try and set it myself," I told him. "I was hoping I could make up for some of the things we missed and give you lots of time with your father. I'll try and stick to the same date when we try again.

"I don't know what went wrong. There has to be a road connecting so maybe he's somewhere that there isn't a road … maybe an island and I just brought us here because I've come here so many times before. I'm really sorry. We'll try again in a few days when I've rested."

"It's okay," Paul said.

When the bed was put together we went out to the living room. Ray and Denis had set themselves up already.

"Who's hungry?" I asked.

"We're not eating anything cooked in that kitchen," Ray said.

I sighed. "I get it … it's a dump. I was never home to do much with it. There's a place a few blocks away that'll be open for a couple more hours. We can head up there for something?"

"Sounds good," Ray said.

I went to the spare room to get some cash. After I got on the chair I started putting boxes of photos down on the desk to get at my secret cash boxes in the back. Paul found me and was unimpressed with the mess.

"Two bikes, just like I told you. And a lot of junk. It's not like you didn't have secret junk rooms in your place. Here, can you put these on the desk please?"

"Yeah," he said. "But the rest of my place isn't a health hazard."

I ignored that. When I found the cash box I wanted I took it down and started counting out four piles of five hundred dollars each.

"Geez Anna, how much money is in there?"

"Over twenty-five thousand in unmarked small Canadian bills," I answered pausing my counting. Then I took one of the piles and put a hundred in one pocket and the rest in the other.

"Cash only," I said and gave him one. Then I got up on the chair and put the box of money and the boxes of pictures all back up on the shelf.

"But where did you get it?" he wanted to know.

"I had to get paid for my criminal career somehow. I can't put it in the bank without signing a letter saying where it came from and I have to spend it before they change the style of the bills so I don't get attention for it. And if you're spending a ton of US dollars around here you're going to draw attention to us."

"Anna," he said trying to give it back. "I'm not spending dirty money."

I wouldn't take it. "It's been clean for years plus all that paper up there is a fire hazard … you're doing me a favour."

Paul sighed with frustration and put the money in his wallet. We left the spare room and I took my gun off and put it beside the bed.

"Yours will have to come off too. You're in Canada now … you won't need it and anyone who sees it will call the police. I don't think the Colonel will be much help getting you out of that. Knives off too."

"Rain and no guns," Paul said. "I feel like I've landed on another planet."

I heard the dryer turn off so I went to fold what was in it before it could wrinkle again.

"Can you break the bad news to Ray and Denis and give them their cash? If you need anything while you're here help yourselves." Paul went to explain Canada to Ray and Denis. I found that the dryer was empty so I went to get the basket of clean laundry from the couch and took it to my room.

They were all unarmed when I got back. "Just in case I forget … Mrs. Desmond has a key so she'll let herself in to put the paper on the counter when she's read it. Hopefully I won't be on my long sleep when

172

she gets here … that could give you a bit of trouble. Ready to go?"

Paul drove us up to the Chinese food place where I had dinner with my father. In spite of it being morning for them Denis managed a few drinks. When we got back I put the load of wash in the dryer and fell right to sleep.

Next thing I knew Paul was crawling over top of me going for his gun. I could hear a key in my door. My clock said it was a little past eight.

"It's Mrs. Desmond," I grunted as I shoved him. "Put it away. Ray, Denis." I called more loudly. "It's the lady upstairs. Stay out of sight."

Paul got off me and finished waking up as I quickly got dressed and went down to the kitchen.

Mrs. Desmond had finally gotten the stubborn lock to pop so I took the knob and slowly pulled it open toward me. She looked just as I remembered. I wasn't much taller than she was in spite of her shrinking with age. Her grey hair was cut short and she wore a rainproof jacket over her stretchy slacks and floral button up shirt. Rain dotted the lenses of her glasses.

"Mrs. Desmond," I said leaning close to her to kiss her cheek. "Come in … how have you been?"

"Anna my dear … as well as can be expected," I knew what that meant. Something wrong with everything but she was going to spare me today. Then she stopped and looked at me.

"Your line's been tangled dear," she said.

I looked back at her. Sometimes she went on about my lines and loops but tangling was a new one.

"Tangled," I said. "That doesn't sound too good. Have you had tea yet? I was just getting my day started." I tried to take her to sit at the table but she wouldn't move. I could hear Paul coming up the hall.

"Tangled with another," she said firmly.

"Okay," I didn't know what else to say. I worried about leaving her alone so much. She spent far too much time off in her own little world now.

Then she suddenly put her hand on my stomach.

"Who have you been with?" she whispered.

I could hear Paul behind me so I kept a hand on her elbow and reached back for him.

"Mrs. Desmond, this is my husband Mr. Richards … Paul," I told her slowly. She was fussy about formal introductions so I made sure I did it the way she would want. I had no idea what she was on about and would have to explain later to Paul that the only part of her mind that was thriving at her age was her imagination.

She took a step toward him and took his hand to shake it. Not like a regular hand shake, but she held his fingers and put them to her nose as if she was going to kiss it. Then she gently brushed them along just above her top lip and her eyes rolled up just briefly like mine had done when I was figuring out Denis.

She dropped his hand and then put hers on Paul's chest.

"I found her a few years ago," she told him. "But I never found you, son. I searched as long as my body would let me but my gifts are weak like this. I hoped if I was with her you would find her … and find me."

Paul quickly stepped toward Mrs. Desmond and put his arms around her. "My God Anna … you did it," he whispered, relief covering his face, but I was shaking my head at him.

"Stop encouraging her …" I whispered but he smiled back at me.

"You found him," he said again.

"Did you find any of the others?" she asked.

"About half," Paul said sadly. "I don't have your gift for that. Ray, Denis? Come say hi."

She sampled them both under her nose as she had with Paul, recognizing them immediately.

"Paul," she said. "You should all call me Bee. Now come upstairs for breakfast. Anna will need her rest soon and I can promise you that there is nothing edible in this kitchen. We have a lot of catching up to do. You boys too."

And then I was alone trying to get a handle on what had just happened.

Chapter 36

Paul had left the truck keys on my night table so I picked them up and put on a jacket. Then I hurried out to the truck before anyone could remind me that I didn't have a license and roared up off the street then downtown to the store.

I got cleaning supplies and garbage bags and some basics. Coffee, milk, cereal, toilet paper, and Halloween candy for tonight. Paul could head out later with cash for a bigger shop if he wanted. It looked like now we would be spending a considerable amount of time at my house. The third floor had two small bedrooms so I hoped Mrs. Desmond would let Ray and Denis stay up there. Paul and I would have some privacy and she wouldn't be alone.

When I got back nobody was waiting outside but Paul was watching for me from her window. He waved and I brought in my bags and locked up the truck. First I bagged everything in the fridge and hauled it all up to the cans by the garage. Then I scrubbed it out and had a go at the counters.

My cupboards were mostly empty except for a bunch of non-food things. More tools, papers and parts catalogues. I moved all that stuff into one cupboard and wiped down the insides of the rest. Then I put away the clean dishes and washed out the coffee maker.

By then my one hour warning had passed so I took the candy and the keys up around to Mrs. Desmond's door and knocked. Paul answered and stepped out in a cloud of cigarette smoke.

"You're not burning my house down are you?"

"Not yet," he laughed as he put his arms around me. "Thank you for finding him. Bee says that you never took her rent and always got her groceries for the past four years."

I shrugged. "I didn't need the money and she never remembered anyway. I'm grateful to have her to keep an eye on the place. It let me wander around to find you."

"She doesn't think she would have made it long enough to find me if you hadn't taken care of her," he said quietly. "She has quite the personality ... not many would have the patience."

"I feel bad for being away so much ... I worried about her when I was gone so long," I tightened my hold on him for a moment and let him go then I gave him the bags of candy. "She loves to hand this stuff out ... the little kids will start before it gets dark. I usually come up and help her out with it but you'll have to stand in for me tonight."

He looked in the bags. "It's Halloween ... I'd forgotten."

"She can't tell Alina we're here," I told him. "And if my father turns up tell him you're Mrs. Desmond's grandson doing a favour for the owner. Maybe cleaning out and updating the basement to rent out? He can't know either because he'll tell Alina. His picture is on the TV unit downstairs. Don't answer the phone or clear the messages on the machine ... Alina will know I've been home if she can leave another one."

Paul nodded.

"In ten days Damian will move on the compound and four days after that I will leave," I said quietly. Paul's jaw stiffened briefly. "We can't interfere with the path that brought us here. In two weeks he could start looking for me again so we need to decide if we're hitting the road for a while or what.

"We can take the cash and stay in hotels for a while if we have to but I don't think she can manage all that travel."

"I know," he said. "I've been considering that too."

"Did you ever send anyone here to look for me?"

He shook his head. "I just waited for you to come back."

"Okay. I'm pushing it ... I have to sleep now and I've lost track of

175

the time." I put the truck and house keys in his hand. "Can you come down in a bit and check that I made it to the bed?"

"Yes," he paused. "Bee wants to talk to you."

"You told her everything I told you?"

"She thinks that things are more complicated than that," his stare was hard, challenging. "Important things … maybe left out?"

"I told you everything I can Paul."

"But not everything," he said.

"I have to sleep … nothing else of consequence," I yawned.

He studied me for a moment. Then he put the bags down on the porch.

"I'll take you downstairs and settle you in."

I was glad he did. I didn't remember making it much past the kitchen.

Paul slept next to me when I woke. The clock said seven. It didn't matter much what day it was. I headed to the bathroom and started the tub filling then down to the kitchen. Ray was in there reading the paper. Denis was still sleeping on the living room floor.

"Morning sunshine," I yawned to him. "What day is it?"

"Hi Kiddo. The second. You slept through two nights … hungry?"

"Soon. I want a bath first," Ray had coffee on so I went to look in the fridge. Just the milk and a couple of six packs that I wouldn't have put in there.

"Bee's been feeding us," Ray explained.

"She would enjoy that … you're all going to look like me. She can bake up a storm."

"I feel it already," Ray said putting his hand on his stomach. "Anywhere decent to go for a run around here?"

"Let me get dressed. You can take me for breakfast and I'll show you where you can burn off the cookies."

First I took him up the hill to the dam where there were trails that connected the small lakes and then to the dirt roads under the power lines for something hillier. I'd only ever run dirt bikes up and down the power lines but Ray thought running there would be better exercise than the flat trails provided nobody wiped out on the uneven ground.

We went to one of the restaurants along the old highway for breakfast then to one of the grocery stores in the other end of town. I didn't want to go to the one in the mall by my house because they knew me. I would let Tony keep delivering to Mrs. Desmond and Paul could tell him the same story I'd asked him to tell my father.

Paul and Denis were just going up to Mrs. Desmond's when we got back so they helped bring the groceries downstairs before they went to see her. I made myself a salmon sandwich and salad and sat in the living room to eat then I got a blanket and pillow from my bed to try and get a nap on the couch. Even after two days sleeping it would take a bit to get my energy back. It didn't help that I was starting to need more rest.

I lay with my eyes closed for a while. The door opened quietly and Paul came in.

"Do you want to come upstairs now? Bee still wants to talk to you."

"Hey Paul," I said as I rolled back over. "I was worried you might have forgotten about me."

"Never ... maybe you should be sleeping in the bed. This can't be good for your back."

I sat up yawning. "How are you doing? Do you need a rest too?"

"Bee kicks us out by nine. Ray and Denis have been going out after we leave but I've just been coming down here waiting for you to wake up. Come on," he said helping me up. "She's waiting upstairs for us."

Mrs. Desmond's main floor was much less smoky than it had been two days ago. Denis smoked out of the wind and on the path between the garage and the house. Mrs. Desmond never smoked much anyway.

"Afternoon Mrs. Desmond," I said to her as I kissed her cheek. "These boys aren't too much of a nuisance I hope."

"None at all," she told me. "They seem to have turned out okay without me."

I went over to the cupboard and pulled out her prescriptions. The number of pill bottles had doubled so I started going through them. I pulled out six that hadn't been there the last time I had seen her.

"Six of these are from six different doctors in the past month," I told her. "Three are for the same thing. You're not taking all of them are you?"

"No idea what you're talking about dear," she said.

I gestured to Ray to come over and look at them.

"Remember we agreed that unless you're having trouble breathing or have chest pains you call Alina first?" She just smiled back. "Do I have to go yell at the cab company again?"

Paul was laughing quietly at me now so I threw a towel at him and picked up her phone to call her doctor's office.

"Hello, can I get someone in to see Dr. Keller this week?" I waited as she checked. "It's for Beatrice Desmond ... she has a dozen bottles of pills here and I have no idea what they're for."

"Tell me about my brother," Mrs. Desmond said.

I covered the phone. "Which one?"

"Your mate," she said loudly as the receptionist suggested twenty

177

minutes.

"Eeww," I said to Mrs. Desmond but I had uncovered the phone. I looked over at Paul, he was glaring at her. "No, sorry, two conversations at once. Twenty is fine."

She said Friday at ten-twenty and would the locum be okay, Dr. Keller was away.

"Yes," I told her then, "wait; is that the same locum as last time?"

She told me yes.

"Anna?" Mrs. Desmond said sharply.

I covered the phone. "I'm going to kill him." I glanced at Paul; but he was distracted by the noise Denis was making coming in and hadn't heard me.

Then to the receptionist. "That's fine; he's not an idiot like the locum before him."

"Anna ... don't talk about the doctors like that," Ray mumbled next to me, he was still going through the bottles of pills but the receptionist was laughing. She had heard that before.

I quickly covered the phone as the towel hit me in the back of the head. "You never met him."

Then she wanted my name.

"Rachel Lund. I'm her grand-daughter. You have me down as next of kin."

Paul rolled his eyes. Another name for Anna and the receptionist wanted to know if Anna should still be listed as well.

"Yes, Anna is my cousin and should also still be on her file ... she married recently, its Richards now, not Creed."

She confirmed the time for me and said good-bye.

"Ray, can you tell me what I need to ask about these when I take her in?"

"Sure Anna," then he whispered. "She shouldn't be living alone ... too much of some of these could be bad news."

"I know. I've been all she has for the past few years. She's outlived her family. She just forgets to take them at all when I'm not here. Getting new prescriptions without me is something she hasn't done before."

I sighed. Mrs. Desmond was starting to fuss with getting more baking in front of Denis and Paul had come to see what Ray and I were whispering about.

"At least her medical records show me as next of kin now," I said while I leaned back against Paul. He put his arms around my middle. It was sad to think about it. "I can make arrangements for her when the time comes. I don't know what to do now. I can't leave her alone again."

"She won't be alone again," Paul said quietly. "Don't worry about it … we'll make sure that family is always with her now."

"Thanks," I said and wiped my eyes.

"Mrs. Desmond," I said loudly. "Can Ray and Denis stay in the rooms on the top floor? It's much nicer than my living room."

"Can you imagine the talk?" she asked me. "Unmarried with two single men in my home? And we are on the top floor dear."

I pointed upstairs. "You have two bedrooms upstairs with beds in them and you expect family to sleep on the floor? There will be no talk."

She sighed in defeat so I went upstairs to see what sort of shape the rooms were in. All the lights worked and other than a bit of dust and some boxes of things she must have forgot were up there the rooms were fine. It was just a finished attic so the roof sloped steeply on either side. There was spare bedding in the closet so I pulled it out for Ray and Denis and took it upstairs.

"You just have to make the beds up," I told them when I got back to the table. "I hauled up the bedding. If you're going out in the evening then you're still welcome to my floor. She'll hurt you if you wake her up sneaking in late."

"Thanks Anna," Denis said. Mrs. Desmond had put the plate of baking in front of him and was heating up the oven to make something to reload it with.

"Pace yourself," I whispered to him. "I showed Ray a couple of places you can go for a run. There's a lake with a trail around it too that I forgot about. I'll show you on the map later. The secret is to keep showing interest in what's on the plate but eat slowly. Otherwise you'll just get round."

"Now you tell me," he laughed.

Ray and Denis went upstairs to get their rooms ready and I sat next to Paul while Mrs. Desmond finished putting a couple of pans into the oven. Then she put on the kettle for tea.

"My son says that you can read the family like me," she said.

I looked at Paul. I wasn't sure if I should be talking about it but he nodded and tilted his head to her as she sat down.

"I suppose," I answered. I didn't really want to talk about it because I had only a rough idea what I could say. "I didn't realize it was impolite."

"Well now you do," she said. "What made you want to try?"

I thought about it. "When Damian's men came for me I could tell that they were similar to him in some way but I didn't know how I knew. I guess they smelled the same … maybe tasted? Neither I guess. I don't know what to call it."

Ray and Denis had come back downstairs.

"Paul said you claim to be able to see who their mother is as well," she said.

I felt like every time I opened my mouth I was offending someone. Paul put his hand on my leg under the table and gently squeezed. He didn't let go. It was a warning, but I already had a good idea what not to say.

"Yes," I told her. "But if I don't know who she was ... I can't make a match."

"I never knew such a thing was possible ... whose did you find?"

Paul squeezed a little harder.

"The third of Damian's men who came for me," I said quietly to the table again. I didn't see the harm in talking about one of Damian's dead men. The only person at the table he was a relation to was me. I took a quick look over at Paul and he turned his head away. He'd suspected that's what I was doing by the pond and would have been happier if he didn't have to hear it.

"How do you do it then?" she asked.

"I put what ever you call it about them here." I pointed to the spot under my upper lip. "Then I take away everything that is similar. It takes a few minutes. When I compared what I remembered of Damian and the dead man all that was left was me."

I made a face. "It was dirty and angry but it was unmistakably me. There's a dark poisonous cloud over Damian's line now. It must have been a part of me then."

Paul had relaxed his grip on my leg by then so I took his hand in both of mine. He started to pull it away from me but then changed his mind. I was surprised he even stayed at the table but then talking about the man by the pond was probably less bad than talking about Denis. I didn't want to embarrass anyone else after seeing how much Ray didn't like me talking about it.

"How many are similar to Paul?" she asked. I looked over at him and he nodded. He was looking down now but squeezed back when I squeezed his hand.

"Four," I told her.

"And Ray?" she asked. I looked at Ray and he nodded too.

"Three ... and there were six that I could read but were unrelated to any of the others."

"And my other brother. What does he call himself?"

"Pilot," I still didn't want to say anymore than I had to.

"And what did Pilot tell you?"

I sat quietly.

"Paul says he has told you everything."

"Not everything dear," she insisted.

"Who are my loyalties bound more tightly too?" I asked her. "My line or my mate's?"

Her eyes narrowed.

"I see what you're trying to do," she said. "You are bound to your line ... until you have found one of your mates. Then you are bound to his."

Damn, I thought. It would be easier for Paul to understand my silence if his father told him that I couldn't speak.

"Paul's line wants you to break your silence ... so you must."

I thought about what I had to say to protect Alina and her baby. Could I stop anyone in the family from hurting her or killing her to keep Damian from bringing another soldier into his family? Could I choose between her life and Paul's if I had to?

"I know enough to complete my task. There are others with parts to play that are just as important as mine. I know enough to stay out of their way and not make their jobs any more difficult than they already are. Otherwise I won't say anymore unless I need help or one of the others does."

Paul took his hand from me and crossed his arms. His father was openly glaring at me.

"When did she become so blatantly disobedient Paul?" she asked.

He took a minute to answer. I could tell from his tone that I had stepped in it again.

"Recently," he said angrily.

"Paul ... how is this any different than if the Colonel sent you off somewhere? There would be nothing you could even tell me to reassure me. You'd know what you had to do and enough to keep from endangering anyone else but you would probably never know the big picture."

"It's completely different," he said, he was almost growling.

"You're right," I admitted. "This is completely different. You already know what I'm going to do Paul. He's going to come for me and I'm going to kill him. I'm going to cut away whatever ties him to his long line of lives so he never hurts anyone in the family ever again. And along the way I have to figure out whatever it is that gets us both killed while there is still time to keep it from happening. I know that's not such a big deal to you but it is to me because I really will be starting over on the other side. You won't."

I stood up and started for the door. I hadn't looked at anyone but Paul since I started my rant.

"So I'm sorry if I have no time to fuss with what anyone else is doing because I honestly don't really care. I have enough to deal with in the next few months."

And with that I left and went back to my couch downstairs. I lay down and pulled the blanket up over my head. Either Paul would be right behind me or he would be a good long while so after half an hour I decided he wouldn't come down any time soon. I took a handful of cash from the box then I put on my coat and grabbed an apple. I quietly left through the back gate. Unless Paul was watching from Mrs. Desmond's laundry room they wouldn't see me in the dark.

My first stop was the convenience store a couple of blocks away. I bought a couple of hot dogs and two of their prepaid cell phones. Then I headed the dozen or so blocks in the other direction to another convenience store and bought two more.

I hated not knowing how much I could trust Pilot but I hated keeping things from Paul even more. Pilot had hinted that it wasn't past Paul to try and stop Alina from having Damian's child like Damian would try and stop me from having Paul's. It was just better to keep him in the dark for now. I would tell Ray to go to Alina when the time was right but for now everything had to continue just as it was.

I let myself in the back gate and locked it behind me then I went inside. I was still hungry from the jump and wanted some real food. Paul waited at the kitchen table. I stopped for a moment to see if he would start on me right away and when he didn't I kicked off my boots and took them down the hall to the closet to put them away with my raincoat. I had left chicken in the fridge for my dinner so I put it in.

Paul still hadn't said anything so I took the phones to the table and started unpacking them. He watched me for a minute then he sighed and started helping me get them out of their boxes. I plugged in two to charge on the counter. The other two I plugged in at the table.

"Hungry?" I asked Paul.

"Yes."

So I put on enough rice for two. The two big pieces of chicken in the oven would be enough. I pulled the leftover salad out of the fridge.

"Beer?" I offered while I still had my head in the fridge.

"Please."

I poured it in a glass and put it on the table then I sat down across from him to watch the little charge bars light up over and over on the front of my phone.

"Bee knows you pretty well," he said finally. "She's known you a lot longer this time than I have. She says I'm not going to get past your stubbornness."

I nodded.

"For the record I'm somewhat hurt. If my father hadn't told me to back off about it I would have been quite embarrassed by your behaviour in front of him. Have I done something to make you not trust me?"

"No. This isn't about trust between me and you."

"But it's still a trust thing?" he asked.

"Yes."

"You don't trust someone else … Ray's father?"

I nodded again. "You and Ray don't know if I can trust him. I

182

didn't like him. He treated me like a child which really rubbed me the wrong way. Like you tell a child there are no monsters under the bed … or maybe you do to keep them from wandering off on their own during the night. Maybe that's all I really am. I don't know if he said what he did to scare me or to reassure me … maybe I'm the monster under the bed."

I reached across the table to hold his hand as the rice started to boil. I sighed and got up to turn it down and set the timer. When I sat back down I took his hand.

"I can spin your ring right around your finger now," I showed him. "I couldn't do that before I left. Our daughter only said my trip would be hard on you. I didn't realize what that would mean.

"He made me like this Paul. I doubt myself a lot. What parts of me are really me and what parts are his programming? Are you going to like who I am when this is over and the pieces he gave me are gone?"

"I fell in love with you before any of those things changed in you and I haven't stopped," he said softly looking into my eyes. "I will love whatever you are left with when this is over."

I stood up and leaned across the table to kiss him.

"My love for you hasn't changed either," I whispered in his ear before I sat back down. "It's because of that I'm doing things this way."

We sat silently at the table for a while.

"You know we haven't had a meal alone together since that last night after Sturgis … before you came and found me."

"Yes," I said. "I've missed it."

"Me too."

"This time next year there will be a highchair at the table."

"Yes," he agreed laughing.

We talked through dinner. The easy humour filled conversation we had been so good at during our first encounters. Before he moved on and I found him again. We talked about the bikes I was fixing up and the work we both had no real plans to go back to. It was a huge relief to me that it was still so effortless to like each other so much when the things around us weren't completely crazy and distracting. Compared to before I met him things were completely upside down and backwards but as things went now they were unremarkable and that was welcome. Very welcome.

After dinner I cleaned up the dishes and Paul took the phones up to Ray and Denis then he brought them back down to get their gear.

"I hope the beds are okay … Alina and her friend had those rooms when they lived with me in college. Before I took in Mrs. Desmond and moved downstairs. You can move her boxes into the spare room on the main floor or into the shed in the back. It's the same key as for my door."

183

"Thanks Anna," Ray said. "So what's up with the phones ... I thought you said to keep them off."

"Keep the ones from home off. We don't want them traced. You'll need to buy cards for more minutes. If we're going to be here for a while we need to start being hidden now."

"Makes sense," Paul agreed.

"The truck needs to go ... if one of Damian's men drives by to see your truck with California plates on it then we might as well sit on the front steps and wait for him. It'll fit in the garage but all the stuff in there needs to go. I'm going to buy a mini van or something tomorrow that Mrs. Desmond can get in and out of. At least we can park that out front. Can one of you drive me around to take care of that?"

Denis said he would.

"Paul, I hate to ask this since you don't like that I was a crook ... but would you agree to getting alternate ID?"

"How alternate?" he asked.

"Alternate enough to do time in a Canadian prison just for having them ... but they'll be good enough to pass pretty much any check the authorities want to run on them. No guarantees of course but they'll be the best you can get."

I got out my Rachel passport and driver's license and my legitimate Anna ID to show him.

"No difference," I said. "These are relatively cheap to do; it's the back end records with the government that are expensive. If you want to get in a bar at seventeen the driver's license is enough. If you get pulled over and they run the card you'll be in trouble without electronic records to match. I have a few sets and they've always held up. I wasn't lying to Iverson about that."

Paul looked unhappy about it.

"Don't tell me you never worked under another name before."

"Of course I have," he said shaking his head. "But those were legal."

"These are legal ... ish. I'll take care of it if you give me the go ahead. You don't have to use them but do you really want to find yourself needing them and be kicking yourself for telling me no?"

"She's right Paul," Ray said. Denis nodded in agreement.

"Alright," Paul said finally. "How much is it going to cost?"

"I got it covered," I told him. Then I got out my new phone and punched in the code to hide my number and dialled Kenny.

"It's Bitch Seat," I said when he answered. Denis started to giggle so I punched him in the arm and he shut up. "I have some friends looking for work for a couple of weeks ... do you have anything for them?"

"How many?" he asked.

"Three."

There was a pause. "Yeah, I could use them."

"They'll appreciate it. So how many klicks have you put on that piece of shit you're riding?"

"Forty thousand," he said.

"You need a woman to ride instead," I laughed. "Riding your bike that much is a fetish."

"I have six," he laughed back. "Let's do lunch. Maybe I'll get lucky and make it seven."

"Go pound sand," I told him and hung up.

"That's it?" Paul asked.

"I'll take the payment and your pictures to him tomorrow … they'll be ready seven days from today."

"Come on, I'll take the passport pictures now and the driver's ones tomorrow. Think about doing something different with your hair for those." I put a new storage card into the camera for the pictures to make sure that there was nothing traceable on it and took a couple of each of them in front of a pull down back drop I had in my spare room.

"How much is this going to cost?" Paul asked when I was done.

"I didn't make my dirty money stealing cars … we were into documents for a while. Paid a lot better. My friend still does it. I have enough."

"But how much?" Paul insisted.

"Forty big ones," I said quietly. "You're doing me a favour … that money has dirty written all over it and it'll be someone else's problem after lunch tomorrow."

Paul put his hands on his face and went into the living room.

"Was that Kenny you called?" Ray asked.

I nodded.

"And why do you call yourself Bitch Seat?" Denis was laughing again.

"Back seat of the bike. He would double me in to whatever we were taking … no jacket or helmet. They got in the way when I went under the steering wheel to start it. Remember to do something different with your hair tomorrow … it's wasted effort if we have the same pictures for both."

They said good night and left so I went and joined Paul in front of the TV. "Some of the guys got in real trouble working shipments to and from the US. Drugs going south … guns coming up north. Kenny and I stayed out of that but his brother is still in jail. I was very lucky to get away with the small amount of trouble I got in. Kenny still does favours on the side with the ID.

"I don't want to get into the how's it any different than when the Colonel gives you what you need to do your job argument again. I know

185

my way is wrong … some of the money will go into the hands of people who do some really bad things," I sighed. "The people setting up the ID's are probably the same ones who make them for your Colonel anyway. It's all I can offer to help."

He sighed then he put his arms around me and leaned back on the couch. "So I get to meet Kenny tomorrow?"

"No, you don't. If you're coming you're going to be out of sight or he won't meet me. You'll have to stay out of sight or he'll leave and we won't get a second chance. It'll be crowded so you can keep an eye on things from a distance without him noticing."

"Can you come back up to see Bee tomorrow?" he said eventually. "What I said in the truck … we've been working on it but it's hard to practice on each other … men who have their lines set. She said there's something different about yours and she wants to test us by seeing if we can figure it out."

"Sure … I guess. Did she say what?"

"No," Paul said kissing my head. "That's why it's a test."

"I like Mrs. Desmond just fine … I guess I'm still warming up to Bee," I sighed. "Any etiquette I need to know for that?"

"Only that you have to give permission to anyone but Ray," he answered. "She's somewhat annoyed that you know so many of the rules … my father has always applied them at his convenience but he knows he can't argue when someone else sticks to them."

"I'm always making things difficult," I said. "You know … I've never had a man here in my bed …"

Paul laughed. "Come on then … I can't let a record like that stand."

Chapter 37

Paul left early for a run with Ray and Denis as I was getting up. They had settled on the run around the lake. I suggested the trails up by the dam were better shelter from the rain under the trees but they didn't see a problem. All it would take was one run in the rain to figure out they might need to get some proper outdoor wear. It was maybe six degrees above freezing and once the rain soaked into their clothes they wouldn't warm up for days.

I was finishing my toast and scrambled eggs at the table when Paul barged through the kitchen dripping and swearing about the weather.

"You want to get some proper rain gear while we're out today?" I asked his back as he stomped down the hall to the shower to warm up. He didn't answer and I wondered if Ray or Denis won their race to Mrs. Desmond's shower. Hopefully their language was better or they would get an earful from her. I put on coffee for him and went to the spare room to count up the money for Kenny. Paul had only seen the clean money box that had been the change from breaking the larger "dirty" bills.

Paul was getting out of the shower as I finished getting the parcel ready. It was wrapped in puffy bundles of tissue at the bottom of a plain blue gift bag. As an extra touch I added a birthday card in an envelope for the data card and crammed it into the top.

"Warmed up?" I asked him.

"You were right," he grumbled.

"Coffee's hot. There's a good place for outdoor gear near where we're headed later. If you're going to attempt that again you'll be a lot happier in something that keeps the freezing rain out. Are you eating upstairs or down?"

"Upstairs I guess if you're finished."

There was a knock at the door and I let Denis in.

"Beat Ray to the shower?" I asked.

"Yeah," Denis laughed. "He can be a real pussy about the weather … you got coffee on? I'm not old lady enough for tea."

"Sure Denis. You know where it is."

Ray joined us twenty minutes later. "Bee is baking something for breakfast. Do you know anywhere to get some rain gear Anna?"

"A couple of good places in the mall we're headed to later. Come on, let's get your mugs in front of the camera again."

They were still warming their hands up around their coffees as they came along to the spare room again. I had changed the backdrop and the lights a bit. I also had them sign their new names in the signature boxes cut from passport applications, they went into the greeting card with the data card containing the photos.

"It's going to be easier for you if we have the signatures in your own writing … you'll never practice enough to forge someone else's writing." I explained.

"How's this work today?" Paul asked as we headed back to the kitchen.

"You've never dropped a wad of cash to a slimy ex to pay for forged ID?"

"Ex?" Denis rolled his eyes. "This keeps getting better."

"In his own mind at least," I told them. "You'll drop me off a couple of blocks from the mall at around noon. There's a food court inside. I'll get a seat at the lower section in the south end. You can find yourselves a spot with a decent view at the other end. Get some lunch and try not to stand out. He'll be there about one-thirty."

"Sounds easy enough," Paul said.

"Here's the hard part," I turned my attention to Paul. "You have to

187

promise that no matter what you see you'll stay in your seat and save what you have to say to me for later."

"Is he going to be armed or something?" he asked. "I'm not putting you in danger for some cards ... not worth it."

"Nothing like that Paul. He needs to worry about me snapping him in two ... promise you'll be silent and stay put?"

"I have to promise without knowing why?"

"I guess not," I sat back in my chair.

"Kenny doesn't trust anyone when it comes to his side business. I don't trust him either. He humiliated me once and even though I didn't turn on him when I got caught with the car he took me to steal he still thinks I might have it in for him.

"I'm going to be checking him for a wire. I'm going to have my hands on him, in close like we get along really well. It has to look easy and comfortable or it just comes off like I'm trying to get a cheap thrill. He's going to be doing the same thing.

"I prefer a public place so that's how it goes. If I'm not satisfied I won't offer the bag and if he isn't he won't take it."

"He better not be satisfied," Paul grumbled. "I'll stay put but I don't like this at all."

Paul dropped me off a couple of blocks from the mall so that I walked past a gas station on the way there stopping for cigarettes and a free book of matches. The clerk looked at my stomach and gave me a disapproving look so I just smiled and ignored her. I would give the cigarettes to Denis. I just needed the matchbook.

When I got to the mall I made a couple of small purchases on the way to the restroom. In the stall I took out the matchbook and a pen and wrote inside Mark Turner 34 John Lund 32 Daniel Webb 28 with heights and weights and closed it back up. They were the names and ages for Ray, Paul, and Denis in the order their pictures were on the data card from the camera. Kenny would give them some valid address. The matches went back into my pocket.

I entered the food court from the south end not looking up to where Paul and the others would be, ignoring them. I had no idea if they ignored me. Not likely, but sitting up top at the other end they were hopefully far away to avoid attention. Kenny would have spotted me in the mall already and would be watching to make sure I was alone. I knew I would be waiting for a while so I got some tea and a sandwich and hung my coat on the chair behind me. It was only one.

Kenny was late. It was twenty to two when I heard his voice beside me. I had almost fallen asleep in my chair.

"Anna ... surprised to see you come crawling back." Sounded like he'd reconsidered the odd proposal he'd given me a couple of months before. I looked up and he was smiling at me so I stood up to hug him.

"Only because I have to," I told him as I put one arm around his back under his coat and ran the other up his chest. I thought I felt the strap of a shoulder holster with my forearm as I felt his back but I wasn't sure. His hand was on my back and as I finished feeling his chest he skipped his hand under mine and grabbed the front of my bra while I was close enough for his open coat to conceal it. Then he kissed my cheek closer to my mouth than he ever had when we'd done this before and his hand dropped to my stomach.

"I always knew you were easy," he said.

"Mmm. Just keep telling yourself that," I mumbled to him then I threw my head back and laughed.

"Buy me lunch," he said. He hung his coat up on the other chair at the table. I picked up the blue gift bag as he put his arm around me and took me to one of the food counters.

"So who's Mr. Right?" he asked as he dropped his hand down to my butt. "One of those three gorillas up top?"

"No idea."

He ordered. I paid. We waited.

"Doesn't matter," he said. "You're not the only one who didn't come alone … there won't be any trouble as long as they stay put."

That was a new move for Kenny. He and I used to be just steps in the middle for these transactions and I wondered what he had gotten himself into. Who had he made trouble for that required him to go out with protection or worse yet what kind of people might he be trying to prove himself to. He had his arm back around my waist and stuck his nose in my ear.

"Let's see how strong his stomach is," he said as he moved his mouth closer to mine. I stepped back a bit and watched his eyes as I slowly ran the tip of my tongue around just inside my top lip. He lowered his eyes to watch.

"Yeah … you like that," I whispered to him and slipped the arm I had used to feel his chest around him. I hesitated momentarily when my hand brushed past a gun under his arm but I pushed myself in closer until my hand was on his back. Then I kissed his cheek and started working my way to his ear.

"What the hell Kenny," I whispered as quietly as I could; my lips out of sight from whoever he had come with. "Should I take the bag and walk away?"

"Mm mm," he whispered. "We'll always be good at this … solid."

I hoped he meant our deal was solid. If he walked away with the money never to be seen again we'd have to make due with identities that Damian could trace.

He made me carry his tray to the table for him and I had to wait while he ate. Then he wiped his mouth and started patting his pockets.

"Damn … I think I left my smokes in the car."

I sighed and offered the package I bought. He took one and put it in his mouth then he stood up.

"Sorry I missed her birthday," I said as I gave him the gift bag. He took it. "I'm terrible with sizes … there's a gift receipt in with the card in case she needs to exchange it."

"Thanks … she always liked you."

By she he meant him. Then he started rooting around in his pants pockets. "Got a light?"

I gave him the matches and he put them in his pocket.

"Don't call me again," he said as he walked off. As I watched him leave four men got up from another table just a few feet away and joined him. They disappeared into the mall.

I finished my cold tea and stayed at the table. Kenny would be out of the mall and on his way as quick as he could. He wouldn't want to be caught carrying all that cash. That plus the photos and signatures would get him in a lot of trouble.

Paul came and sat with me. "Ray and Denis are making sure they left," he said.

"Paul … tell them to come back. That could have been really bad. Kenny had a gun and he knew you were up there. Those four are probably armed too."

"They'll be fine," Paul said.

I wasn't happy about it. "I'm sorry … Kenny never took it that far before. He was trying to push you because he saw you all watching me. I thought I felt a gun on him … I had to get close to him at the counter again to be sure. He was armed. Two of those guys with him were in to some nasty things with his brother. Please call them back. Kenny is going to get as far away from here with that stuff as he can."

Paul sighed and called Ray and told him to return right away.

"Wasn't there another way to do that?" He asked. "I really want to straighten him out now."

"You're sweet," I kissed his cheek. "So would I. The alternative is undressing for each other on some dirt road in the middle of nowhere. That's why I prefer the way we did it."

"At least he wouldn't have touched you," Paul said. Then he reached in my pocket and took out the cigarettes. "Not again Anna."

"No … part of the exchange. Denis can have the rest. The cigarettes are a prop … a reason to give him the matchbook. I'd written instructions inside it."

"Are we going to have to do this again in a week?" he asked as Ray and Denis joined us.

I shook my head. "That will be a lot easier … but you still can't straighten him out for today."

"I still don't like it."

I sat out in the mall while they got their rain gear, then we headed home. Denis said he would take me car shopping the next day after their run which was fine. I needed a nap before dinner so when we got in Paul and I headed downstairs for some time alone. I needed Paul for a while to get Kenny's attention out of my mind. So did Paul.

Chapter 38

I didn't make it back upstairs to Mrs. Desmond's for her test until after dinner. Even though my fridge and cupboards were full Denis wanted takeout so they ordered and I cooked for myself. My time at Paul's had turned me around from fast food. Denis on the other hand was still treating every night like shore leave. Paul said he wasn't coming home completely drunk any more like the first night but he was still coming home with women's names and phone numbers in his pockets.

Mrs. Desmond wanted to see how well they could test my line through my lives to see how strongly it was connected to me. Or something like that. Other than what Paul had explained to me in the truck I had little understanding of how their lines actually worked. Pilot had told me that Paul's would be strong like a chain. Mine much weaker. Anyone not like us wouldn't have one at all.

When I got in she was still working on the dishes. I'd put in a dishwasher upstairs but she still preferred to wash by hand. Denis was outside having a cigarette and Paul and Ray were watching the news laughing and trying to remember if they had heard any of it. Most of it was local or Canadian so it was almost all new to them anyway. I dried and put away for her and made sure that the leftovers were in the fridge.

When we were finished she sent Paul outside with Denis. She was going to have them come in one at a time to see how they would do.

"What's going to happen?" I asked her.

She shushed me. I sighed. Mrs. Desmond was fine but Bee made me feel in no uncertain terms that family children like me should be seen and not heard. Whatever being a child meant.

She closed the kitchen curtains and told me to stand up.

"Ray," she said. "There is something different about this one. That's all I will tell you. I just want you to tell me what's there … you can check for attachment just don't test it. Understand?"

"Yes," Ray said. He got up and stood close in front of me then he held his right hand over my chest. Paul had said that I had to give permission to anyone other than Ray so he didn't ask and I didn't say anything. His other hand went around my upper arm. I didn't get the feeling that it was necessary. More that he was comfortable with me and didn't have anything else to do with that hand.

"I'm going to start now Anna," he said. "You won't feel anything."

He was telling me, not asking so I nodded.

His fingers were spread and they moved gently like they were handling whatever his distant gaze was seeing. Then he looked a little puzzled and held his hand still.

"She has two lines," he said.

"Yes," Bee said. "Tell me about them."

His hand moved a bit more. "One is soft … not attached to her. It stays close to hers though. When I get near it moves closer … almost hiding behind hers," he smiled then. "It's the baby's. But why doesn't the baby have it?"

"It won't move into the baby until just before he is born," Bee said. "If the mother were to die now the child would not be seen again. It will loosen … separate from hers and move into the baby only when his birth is imminent. The mother can feel that sometimes but of course she doesn't know what it is and is usually too caught up in labour to make much of it."

"What else do you notice?"

Ray's hand moved a bit more. He looked a little confused.

"Anna's isn't what I expected … it's stronger. There is almost something male to it. Just a bit." Ray said. "It's something I've never felt in a mate. I don't know what to make of it."

"Yes," Bee said as Ray put his hand down. "Curious, isn't it? Have you done much of this before Ray? You're quite good."

Ray nodded, almost shyly. "A long time ago."

"Be receptive to teaching any others who wish to learn," she told him. "Go get Denis now … you may stay as long as you don't interfere with Denis' test."

We waited for Ray to come back with Denis.

"When you said my line was tangled … did you mean with Paul's?" I asked her. "Is that why the baby's line is in me?"

"No dear," she said. "Now be quiet."

I crossed my arms. What if I said no thank you, I thought. Like yesterday when I wouldn't talk about Pilot. I was thinking about doing that now … but Paul needed this for our daughter so I would let them do it. What Ray found was interesting but Bee said he was pretty good at it so I didn't expect Denis or Paul to find as much.

When they came back Ray sat down next to Bee. She told Denis the same thing that she had told Ray.

"Anna," Denis asked. "Do I have your permission?"

192

"Yes Denis," I told him. The way he asked seemed awful formal but I guessed that was the way things like this were done. Mrs. Desmond had always been firm about etiquette even before I knew she was Paul's father.

Denis put his hand over my chest. He didn't stand as close as Ray did and kept his other hand at his side. He quickly found that there were two lines in me but didn't figure out why as Ray had.

"Do they seem the same?" Bee prompted him.

"No ... one is stronger ... firmer."

"Are they both attached to her? Don't test their strength ... just feel for attachment."

"No. The stronger one is attached."

"Please get Paul now Denis, then come and take a seat."

While he was getting Paul she spoke to Ray. "What Denis found was the most I had expected from all of you. You did well."

Denis and Paul came in and Denis sat down. I leaned back on the counter now since my legs were getting tired. Wandering around the mall was more exercise than I was used to these days and I wanted to soak in the tub and put my feet up.

"Paul," Bee said. "Something is different with your mate from what you have seen in the others. You may be more sensitive to it than they were ... remember just feel what is there. Do not test its attachment. You already know how to do that from these two."

Paul stood close as Ray had and put his left hand on the counter and his right over my chest. Suddenly I felt an unwelcome pressure in my ribs and I quickly brought my right hand up under his, blocking it. Paul drew his hand back in surprise and rubbed his palm on his leg.

"What the hell was that?" he asked.

"Anna dear," Bee said. "What did you do?"

"Pressure ... it was intrusive," I tried to explain. "I didn't like how it felt."

"You shouldn't have felt anything," Bee said. "But I haven't seen this done with a mated pair when there is a child ... what did you feel Paul?"

"I got a shock," he said as he looked at his palm, wiggling his fingers.

"Sorry Paul," I apologized. "I just wanted to push your hand away."

"Perhaps you should have asked permission first Paul," Bee reminded him. "She has good reason to be protective."

I could see understanding in Ray's face. We both realized now that I was protecting the baby. It was an intrusion when there was no permission, even with Paul.

"Okay," Paul said sheepishly. "Anna, may I?"

"Yes Paul." I said looking up at him, watching his face as he put his hand back up and started again. It felt much different. Wonderful in fact. Well, better than that even. More like something I would feel in my bed with Paul but extremely focused in my chest. I took a quick couple of gasps of air.

"Jesus Paul," I whispered. "Make it quick or I'm going to need a smoke."

"Awkward," Denis muttered but Paul ignored me.

I turned my head away from them and tried to think about something else but it wasn't working. My cheeks were hot with embarrassment, breathing deepening. It had all happened in the space of a couple of seconds. I could feel exactly where he was focusing in me. It was like every night we had spent together getting rolled into one.

"Anna, compose yourself," Bee hissed at me.

"You go compose yourself," I growled at her and I put my hands behind my back. My right hand went around the fingers of my left and I started to squeeze as I tried to distract myself from the intense pleasure with discomfort.

The pleasure started to decrease as I squeezed my fingers even harder. I closed my eyes and relaxed my breathing trying to keep strength in my right hand.

"It's my daughter's," Paul said quietly. His voice sounded further and further away. "She was protecting it … it stays so close to hers."

Bee said something. I wasn't really listening. The pleasure in my chest was building again so I put more force into my grip and something popped in my left hand cancelling it out.

"Hers …" Paul said. "Isn't all hers, is it?"

Bee didn't say anything.

"It's like there's something stuck to it … through it. Making it stronger than it would be on its own."

I risked opening my eyes and looked up at him. His brow was knotted together, little beads of sweat on it from the effort of what he was doing. His mouth opened a bit; quickly a couple of times like he was trying to say something he didn't know the words for. The pleasure in my chest grew again and I reacted by tightening my grip on my fingers even more. Another small pop, something shifted in my hand and the pleasure subsided again.

Then suddenly the pleasure disappeared replaced by a huge feeling of more invasive pressure. He was doing something in there he shouldn't. He would damage me … take something if he kept it up. I released my hand and brought my right around to block him with my palm like before. The pain in my left hand now that the pleasure in my chest was gone startled me and I felt real power surge in my right as I thrust it at his chest, not his palm.

He reacted instinctively like a soldier to a suddenly drawn weapon, grabbing my wrist with his left hand and holding it out and away from us. I heard growling and then cold air flowed in over my teeth when it paused. Paul looked at me, flinching at the look on my face and then to Bee. He didn't know what to do.

"You're not taking it," I whispered through my teeth.

"Sshhh," Paul whispered in my ear. "Sshhh …"

After a moment the growling stopped and I turned my attention to the soft humming and snapping I felt in my hand. Other than Paul and I breathing hard it was the only thing that seemed to be moving in the room. I couldn't see my palm but I could make out a soft blue glow between my fingers and the odd blue arc of light circled from my palm around my hand before it re-entered through the back of my hand.

"Anna," Bee said loudly. "Do you have control of yourself?"

I nodded. I hoped I did anyway. What I had done when Paul first started was weak, like brushing dust off. This was an attack.

"Don't move yet Anna … Paul step away."

He looked at me then cautiously let go before going to stand near Bee.

"Anna … you need to take that back. You can't let it loose at anyone. I want you to imagine your other hand opening up … like an eye."

I closed my eyes and pictured it. I could actually feel it, like my palm was gone and there was a tunnel running into my arm. It hurt … my twisted fingers were still behind my back. I nodded.

"Now put your hands together and let it flow back in to you."

I did as she said. It felt odd … the blue arcs that had been circling my right hand now entered my left, pulsing for a minute until they faded and stopped.

"Anna … your hand," Paul said.

I looked at it, palm up, two fingers were bent in the wrong places and starting to swell. The whole thing hurt.

"Composing myself," I said. "It didn't hurt at the time. It helped to distract me from feeling what you were doing to me."

Ray got up to look. He cautiously stayed away from my right.

"You dislocated two fingers," he said. "Denis, can you run upstairs and get an ice pack from the bag in my room please?"

Then he looked at Paul and nodded. I thought he was letting Paul know it wasn't too bad and Paul came over and put his arms around me. Ray was still examining my hand.

"I'm sorry," he said. "I had no idea that you would feel anything. Was it that bad?"

"No Paul," I whispered. "It was that good."

"Really?" He had put his lips near my ear and was brushing them

195

over my skin. "I never made you do that before."

"Paul ..." I swallowed, starting to feel like I would need distraction again. "Not in front of—Ray!"

There were two quick painful snaps as he fixed the dislocated joints.

"Sorry Kiddo ... it's easier if you don't know it's coming," he paused, looking at Paul. I understood why he did it that way but I was still glaring at him. "You're not going to hit me for that, are you? Someone hit me once when I set their broken finger."

"Ray ... that was ten years ago," Paul said. "And I said I was sorry."

Ray harrumphed. Denis had already crushed the little plastic pouch in the ice pack so Ray put it on the back of my hand. It was cold and it seemed to help with the pain. I took a seat next to Paul at the table and waited for Bee to either say something or stop staring at me like I'd turned orange. She did neither so I closed my eyes and rested my head on Paul's shoulder.

"What just happened?" she finally asked.

"I—" Paul and I answered at the same time before we stopped.

"Anna ... what was Paul trying to take?" she tried again.

"I don't know," I told her. "I think whatever he found stuck to my line."

"Mmm," she thought. "Is that true Paul?"

"Yes Bee," he said. It sounded like he felt terrible for doing it.

"I'm not sure whose behaviour I'm more puzzled by," she said. "Anna, you have part of a man's line reinforcing yours and you tried to attack your mate. Paul, I'm disappointed that you would try and take it from her particularly after she gently blocked you once and I told you to just look."

"Yes Bee," he said again.

"Where do you think you got it from?" she asked me.

I knew but I had no idea how. Paul had never asked me what had happened with the man on the hill and I hadn't volunteered it. He didn't like Andre much.

"The man on the hill," I said quietly. "I cut his line from him when I killed him. My hand was on his back when he died ... making sure. I couldn't reach to search him properly when I was standing on his head."

"That's hardcore Anna," Denis said. He sounded impressed but Ray elbowed him.

I shrugged. Hadn't really given it any thought.

"Pilot told me I'd cut it loose ... maybe part of it stuck to me."

"Can you read it? Does it match his?" she asked.

I sighed and closed my eyes. First I remembered the man from

196

when I tracked him as he ran along the slope and stored it under my nose. Then I put my fingertips on my chest to read the spot in me that Paul read and put that under my nose too. I took a deep breath to clear my mind and began to look for anything similar. Nothing, so I shook my head slowly trying to move my samples around and tried again. Still nothing. I continued to check until I started sneezing.

"Excuse me," I said as I put my elbow over my nose as I sneezed a few more times. "Nothing similar at all."

Bee nodded. "I didn't think you would find anything. We travel along our lines … you have the end he hadn't used yet. Untouched. That is what I meant when I said your line was tangled with another. It got tangled with yours when it was free of him … before it could drift away. Your line loops too. The four of you have looped now. Your lines exist elsewhere now and into the future but Anna has looped them back here … moved them … and you have travelled along them to this place."

"Time and place," I said quietly. Then I understood. "The three men … that's why I knew where they would be and what they would be thinking when they got there. Somehow I knew where their lines would be. It's how I knew the first one was moving for a better shot. That he was hoping to get me first while I was still in the open before he finished Paul off. I knew when the other two would be at the pond and what they would do after they got there. You were right Paul … your father would be able to explain what happened to me.

"What about the blue light in my hand?" I asked her.

"We all have it. Inside us," Bee said. "Pilot could sometimes control his in such a way. You use it to travel also … you drain it. It needs to recharge. You must never use it on anyone like us unless you are completely focused on the outcome."

"I didn't do it on purpose …" I told her. Paul tightened his arm around me. He knew I didn't. If his reactions weren't so fast I would have hit him with it.

Bee sighed. It was getting late for her. "Go and get some rest now child."

No point in arguing with her. She was right. I was tired too.

"Grown up talk, I get it," I got up and kissed her cheek. "Good night Mrs. Desmond. Ray, Denis, 'night." I yawned. "See you downstairs Paul."

Chapter 39

I put the ice pack in the freezer while I had my bath. It was probably too hot but after all the walking and standing I wanted to be sure that I wasn't up half the night trying to ignore the aching in my legs.

Paul was quiet when he came down later. I'd fallen asleep on the couch.

"Anna … wake up Sugar. The ice came off your hand," he said as he gently shook my shoulder. He didn't sound like himself. Apologetic and I couldn't guess why.

"What's the matter Paul?" I asked him. He didn't look right either. It was guilt I'd seen only briefly on his face only this time it wasn't leaving. He helped me sit up and put the cold pack back on my hand. It was stiff and sore from the swelling and the popped joints were bruising but it felt a lot better now that everything was connected properly.

"Ray says you should have it off and on for a while."

"Okay," I consented but I wondered if he had just woken me up to tell me that. "Are you turning in?"

"I thought I would go out with Ray and Denis tonight. I just wanted to get you tucked in so you weren't waiting up on the couch for me."

"Oh."

I went and got in bed and he sat with me for a while.

"What's troubling you Paul?"

He sighed and didn't say anything but he didn't get up either so I waited.

"What I tried to do to your line tonight was terrible," he said finally. "Bee explained it's like a skin graft … it's yours now. In time it will be indistinguishable from yours … yours will just be that much stronger. The only part of our lines we own is the part we have used. I thought it was part of another man's and after seeing you with Kenny today all I wanted was to get it away from you. But it's you now … it would be like me trying to take away your arm or leg. My father is very angry with me."

"I don't really understand," I told him. "What about what I tried to do to you? If you weren't so quick …"

But Paul shook his head.

"My father says I deserved to be hit with it," he sighed. "I did one of the worst things a man can do to his mate. My family can decide that I'm not worthy of you and send me away. I'd be bound to that decision … but since you are so aware of us and who you are Bee has decided to leave it up to you. If you feel that what I did was unforgivable and you want me to leave I will. You won't see me again. Damian has tried to harm you too so he couldn't be left in charge of our daughter. He has proven himself unworthy countless times and Bee feels the fate Pilot has chosen for him is fitting. Ray has agreed to see to her upbringing."

Cold sunk into my stomach. I didn't understand why what he did was so wrong but the potential consequences for him made me well aware of how completely wrong it was. Just as wrong as what Damian had tried to do to me.

"What exactly do you mean by leave Paul?" There was no chance whatsoever I would ever want him to go … I knew that soon I would have to find a way to make him keep his distance while I dealt with Damian but that was temporary. Something brief I hoped we could get through. But this would be punishment for both of us.

"I would … Ray and Denis would make sure," he struggled for the words. "You would never see me again like this … I would be waiting to see you on the other side."

I felt sick. Maybe for someone like him who had lived so many times it wasn't such a big deal but for someone like me who would only remember one life at a time it was barbaric. I remembered how he had just surrendered to Damian when he thought Catherine was dead and how he was so ready to start over when he thought I was dead. It disgusted me that it was so easy for them to hit the reset button. And I thought I had a problem with running when things got tough. I was learning to stick it out. To deal with what I had before me rather than take off and avoid it. He would have to learn how too.

I couldn't see his face. The bedroom was dark except for the hall light that shone in on the foot of the bed next to him. I wasn't going to minimize the importance of his family rules. I was certain that they were there for a reason even though this one was completely ridiculous.

"Let me make sure that I understand this," I said. "You did something possibly unforgivable … yes?"

"Yes," Paul said.

"And punishment for you is getting to run away from your guilt and start over with a woman who won't remember what you did?"

He shook his head.

"So who is the one who would really be punished for this? Doesn't sound like you would be at all."

He didn't say anything.

"I appreciate the need for order and rules in the family … but from my perspective spending what could be the last few months of my life without you isn't really a fitting punishment for you at all. Maybe it's a lot more complicated than I could ever understand," I paused. "If you really feel that you have done something so terrible then you should have to face me every day until your guilt goes away on its own."

"You're far too generous," he whispered.

"If you think you're getting off easy then that's because I'm far too selfish and naïve. I don't understand what happened tonight or why it's a big deal. I'm more upset by what I tried to do to you. I can't make that up to you if you're not here. I'm sorry if this sounds blunt but perhaps humility is something that you have lost touch with through the course of your long life."

He just nodded.

"I forgive you. I don't know if you forgive me … I have no idea what I could have done to you but I'm sure it wasn't good. I don't know what else to say … are you still going out?"

"There is nothing for me to forgive. I guess I'll go with them for a bit."

I sat up and put my arms around him.

"Come back to me tonight, promise?"

"Yes. I promise."

He got up to leave, straightening his shirt and zipping up his jacket.

"Wait Paul … I haven't been back much more than a week after what I did to you. We both have things we feel terrible for. In a few days can we get away alone for a while? Take the truck and go? If things go wrong in a few months I don't want to think I spent every night patching things up with you after an evening at Bee's table."

"Yes," he said and came back to kiss me. "Goodnight Sugar."

The next day after their run and breakfast Denis took me car shopping. After looking at a few minivans I quickly realized that the back seats were too small. It was hard enough to get myself in them much less anyone bigger so we went back to one of the smaller used car lots in the south end of town so I could take another look at a nice older sedan I had passed over while I was focused on vans.

All it needed was winter tires and a tune-up. Price was a little high but after pulling out cash Rachel drove out in a beautiful nineteen-seventy something Lincoln Town Car. We spent an hour in the tire shop then I ran into the parts store before we went home and got the tools out. Now Ray and Denis could get Bee around while Paul and I were away.

Paul seemed more like himself after a little more sleep. He avoided his father but otherwise got along with Ray and Denis like nothing had happened. I wondered if he'd only come down the night before to say goodbye. Maybe he felt so bad about what he had done that he had planned on going back upstairs and telling them that it was time for him to go. But then he couldn't run out on me and changed his mind, deciding to tell me instead.

The following day was Friday and Ray came with Bee and I for her appointment. We got everything sorted out for her and Ray was pleased with the locum. Maybe he would want to stay in Toronto with Alina when he finally went to see her.

Paul and I were having a late breakfast the day that the ID would be ready when there was a knock at my door. Ray and Denis would just knock and walk in but the door stayed closed.

"Expecting anyone?" Paul asked quietly.

"If it's Kenny he's hours early … are you ready to meet my

father?" I asked as I quickly picked up my plate and cup.

"What?" Paul asked.

"You're John Lund, Bee's grandson, doing a favour for the owner. Make it sound like I'm still in the States and won't be back for a long time."

He sighed. "I get to meet him for real eventually, right?"

There was another knock.

"He knows I'm never up this early so he'll keep knocking for a while trying to get me out of bed. We can ignore him but he'll just keep coming back."

"Okay ... get down the hall."

"Thanks Paul," I told him and gave him a quick kiss before disappearing with my breakfast. I didn't want my father to see an abandoned second place set at the table. After closing my door most of the way I stood behind it and put my plate on top of the dresser.

Paul fiddled with the lock for a moment and opened the door. "Yeah?" he said.

I was right about who it was. I heard my father's surprised voice. "Who are you?"

There were a few seconds of silence.

"I'm the man holding the door open," Paul sounded irritated. "Who are you?"

After a few more seconds. "I'm John Creed. The uh ... owner's father. Is Anna around?"

"John Lund," Paul said. "Sorry, I wasn't expecting anyone. No, she isn't ... you want coffee or something? I'm letting all the heat out."

"Sure, thanks," my father said.

"Have a seat, do you mind if I finish my breakfast?"

I heard chairs slide on the lino.

"No ... I thought I'd be waking up Anna if she was around. I'm sorry for interrupting. Is she going to be here later?"

"Mm mm," Paul said. His mouth was probably full. "I haven't met her. Bee Desmond upstairs is my grandmother. She asked me to come do some work down here for the owner. I'm ... between jobs at the moment so I can stay here as long as I'm working on it."

"What do you mean?" my father asked.

"I have to pack up her things for storage and get it ready to rent out. Carpet, paint, repairs. I might rent it myself when the work is done if I can get on around here. My grandmother doesn't have any family nearby and shouldn't be on her own any more," he paused and spoke more quietly like he was confiding in my father. "She says that the owner met someone in Nevada ... one of the bikers who picked her up off the road after her accident. She wasn't in any shape to bus home after they kicked her out of the hospital ... she's living with him now."

"Anna … with a man?" I could hear the disbelief in my father's voice. "Growing up she never slowed down enough to chew her food then she took off at sixteen and I've hardly seen her since."

"That's what I heard anyway," Paul said. I could picture him shrug.

"Her sister sent me to check on her … she got a call from some doctor in California a few weeks ago about an accident. She said he checked out. But you said Nevada."

"Gran's memory isn't too good. She gets my name wrong half the time."

My father laughed. "Anna's good for looking out for her … but if she's taking in an old lady she should think about slowing down and being around more."

"I hear that," Paul said. I could hear his cutlery on his plate.

"I guess it's good news she might be settling down. Taken me by surprise is all. She and her sister were so much alike until we lost their mother. You have kids John?"

"Mm mm," Paul said, mouth full again. "Oh, that. I keep hoping my ex-wife will change her mind about me." There was a pause.

"Alina buried herself in school and moved away … workaholic," my father went on. "Anna just seemed to self destruct. She could have done so much with her life … hands down smarter than Alina who is brilliant. The police stopped calling me to pick her up … eventually they would just bring her home. Usually drunk and starting trouble at some party; she fell in with some bad kids for a while. I don't know how she pulled off school. Finally she did something she couldn't talk her way out of and they charged her … when they got her out of the stolen car she was driving she was so smashed she could barely stand. She seemed to stay out of trouble after that but then she rode off one day for good. Didn't see her for two years … maybe she's ready to stop running."

There was silence for a few seconds.

"I guess Alina found her own way to run too," my father said. "Sorry to unload on you … the only news I ever get about Anna is that she survived another season on that damn bike. Maybe the accident was a wake up call for her."

"No worries, John," Paul said. I could hear his chair move as he stood. "Gran doesn't expect to see her here any time soon. Anyway, I have to figure out how I'm going to make room in the garage for the bikes in the house. Sorry to rush you off."

"I understand," my father said. "Just two years of cleaning up Anna's disasters was exhausting … I don't envy you at all dealing with this place. I'd still do it if she'd let me. I'll wait to hear from her I guess."

I heard the door open.

202

"Thanks for your time John ... one day I'd like to shake the hand of the man who could tame that one."

"Yes sir," Paul said and I heard the door close.

There was silence in the kitchen so I wondered if Paul had walked him out to his car but after a minute I could hear him coming down the hall. Paul found me behind the door.

"I think he worries about you a lot ... any reason why you try so hard to avoid him?" Paul asked.

"I'm not," I said. "He can't know we're here ... he'll tell Alina then Damian will find out."

"I don't mean now. I meant the last eight years," he said softly as he put his arms around me.

"I can't explain," I sighed. "We all fell apart when we lost her. I'm not the only one who hid ... but I guess I was harder on him than Alina."

"How much trouble did you get in?"

"Officially ... once," I told him.

"Uh huh ... I guess it doesn't surprise me. You don't drink like that now."

"No," I agreed quietly. I could feel my eyebrows pushing together as I looked down. "Not for a long time."

"I keep learning more about things I already knew about you. I think he's happy you've stopped running."

"Have I? I'm hiding behind the door." I felt the sting of tears. Paul hugged me tighter.

"He's a nice man. I understand how he feels ... worrying about his daughter. Think about seeing him more when things settle down, okay? Don't let it go on too much longer. I'll owe him an apology when he finally does shake my hand."

"Okay Paul," I said as I wiped my cheeks.

He kissed me and relaxed his hold around me.

"So we're expecting Kenny here?" he asked.

"Sorry ... yes. At the same time he arrived at the mall."

"That man under our roof?"

"I ask too much," I sighed. "It won't be like last time. He'll have some excuse for coming by but he'll just be here to drop your ID off."

"You ask an awful lot ... now come to bed. I need you for a while before he shows up."

Chapter 40

I tried to talk Paul into going up to Bee's while I finished off our business with Kenny but he wouldn't. He told Ray and Denis that he was coming and he promised not to squash him but I had the feeling that if Kenny provoked him he might change his mind. All I could do if that happened was hit Kenny first. Hopefully it wouldn't come to that. It wasn't that Kenny was all that bad. He just never seemed to get over the crush he had on me when we were kids. Never felt that anyone else was good enough for me.

His friends however were a problem. Kenny should come alone but then he should have met me at the mall alone too. After I thought about it I realized that I should have gone alone to the mall too. Not much I could do about not being alone here in my own house. Since Paul knew he was coming there was no way I could get him out now.

So with that I was nervous. Nothing like sitting on a mountain of testosterone waiting for just the right spark to set it off. Paul and I sat at the kitchen table with a map deciding where we would go when we left in a few days when Kenny knocked. Paul quickly put the map away and I answered the door. The less Kenny knew about us the better.

It was raining hard and Kenny had his hands shoved deep in his pockets, pushing up his collar to keep the rain from running down the back of his neck.

"Hey Anna," he said. "My brother wanted me to pick up his bike from you next time you were in town. Now a good time?"

"Sure Kenny," I said. "Come in out of the rain while I get the key. Battery will need a charge but everything else should be fine."

Kenny stepped in and closed the door before he noticed Paul. I went down to the spare room to get the key for it from its hook and hoped for the best. Before I got to the room I heard the front door open and close, then a bit of shuffling and quiet voices. Shit, who else joined the party? I couldn't decide which would be worse. Kenny's friends or mine.

When I came back Ray was at the table with Paul. As I rounded the corner Kenny was quickly doing his pants back up. His coat was undone and his shirt was untucked. Denis calmly leaned against the wall like they were waiting for a bus together or something.

I tried not to notice. "Got the key Kenny ... you want coffee?"

"Yes," Denis said. "He would love some. Right Kenny?"

"Um, yeah Anna. Coffee sounds good."

I tossed Kenny the key and tried to ignore the ridiculous male posturing that had filled the room. Kenny hadn't taken his eyes off Paul except to catch the key and Ray and Paul hadn't taken their eyes off Kenny. I was easily two inches taller than Kenny so next to Denis he looked tiny. I made myself busy getting out cups and hoped this would be over soon. If they hadn't come down Kenny would be loading up the bike while I looked over the ID and he would be gone in a matter of minutes. Now I had no idea what Paul had planned.

Denis took a step toward me. I hadn't noticed it on the counter before since I was focused on the coffee and trying to ignore everything else. He put his hand out and slid an envelope over to me. On top of it was a gun. I sighed. Paul got up and put his arm around my waist, his lips to my ear.

"Sugar," he said loud enough for Kenny to hear. Then he slowly dropped his hand to my butt. Out of the corner of my eye Denis elbowed Kenny who quickly looked up at the ceiling. Paul put his hand back up.

"Why don't you tell your friend who we are. Perhaps he would be kind enough to keep an ear open … in case anyone asks about us."

I had an idea what Paul was up to now. Kenny was apparently connected to the same sorts of people Damian might use to try and find us and they'd already found me once through him.

"Kenny," I sighed as I pushed the gun off the envelope, "I'm not sure why you would disrespect me by bringing a gun through my front door."

I filled a cup for Kenny, just sugar I remembered, and took it to him. His hands shook a bit as he took it. Then I got coffee for the others before I took the envelope and opened it. I had a small magnifying glass in a drawer so I took it out. I opened the first passport and started examining it.

"Drink your coffee Kenny," I said. He looked at Denis who nodded so he drank.

"I see you fixed the problem with the r's," I told him. Then I moved on to one of the driver's licenses. I was impressed. They were good a few years ago but they were even better now.

"We're not really here Kenny," I told him. "I'm in a bit of trouble. The man next to you is Denis Martin," I gestured to the table, "Ray Jackson," and then tilted to Paul who still stood next to me, "and my husband Paul Richards."

I had the driver's licenses and passports out in pairs now double-checking the spelling and information on them. When I was satisfied with the last one I put it down on the counter and walked up to Kenny. Paul stayed where he was.

"You're still standing. You must have been completely kind and co-operative with my friend Denis." I looked over at Denis who nodded in agreement.

"As I said, we aren't really here but that doesn't mean that someone won't think we are. If anyone asks about us we would hope that in return for my hospitality and my forgiveness for your bringing a gun in my house you would let one of us know right away. I would also see fit to throwing a big fat envelope your way. And of course you wouldn't remember us at all if you were asked.

"How does that sound?" I asked him.

"Good," Kenny said. He sounded relieved.

I took his empty cup. "Did you bring the truck or do you have the trailer?"

"Truck," Kenny said.

"Denis, would you return Kenny's gun and help him load up his brother's bike? It's in the shed in the back."

"Sure," Denis said. "Come on Kenny."

He gave Kenny back his gun and put the rounds in the envelope the ID had come in. That he put in his own pocket. Denis opened the door and stepped out of the way so Kenny could walk past.

"Mister Richards," Kenny said, "don't let her down. She deserves the best." Then he disappeared out the door with Denis close behind.

"I know that," Paul said when they were gone.

I clung to him relieved that it was over.

"You make a good good cop; A nice complement to Denis' muscle."

"Here Ray," I passed him his new ID, then gave Paul his.

"I think he still loves you Kiddo," Ray said.

"Kenny?" I asked. Thanks for bringing that up, I thought. "Yeah, I think you're right. He's never figured out that I never felt the same way."

"Never?" Paul asked. "It's okay if you did."

"Never, okay?" I snapped back at him. "Had enough of my troubled past dragged up today thank you," I grumbled as I stomped down the hall to my room and slammed the door. Between my father showing up and moping all over my husband about how I was an irresponsible teenage drunk and Ray pronouncing Kenny still in love with me I felt like nearly everything I had run from stood naked in the kitchen with them. Paul shouldn't have even let my father through the door. Now I felt like my past was a heavy anchor around my neck holding me back.

I curled up in the corner of the bed by the wall and pulled the blankets up over my head. Enough had changed in the past few months for me that I didn't need any of that any more. Wasn't it obvious that I had gotten on with things? I sighed. Could they try any harder to annoy me?

Paul quietly opened the door a few minutes later and I heard him laugh quietly at the lump under the blankets.

"Anna? Anything I can do?"

I sighed. You can piss off, I thought. I felt like he could see all my faults even through the blanket.

"Are you sure?" he tried again.

"Paul, if I wasn't so busy getting drunk and starting fights I probably would have been capable of loving someone but I was an angry kid. I don't know how many times Kenny got me out of trouble but he finally gave up waiting for me to return what he felt and turned on me. Maybe I should have tried to pin the stolen car on him but I didn't ... maybe I felt like I had something to prove. Maybe I did care about him then after all. It doesn't matter now."

"Maybe it does matter," he said cautiously, "if it's still bothering you."

"Maybe if you and Ray and my father weren't trying extra hard to irritate me I wouldn't have to hide in my own bedroom! I think I was more than patient with you all ganging up on me!" Oh, I was mad.

"Okay Sugar," Paul sighed and patted my hip.

I stuck my tongue out at him under the blankets. He went down the hall and I heard him talking to Ray.

"Sorry Ray ... it appears we've all been out of line," Paul said.

I could hear Ray laughing. My temper was rising again if it had ever cooled off. I quickly sat up and hurled a book out the open door into the hallway. It flew through into the bathroom and banged into the accordion door for the laundry closet. They ignored it.

"How is she sleeping Paul?"

"Not well. The shouting we hear upstairs is nothing compared to being woken up by it. The fire and Alina, telling me to get out from under the tree. The worst is when she's yelling about someone putting their fists on her sister. I can hear the exhaustion in her when it's over. She doesn't wake up ... but most nights it goes on for a while."

That was news to me. I'd been having dreamless sleeps since we jumped here. Woke up tired but I thought that was just part of being pregnant and starting to be uncomfortable. I didn't know I was keeping Paul up. He should have said something. I sat up in bed and crossed my arms.

"Why don't you suggest something to help her sleep? I have something safe she can have. It's for morning sickness but it will help her be drowsy. She has a long way to go to be so tired already."

Next I threw a glass. It exploded against the wall. Sleeping pill my Royal Canadian ass. If I was going to have a lousy sleep then they could too.

"Jeez," Paul said.

"Fantastic bad mood," Ray laughed quietly. "Try not to let the hormone attack get to you. She doesn't mean it ... she's just along for the ride."

"Walk west 'til your hat floats," I yelled down the hall. I'd feel better if I wasn't out of dishes.

"Good luck," Ray told Paul and left. Hopefully in fear. I sat in the middle of the bed waiting for Paul. I saw him in the hall picking up glass but he didn't look at me. Then he ran the vacuum and I could hear him putting dishes into the dishwasher and turning it on.

Eventually he quietly came into the bedroom and sat down behind me. He didn't say anything and after a few minutes pulled my hair out of the way. Then he started working the knots out of my neck and shoulders. I sighed. It felt good. Like little electric pops in my brain erasing all the anger from my tantrum. As he worked his way down my back he reached up my shirt and undid my bra then he helped me pull it off through my sleeves.

"Mmm," I sighed, "I don't remember any dreams Paul ... I'm sorry for keeping you up."

"Sshhh ... think about Ray's offer. I can look after you but I can't make you sleep. You need your rest."

"Mm hm." It was so hard to talk when his hands were on my back like that. "Tell Ray I said okay ... and sorry about the hat thing."

"Okay Sugar," he said. "Lay down now and get some sleep. I'll stay with you."

We lay still, Paul's hand on my stomach. She was moving for him as I fell asleep.

Alina

Chapter 41

Paul woke me quietly our first morning in Edmonton. After making a slow trip across British Columbia we settled on the hotel in West Edmonton Mall for a couple of days before we would head south to Calgary then back to my place for Christmas.

He had pulled himself in close to me, a long jewellery box in his hand.

"Happy Birthday Anna," he said softly.

First day in December. I reached up and put my hand on the box but he didn't let go.

"You can't open it just yet. I want to explain."

"Okay," I said tucking my head into his chest to listen.

"I know you're not much for this kind of thing but it's a traditional gift in the family ... something we give our mates. Like exchanging rings but longer term. I got it when we were in Reno. I brought it along thinking there might be an occasion I could give it to you."

"Okay," I said then I tilted my head up to his neck to put my lips on it.

"You can open it now," he said. Inside was a heavy gold necklace woven to look like a ribbon. The lamp light shimmered along its surface like it was alive.

"It's really beautiful Paul," I said softly. It really was. "Thank you."

"You'll wear it?"

"Of course," I would be happy to. He was pleased.

"Sit up," he said, "I'll help you put it on."

I held my hair up out of the way and ran my finger along it, feeling how smooth it was as Paul closed it behind my neck.

"What's the tradition behind giving it?" I asked.

211

"The shape symbolizes our lines ... and when it's closed in a circle it's our promise to be there again for you. Not too long ... it should reach to where your line is ... that's perfect." He reached around to feel it on my chest.

"Is there something I should give you in return?"

"No ... it must be beautiful," he added in my ear, "but never more beautiful than the woman receiving it."

"I like that tradition," I giggled as his hand started to drop lower. "Did you just make that last part up?"

"New tradition," he whispered, pulling me over.

"I like new tradition too."

Our days since leaving my house had been quiet like our nights together when we first met. Food, sex, sleep. Paul looked more like his normal self. He'd gained back much of the weight he lost while I was away and seemed to forgive himself for whatever he'd tried to do to my line. We ordered in room service and pulled the table up to the window to eat looking out over the city.

"Can I ask you something without coming off as insecure or paranoid?"

He laughed. "I can't picture you as either ... sure."

"Do some of you have more than one woman like me?" I couldn't stomach sharing him with someone else even in the interests of the family.

"By some of us do you mean me?"

"I told you it would sound paranoid and insecure," I frowned at the table.

"You really worry about it? I guess we've never talked about how that works," he paused. "Come on let's get your feet up. You did a lot of walking today."

We brought our unfinished drinks to the bed. I thought he was trying to change the subject and hoped he knew better.

"Do you remember when you told me what you felt about Damian? It was like what you feel for me but weak." He could see I didn't want to talk about that. "I'm sorry ... I need to relate it to something you understand. If I wasn't in your life you would have been as attracted to him as you were to me. Alina felt it strongly ... we can have that effect on women who aren't like you. With you my attraction to another mate would be as weak as yours was to him. No comparison."

That I understood.

"Why didn't Catherine want him any more ... she felt that way at first."

"He ..." then Paul hesitated. "He took what she was willingly offering. He beat her and he took it."

"Why didn't what you tried to do to my line cause the same thing?" I didn't like saying it out loud but he didn't seem too bothered by it.

"I wasn't trying to hurt you … I didn't force you to give me something you could give me. Like I said, it's complicated … and to answer your question I don't have another."

"Do all the women have two?"

"Again, usually," he said.

He said he wouldn't be attracted to another mate but other women could be strongly attracted to him. My mood soured as I realized what I might have to do to drive him away for a while. Mistrust him. It was simple.

"I get it," I sighed. "I'm sorry for asking … sometimes I feel like I'm not giving much back."

He put his hand on my stomach. "You are giving me more than you can imagine every day. Keep doing what you're doing, okay?"

"Okay Paul," I said. "I felt pretty shallow asking that."

"Don't worry about it. Keep asking questions like that when you have them, please? I don't want there to be any misunderstandings. What made you want to ask?"

I struggled inside for a minute and decided that now was a good a time as any to start to really sound paranoid and insecure.

"When we were out today … I noticed how some of the women looked at you. Their interest bothered me after a while."

"Awe, you have nothing to worry about Sugar. You know that don't you?"

"Yes," I told him, "after I lost my mother I ruined my ties to everyone in my life and never let myself get close to anyone until I met you. Today I kept picturing myself alone again … it wasn't the peace I pretended it to be."

That part was true. I liked that I wasn't alone any more. I took a deep breath and wiped my eyes surprised with how I felt.

Paul didn't say anything right away. He put his hand on the side of my face and kissed my forehead.

"Are you jealous?" he whispered.

"Yes," I said but I shrugged. "No. Selfish. Territorial. I've found a reasonable excuse to be back on the road running and I've dragged you along with me."

"We can go back to your place first thing tomorrow," Paul offered.

"Not there … I'm homesick for your place. It's the first place I've felt settled since I was a kid," I sighed. "I want off the roller coaster … my mood is all up and down today. I'm sorry."

"Nothing to forgive. I have to go make sure the truck is still there … did you want to come along or stay here?"

213

"I think I'll wait here for you."

Chapter 42

I'd fallen asleep in our bed when I heard his apology in my ear.

"Sorry I was gone so long ... everything's okay."

"I tried to wait up," I told him.

"I went to call Ray but my phone is low on minutes. I needed to find a place to buy more."

"'kay," I said. My eyes were closing again.

I heard a beer can open then he called Ray. They talked for a bit. It was like the briefing after I got back from seeing Pilot only I could hear just half of it and it was just as boring. But I paid attention for the next part.

"Something happened in the parkade when I was checking on the truck Mark," Paul said. We used other names on the phone. "I caught a man watching me. I had to go past him to leave and he took off."

"No, I don't think so ... he seemed curious, cautious."

"Maybe ... but she wasn't with me."

"I guess ... if he wants to speak with me he might hang around. Truck's in the hotel parking. He'd know we're here for a bit."

"Yeah, we're on schedule ... talk to you again."

"Bye."

I opened my eyes and watched Paul. He sat without moving like he was deep in thought; not really watching what was on the TV.

"Family?" I asked. He jumped. "Sorry."

"Could be ... I thought you were asleep."

"I tried ... no luck yet."

Paul didn't say any more. I watched him brooding there on the couch for a long time before I finally nodded off.

Suddenly the door burst open. I opened my eyes to see what it was but fear from the noise left me paralyzed. Paul jumped for the dresser where we'd hidden our weapons but he didn't make it. Two of them had him, arms behind his back. He struggled and got an arm free as a third stepped into my field of vision and hit him hard in the jaw. I heard his teeth snap together as one of the men behind him got control of his arm again. They were all as big as he was. The third hit him hard in the stomach so the air shot out of him and again in the side of the face. Paul was dazed, his head sagging. The two men behind him threw his arms over their shoulders and followed the third man to the door. I heard it open then click shut behind them.

I was breathing hard frozen in place. As my pounding heart slowed I started to be able to move again. Which was the one he had seen in the parking lot? Why didn't they want me … maybe they were just getting rid of Paul. Someone else would be coming.

As soon as I could get myself up out of bed I got my gun from the drawer and grabbed my phone. Then I turned off the lamp and squeezed myself into the corner behind the couch. I dialled Ray. Woke him up.

"Mark … it's me …" My God, did I really sound that hysterical?

"Rach? What's going on?"

"The man from the parking lot … two more … beat up … took him." I was thinking so clearly but my words were so confused. Why was I shaking so hard inside? I had the presence of mind to get the names straight at least.

"Danny! Try phoning John!" Ray sounded like I thought I felt, which was a lot more collected than I sounded.

"I have to go. I don't want them to hear me in here." I disconnected the call and turned the phone off. I didn't want the ringer to give me away when Ray called back. I put the phone on the floor and slid as far behind the couch as I could without moving it.

I didn't have to wait long. The door opened slowly. The shadow of a man stuck into the room, lit from behind by the light from the hotel hallway. I forced myself to settle my breathing and shoved my head down as low as I could. My thumb turned off the safety. The soft click seemed deafening to me but I'd never noticed it before. Hopefully he didn't. The light just inside the door came on so I silently made sure I was as small as possible in my corner. Then I heard a couple of quiet footsteps as the door pulled itself shut. He would be far enough into the room to see that the bed was empty.

Another light came on, the bathroom one this time. I wondered which one of the three it was. Looking for me. Maybe it was someone else. I wished I had my knife. It was so much quieter than the gun but I had left it behind. It was in my dresser back in my basement suite. Some of the metal rings holding the shower curtain to its pole moved quietly. Then he stepped into the main room.

There were a few more steps. He'd be able to see I wasn't behind the bed. His eyes would still be adjusting from the bright lights in the hall and bathroom so I stayed still hoping I had a bit of time where he could only see me if I moved. My lungs were starting to complain though; since I had slowed my breathing to be quiet I was feeling short of air.

He took something out of his pocket. I held my breath as he put it to his ear.

"Did she call again? She's not here," Paul said.

I let air into my lungs again and put the safety back on.

"Paul? I'm here," I said quietly, putting my gun by my phone and trying to get up. His ears focused on my voice and in two strides he was beside me. I threw my arms around his neck when he knelt down and pulled him into the corner with me. The panic I had been ignoring was making me numb again.

"You got away," I whispered. My voice was shaking again.

"Sshhh," he said. He put the phone down and started pulling me out of my corner. "You're really wedged in here."

When I was out from behind the couch he got me back in bed and covered me up then he turned on the lamp and went to pick up his phone. He got mine off the floor too and my gun.

"Why do you have your gun out?" he asked as he checked the safety was on and put it back in the drawer with his.

"Give it to me ... they'll come back," I told him.

"You don't need it," Paul said.

When he came to sit on the bed with me I grabbed his face and pulled it close, examining his cheek.

"No marks," I said. Nothing on his jaw either. I pressed with my fingertips where he had been hit but he didn't react. "Doesn't that hurt?"

"John?" Paul's phone spoke. I didn't realize Ray was still on the line and Paul had turned the speaker on. "What's going on? What about the gun?"

"She was hiding in the corner with it ... did you hear the rest?"

"Yes."

"Anna," Paul whispered in my ear, then louder so Ray could hear. "What happened?"

I looked back at him dumbly. Maybe he had a concussion. Maybe he didn't remember.

"Sugar?"

"Why don't you remember?" I was looking at his eyes. Pupils were the same size so I started feeling his head for bumps. "How hard did they hit you?"

He took my hands off his head.

"Nobody hit me ... what do you remember?"

I guess I had to humour him ... maybe it would trigger his memory.

"You were on the couch when I fell asleep," I pointed to it. "Next thing I knew three men burst in. Two had you from behind before you could get to the drawer ... the third knocked you out."

I felt the side of his face again.

"I couldn't move; they dragged you out ... the door clicked shut. I don't know how long I waited until I could move. As soon as I could I called Mark ... then I hid. Mark ... he doesn't remember."

Paul sighed. "I went down to the pub for takeout. Mark called when I was on my way back up. You were scared, slurring, said I'd been taken. I found you in the corner."

216

He gestured to the dresser. His grease spotted paper bag of takeout sat on top.

"No …" I shook my head. It didn't make any sense.

"Take me off speaker John," Paul did and went into the bathroom with the phone. I counted to sixty then I pulled the cover off the bed and followed him while I was wrapping myself in it.

"Why don't you believe me?" I asked him. His back was to me and he turned around. "I don't like being whispered about behind my back."

He sighed. "I think you're right Mark … we'll sort it out." Then he hung up.

"Come back to bed … you had a bad dream," Paul said.

He put his arm around me pressed his hand on my back to move me but I held my ground and stared back at him. I'd be happy to accept that if he could make it make sense. I raised my eyebrows at him. Go ahead, I nodded.

"You couldn't move because you were asleep … Ray says sleep paralysis. You didn't take anything before bed, did you?"

I shook my head.

"Maybe you were dreaming when I went out … that's why you heard the door close," he pulled my arm out of the blanket and put it on his cheek.

"I'm not hurt," he said softly. "See."

"I see," I agreed. I couldn't argue with his untouched face. This time I let him take me back into the room. I put the cover back on the bed and got in. "Sorry I interrupted your snack. I guess I got too worked up about being without you today."

Paul offered me some of what he brought back. I picked. Never had been a big late night eater.

"Will you go out with me sometime?" he was wiping his hands on a paper napkin.

"Like a date?"

"Yeah," he winked at me, "we never really dated."

I thought about it. "I'm free tomorrow."

"So you'll go out with me?"

"Yes," I was smiling now. That cheered me up so I suggested something he would like. "Some place nice?"

"But not too nice … I hate wearing a tie."

I agreed. A tie was a terrible thing to do to a man.

"I have to go shopping," I told him. The things I had packed were more practical for travel. I'd get something nice but not too nice. Then Paul and I would go out on a date.

Chapter 43

The next morning we split up in the mall to shop. I found a dress almost the same colour green as Paul's eyes; just a shade or two darker. It had short flared sleeves and fit tight up top. The loose skirt draped and clung to me and came down to cover just the tops of my knees. Three small pearl buttons closed the front of the bodice and a wide ribbon covered the seam where the skirt and the bodice met. The neck was low enough that my necklace from Paul wasn't covered by it at all.

Paul called as I was heading back to the hotel. He was already there and wondering where I was. When I got in I stashed my things in the closet out of sight. The dress was in a garment bag so he couldn't see it. He'd ordered up some lunch then we both got a nap in before getting ready. I planned on making it up as late as Paul wanted to stay out.

I got the first shower and after blow drying my hair loaded it up with rollers.

"Not a word," I told Paul. He thought it was pretty funny. I guess he never thought he'd see me like that.

Then he got the second shower and dressed in the room while I finished up in the bathroom. He knocked, my hair was done but I was struggling with the makeup. Alina usually did it for me when we went out which wasn't often.

"Ten minutes?" I called back.

"Just making sure you didn't go to sleep in there."

Sure you were, I thought, you were hoping to get another laugh at the rollers. Then I laughed when I backed away from the mirror to study myself. Couldn't blame anyone for thinking I was Alina. I pulled the pantyhose and the dress on but I couldn't zip it up. I put the lipstick in a little purse and perfume on my neck and wrists.

Paul was pacing when I got out of the bathroom. Nervous didn't really suit him but there he was.

"Can you zip me up?" I asked taking him in. He had medium gray dress pants on and a deep blue shirt. Top button undone. There was a darker gray blazer on the bed. Black dress shoes and belt.

"Look at you," I said.

"Me ..." he said softly; his voice wandering with his eyes. "I thought you were beautiful before ... what did you ask?"

"Zipper please," I laughed. I carefully turned around in my precarious shoes and lifted my hair out of the way. The back of the dress was cut down a bit and my hair was so long now it covered most of the zipper. He slowly did the zipper up and put his nose to my neck.

"What is that?" he whispered in my ear, smelling my skin as his hands ran down the smooth fabric of the dress, feeling my curves underneath.

"I can't pronounce it."

"Mmm. We better go or we won't make it out of the room," Paul said. I agreed. He took my hand and slowly spun me around. Then he stopped me facing him and ran his fingers over my necklace. I was only a couple of inches shorter than him now.

"Wait … you're missing something."

He got a small box out from under his jacket. There were two pearl earrings inside. Screw on backs. Each had half a dozen pearls hanging down at different lengths on fine gold chains. He helped me put them on.

"Get your ears pierced tomorrow … we can change them to posts. These are hard to find."

"They're lovely … thank you."

Paul got caught with his hands all over me in the elevator when the door opened in the lobby. It never embarrassed him when he was the one being forward and it took a good minute for my cheeks to stop feeling so hot.

It was a longer walk than I thought it would be and we took our time. I held on to Paul and avoided wiping us both out in my shoes. He kept saying how good I looked until I told him I was going to worry what he might really think about how I usually dressed.

"I won't promise to stop … but for now I think I've made my point," he said, but was right back at it a few minutes later.

We found a steak and seafood place that was quiet. It was earlier on a weeknight so we got a table. There was a second level above part of the restaurant. I thought it might be more secluded but from my seat I could see a chain with a sign that said 'Private' blocking the stairs so I didn't bother asking about it.

While we ate I noticed a man up on the second level watching us. Or I thought he was. He came and went a few times and disappeared when he caught me looking. I thought about the man Paul had seen the night before.

"The man you saw … what did he look like?" I asked.

Paul finished his mouthful while he thought. "Shoulder length blonde hair, rectangular shaped glasses … thick black frame. No facial hair. Why?"

"So it's not the man up there who I keep catching watching us." The man I saw had short dark hair.

He laughed a bit. "Maybe you have a fan?"

I shook my head. "He's not acting like that."

Paul seemed to brood again for a moment. "I don't like to ask you to intrude but my father always did. Is he family?"

I reached for Paul's hand and started absently playing with his ring as I extended my sense like I had at his table. What I picked up was confusing. I lifted my eyes to Paul's and let my mind wander. I decided to tell him what I found and as I spoke I fit the pieces together.

"Yes … and no," I told him, he raised his eyebrows.

"His loyalty isn't to anyone I've met. It's solid to someone sitting up there. I have no way of recognizing them like your father does … I wouldn't remember meeting them before."

"Them?" he asked.

I nodded. "Six. Five men and one woman. She's connected to the one they are loyal to …"

My focus wandered again, centering on her. Then I smiled.

"Our child isn't the only one coming."

"You got all that?" There was amazement on Paul's face. "They must be interested in us … have someone who can read. Maybe the one you saw up there."

"So this has turned into a working date? We'll have to do this again."

"Yes," he smiled at me and we went back to our food for a while. The man kept checking on us.

"So what do we do?" I asked.

"I'm not just going to march up there," he said as he finished his glass of wine. He was cautious.

"Is there a tradition for when you find someone?"

"Usually we drink," Paul said.

"That's not very imaginative," I said and Paul shrugged. It was about what I expected from a bunch of guys.

"I have an idea if it's okay with you." The waitress had spotted that we were done and was on her way over. "Order a drink then nod like you're giving me permission. He's watching …"

I quickly pulled one of the dirty hundreds out of my purse and folded it up ready for the waitress. Paul talked to her about the scotch they had and ordered. I looked over at him and he nodded. The man still watched us.

"Can I ask you something?" I leaned close to her so I could keep my voice down.

"Of course dear," she said.

"Is there a fellow sitting up top there … blonde hair," I indicated to my shoulders, "glasses, black frame … squarish?"

"Keith?" she answered.

"Yes … we'd like to send a round to him and his table. Can you tell him we're friends from way back and would like to send up a … traditional hello?"

She looked at me like I was trying to have fun with her so I gave her my sweetest smile. "We appreciate it's a very unusual request … this is for their drinks. The rest is for you." I slipped her the hundred. She looked at it with surprise.

"My pleasure," she said and gathered up our empty dishes.

"Ice broken," I told Paul.

I excused myself to the washroom to touch up my lipstick. When I came out the waitress had returned.

"The gentleman upstairs says he would like to thank you personally. Can you stay a while?"

I looked at Paul until she looked at him. Then he nodded.

"So the rest is up to me?" he asked.

"Isn't there an easier way to do this? Second Tuesday in October at the Space Needle or something?"

"We could never agree," he laughed. He reached across the table and I took his hand. We chatted for a while then I had a concern.

"Paul ... they will think I'm like I was before. We shouldn't bring up anything other than my ability to read."

He nodded. "I was thinking the same thing. I don't know what sort of agenda they might have ... if any. They're not loyal to Damian but they may not like what you have planned." He thought a minute. "Hopefully we can make some friends—

"Wait," I interrupted him. "She's left ... one of them is coming down."

We kept our attention on each other. I waited for Paul to look up first when he approached our table then I followed. It was the man with the black glasses but his blonde hair was tied back.

"I must admit nobody has ever bought me a drink in my own place," he said. Then he reached his hand to Paul. "Keith Waters ... this is my restaurant."

Paul stood and shook. "John Lund ... my wife Rachel."

I stood too. Keith took my hand.

"Perhaps I could speak with you privately for a moment, John."

I sighed and shook my head. Grownup talk.

"You may excuse me," I said. Paul nodded to me so I went down the hall to the ladies room for the second time in twenty minutes. My lipstick didn't really need any attention so I used the restroom then counted to one hundred. When I came back Paul and Keith were talking quietly with their heads together. Neither seemed tense or uneasy and both smiled as I approached. When Paul saw me he stepped back from Keith and reached for me. Keith's eyes dropped briefly as he noticed my stomach.

"Paul says you don't appreciate being left out," Keith said.

I looked at Paul for an explanation. The conversation had started with us not using our real names.

"Keith and I have been good friends for a very long time," Paul explained.

"Anna," I said holding my hand to him again. This time he kissed it.

"Russian?" he asked.

"On my mother's side."

"Interesting … she who will rise again."

"Yes," I said. The corners of Paul's mouth came up a bit.

"Well, you must come up and join us. My wife hasn't been feeling well so I convinced her to go lie down in the office for a while."

Perhaps Keith didn't know yet that his wife was pregnant. I certainly wouldn't bring it up and was quite sure that Paul wouldn't either. We followed him up the stairs. I held on to Paul's hand. The carpet was thick and my shoes felt awfully unstable.

There was only one table occupied up top. Three men waited there; the man with the short dark hair watched us from the railing.

While Keith introduced Paul to the ones at the table I stared back. After absently hearing their first names I realized who he was. I gently slipped my hand from Paul's and approached him, pausing within arms reach.

He looked at me for a moment longer.

"You must be the reader," he said. "Your husband requires too much explanation."

"Anna Richards," I nodded to him and offered my hand.

"Patrick Fletcher." He shook.

"I believe I owe you a cigarette," I told him.

"Yes," he laughed. "I remember Andre. I don't smoke."

From the corner of my eye I could see Paul look over.

"Well, let's not make a spectacle of ourselves." He gestured to the table. Keith had pulled over an extra chair and we sat down. Patrick took a moment to whisper in Keith's ear while Paul was whispering in mine.

"What was that all about?"

"I remembered that one."

Paul looked at me for a moment.

"Patrick says you are a good reader … perhaps you could show me."

I looked at Paul; the last thing I wanted was to embarrass him in front of his good friend. He nodded to me so I looked back at Keith.

"Whose line am I part of?" he asked. I hesitated and spoke quickly to Paul.

"Can I speak of your line if I need to?" he nodded.

"And what about mine?"

"You represent your line here … use your discretion."

I looked at Keith.

"Mine," I said immediately.

"And Patrick?"

"Also mine," I replied. This was easy and probably answers he already knew.

"And the others?"

I pointed to the other three one at a time. "My husband's, related to another I have met who is not part of one of the three lines, not related to anyone I have met before."

The table was quiet for a minute.

"That was almost too easy for you … is there any more you can do?"

I looked at Paul again. Keith was pushing farther than I felt comfortable but Paul nodded to go ahead.

"I've had some success tracing family lines where the exact relations have been forgotten."

Now there was silence around the table.

"You could help Patrick and I settle a bet … with what you know of the family can you tell us if we have the same parents?"

"Only if I've met them both …" but I felt a solution come to me as I said it. "Maybe I can find a way around that."

If I could figure out how a sister and brother were related then I could figure out the sisters from men I had met.

"Yes," I said to myself more than to them. "It might work. Amuse yourselves … this could take some time."

I stood and walked to one of the other tables and took one of the nice cloth napkins. I was going to need it. Then I took my shoes off and felt the joints in my feet straighten out on the carpet. I walked to the wall opposite the railing and started. First Ray and me. I didn't think it was rude to use Ray. Whatever I learned I wouldn't mention him.

After placing my memory of Ray under my nose I put myself there too then I started looking for similarities. Nothing came right away so I wriggled my nose and kept going. Then I shook my head. Still nothing. I worked on it for several minutes without success. Maybe it was more difficult than a simple subtraction like finding who the mother was. I opened my eyes briefly and looked back at the table. They were all watching me so I closed them again.

I decided that looking for things that were the same wasn't going to work so I looked for opposites. Things that were completely different and started removing them one at a time. I was slowly moving my right hand back and forth in front of my face as I worked, feeling my cheeks warm as I exhaled on my palm when it passed in front of my nose. As I kept removing the opposites I matched I became aware of a quiet hum … first in one ear then the other as my hand moved. Then a hand on my wrist gently pulling my hand from my face so I started slowly turning my head back and forth as I worked. I seemed to need to fidget to focus.

The gentle movement helped.

I was surprised when I had nothing left to match. Sisters were a mirror image of their brothers. A soft reflection. My nose started to tickle so I covered it with the napkin in my left hand and sneezed a few times, then I shook my head to get myself out of what ever deep state I had put myself in.

When I opened my eyes Paul was next to me holding my right hand still away from us, pointing it at the wall.

"Paul?" There was concern on his face.

"I didn't like that so close to you," he said. When I looked at my hand I could see the blue glow in my palm; arcs of blue light occasionally jumping around and entering me through the back of my hand. The men at the table looked uneasy.

"I didn't realize I did that," I closed my eyes and pictured my left hand opening up, the hole widening until it covered my entire palm. It felt like my forearm was hollow. I put the napkin between my hip and the wall to hold it and put my hands together. The blue light obediently flowed back into me.

"Sorry about the light show," I whispered to him. "I don't think it will hurt me … it is mine after all."

"Anything?" he asked.

"A piece of the puzzle … I'm having to figure out how to make the pieces I'm missing but once I know how it shouldn't take this long if I'm asked to do this again. I have everything I need … I think. Now it's just a matter of making comparisons."

Paul softly put his lips to my ear.

"I love you," he whispered.

"I love you too," I replied then I sighed and rested my head on him for a few seconds. This was tiring and I wondered if I was spending energy to do it. And how much. Nothing I could to about it now. I closed my eyes and got back to work. I didn't hear Paul return to the table.

Since Keith and Patrick were from the same line as me I would compare them both to Pilot and Ray … see if the woman who was left was the same. It was possible that some of Ray's other relations back at the compound could be the father but I would start with the two I knew best. I didn't know who Pilot's mates were but I knew who Ray's was. It was the easiest route to go. If I had to find Pilot's mates I could be at it a while and have a lot to remember. If I struck out there I would have to try hard to recall the other three men and compare them to the same mates I found with Pilot.

I decided to make sure I had Alina first and then make sure I could make Paul's sister match her. I hadn't seen her in so long so the quickest way would be to find the opposite of Paul … then compare what I got to what I remembered of Alina. Hopefully they would be the same. If they weren't I might have a problem. It was harder than I thought to find his opposite. My first attempt was close to Alina but in no way the same. I had to go through the pieces of him that I had and reverse them ... not losing any. My second try was a match. I tried a third time to be sure I could do it again and I could. After each attempt the sneezing started and after the third I opened my eyes and sat down. Paul had returned to the table but came back over.

"You've been standing there for almost an hour ..."

"I'm learning," I explained. "I had to figure out how to match a brother and sister ... then to create that match where I don't know the sister. I'm the only one I know and I wouldn't be their mother."

"You look exhausted," Paul said. "You don't have to do this all right now. We've been invited back tomorrow."

"I think I'll be asleep tomorrow. It feels like I'm using a lot of energy to do this. Maybe it's just tiring out my brain. Make hay ..." I smiled.

"If you're sure," Paul said. He seemed to be leaning a bit then he chuckled. "I'm going to have some hangover tomorrow."

Oh well, I would be holding him up on the way back to the hotel while I carried my shoes.

Finding the mother felt like it went much faster but that was only because I had done it before. First I compared Pilot to both Keith and Patrick. There was no match. Then I compared Ray to both of them also found no match but there was something interesting. The woman I found when I compared Pilot and Keith was the same woman I found when I compared Ray and Patrick. They had the same mother ... different fathers. But their fathers were very close, probably father and son. I worried I had done something wrong and had to check with Paul.

I didn't open my eyes. "Paul?"

I didn't hear him so I lifted myself a bit out of trance I seemed to be in and heard their talk and laughter so I came out all the way and stood.

"Paul!" I said more loudly this time. He slowly turned his head and looked over then made his way to me.

"You okay?" It came out yokay. I'd never seen him so loaded.

"I think by now he's forgotten what he asked ... I have a question."

"Shoot," Paul said.

"Can a woman be mated to both a son and his father?" I asked.

Paul shook his head. "More like handed down."

"When I'm in charge that's the first thing I'm going to change," I told him and he started laughing. "I think I have my answer ... just have to check something. Go sit down before you fall on your face."

"Yes Ma'am," he said and swaggered off to the table.

I sat back down and first compared the woman who was Keith's mother with Paul's sister Alina, then the same for Patrick's mother. They were indeed the same. Alina was the mother of both.

Finally I just made a quick comparison of Keith and Patrick like I would have before I got my idea. The answer amused me. They were close enough that I probably would have given a fairly confident yes as my first answer but after a lot of learning and work I found that the relations in the family were definitely worthy of a thoughtful examination.

I put my shoes back on and sat down next to Paul. He was talking with the man I'd identified as being from his line and none of them seemed to be letting their reunion tradition down at all. My daiquiri was just pink water now but I didn't mind. It was tasty but a little too sweet for me. I put my hand on Paul's leg under the table and he put his hand on top and curled his fingers around in between mine. I wasn't sure how much more reunion he could take before I had to push him back to the hotel in a shopping cart. My eyes closed as I leaned against his shoulder.

"How long was I over there?" I asked Paul.

He checked his watch. "Couple of hours? Keith's down sending up more food."

"Sounds great ... I need to refuel."

"Got it figured?"

I nodded. "I did the obvious comparison last ... my answer would have been wrong." I put my head back down and waited.

"Okay."

It was almost twenty minutes before Keith and the waitress I'd given the hundred to came up with trays filled with food and more drinks. I could have fallen asleep on his shoulder if my head didn't bounce every time he laughed. Paul had gotten me another daiquiri but was sticking to water now himself. Self preservation had set in.

"House special," Keith said.

"Prepped too much salmon?" Patrick asked.

"That's why it's the special," Keith laughed. Special or not, it was really good. Once everyone was settled Keith turned his attention to me.

"That took a while ... trying to get out of it?" He winked.

"No," I said between bites. "It was a complicated question. I spent most of the time learning to make inferences about people I haven't met."

"How do you mean?" Patrick asked.

"I'm the only woman like me I've met. I had to figure out how to find the ... fingerprint I guess of a woman from her brother. After that it took some time to compare the men in your line with the women's fingerprints I made." Not entirely true but I couldn't explain who I targeted first without talking about Ray and I was sure that he would be very uncomfortable with that.

"And?" Keith asked.

"The obvious solution was to just compare you and Patrick ... I did that last. You're very close. Close enough that I might have just said yes when you asked." I paused for another bite. And for effect. I felt pretty pleased with myself.

"But I would have been wrong. The differences in your fingerprints are very subtle but definitely there."

"So the answer is no?" Keith asked.

"Correct."

"Ha!" Patrick said. "I win."

"Hold up," Keith said. "I want to hear why before I concede ... there's a lot at stake. How are we different?"

I wanted to fill up and get some sleep but I did need to provide an explanation.

"The same woman was your mother ... but your fathers are different. Close but different," I explained.

"Who are they?" Keith asked.

I looked to Paul again. He nodded to go ahead.

"My husband's sister," I told them. Paul grabbed his water to fix a sudden problem in his throat. "I've never met her ... I had to teach myself how to create her fingerprint from his."

"How do you do that?" Patrick asked but Keith motioned for him to hold his thought.

"And our fathers?" Keith asked.

"I wouldn't even ask his permission to tell you. I'm sorry ... your father is the father of Patrick's father if that makes sense."

"No, you're right ... I know who Paul's sister is mated to. He can be a little funny about things. This won't be spoken of again."

"Agreed," Paul said.

"So I win," Patrick said. "Never bet against a reader when it comes to family."

"Yeah, but you never had a better answer than 'just because.'"

"So I win," I said. Keith grinned and was nodding and pointing at me.

"Uh," Patrick didn't sound happy. "She can only win if she knew the stakes before she started."

"Nope ... we both lose. Tomorrow Patrick, or don't come in. Paul, would you consider permitting your mate to try and teach what she can do to Patrick? It's a shame that a gift like hers is going to be lost."

Paul thought about it. "We can stay a few extra days ... Patrick you're welcome to come stay with us for a while later in the new year when we're home again."

"Thank you Paul," Keith said. It seemed to make Patrick happy but Paul wasn't too taken with the idea. Maybe he had agreed as a courtesy. Keith's reasoning seemed sound though I didn't like being reminded that all I was learning would be gone at the end of my life. And nobody had mentioned my light show. I wasn't sure how to take that.

While we finished eating Keith's wife came looking for him. She was young. Not much more than nineteen, maybe twenty. Her name was Marie and she didn't look pregnant at all but I could definitely feel her son. She was surprised that Paul and I were here and I got the impression that Keith never let anyone other than his buddies sit at his table. Keith said Paul was his best friend in high school and they lost touch quite a while ago. She had long straight red hair and more freckles than me and was an inch or two shorter. Keith excused himself and walked her out to the car so she could drive home.

When he came back he said she had classes the next day and would come back after that. She studied upstairs here or in Keith's office and had been waitressing in the evening but the school load was catching up with her and she was just too tired to be on her feet much past dinner. I knew it was the pregnancy and they would find that out soon enough.

By the time he got back Paul had decided we should return to the hotel. I'd hoped to stay awake longer but answering Keith's question had worn me out. Paul was thoughtful and a little distracted but had no problem finding his way into my dress as soon as we got into our room. He didn't even get his clothes off and was still wearing them when I woke up the following morning.

Paul smelled like he'd been sweating alcohol out of every pore. I quietly got out of bed and ordered myself breakfast and a pitcher of orange juice and a thermos of coffee for Paul then washed off the makeup and hairspray in the shower. When I got out Paul's phone was ringing and there was a knock at the door so I answered the phone on the way to let breakfast in.

"Hey Mark," I could tell from the number.

"Rach? Hi."

"Just a sec …" I opened the door and let room service put the tray on the dresser. Paul was still a snoring heap under the blanket on the bed.

"Sorry Mark," I said when we were alone again. "Doorbell."

He laughed. "Just wondering how you're feeling about the other night."

"You were right … and I'm feeling a lot better. We went out last night … John will be in rough shape if he ever moves again."

"So it was what we thought?" Ray asked.

"Mm hm," I answered around my toast as I poured a glass of juice.

228

"Sorry, I'm starving. How are you doing?"

"Quiet here … Gran's teaching me to cook."

That was a surprise. I giggled. "You mean bake?"

"Isn't that the same thing?" Oh dear, he sounded like he really thought it was.

"Yeah," I said. Now I was shovelling in eggs and fried potatoes. Maybe once she'd shown him how to bake with eggs he'd venture out into cooking them.

"Is that Mark?" Paul's voice came out from under the blankets.

"Mm hm, you want him?" I asked.

Then to Ray. "The master rises and desires conversation with you."

"Put him on," Ray laughed.

Paul pulled the blankets down enough to see and I gave him the phone. Then I closed the curtains and got him the bottle of pain relief and a glass of juice.

He looked at them and at me and said, "I love you."

I blew him a quick kiss before going back to my breakfast then he said to Ray, "I know you know I love you." He tried to laugh but just wound up holding his head together so I took out three of the pills for him and got him a cup of coffee. I'd stopped regularly drinking like that long before I ever started getting hung over and hadn't been hung over since the last time Alina and I tied one on. It was something I never cared to do again.

Paul had gotten the pills down and was talking quietly to Ray. I tried to be as silent as I could with my dishes knowing Paul felt every little tink bash its way into his head. When my breakfast was gone I finished dressing and took a few hundred from our stash and put my phone in my pocket. Then I knelt beside the bed until I had Paul's attention.

"Sorry to interrupt. Phone up for breakfast if you want some … I didn't know when you'd be up or if you'd want any. I'm going down to the mall for a bit. Hour, hour and a half maybe."

"Okay Rachel," he said. I kissed his forehead and hurried downstairs.

My first stop was a jewellery store I'd noticed on the way back from our date that had a sign in the window advertising they did ear piercing. It wasn't as bad as I thought when they put the light blue stones in my ears but they started to burn on the way out of the store. I realized after that the colour of the fake aquamarine studs was the same as the blue light I could make in my right hand. And of my eyes.

Next I went back to a department store and got some softer makeup for wearing during the day. I had the lady show me what to do with it and put it on me. Paul liked it on me so I figured why the hell not.

229

We might not have a lot of time left; about fifteen weeks by my count and making him happy made me happy.

I checked the time on my phone and hurried back; already twenty minutes long on my estimate. The mall was easy enough to find my way around in but bigger than I thought and I'd taken a long time in the department store.

When I got back in to the room I put my prizes in the bathroom and found Paul upright on the couch. Showered and changed. He'd turned a lamp on.

"You going to walk away from this one?" I asked.

"Mmm," he said. "Any hangover you can walk away from. Can I get more coffee please?"

"'course," I refilled him and joined him on the couch. "Bee's teaching Ray to bake. It's good news for everyone."

"Yeah," Paul said sipping his coffee. Then he blinked a couple of times when he noticed my face. "That's pretty. Why the big change?"

I shrugged. "I'm going to be raising a girl so I thought I would try acting like one. Is it too much?"

"No," he smiled at me then he pushed my hair back behind my ears. "Ears too? You didn't have to do that."

"They said six weeks but I'll probably be able to take them out in three. I think I like them. Starting to hurt a bit now though."

He kissed my ear. "I love you either way, you know that don't you?"

"Yes Paul," I sighed and moved closer to rest my head on him careful to not lean on my ear. He sipped his coffee quietly.

"Can I ask how you know Patrick?" he asked. I saw that it bothered him the night before and figured he would bring it up.

"Andre took the cigarette from him," I told him.

"He worked for Damian then?" Paul sat up straighter beside me so I turned to face him. When he put it like that it didn't sound very good at all. I closed my eyes and recalled the Patrick I knew then.

"No more than Andre did," I told him. "Bee was a girl then. There was nobody to bring everyone together … Damian, Patrick and Andre all got there by different routes. They hadn't known each other more than a few months. Patrick was loyal to the Service and like Andre he didn't like the Lieutenant. He believed strongly in the chain of command so he was as loyal to him as he would be to any Lieutenant but not to him personally. He was shining him on hoping it would look good … hoping for promotion. Everyone knew Damian got ahead on the backs of his men. He didn't care about the cigarette … he saw an opportunity to help himself get ahead.

"Andre played the same games only he made sure that he never moved up. There was no place else for someone who liked what he did so much. He knew the war end and he wouldn't get by back home with such a bad habit. The front line was the only place for him."

"Are you sure?" Paul asked.

"Yes. I don't feel any tie to Damian in any of the men we met last night."

"Alright."

"Why didn't they ask about the blue light?" I asked Paul.

"They don't know what to make of you. They did ask me. I told them I'd only seen it once before when you were concentrating really hard and you had it under control. I said you didn't understand anything about it and I was making sure it stayed that way."

"I guess that's the best answer," I agreed. "I hope I did a good job of being a good obedient mate for you last night."

"The best," he said, smelling my clean hair. "I know you don't like being treated like a kid. I appreciated it. I don't have to worry about you not being able to look after yourself or play your part with the men. You're a lot more than they think you are."

"How am I supposed to teach him?" I'd thought about it as I was falling asleep the night before and hadn't come up with anything. "The only solid relation I have to work with is you, me, and her … and I don't think I want him touching her."

"Marie is Damian's sister," Paul said. "We don't take mates in our own line. Maybe better to not bring that up either."

"I'll see if he'll talk about relations he knows. There's probably something there we can work with. Has he always been able to read?"

"Yes, but just matching us from before to us now."

"You're not pleased that Keith asked are you?"

"No … I don't like you sharing something with someone else that you can't share with me. But it would have been a huge insult to Keith had I refused," he admitted.

"We never tried."

"I know I can't," he said giving me a weak smile. "My father tried."

"Okay. Can I get you anything?"

"No thanks. If my stomach keeps behaving I should be able to manage lunch. We're expected after one sometime."

"Alright." We sat quietly on the couch trying to get a little more energy back.

"Do they think I think she's a boy?" I asked him. I was trying to make sure we had all our notes compared.

"I told them you didn't want to find out ahead of time. Of course they think she's a boy and believe that's what I think too," Paul said. "And the same Daytona story we told the Colonel. Better to stick as close to the truth as we can. Less chance of getting caught on a lie."

I felt the same way. He was starting to think like me.

"Okay ... I need a nap if we're going to be out that late again tonight," I told Paul.

"Yeah," he said and joined me.

Chapter 44

I fell asleep right away and woke up suddenly on the cold ground staring at a pair of men's dress shoes. Couldn't move; not even my eyes. There was heavy breathing above but I couldn't see the man making the sound. Then footsteps behind me and the shoes turned. They pushed the blood they were in around the toe of one foot as he pivoted. I would have been able to smell the blood if I had been breathing.

"Anna—"

Alina's scream was quickly muffled and cut off as he stepped over me to her. There was struggling and he dragged her back to where I was. Her feet bounced as he threw her into the wall. She started kicking but he was pressed in close to her, air wheezing in and out of her lungs.

One of her shoes came off and landed in my blood. Slowly her feet kicked less and less and the sounds in her throat stopped. I waited for the blood to start flowing down her legs. The dream would be over. Then I would wake up and shake it off. I'd hold on to Paul and push what I was seeing from my mind. It took so long but eventually it did ... slowly at first, then faster, as it ran down her legs and onto her shoe. Finally just a trickle as her foot curled up and trembled once. Then again.

Drop her, I thought, please wake me from this.

He did. I didn't.

His heavy breathing paused so he could swallow. Alina and I were both strong. We both struggled and he'd had to work for the pile of bodies on the floor. I lay still and didn't wake up.

His heels came up as he squatted next to us. He was doing something to her I couldn't see. He'd taken her life. Couldn't he just leave her alone now? Then he turned to me and put his hand on my neck feeling for a pulse I suppose. I knew I didn't have one. He put his hands on the side of my face and turned me to face him.

It was Paul.

"Anna ... God I love you Anna," he said quietly. "I'm so sorry. I hope it won't have to be like this next time."

"Bastard!" I yelled and pushed myself up in bed. Paul was already sitting. He tried to hold me but I pushed him away and landed on my feet beside the bed, backing into the wall and breathing hard. I felt his hand on my neck making sure I was dead before I realized it was my own hand, convincing myself I was alive.

After a few gasps I realized I was awake and got my bearings. Then I almost dove back into bed and grabbed him tight. My eyes closed and I tried to relax.

"That sucked," I said. "I thought I was still dreaming."

"Sshhh," he said. "Sshhh."

"I'm sorry," I said after a few minutes. "I didn't know where I was."

"Do you want to tell me about it?"

I shook my head. I didn't want to have that dream ever again. Damn Pilot. He should have spared the bit about Paul hurting me and done what Lieutenant Nielsen had. Sent me straight after Damian. Given me a knife and pointed me up the fucking hill.

"It was the dream where he killed Alina and me again, but this time at the end he knelt down and held my face to his … I woke up."

"I wish you had more good dreams," he said.

I tucked my head under his chin. "The good things all happen when I'm awake. Do you ever get nightmares?"

He stroked my hair.

"I went through some bad spells … drinking, dreaming. Not being alone any more helps."

"I'm sorry," I whispered. Sorry for asking. Sorry for intruding. Sorry to hear that. Sorry for leaving you alone for so long.

He moved his hand to my stomach.

"She's getting big … how long now?" he asked.

I was glad to change the subject. She seemed to like when he touched her; we could feel her move.

"Fifteen weeks … beginning of April now if we don't lose any more time. She moves more for your hand than for mine."

"We should get going … it's almost two," he sighed.

"Mm," I said.

After changing out of the clothes I'd been sleeping in into jeans, black runners, and a long sleeved stretchy T-shirt I put my hair up and touched up the makeup. Paul was dressed more casually like the men we met the night before. Keith had been dressed better, like his waiters, to help out when the restaurant was busy. It was Friday so I guessed it would be.

Paul bagged up our cash, guns, and my pearl earrings while I was changing. His clothes from the previous night and my dress were in the hotel dry cleaning bag.

"Keith has a safe we can put the bag in for the evening so we can get the room made up," he explained. That was good. I didn't want to have to spend the night guarding it between my feet. Paul stopped at the desk to ask the room be done.

When we got to Keith's the waitress showed us right upstairs. There were five men at the table but not the same five as the night before. Keith and Patrick were missing and there were two others we hadn't seen before. Paul was behind me so I reached across him and grabbed the railing. He bumped in to me.

"Anna?" he asked as he pushed a bit but then he saw the two new ones and stopped. I started to carefully assess them both but their presence had taken me by surprise so it took a moment to be able to focus.

"She's protective of you," Keith's voice whispered behind us.

"Yes," Paul replied quietly, "very. She's one of my best. You don't want to be the man who tries to get to me past her."

Keith didn't comment. Part of me wondered exactly what it was Paul told him I did. I would have to ask him later. It only took a minute to learn what I needed about them. I let go of the railing and took Paul's elbow.

"What's holding up the train?" Patrick's voice from half way down the stairs.

I turned to apologize to them and had to cover my mouth to stifle a laugh. Both were shaved bald. Completely, shiny, bald. I didn't comment; I was very glad I hadn't taken the bet.

"Marie hasn't seen it yet ... she's going to kill me," Keith said.

Paul patted his back. After Keith introduced us to the two we hadn't met he took us down the other stairs to his office to lock our bag in his safe. At least we didn't have to worry about the cleaning staff finding the things in it and I tried not to worry that we wouldn't get it back. Paul wouldn't have given it to him for safe keeping if there was any concern about that at all.

When we got back upstairs I pulled Paul aside. Keith was arranging lunch and Patrick was waiting to get started with me. It was going to be hard to look at him for a while without laughing.

I lifted my chin so I could whisper right into his Paul's ear.

"Paul ... the one in the red shirt is ours. I guess we've been busy."

He smiled at me and kissed my cheek.

"The other is Ross's line ... the ones that aren't in our lines don't seem to be as independent as I thought."

Paul nodded. "Most of the mates are from outside our lines. My father says the ones who've been around the longest like us mated before the other ones started showing up."

That made sense. When I thought about it the first three lines seemed as unrelated to each other as the ones like Ross seemed related to them. Maybe the first three just called themselves brothers. It would give them authority over any newcomers.

"What exactly did you tell Keith I used to do?" I asked Paul. My arms felt like they wanted to cross so I put one around him and the other on his chest. I didn't want to look like I was challenging him in front of his family.

"What do you mean?" he asked so I repeated what he had said to Keith.

"Oh, that. The men are always protective of the man they are loyal to. It's unusual for a mate to be. She usually needs protection," he paused. "I know you can look after yourself but I have a deep need to protect you too."

"And?" I asked. He hadn't given me the whole answer.

"And you served under me until I knocked you up …" he admitted.

"I see … it's not like you to tell a fib," he looked a little sheepish. "But that's exactly how I got knocked up."

He laughed. "Yes. They need to have a healthy respect for you. Like my men back home."

I understood. "I didn't mean to cause a problem on the stairs. I'm protecting the baby and me as well as you."

"You didn't," Paul said.

I remembered how helpless Catherine was. Like a toy in Damian's hands. But she wasn't afraid … just incapable of defending herself. Angry and sickened by the violence. She stayed so still to try and protect her lover. She was loyal to Paul then; willing to sacrifice herself to give him a chance. Paul put his hand under my chin and pulled it up to kiss me.

"Get a room you two," Keith said. He had just come up the stairs and was walking past. Paul looked right at him and kissed me again. I giggled and tried not to turn pink then he turned us around so I was between him and the wall.

"Ray wants to know more about what you found out last night … but he doesn't want you to tell him. He wants me to."

I didn't really understand the difference but Keith said he was funny about things so I would go with it.

"Keith and Ray are both Pilots," I told him. "They're … brothers? Does that work? Different mothers."

"That works," Paul said.

"Patrick is Ray's. I guess he inherited your sister from Pilot? Does that make sense?"

Paul nodded. "He was interested in which one was his. He'd like to visit some time after we get back. Ray says you can talk about him to Patrick to help him learn … but Patrick needs to keep it to himself. He should understand that already."

I agreed.

Lunch was coming up the stairs so we joined the rest of them to eat. I only had a couple of hours with Patrick today before Marie would arrive so we needed to get to work. Keith explained that the two who were missing from last night would be with us by dinner and he would need to open the top floor up to customers. We would keep our table but would have company through the evening.

Patrick pushed his plate back before I did and looked over to see if I was ready but I wasn't so I decided to start off by making sure I would be listened to. I waited until he stopped looking at me.

"Patrick," I said a little sharply. He looked back. I tilted my head to where I'd been working on Keith's question the night before.

"In the corner please. Take your napkin."

"There?" he asked. I just looked back.

"Okay," he took his napkin and went over to wait.

"What are you doing?" Paul whispered to me.

"Even though I'm the kid he needs to know he's my apprentice."

Paul put his nose in my ear. "Okay. I know you only take shit from them when you choose to."

"That's right."

I went over to join Patrick at the small round table in the corner. There were only two seats so we sat across from each other.

"So," I said to Patrick, "ready to start?"

He nodded.

"How are your manners?" I asked.

"Fine?"

"Ground rules first then," I sighed. "I only provide information about a relation if I'm asked by the man it pertains to. But in the course of answering his question I learn a lot about other relations ... build on other answers like last night. I won't share those answers even to the men they pertain to. They must ask their own questions.

"I'll share with you while you're learning but you have to understand how completely personal that information is. Even Paul doesn't know the extent of my knowledge of the family and nobody else can know yours. It protects us in a way ... if the third line knows what a resource we are it may decide to silence us or try and take that information from us. Your discretion protects us both, as does mine."

"I understand," Patrick said. "Where do we start?"

"Your questions first."

He thought a bit. I noticed Paul kept glancing over as did Keith.

"What was that blue light?" I suspected that was Keith's question. My guess was he wanted to make sure that I didn't understand it. That was fairly close to the truth, my understanding of it was quite limited though a lot more than Paul let on.

"I did it once before ... I was really focused on something and I

236

guess it got out. Paul was upset with me. I think my self control is lacking because I'm just an over-informed child this time around. Like bed wetting maybe? I think I made him feel awkward in front of you. I know he's disappointed in me."

I sighed and leaned toward Patrick. "I don't understand what I did. I think it's more like we feel about hearing voices. Do you think I could be crazy?"

Patrick laughed. "No, I don't think you're crazy."

I acted relieved. "I just don't want to embarrass him like that again."

"What relations can you find?" he changed the subject.

"I can find a sister's fingerprint from her brother's and probably the other way around but I haven't done one yet. I can remove the father's print from the son's and what is left of his is the mother. Each one is time consuming … it leaves something here." I touched under my nose. "That's why I kept sneezing. To clear it I think otherwise what's left might interfere with my next comparison. It's tiring."

"How?"

I thought as Patrick waited. How was the question.

"You do it here, don't you?" he asked pointing under his nose.

"No, here," I shook my head and laughed pointing under mine.

"Fine … yours it is," he said. "I'll focus there."

"I …" but he was already leaned back in his chair with his eyes closed.

"Ready?"

"Yeah," he sounded drowsy already with concentration. I felt the same way.

"I'm going to put two prints there. Don't say the names."

First I put in Paul then I put in Warren, the man in the red shirt.

"Do you know who they are?" I asked him.

"Yes," he spoke even more slowly.

"When I look at them closely I see a lot of things. Words, colours, feelings …" I said.

"Shapes, smells … I feel like parts of me are being touched," he continued, "other things I can't describe."

"Very good … you're going to help. We're going to start by taking things from the son and father that match. Keep what's left separate. We can't mix them up or we're starting over … no harm done just extra work. There will be things left over in both prints. We can ignore the father. We're only interested in what's left in the son."

"Okay."

I started with something I found in Paul and Warren and removed it from both. Patrick picked it up quickly and I watched as he did the work. By the time we were done he was as fast as me. All that was left of Warren were pieces of me.

"Well done. I think male energy is stronger … more concentrated. You're fast and accurate. Now focus on what is left of the son … can you match it to a mate you have met?"

"Yes," he said quietly, "does the son know?"

"He doesn't, the father can tell him." I sneezed. "Next one we'll do in you. You're going to find my brother … your father."

"Auntie?"

I laughed.

"You do it this time." I focused under Patrick's nose. He didn't seem to notice.

"I'm not reading anything."

"Put me there," I prompted.

"Right …" He did and I read myself.

"Tricky part is not losing anything or getting what you've done mixed up with what you haven't," I explained.

"Okay," Patrick sounded even dopier.

It took him two tries. His first attempt was more like Keith than like Ray. I suspected that was because he was familiar with Keith. Second attempt he nailed it. Then he proceeded to find his mother and reverse her into Paul.

Show off.

I was pleased, his quick success made me look good.

"We need to clear again and then we can wake up," I told him, vaguely remembering Paul's voice saying Marie would arrive soon. "I think we're out of time today."

He sneezed first and his eyes were already open when I opened mine. Then he took in a deep breath and sank back in his chair.

"Do I look as tired as you do?" he asked me.

"Uh," yawn, "huh." Patrick yawned in reply and nodded.

"Do you think you can practice that on your own?" I asked him.

"I can … you just made up teaching that?"

I nodded.

"Thank you, Anna. You're a good teacher." He stood and helped me up then he kissed my cheek.

"Most welcome Patrick. You're a good student," I replied.

We took our places back at the table. Paul had kept one empty next to him for me. When I sat down I closed my eyes and leaned on him.

"I don't know how not moving could be so tiring," he said. "You'll sleep well tonight."

"How's your head?"

"Sore … I don't think anyone is drinking tonight."

I closed my eyes and tried to get my energy back. When I opened them Patrick had come back up with coffee for himself. There was an empty seat left next to Keith. For Marie I supposed. It didn't take long for her to arrive. We already had customers taking seats upstairs with us so she kept her voice down but her displeasure with Keith's new look was obvious.

She glared at him then at Patrick.

"What stupid bet was it this time?" she quietly demanded. Keith and Patrick both looked back at her innocently. Paul snickered. They both looked afraid of her. Keith more so than Patrick.

"At least you both lost ... who did you lose to?"

They pointed at me. I tried to look aghast. Marie was furious.

"Blaming our guest," she quietly fumed. "I hope it grows back in patches."

Then she spoke to me across the table. "I'm so sorry Anna. They try and have this old boy's club thing going but they just wind up making fools of themselves."

"Marie, you're more patient than I would be," I elbowed Paul and he pulled himself together. The other men were still laughing and at least I could keep mine in line.

Chapter 45

I hurried down to the ladies room to give my legs a quick stretch. Marie was waiting for me when I got out of the stall.

"Hi Marie," I said as I washed my hands. She disappeared into another stall and started talking.

"You know I was sixteen when I met Keith ... he was thirty. Grade eleven. My parents found out when I was in grade twelve. They freaked out on me but there was nothing they could do ... they couldn't prove we were sleeping together."

Please Lord, I thought, I never wanted to hear this come from a woman on a toilet.

"Keith insisted I finish high school and put me through my first year of university. I was still living at home until my eighteenth birthday when we got married and I moved in with him. They had warmed up to him some by then ... couldn't really be against someone who felt my education was so important even if he was almost twice my age."

She stepped out of the stall and turned both the hot and cold on full.

"I'm second year now. We quit being careful when we got married and have been trying ever since." She looked at my stomach. "Was it hard?"

"Was what hard?" I asked.

"Getting pregnant."

"Oh, that," I said. "Nothing's a hundred percent … not unwelcome though."

I waited for it; for the woman I just met to talk to me about reproduction in a ladies room.

"I'm a week late," Marie said. "I told Keith I saw the doctor and he's flooded with late stressed out university women right now. I'm taking six classes and working here most nights. I told him the doctor said to quit the job or take a couple fewer classes next semester or he's going to have me on tranquilizers. But I'm so tired and the last couple of days I threw up between classes. Keith is so down about us not being successful I just don't want to have to tell him no again."

She looked down too. I'd never thought about having children until it happened to me. There was nothing I could draw on to relate to the frustration and failure they had been going through. What I did know was that I liked her and I wondered if we'd always gotten along.

"You already told him the doctor said no. You should find out. At least you won't have that worry on top of everything else." I offered. "I'll come with you to the drug store if you want to do it now."

She seemed to brighten a bit then her expression changed. "Keith never lets me run around the mall alone. If he can't come with me one of his buddies does. There was a girl my age raped a year ago … they never caught the guy."

"You won't be alone. I'll take care of it. When they hesitate we'll run for it."

Then she cheered up. "Okay … I can show you around here a bit."

When we got back upstairs I stood behind Paul.

"My calves are cramping up from all the sitting … I need to walk around or they'll be in knots. Marie's coming with me," I told Paul, loud enough for Keith to hear.

Keith checked his watch. "I have a section to cover now, can you go with them Paul?"

Paul started to stand so I pressed my hand hard on his shoulder and my other around Marie's waist.

"I will guard this young one with my life," I told them. I was dead serious but she didn't know that and she covered her mouth as she laughed.

Keith hesitated and looked at Paul who nodded at him. "Well …" he said.

"'kay … bye," I said as Marie started dragging me to the stairs.

We hurried down and to the main door to the restaurant. I cast my senses back to the table and felt Warren coming down the stairs as we walked out into the mall.

"Bet he changes his mind," Marie said not slowing down. We

240

took a right when we got to the main concourse and I quickly looked back as we rounded the corner.

"You're right … Warren. He could have sent someone in a less obvious shirt. He'll be easy to keep an eye on wearing red."

"Grrr," Marie laughed. I noted the stores as we walked by then I pushed her into a record store.

"You like music?" I asked.

"Sure," she said. We looked around for a few minutes. She found a couple of CD's on sale she'd been looking at for a while so she got them. When we left we cautiously approached the door and spotted Warren on a bench two stores down. I looked the other way and there was another bench with a jewellery kiosk just past it. A garbage can and a couple of decorative fake trees.

"When he looks the other way we'll run and hide over there," I pointed.

She nodded. "Have you done this before? This is turning into the most covert girls' night I've ever been on."

I laughed. After a minute Warren checked his watch and his attention wandered. A couple of women in short skirts walked past him heading back the way we came and he obediently watched them go.

"Now," Marie said and we ran to the trees behind the kiosk. It was hard enough to see Warren on his bench so hopefully he wouldn't see us. After a couple more minutes he went to peek into the music store, then he walked in the door. We waited. When he came out he was on the phone so I quickly took mine out and turned the ringer down. After another minute it rang. Keith must have had to go and get Paul.

"Hello?"

"Hey Rach," Paul said. "Where did you two get to?" Wow, direct. I thought he would at least try and sound interested in what we were doing.

"There's a smoke shop … Marie's thinking of getting her dad a humidor for Christmas," I told him.

Marie covered her mouth to stifle her laughter. I heard Paul's palm rustle on the phone then after a few seconds Warren went back the way we came. The smoke shop was six stores back.

"Pardon Marie?" I called out like I was trying to hear her across the store. "I have to go, love you."

She grabbed my hand and we ran to the stairs to the second level of the massive two story mall. We didn't stop until we got to the drug store.

"What did we just do?" Marie asked me.

"Gave Warren the slip."

"Is Paul going to be mad at you?"

"Not our fault Warren got there after we left. We had no idea he

241

was following us. And besides, do you really want to hang out in the family planning aisle with him?"

"Eew, no." she laughed. She got a box with two pregnancy tests in it. I got some time for our phones and a bottle of Advil for Paul. I had a feeling that he would be using my minutes up fast tonight. The Advil was for the headache I was making worse. We paid and left as my phone rang again.

"Hello?"

"Rachel … are you two okay?"

"Hi … yes. She's showing me the pirate ship."

More palm rustling on phone. Marie was grinning. We were nowhere near the pirate ship. I'd read the brochure in the room.

"What the hell is that?" I exclaimed. "A submarine?"

I gestured for Marie to answer. She was close enough for Paul to hear her.

"Mm hm. We can go in it if you want. Keith and I made out in there once … third base."

I burst out laughing. "Maybe next time … can we go on the ship?"

"Uh huh. Let's go." She was enjoying getting in on the deception.

"I'm low on minutes," I told Paul.

"Oh, okay … bye."

"Bye," I told him.

"Do you want an easy way to make up to him for giving him the run around tonight? A place I worked last summer … they're hiring me back for some shifts heading up to Christmas. Get you a good discount."

"Sure where?" I asked. I'd found a couple of hundred in the back pocket of my jeans when I put them on.

"You'll see."

It was one of those adult places with some naughty underwear on the mannequins in the window and a wall blocking most of the front door so that you had to walk around to see what was inside. There weren't any other customers other than us.

"Carla?" Marie called and a middle aged woman came out of the back.

"Marie," she smiled and hugged her. "Who's your friend?"

"Anna," Marie introduced us. We saw that Carla's hands were full of Christmassy red brassieres so Marie offered, "I'll wait on her … let you know when we're ready."

"Thank you!" Carla disappeared.

"I think we're the same size … you'll want something your stomach won't outgrow too fast." She tore through the racks as my phone rang.

"Hello?" I answered while I looked at the shelves of adult toys and potions. This is what I thought of when we were going to Willy's Toy Shop. Only this was Carla's.

"Enough Rachel. Where are you?" Paul was losing patience.

I acted offended. "So a woman can't pick up a little something to surprise her husband without some other man escorting her? Tell Keith we're at Carla's and see if he doesn't blush when he explains that to you. Then we're probably going for ice cream or something and we'll be back in time for dinner."

I waited through the rustling. I had been talking about Marie and I both surprising our husbands. With different things of course. Marie was still pulling things off the racks but she was slowing down. While I waited I felt around the store and the mall out the door for Keith's men or Paul or anyone else I would have to be cautious of. There was nobody.

"Um sorry," Paul said. "Dinner's at nineteen-thirty."

"Okay John."

He hung up.

Marie took me down to one of the change rooms. "What colour does Paul like?"

"I don't really know … he liked the green dress I wore last night."

"Okay … I don't have any green that won't make you look like a Christmas present and I find bows on pregnant women to be intolerably tacky. Like someone is going to be dumb enough not to know what's under the gift wrap. Here."

She gave me a purple teddy. The panties were stretchy satin as was the push-up style bra on top. The sheer short skirt that hung from it was a little stretchy so it didn't have too much bulk now and would still fit in a couple of months if I was still in the mood to put it on, as she put it. Then she made me come out and model it.

"Carla? You have to come see this," she called so Carla came in.

"That's very nice," she said. "Your stomach is just the right size to model things like this … my advice is to put it on after, honey. When he's tired but won't resist going again. Otherwise it'll be over so quick you won't feel like you got your money's worth and you'll be back in here complaining to Carla."

Marie and I laughed. I'd save the modeling for Marie in a few months. I wasn't into doing that at all. Then Marie gave me a couple of others to try. I settled on the purple one and a black one. The top on the black one didn't stretch like the purple but the front seam was open so there was room for my belly. Carla gave us Marie's staff price and sent us on our way.

We still had half an hour until dinner so we took our time walking back. There was ice cream at a chocolate shop we passed and I got a box of dark chocolate caramels for a craving I suddenly had. I tucked them in with my lingerie. We got bubble gum ice cream cones because we both remembered liking it as kids. It was still just as good. I kept scanning ahead and behind for anyone who could be following us, friend or otherwise, but there was nobody.

Marie was a lot like spending time with Alina. Quick to laugh and crude to the point of being blunt. It was hilarious and I had no trouble keeping up with her jokes and sense of humour. We had to finish our cones outside Keith's restaurant before we could go in.

"Will you come in the restroom with me?" she whispered.

I nodded so she took my hand and we walked in together. Nobody was at the railing on the upper level watching for us so we headed down to the ladies room. Patrick would have spotted us anyway. We made it past the stairs up without being stopped and safely into the washroom. Marie put her bag of CD's on the counter and took the other one.

"Here goes," she said. Her hands were shaking a bit so I gave her a hug and smiled warmly.

"I think you already know what it will say or you wouldn't be making sure," I told her.

"You're right," she smiled back. Then she showed me her crossed fingers and went in. After a minute I heard the cap snap back on it and she passed it to me under the door.

"Here," she said. "Tell me what it says ... I can't look."

"Okay," I took it and watched until the window showed a plus sign.

"Do you want to do the other one to be extra sure or is one good enough?"

"Anna! What does it say," she demanded.

"It says congratulations Marie ... go tell your husband."

"Yes?" she squealed and burst out of the stall and threw her arms around me.

"Yes." I showed her. It wasn't the reaction I'd had when I'd found out but I hoped it would be something close if Paul and I were lucky enough to try again sometime.

She checked her watch.

"Should I tell him at dinner ... in front of everyone?" she asked.

"You know him best. Maybe he'd rather find out privately ... then you can decide together how to tell everyone."

She considered that. "No. He's such a prankster. We have some cakes in the fridge for things like this. I'll get one out and set something up with a waitress I trust to be quiet about it."

"If you're sure," I told her, but I guessed that anyone who would be fine with getting to third base on a tourist submarine would have no trouble with a baby cake.

Marie and I split up at the bathroom. I went upstairs to find Paul and she went to the kitchen. The restaurant was still packed but I noticed that a lot of the customers were having desert or coffee so it was probably going to quiet down soon. I took my seat next to him and put my bag between my feet.

"What's in the bag?" Paul asked. Carla's bags were plain brown paper. Appropriate for an adult shop. I picked it up carefully to keep Paul from peeking. Didn't matter though. The things I bought there were well wrapped in tissue. I rooted around and pulled out the Advil.

"There you go," I told him as I put the bottle on the table.

"Fantastic," he said taking a couple then he shook it and had a few other takers.

"What were you two doing?" he asked. Keith listened across the table.

"We were up to something. I felt Warren behind us from the moment he started down the stairs. Nobody is getting even close to us. The other two will be entering the restaurant in a few seconds." I said just to prove my point. I'd made a quick sweep of the entrance and lucked into spotting them. Keith stood up to look and then sat back down.

"They're here," he said but he still didn't seem very pleased with me.

Paul understood that protecting Marie now was as important as protecting me. Keith didn't yet. The only difference was that Marie would need the protection if there was trouble. I wouldn't.

"I like her a lot. She's so much like Alina it's uncanny."

Paul laughed. "You two have always gotten along. I'm not surprised you found some reason to take off together the first chance you got. So what's in the bag?"

"I know where our child will get his impatience from, Paul. You want me to show you here?"

He grinned and shook his head. Marie came up and took her seat next to Keith. He put his arms around her, relieved that she was back. She gave me a quick smile over his shoulder and they whispered for a while. He seemed to calm down after a few minutes.

"Is Keith mad with me?" I whispered to Paul.

"He's not convinced you can take care of his girl," he answered.

I shrugged. Whether he believed it or not I was.

Dinner was great. Fettuccine Alfredo with prawns, salad, and garlic bread.

"You want cheesecake Anna?" Marie asked. "Keith's is the best. Paul?"

"It is Friday," I laughed. "Cheesecake day."

Keith went down to order desert. He came back looking puzzled.

"They had to scramble to get more ready … she'll bring it up in a bit. We don't usually run out of cheesecake."

I got it. Marie's waitress friend had told him that so she could bring up the cluttered tray of deserts instead of just Keith's baby cake. She was up in a few minutes to get our dishes and apologized to Keith.

"We had a run on it … big family here for dinner ordered a round for their table. We had to put candles in all the pieces. Shouldn't be too much longer."

She left and came back for the rest of the plates. Marie wasn't even nervous. I guessed that she was in on the pranks even though she wasn't happy about the friendly bets.

When the waitress finally came up with desert she started with Paul and me, then worked her way around the table skipping Keith and Marie before going back to them. Keith was talking to Paul and not paying attention to the cake being set down all around him. Marie first, then she put the little pink and blue cake in front of Keith. She rested her hand on his shoulder to get his attention off of his conversation with Paul before she made off back down the stairs. I quickly glanced at Marie while Keith looked down. Her grin was huge and she looked like she was about to vibrate off her chair. Paul had noticed the cake as soon as it was put down and slipped his arm around me.

"Is this what you were up to?" he whispered.

"Mm hm."

Keith was picking up his fork to dig in then he paused.

"Marie?" he asked then he looked over at her.

"Yes!" she exclaimed, practically bouncing in her seat. He gently put his arms around her and I spotted tears in his eyes as he buried his face in her hair. There were tears on her face too when I looked away. After they came up for air there were handshakes, then I took a couple of bites of my desert. Marie was right. It was the best.

When I looked up and they were gone. I elbowed Paul and tipped my head toward their empty chairs. He shrugged. The little smirk on his face told me he knew where they had gone and it wasn't long after our desert plates had been cleared that I knew for sure. Keith sat down pink cheeked and Marie's shirt was misbuttoned. She had an extra button hole up top.

"Buttons," I whispered to her across the table, resting my fingers on the collar of my shirt.

"Oopsie," she said as she started to fix them, "Keith wanted to make extra sure."

She had turned toward him for a little privacy but when he saw her hands undoing the buttons he took her elbow.

"Not here," he said softly and she laughed as he took her back to the stairs.

"Extra, extra," she called back to me.

Everyone called it an early night. Keith and Marie were gone a lot longer the second time and when they came back he brought our bag up with him. He said we could come back same time tomorrow, just like today. It would be just as busy upstairs the next two nights but by Monday we would have it to ourselves again. We had originally planned on leaving the next day but Paul figured if we only did one night at each of the stops we planned next we would be back on schedule if we stayed until Thursday.

As soon as we got in the door Paul made sure I had my bag in hand and shoved me in the bathroom.

"Go change," he ordered.

I started with the purple. It didn't stay on long and when Paul was almost asleep I crept into to the bathroom and put on the black one. Paul laughed and begged for mercy and it stayed on a little longer.

Chapter 46

It was Monday at dinner. I felt like all we had done was eat since we found Keith and his part of the family. Paul had spent Sunday hung over again so Marie had taken me around the mall some more. We didn't complain about Keith tagging along. They'd been inseparable for the past two days for which they could easily be forgiven.

Patrick nudged my shin under the table with his foot just after dinner came up. I thought he was just rearranging his legs but then he did it again so I looked up. He looked puzzled.

"Anna," he said, "I have a question about my … homework."

I nodded back even though I hadn't given him any.

"I'm not sure how to describe it. Can I show you?"

"Now?" I asked. I had no idea what could be so urgent that we had to sit with our eyes closed while our food went cold.

"Yes," he said firmly. "It'll just take a moment."

I leaned back in my chair and closed my eyes.

"Come to me please," he said. I relaxed and cast my sense to him. "Ready? Follow."

He shot toward the entrance and quickly disappeared.

"Slow down … I lost you," he came back and led me out into the mall. I strained to keep my focus. I had no idea how he had been coherent and looking that far away. He stopped at a man coming toward us placing his sense in him. I read him too.

"What do you make of it?" he asked. But I was already pulling what I could. He was Damian's.

"I need a minute Patrick."

I had been able to read the intentions of the first three of Damian's men quite by accident so I tried to do the same on purpose. I felt my eyes roll up as I jumped back along his line, rewinding his past few days. A taxi ride, the bus, anonymous travel … he wasn't supposed to be here. Should be in Calgary. Hadn't told anyone … just gotten bored. So much for absolute loyalty in this one.

"Holy shit," Patrick exclaimed. "How are you doing that?"

"Sshhh," I told him. I had no idea he'd be able to see what I was doing. The man had come down to where the restaurants were … very close. I watched as he was seated just below us. Stupid coincidence but then why wouldn't he eat at the best restaurant at the arguably the biggest tourist attraction in the city. He didn't know we were here and nobody but Patrick and I knew about him. The man couldn't find out any of us were here. I decided I would deal with him. If I did it quickly he wouldn't have a chance to tell anyone where he had snuck off to or about me. Then I could be sure that Keith and his group were kept hidden. I pulled back into myself and felt around for my napkin and cleared the man from under my nose. Patrick was looking at me when I opened my eyes. He had the sense to keep quiet.

As I thought my food was almost cold.

"Eat … then we'll talk," I told him. Paul looked puzzled so I just shrugged. "Stupid reader tricks." I explained. He seemed to lose interest. I kept my focus gently on the man downstairs. The restaurant wasn't busy so I didn't think Keith or anyone at the table would go downstairs.

"Patrick?" I said when we were done. We took our napkins and went to the corner to sit down.

"What was that you did?" he asked right away. "He's like us but I don't know him."

"I do … in a way. Please remember the ground rules … nobody knows that I can do it except Paul but he doesn't really understand it. That man is very loyal to my other mate … do you know who that is?"

Distaste showed on his face but he didn't say anything.

"I feel loyalties as well as fingerprints. I don't know the man but his loyalty is to the other line. I have a sort of affinity to them. I don't know how, but I can see where his line has been and where it will be. Then I know what he's done and will do. I can only do it with that line … not the others."

Patrick nodded. "That was intense … I saw where he'd been the past couple of days. You did that?"

"Yes." I thought about what I would say next.

"He's not supposed to be here. He's hunting me. Should be in Calgary but he decided to come up here for a couple of days for R and R I suppose. By some bizarre coincidence he chose to have dinner downstairs. No idea we're here."

"So we let him go?"

I shook my head. "Patrick ... I'm going to take him out. The man he's loyal to will think he disappeared in Calgary. You'll all be safe. This place won't come in to it at all."

He looked alarmed. "No ... you can't do that alone."

We were leaning closely together. "So we leave his body in a hallway around here? They'll be all over this place. I can do it ... away from here. There is a child to protect now ... we can't take any chances."

"But what about Paul's child?" Patrick demanded.

"Follow me," I closed my eyes and waited for him, then I took him back to the man and ran his line forward. Images of leaving the restaurant then startled that I'm walking beside him. A service hallway, his knife, then it's dark, the smell of dirt and pine. My face in a blue glow that blinds him in the dark. Pain, his knife hits something soft, more pain then warmth down his chest in the cold. Weakness, numbness, my blue face standing over him.

Suddenly we were looking at each other as his line ended. Patrick looked a little green.

"See ... no problem," I whispered. "It's what I do."

"You can tell Paul if and when my absence worries him, otherwise I'll be in touch when I get back ... swear on Keith's son's life Patrick. Not a word. And I swear I'll keep him safe too."

"I hate this a lot ... I can't find fault in your logic."

"No, you can't."

"I swear Anna."

I watched the man on the floor below while he finished his dinner, then desert and coffee. He paid and made a stop in the restroom before he left and walked back in to the mall. I'd slipped my steak knife up my right sleeve blade first. It was crude but it would do.

"Washroom," I whispered to Paul. He was talking so he just nodded and patted my leg as I got up.

I quickly used the restroom then walked out into the mall. Still focused on the man I had no trouble catching up with him. As I followed him I thought about the logging roads up the hill from my home. I knew them well from dirt bike riding with Kenny. I pictured a section a couple of miles in ... a hidden footpath that led about fifty feet from the gravel road. Kenny and his friends and I would go up there and drink some afternoons. That was years ago and the path would be grown over. It could be months or years before anyone found him there. We passed a few more stores as pressure grew in my back. I stumbled as I was pushed from behind ... it wanted to take me. I would drain the man on the trip; take more than I needed to get back. He wasn't worth sleeping off.

I took his elbow and smiled up at him. He was surprised and

tensed his arm but then he smiled back at the sweet thing holding him for a moment before recognition appeared on his face.

"Hello handsome," I said.

"Uh, hello."

"What do you say we go somewhere more private?" I asked him. I kept my focus on our destination. It was hard to smile with the pain of the pressure but all I would need was contact with him when he made a move on me and we would be in the forest alone in the dark. He put his other hand on my forearm and gripped it tightly. I put a little fear in my face and pulled on my arm like I was trying to free it but he grinned and tightened his grip.

"Be quiet," he said. "I have nothing to lose if I kill you here."

I stopped pretending to struggle and walked with him. He wouldn't phone anyone until he was done with me. He guided me into the first service hallway we came to. The back doors to some of the stores went down one side then he took me around a corner to another long hall where there were more doors.

"Damian wants you for himself but he can't be choosy."

I stared back. He spun me around so he had my forearms and pushed me hard back into the wall then he pressed his lips into mine. I relaxed in his grip and kissed him back. There was a low growl in his throat as one of his hands let me go and dropped to his pocket. I heard his knife snap open and as he drew his arm back I let the pressure take us.

Blue light filled the small forested clearing. My hand appeared to burn with it. I had taken so much from him it must be the excess … hopefully enough to get me back so I didn't have to spend any of mine. I located him quickly and turned to face him, taking a couple of steps back. He was disoriented and confused. I held my palm out at him so the brightness toward his face partially hid me in the blind spot behind. He didn't say anything. I reached into my sleeve and took the steak knife. Then I let Andre out.

The man stepped toward us as we stepped to the right. He made the first move, lunging to the left while bringing his knife up at my belly, but the light had hidden Andre and me and he misjudged how far away I was. He was close, inches to spare, but not close enough. Andre spun while his weight was still shifting and sliced deep into his side as we danced away back out of reach.

The man swore and caught my hair swinging behind. Andre and I were stopped in our tracks by the sudden tug at the back of my head. The man slashed at us again and scored a hit low on my back through my shirt before I could get out of the way. I didn't feel it but my skin started to feel warm, trickling down to my butt.

He laughed as I stuck my blue right hand at his face causing him to flinch and let go of my hair, his hands to his face in defence. I kicked him in the nuts as hard as I could and he grunted and dropped to his knees. Something pulled in my stomach, just a muscle. Andre ignored it and ran the serrated blade deeply along one side of the man's neck. Warmth covered my hand. His blood was black in the blue light. He brought his hands up but his stomach was heaving from the blow to his crotch.

Then Andre made the knife go just as deeply into the other side of his neck and we disappeared back out of reach again. I lowered my arms and stood, breathing hard. It was too late for him to protect his neck. The blackness covered his light coloured clothes and I could hear the air leaking out where it shouldn't.

"Good night," Andre said as the man sat back on his feet, then after another half minute his head leaned to the side, its shifting weight toppled him over.

The only sound now was my own breathing. Andre was gone. The man's body was partly hidden in the underbrush. Thick salal and fern. Nobody had been here in a very long time. A quick check of my pocket verified that my phone was still there so I slipped the knife back in my sleeve and pulled out the phone. No Signal. I thought as much. They used radios up here. No cell service. That reminded me to check his. I found the phone in his coat pocket and quickly took out the battery so nobody could find him by the signal just in case some miracle allowed it to be picked up.

I studied my palm. Paul had pulled it away the last two times so I never had the chance. My skin seemed to bubble and roll beneath the air that appeared to glow just above the surface, like a pot of water only thicker. Where a bubble burst blue light would arc around to the back of my hand. Cautiously I touched it. There was no heat or tingling. My skin felt normal. I put my palms on my cheek; no difference then ran my fingers through my hair. Other than the blue light there was nothing in the feel of my hand that would give it away.

I opened the palm on my left hand and tried to take the energy back. It flowed in for several minutes only to reappear back in my right hand. It was extra … more than I could hold. I would have to focus well on where I would return to. Didn't want to show up in the lobby with that … or the cut on my back.

There was still pressure left from the jump here so I focused on the bathroom in our hotel room. I could clean up there and not worry about blood on the carpet anywhere else. My eyes closed as I concentrated. Long minutes passed. First a nudge from behind, then I caught myself as I tripped over the man and almost went face first into the brush next to him. There was pain now from the top of my head down my spine and in the cut on my back. I saw nothing in my mind but the hotel bathroom just the way I had left it. When I was sure that the pressure would take me whether I did anything to help it along or not I squatted down then suddenly straightened my knees and disappeared.

And with great relief found myself where I wanted to go. I could have been walking several miles down the logging road in the dark now using my hand as a flashlight until I had enough cell signal to call Ray for a ride if it hadn't worked. Then what? Steal a car and try and jump to the parkade below? My palm still glowed though less brightly. I opened my other hand up and took in as much as I could but I still couldn't make it all go away. Damn. I put the seats down on the toilet and sat resting my head on my arm on the counter.

My cell phone rang and I got it out of my pocket. Paul's number. If he was calling then he was worried, which meant Patrick had told him what I was doing.

"John," I said.

"Rachel," he said. Keith's voice in the background. I couldn't make out what he was saying. I waited but Paul didn't say anything. Likely deciding how to give me both barrels over the phone. It hadn't occurred to me until now how pissed he'd be.

"I'm in our room … bring Keith. He needs to hear about this complication."

"Keith … come with me," Paul said but he didn't say anything to me. He was less than ten minutes away. Much less if he hurried.

"Do we have the stuff for stitches?" I asked him. Ray had packed a fairly large first aid bag for us.

"What? God damn it Rachel."

"Patrick—," I started but he interrupted.

"What Patrick said doesn't make any sense." Paul must have been nearly running. I could hear his hard breathing. I put the phone on speaker and put it on the floor. I was suddenly faint and eased myself down to the lino on all fours resting my head on my crossed arms. After a minute I could hear them running down the hall and the key in the door. My phone beeped twice as he hung up.

"Anna?" he called as they stepped in.

"Bathroom."

He pushed the door all the way open as I carefully righted myself.

"Jesus," Paul said as he knelt in front of me. He took my face in his hands and started looking for the cut. I realized that the man's blood had been on my hand when I'd put both hands on my cheeks to compare how they felt, then I'd run his blood through my hair.

"That's not my blood," I glanced up at Keith and told him. "Nobody is getting to your child."

His brows pushed together. He didn't know what to say.

"Are you hurt?" Paul asked; all business. "You said something about stitches."

I reached around and pulled up the back of my shirt.

"He got hold of my hair and managed to tag me here before we could get out of the way."

"We?" Paul asked. He was looking at the cut now.

"I let him out to fight," I said.

"Keith, can you get me the red bag from the closet?" Then he muttered when Keith was around the corner. "If I could I'd kick his ass for letting you get hurt …"

Paul helped me back up on to the toilet seat so I was facing the counter again. Keith brought him the bag. I noticed that the blue had faded more from my hand so I kept my palm down on my leg. Good. Less to explain.

"Paul, will you please tell me what just happened?"

"Anna," Paul said, "how 'bout you tell us both."

He started going through the bag and getting things out. I pulled the bloody steak knife out of my sleeve and dropped it in the sink.

"Sorry I swiped your knife Keith," I said. Paul just sighed.

Then I took off my shoes and socks as my foot started to throb.

"I didn't think that would bruise." The top of my foot was darkening around a big lump. I must have hit it just right. "Hurts more than my back."

"How did you do that?"

"I kicked him in the junk after he pulled my hair. If he was going to fight like a girl so was I."

"Was," Paul said. He wasn't asking.

"He won't bother us again," I said quietly.

Paul sat on the tub behind me and started cleaning the cut.

"She killed him?" Keith blanched.

"Yes," I answered. "I want to get the blood off and change then I'll answer what you want. It's over now. You're safe here Keith."

"I'm freezing you," Paul said. His voice tighter but with what I couldn't tell. Disappointment maybe. Resignation. "It's going to sting."

"I know Paul," I said. It stung.

While he was sewing me up Keith's phone rang. Patrick and Warren had taken Marie home. Patrick said the place was safe so Warren stayed to watch from the street and Patrick was almost back. Keith told him where we were and he was coming.

"He said he watched what happened … he's upset," he explained.

I was out of the shower and dressed by the time Patrick got there. Paul had cleaned my cut a second time after I was dry and put a bandage on it. Patrick brought a bucket of ice and a mickey of whiskey. They were on their seconds drinking from the hotel plastic cups before any of them spoke to me.

253

"What the hell happened, Anna?" It was Paul.

I got up and turned off the hall light, then the lamp. The blue glow in my hand was obvious in the dark. What was left of the energy I had taken from the man.

"I drained him on the trip out … this is all that's left of it. I'm not wasting a day sleeping because of him. It was so bright in the forest. It was the blue glow we saw Patrick."

I turned the lamp back on. I would tell Paul. He would understand what I was talking about and could tell Keith and Patrick whatever he wanted.

"He was supposed to be in Calgary … didn't tell anyone he was coming up here. Just wound up downstairs. I followed him into the mall. When he saw me he took me into a hallway, where the back doors are to the shops. I was ready to get him out. The pressure was so painful. He pinned me to the wall and started kissing me so I relaxed and let him. I would have hurt myself struggling. He used one hand to pull out his knife. When he made his move I reacted and took him away. If we killed him here they would be down on us in no time. Keith's done nothing to deserve the attention I'm getting.

"They won't find him here and Damian will think he disappeared in Calgary. They have no reason to think anyone is here. It had to be tidy."

"Where did you take him?" He sounded less mad. Hopefully he understood my reasoning but he wouldn't be any happier about it. I looked at Keith and Patrick.

"Tell me," Paul said.

"He's in the forest up the hill from my house. Miles into the bush. I don't think anyone will ever find him." I rubbed the side of my stomach. The pulled muscle was painful. I got off the couch and went to lie down. That felt better.

"How can she be so indifferent?" Keith asked.

Maybe it was so many years of the old boy's club that kept him from accepting me. I could only guess. But then most of the men at Paul's were like that too. Ray and Denis liked me, Ross put up with me. The others just kept their distance. I hadn't realized how far I was from what I should be. Paul came over and sat by me on the bed. He gently pushed the hair from my face.

"She isn't," he said. He knew everything I'd been through and what I'd struggled with. "Anything else hurt?"

"My arms … where he grabbed me and threw me in the wall and I pulled a muscle in my stomach. But the back is the worst. Is there something for pain in the bag? I feel like I've been hit by a truck."

"Yeah, but I'll have to ask Ray what I can give you." He pulled out his phone and dialled.

"Hey Mark." He listened for a minute and frowned. "Fill me in later … Rachel's had a misadventure … what's in the bag that I can give her?"

"Okay … no … later."

"Bye Mark."

"Denis isn't entertaining women in my bed is he?" I asked.

He shook his head. "Ray took Bee in to the hospital with trouble breathing. He says it's under control now. Don't worry he's taking good care of her."

Paul went in to the bathroom where he had left the first aid bag. I did worry but I was very grateful that she wasn't alone.

"Patrick," I asked, "how far away were you when you saw what happened?"

"Still at the table," he said.

Paul was pushing up my sleeve and rubbing it with something cold then there were two pricks in my arm.

"Sorry … he said something to help you rest too," Paul said.

"'kay Paul. I guess my secret's out."

"Yeah. Close your eyes."

I wasn't sure how long it was until I heard them pour another round and I started to feel heavier. I was sleepy but I didn't sleep. Just floated.

"Is she insane?" Keith asked after what felt like a very long time.

"No," Paul's voice said. He sighed getting ready to explain. "You and her brother have the same father. One of the first three. She's met them all. One, her other mate tried to kill her. She found my father a few weeks ago. And your father shortly before that. He's hiding now. I think he made her like this but she won't talk much about it. She tries to accept what she is; the gifts he burdened her with. But she's not insane."

"If she does prove to be insane you have to put her down Paul … even with your son if she's a risk to other children," Keith said.

Paul sighed. I could picture the expression on his face; his mind looking inward, knowing Keith was right and hating himself for having to agree with him.

"I don't believe at this point that she is," Keith continued. "She's reckless but she made Patrick swear on my son that he'd keep quiet until she got that man away from here. She seems to be more focused than we are on protecting ourselves. That line has made us all suffer for too long."

"How did she get him out of the mall?" It was Patrick. "I thought he killed her … she just disappeared."

"She did disappear," Paul said. "My father says she can move her line. Or her place on her line. Can take others with her too. It's how she found my father. She wished for him and took us there. Me, her, and two others. I don't know how she does it. She doesn't either but she's getting better at it. She disappeared with him and they reappeared with him some miles ..."

I couldn't make out the rest of it. I had floated a long way into a dark echoing tunnel and couldn't piece their words together any longer.

I slept.

Chapter 47

I dreamed. Alina was begging, crying, Damian was laughing. My ear was pressed against door 1502 and the sounds were faint. Her building was so soundproof there was no way her neighbours would ever hear what he was doing to her inside. I put my hand on the doorknob and turned it as slowly as I could. When it was turned all the way I pushed it open and stepped inside closing it behind me.

Alina was curled in a ball on her sofa. There were bruises on her arms and what I glimpsed of her face.

"You make me sick Alina," he laughed at her. "You're disgusting. Nothing but a warm place to stick it until you got down to doing your job … now I've rented your womb out cheap. If I could have loaded it up without having to listen to your mouth run all the time I'd be the happiest man alive."

He took two hard steps toward her and raised his fist. She cried out and put her bruised arms over her head again, pulling her knees in tighter. He spat at her.

"Damn you Damian …" I whispered.

He paused and turned to me.

"This is grand," his angry face lit up. "Two for one."

Then I noticed the gun shoved in the front of his pants. There was blood on his shirt where the handle pressed into his stomach. The bastard must have hit her with it. He took the handle and pulled it out … it was too long, there was a silencer screwed into the end. When he had it almost pointed to me I would jump to Alina and get her away.

I watched the gun come up, ready to go. But nothing happened.

There were two quick puffs of smoke from the barrel I felt in my chest.

"Anna!" she screamed.

I tried to get to Alina but things stopped working. The pain brought me to my knees, then to the floor. More pain as my body started demanding oxygen and the room started to lose its colour.

"If you hurt my son or try and run away I'll do to you what I did to her. I guarantee it."

My vision failed as he battered the bruised arms that tried to protect her head then he turned his back on her and walked to her door. The last thing I felt was a viscous kick to my belly. The door slammed shut.

Alina cried. She wanted to cry hard but it sounded like it hurt less to be silent so her sobs gave way to the sound of air wheezing in her throat and desperate attempts to sniffle to clear her nose. I heard her come close then her arms were around me as she pulled me up. My head sagged back and my arms stuck out awkwardly as she held me tight around my ribs. She put a hand behind my head to steady it and hold it to her shoulder then she took me up away from the bloody carpet.

"Mom?" she called. "Mom? Are you here? Is Anna with you now?"

Her voice grew tighter as she tried not to cry again.

She was taking me to the angels. To our mother. She was such a good big sister.

"Please mom. I can't leave her alone here … please come get her. Take care of her."

She smelled of whiskey.

"Mom … mom. Come on … mom … wake up. Please."

Rough stubble caught the hair on top of my head and pulled it over my face.

"It's like this every night. Please Anna, come on, try and wake up."

My ribs moved as air came in and went out again and the arms around me were so much bigger and stronger than Alina's. I reached up and held on to Paul. Even in the lamp light my hand still glowed faintly but it didn't hurt him when my hand was on his back. I pulled my arms in between us to hide myself as my eyes closed again.

"Sshhh," he said, "bad one."

"Mm hm, he left her Paul. He beat her and he left her," I sighed. "She's safe now. He won't get to hurt her again. I'm going to cut his fingers off and shove them down his throat before I let him die."

"Who's safe now? That Alina she was talking about?" Someone whispered. Keith or Patrick.

"Her sister … Damian took her. Tried to use her to draw us out. It's been hard on Anna to be so helpless to protect her."

"It's okay now," I told him. "Tummy hurts."

Paul gently put my head back on the pillow. "Ray thinks ligaments. Not muscle. Could be sore for a while. He says you're going to have to go home if you keep doing things like that. He says be good little sister."

"Okay," I smiled. Ray went to a lot of trouble to look after me too. It sounded like Paul told him what I did; he would be worried. "Tell him I'll be good. He likes to hear that."

"I'll get you another shot. Just a sec," Paul said as he got up.

I studied my palm then I opened up my other hand and tried to take the energy back. Keith and Patrick watched as the last of the blue light disappeared. I sighed with relief.

"You can take that?" Patrick asked.

"Yes … if I use up my own to get around I have to sleep for a couple of days to get it back. Nothing can wake me up." I told him; then more quietly. "I don't have a lot of time left … I'm not wasting what little I have sleeping any more than I have to."

"What do you mean?"

I closed my eyes and didn't answer. Shouldn't have said it. Paul came and gave me the shot.

"What does she mean Paul? She says she doesn't have a lot of time." Patrick again. Keith still wasn't talking to me.

"She thinks Damian will come for her before the baby comes … she doesn't think she'll make it," Paul explained sadly. "She won't talk about it … don't bring it up to her again."

I woke up alone. The room was dark but after I carefully got out of bed and opened the curtains it was bright. Outside was cold and sunny. Paul wasn't in the room. No note. I didn't really care. Whatever he'd given me left me feeling like I was drifting … everything was good. After I dressed and tied my hair back I got some cash and took my key and phone. I wanted coffee. One wouldn't hurt. If I didn't wake up at least I'd feel like a jittery piñata dangling from the ceiling. That would be more fun than hanging around in the room. I had no intention of spending the afternoon and evening at Keith's restaurant again. I didn't fit in with them at all and just wanted to go home.

I got some food and a small coffee in one of the food courts. After I ate I took the coffee to a bench and sat down with it. I was still loopy. It was good going down but it just made me feel queasy once it was in my stomach.

"There you are," it was Keith. "Paul said you're not answering."

He sat down with me as I took out my phone. It was off so I held the power down but it didn't come on.

"I didn't notice it was dead. Can you let him know?"

"Yes." But he didn't call. "Look, Anna. I wanted to say thank you for what you did yesterday. I haven't been very friendly to you this week and I'm sorry. You've always been so loyal to Paul. Sometimes you don't think first and it gets you into trouble. Too willing to put yourself in the way for him and last night you did it for us.

"I can see how upset he's been that he can't do anything about it. I think he accepts it now for the most part. It's who you are."

He hesitated. "If you weren't in my line I would talk to him about

258

taking you as my other mate."

I opened my mouth but I couldn't think of a reply to that. Should I be flattered? Two mates was something I didn't want. Three was both silly and indulgent.

"Oh," he said, "I thought you knew how that works."

I shook my head. "I don't, but you're not going to get away without telling me."

"I guess not now that I've opened my mouth."

He quickly called Paul and explained about my phone and where we were.

"I would have to ask permission to try from your unborn child's father. When you're expecting and most connected to him. If he thought I was unworthy he would have to have a good reason. There are rules for that. He couldn't refuse if I was worthy. If you would accept me in your bed ... then we'd be connected as mates. Your first is chosen for you. Any other attention toward you from any of us is forbidden.

"I'd be the first one responsible for your child if something happened to his father ... it's not something we enter into lightly. And he would be responsible for mine if I found you first and something happened to me," Keith said.

"And no concern about how she would feel about her husband's buddy showing up at the door with flowers and cheap aftershave?"

"Not really," he shrugged, "from our point of view we're ensuring the survival of our children. I've seen Paul with you ... it would be a load off my mind to have someone like him backing me up with Marie and the baby. Even with you he would still be responsible for her ... without you they would become a mated pair."

"Has he asked you?" I blurted without thinking. The filter between my mouth and brain was off as I continued to feel like I was floating above the bench.

His eyebrows went up briefly. No doubt Paul would hear about that.

"He wouldn't be interested while he has you ... but if he didn't and he did ask I wouldn't object."

"You can inherit one too?" I asked, trying to change the subject.

"Yes ... If I had two I could let one go ... one of my sons with the other mate could take her. And sometimes when a new one splits I could be chosen for her. It's complicated."

"It's all complicated," I had resigned myself to Paul's family getting more and more complicated.

"Come on," Keith said helping me up, "Paul's coming to meet us and I need to get to the restaurant to open."

Paul met us on the way.

Keith had to hurry but said that Maria wanted to hang out in our hotel room with me. He'd told her that I'd turned my ankle on the stairs and caught myself but hurt my back and pulled muscles. Keith said he'd send sandwiches or something cold that wasn't so likely to make her sick. That sounded good. I didn't realize I'd wandered so far into the mall and all the walking made everything I'd hurt the night before hurt more.

"Do you need anything for pain?" Paul asked when we got back to the room.

I didn't like how it made me feel so I shook my head.

"I still feel funny … I went looking for you."

Paul plugged my phone in to charge.

"You couldn't use the phone?" he asked, starting to sound angry. "That's twice in two days I've had to look for you. You ran off again last night."

"I didn't … I told someone where I was going. I didn't want to worry you."

"You told Ray where you were going too … and you were gone for two months. And last night you took off after someone." His voice was rising now so I waited for him to cool down. I had no idea if anyone was in the adjoining rooms.

"So I tell you and there's a big mess in a hallway here? There's police … then Damian? Maybe you want the next one done publicly?"

He fumed, staring at me. I was right and he knew it.

"You still could have used the God damn phone." His voice was still raised.

"You could have used the God damn pen and left me a note. Every time I wake up you've run out the door again," I hissed back.

He covered the distance to the desk in a few steps and yanked the drawer open. Then he pulled out the hotel notepad and threw it down.

"I'm going out," he said loudly as he gouged it deeply into the paper with a pen. Then he stormed past me to the door.

"Now who's being childish?" I called out to his back as he went out. Take that mister all grown up.

I roared at the closed door and went to lie down until my head stopped spinning. I was being childish too but I'd be damned if I was going to admit it first. He hadn't seen stubborn yet.

My cell phone ringing a couple of hours later woke me.

"What," I said, snapping the 't' with my tongue. I was still very sore and short tempered from our fight and on top of that he should have known he'd wake me up. "Are you having a good time being out?"

"Marvellous," he said, but he didn't sound like he was marvellous. He sounded lost and lonely without me. I felt that way too but I wouldn't admit it. "Marie should be there in a minute."

"Good," I told him, "I'm looking forward to spending some time with somebody capable of being nice."

I could hear him sigh loudly in my ear. "Patrick is going to keep an eye on you from here."

All the way from the restaurant? There was no way I could look that far and I didn't like being spied on. Since what I taught him was so new I decided there had better be some rules about it.

"I'm keeping an eye on myself … can you please remind Patrick of his manners. I didn't ask him to so he needs to keep it to himself."

"Argh," Paul said sounding defeated, "I asked him to."

"That's just as rude. Now you have bad manners too. Good job." There was a knock at the door. Marie. He hung up on me. So be it. I took a couple of deep breaths as I walked to the door to let her in.

Marie brought iced tea and sandwiches and her bag of books. She was excited to get to spend some time away from the man table at the restaurant and with me instead.

"What colour did Paul like best?" she asked.

"The black I think," I felt my cheeks warming up and looked down at my food. "He didn't say."

"They never say," she laughed, "but it's usually the black. They won't complain about the other ones either. Keith's the same way. He won't ask me to change out of the red or blue but if I wear black he's crazier for me."

I thought about Paul. Maybe wasting our time being stubborn wasn't the best thing right now. Neither of us was wrong and our fight was stupid. I decided to apologize after he did first.

Maria put her sandwich down and covered it up with a napkin then she made a face and grabbed her bag before running with it to the bathroom. I heard the sandwich come up and gave her a minute.

"You going to be okay?" I called.

"Yeah," she said. "I brought my toothbrush just in case. Can I use your toothpaste?"

"Of course."

"When did mayo become the work of the devil?" she asked me when she came out. She sat back down on the couch without looking at the food. I'd finished mine while she was in the bathroom so I packed the rest of it away out of sight.

"I'm sorry you hurt yourself," she said. "You didn't fall on Keith's stairs did you? I told him that carpet was lumpy and too thick."

I shook my head. "But I'll be careful on those ones. I need to lie down. Do you want to use the desk?"

"Okay." She got her books out and sat down. I couldn't sleep and listened to pages turn. It was relaxing. It reminded me of when Alina with me, studying at the table. We were just near each other, together. Not being alone. I'd been alone for two years before that and her quiet

261

company was nice and not demanding.

After a while she sighed. "I'm warm … I think I'm going to fall asleep here."

"I can fix that." I told her and started to get up. I could turn up the air conditioning for her and get under the blankets but she got up first.

"No, I need a nap. I have my courses pretty much nailed and if I don't know it by now I'm screwed anyway. Six exams in four days next week so I need rest more."

She started to pack up.

"Are you going back to the office?"

"I guess." She didn't sound too enthusiastic about it. "The smell there is terrible now. It's not the food so much as the cooking. I'm okay if I can make myself believe it wasn't cooked but it's hard to trick myself about it there when that's what they do."

I made some room.

"There's a couple of spare blankets up in the closet and it's cooler over here away from the heater. You can nap with me."

"Really? I spend so much time alone now. I like being here with you. It's cozy like I've known you forever."

"I know what you mean," I told her. I knew why. Paul said Marie and I had always gotten along but she didn't know that. She brought a book and got the blankets and put one over me then she lay down close beside me.

"Were you fighting?" she asked.

"Why?"

She pointed at the desk. "Notepad … he wrote through eight sheets."

We laughed.

"It was childish. Paul gave me something for the pain in my foot and back last night and I was still high from it when I woke up. His best friend is my doctor. He sent a bunch of first aid stuff with us so he told him what to give me. I went to look for Paul when I woke up because he went somewhere and didn't leave me a note and I didn't notice my phone was dead so he got everyone looking for me.

"I'll apologize for being unable to use a phone when he apologizes for being unable to use a pen … he wrote that note when he stomped off."

Marie laughed again.

"You're right to apologize second … he was stupid first. He was sure gloomy this morning but I think he'll start sucking up soon … he's setting up a surprise for you or something."

"I'll be nice then Marie. I've been on my own since I was sixteen. I guess I'm still getting used to having things done for me. Always just looked after myself."

262

She was thumbing through her book.

"I thought you two had been together forever. You seem so connected."

"I guess," I told her. "We met last spring and spent a couple of nights together here and there through the summer. It was casual, intense … he's addicting. But nothing we ever thought would be long term. I was so busy with work I didn't realize I could be pregnant until I was two months late. So I found out for sure and went to tell him. I never left. We got married at the beginning of November."

Marie laughed. "Now I feel like the old married woman and I'm only nineteen."

"I think Paul and I give each other the pieces we were missing in our lives. We both want the baby so much. It's turning out really good."

"I'll set you up with some really sleazy things when you're back in shape … that'll turn out really good." She winked at me. "Now sshhh, I'll read to you a bit. Keith gave this to me when we got married. Shakespeare sonnets."

I turned on my side with my back to her and she read a few of her favourites then she yawned and put the book down.

Chapter 48

I heard the key in the door. Marie was cuddled in close behind me with her arm around my ribs. Her breathing didn't change so she hadn't been woken by the door opening and the sound of all the feet on the carpet. I figured it was Paul with Keith and Patrick. I couldn't be bothered to read and find out for myself. Or open my eyes and look up. They stopped at the foot of the bed.

"Funny how they do that when they're pregnant," Keith whispered.

Paul laughed a bit quietly.

"Here goes," he said, "hope she's not still pissed."

He came to the side of the bed and got down on the floor near me and pushed my hair back behind my ear.

"Sshhh Anna," he whispered, "it's me."

"Hi Paul," I whispered back.

"Are you still mad at me?"

"Only if you're still mad at me." I could hear someone coming over to Paul but I didn't open my eyes.

"I'm not … I brought someone to see you."

I felt weight on the bed near me and someone else behind Marie so I opened my eyes as a hand went on my arm.

"Hey Kiddo," it was Ray. Keith had pulled Marie off me and was waking her up so I carefully pushed myself up and hugged him.

"Ray … it's good to see you," I said. "But you didn't have to come all this way. Paul took good care of me."

Paul glanced at Marie. "House call."

I got it.

"House call," Ray repeated. "I didn't think Paul could talk you into checking in with a doctor after you fell so we decided I should come to you."

"I'm good," I told him, "but I missed you so I'm glad you're here."

Keith had Marie up but she was sleepy and out of it.

"She threw up from the mayonnaise … her book is on the bed here somewhere and the rest are on the desk," I told them. "Toothbrush might still be in the bathroom."

"I'll get it," Patrick said. I hadn't noticed he was with them. Maybe Ray had come to see him too. There would be hangovers tomorrow.

"Are you still sore?" Paul asked as he stood up.

"Yes," I answered. The cut on my back ached and so did my foot and stomach from walking around before lunch.

"I'm going to get Marie home … then I'll be back," Keith said.

"See you Marie," I said. She waved.

"Who's looking after Bee?" I asked Ray after Keith and Marie were gone. Patrick stayed behind.

"Denis is taking care of her. He knows what to do. He won't be on his own with her for long," Ray answered. "Now let me see what you did."

I sighed and lay back down with my head at the foot of the bed. "You came all this way for that?"

"No. Where does your stomach hurt?"

"Its better today already … my foot and back hurt most." I showed him and he pressed around with his fingers. Then he looked at my foot.

"I didn't think you could do that kicking a guy there," Ray mumbled. "Nothing broken."

He peeled the bandage off my back to get a look at it too.

"Jeez Kiddo, I thought you knew better than to let that happen to you."

"Andre's not used to fighting with long hair … he didn't think it would have to stay out of reach."

"Hm," Ray said as he poked at the cut. "How deep was it?"

"Deep enough … not into the muscle. I had to get rid of the clothes she was wearing. It bled almost down to her shoes," Paul told him.

264

"Okay," Ray said and put a new bandage on it. "Are you taking her back tomorrow or am I?"

"What?" I asked. Nobody said anything about going home.

"I think it's time we headed back Anna," Paul said. "Ray can fly home with you because he needs to get back to see to Bee and I'll drive the truck. I'll be a day behind at the most."

I shook my head. "We're not splitting up Paul."

"You fly her home … I can take the truck back," Ray said.

"Ray … you don't understand. I'm not leaving Paul behind and I'm not getting on a plane." I wasn't angry about it. They wanted me where Ray was and felt I was vulnerable staying in hotels. What they didn't understand was how dead set I was against flying.

"Anna, please …" Paul begged.

"I've had that dream of the crash as long as I can remember and I know its coming. You saw it in the mirror. I'm sorry Paul, there's nothing that will ever get me in the air." I told them. "And besides, Patrick might have questions for me. Right Patrick?"

But Patrick wasn't helping.

"Last night you showed me what would happen and you were bang on. Right down to you getting cut. You should be somewhere safer … not a big mall filled with strangers."

"Wait," Paul said, "you knew he would hurt you?"

I glared at Patrick. He looked away.

"I did … but I also knew I'd be standing at the end of it too. So did Patrick."

Paul's hand was over his face rubbing his eyes.

"You want something for pain Anna?" Ray asked. He looked like he was on Paul's side. I couldn't tell if he was trying to change the subject or was trying to avoid getting drawn in to whatever trouble I was in.

"Yeah, but I'm still half flying from whatever the other thing was Paul gave me and I don't want to sleep any more today."

"Okay," Ray said and he gave me a shot of something.

"Doesn't it come in pills?" I asked.

"I can't get someone who's unconscious to take a pill."

He was right about that but not everyone was unconscious.

I wasn't.

It was almost time for dinner so we started walking down to Keith's restaurant. Ray and Patrick talked quietly the whole way there. I held on to Paul's elbow since whatever Ray had given me was making me wobbly. I wasn't happy that Patrick told Paul I knew going in I would get hurt. I'd managed to convince Patrick it wasn't a big deal and I'd be fine. Now I seemed to be the only one who wanted me around. I had gone from wanting to go home this morning to refusing to leave.

I sat between Paul and Ray at the table. My usual place back home at Paul's. I hadn't realized how homesick I was and wanted to be back as soon as I could as long as it didn't involve flying. My place would do but Paul's would be better.

They were all drinking as soon as we sat down and well on their way to drunk by the time dinner was over. I had to get Patrick away from Ray before he was too far gone to give him the rest of my fingerprints in case Paul planned on sedating me and taking me straight back in the truck tomorrow.

"Patrick, can we talk a few minutes?" I asked him.

"Sure Anna," he said but he didn't get up.

"Over there?" I pointed at the table in the corner.

He got up reluctantly and followed me over.

"Are you mad at me?" he asked. "I'm sorry I said that about you getting hurt but I was really worried about you and I want you to be somewhere safer than here. You just let him take you into the hallway and pull a knife on you."

"I'm not mad Patrick. Like I said it's what I do. I wanted him to try and hurt me to trigger a jump away. It's not easy for any of you to accept. It just turns on and I can't stop myself. I know they want me dead so what else can I do?"

I waited a few seconds before continuing.

"Anyway that's not why I wanted to talk. I want to give you the rest of the fingerprints I have. The divide in loyalties between Paul and Keith feels like it could be permanent and I don't think your group will rejoin with Paul's next time. You'll still be close but Keith and Paul have both matured as leaders. Keith will need you to know what I know and Paul will have his father next time."

Patrick nodded. He understood. "I can't read loyalties ... even with Ray here I can't feel any difference between him and Keith's men. I won't tell them that you think that but I think you're right. It makes sense for me to have the prints if we do split. It won't be a split like that other line but the whole group has gotten way too big especially when the mates start turning up."

"Patrick ... I think the mates are just behind in age. You're all in your thirties. Marie and I are so much younger. You might find more yet."

He smiled. "I hope so. It's been a long time since there were children."

We got down to work. It took almost half an hour and a lot of sneezing but I was able to introduce him to all the others back at Paul's house.

"I'm sorry," I told him when we were done. "I've kept you from Ray. I think our line is well represented tonight."

Patrick laughed. "Yes, we are."

I lasted a couple of hours after dinner but then had to go back. Ray took me. He said he had something else to discuss. When we got back to the room I asked for something to help me sleep so he gave it to me. I didn't want nightmares when I was alone and now that I knew how I would feel in the morning it wasn't so bad. Ray would fly back alone tomorrow as long as I promised to try and stay out of trouble and let Paul and Keith look after things.

Ray took a map out of his bag. It was the logging roads around my house.

"I found it in your junk room," he explained. "I need to know where he is."

"Why?" I asked. I didn't think he'd be found so soon.

"He cut you Anna. If someone finds him soon your blood is on his knife. Denis is going to go and get it and make sure that there is nothing else that could get you into trouble."

I marked the spot on the map for him.

"I didn't want to ask you over the phone," he said. "You never know with cell phones. We'll destroy the map after Denis cleans up."

"I should have thought of that … I was just focused on getting back here. Otherwise I would have had to walk for miles out of the bush in the dark until my phone worked to call you."

"I was a little hurt that you were in the neighbourhood and didn't stop by and say hello," he laughed. "Alright … you rest up and I'll see you in the morning for a check-up before I fly back tomorrow afternoon."

I changed into pyjamas and he tucked me in. Whatever it was he gave me was working.

"Ray, can you please ask Patrick to keep an eye on me here? You have to tell him I asked or he won't do it."

"He can do that from there?" Ray asked.

"He's very good," I told him and drifted off.

Chapter 49

Ray slept on the foldout couch in our room. I passed on a shower since I was still woozy from whatever he gave me the night before but my back felt better. Paul was stirring by the time I was dressed so I got out the rest of the Advil and ordered up breakfast for me and coffee and juice for them. I kept the curtains closed and sat on the bed to wait quietly for room service.

"Anna … Sugar," Paul whispered. He didn't sound very good.

"Hey. Sshhh," I told him. "Coffee is coming. I'm sorry I woke you up."

"Why didn't you tell me that man was here?"

I understood now what bothered him most about the other night. He doubted my trust in him again. Or still. The same reason he was so angry with me when I returned from finding Pilot. For Paul nothing was more important between us than trust. I lay down facing him, my face close to his blanket covered head. He must be hurting if he wasn't taking it off yet.

"This isn't a trust problem Paul," I said softly. "I don't consider everything when they're around ... I get more focused on finishing them off than I do about getting help. But I don't get in over my head. I think about your safety ... not your feelings."

I put my hand on his shoulder and rubbed it gently so my hand moved on the blanket but I didn't move him on the bed. It was so much easier to fight with him when he was too hung over to get mad.

"Anna ... if something happens to me you have Ray to look after you and our daughter. Our daughter is more important than we are. I know it's hard for you to accept but I'll be back with you again. If something happens to you I lose her."

"I know you don't like me very much right now. It's okay."

He didn't say anything. That was okay too. He wasn't going to lie and say it wasn't true.

"Did you go back to sleep?" I whispered.

"No."

I waited but he didn't have any more to say to me.

There was a knock at the door so I kissed Paul's head through the blankets and went to answer it. I let room service put the tray on the dresser and locked up again. Paul staggered into the bathroom to get sick and crawled back into bed waking Ray up. I got juice and coffee for Paul again and he got down some Advil with the juice before going back under the blankets. Ray managed being upright a lot better so I shared my toast and fruit with him.

"Paul, can I give you anything?" Ray asked him.

"Uh," Paul said. I had no idea if that was yes or no but Ray seemed to.

"Where's the bag?" he asked me.

I pointed at the top of the closet as I was chewing.

"How come you're not that sick?" I asked Ray.

He shrugged. "Paul can't hold his liquor."

"What are you giving him?"

"Morphine and Gravol ... same as he gave you."

"Can I do it?" I asked.

"What?" they both said.

It made sense for me to learn. "Sorry, is that some secret grown up

268

knowledge I'm forbidden to possess? Because Paul might have been grateful for it last week."

Ray laughed.

"At least I wouldn't have had to focus my eyes enough to do it myself," Paul said.

"Okay Kiddo," Ray said then he showed me what to give him and how much. Then he had me fill the syringes. He gave Paul the first one and I gave him the other.

"So you did this yourself last week and it still took you two hours to get out of bed?" I asked Paul.

"A 'you're welcome' would be sufficient," Paul mumbled.

"You're welcome Paul," I said. "Try some coffee … I'll get the lights."

I turned them all off and left the curtain open a bit so nobody got hurt fumbling around in the dark then I closed up the sofa bed while Ray was in the shower.

"I just don't like some of the things you do," Paul said.

I went over and sat on the bed with him.

"Would you recognize me today if you hadn't seen me again after that first night?" I asked him.

He put a hand on my face. "Yes."

"Keith said we're most connected now because of the baby … will you still want me after she's born?"

"He apologized to me for that. He should have told you to come to me. And yes … you'll want me too."

"I just keep disappointing you," I told him. "One day you're going to throw up your hands and leave. I don't know how to stop pushing you."

"It'll be okay," Paul said but he didn't sound convinced. Maybe it was the hangover.

"Okay," I tried to kiss him but he dodged my lips.

"Threw up," he explained but now I didn't feel convinced. "Did you kiss him back?"

"I couldn't have stopped him … I wanted him to drop his guard."

"That's not a no," he said.

"It isn't." I got up and topped up his coffee.

"Go shop or something. Get out," Paul said. He lay back down with his back to me.

I took some cash and my phone and left. First I replaced the blood covered clothes that Paul had to throw out then I got a hot chocolate at a coffee place and wandered around for a while. Quite by accident I was on my way to making Paul leave. Much sooner than I wanted. It hurt a lot. I wasn't ready to let him go yet. It was almost two hours before Paul called. By then I had found a bench to warm.

269

"Mrs. Lund," he said.

"Hi Mr. Lund."

"I miss you."

I was relieved. "I miss you too."

"He's leaving in a while … meet us for lunch?"

"Okay," I answered and we said goodbye. Ray would have talked it over with him. He was good at that. Ray was a good man. I was happy that Alina would have him to look after her. Just him. When Damian was gone Alina and I wouldn't have to have anyone else other than Ray and Paul.

Patrick took Ray to the airport after lunch and Paul and I spent the afternoon together in our room. He asked me to put on the black teddy and when we finally got out the door again he took me shopping at Carla's.

We stayed with Keith and his family a few more days before we made our difficult goodbyes and drove south to Calgary for the first leg of our long trip home.

Chapter 50

We hadn't been able to decide between two nights in Hope then straight back to my house or one night then one in Vancouver. We'd stayed a night in Calgary then a night in Banff and were back on schedule after spending a lot more time in Edmonton than we had intended. Paul had enjoyed the company of Keith and his piece of the family and they had tentative plans to come see us in the spring after Marie finished her semester.

Ray told Paul that Denis found what he had been looking for. The man's knife. And that I had made a hell of a mess. Paul wasn't pleased but he shouldn't have asked Denis what I had done to him.

Christmas was less than two weeks away then it wouldn't be long before we could go back to Paul's. I hoped that by then he would be furious enough with me to go back alone if I hadn't gotten him to leave sooner. We had mostly made up after our falling out in Edmonton but I could feel distance in Paul now that wasn't there before. He wanted me as much as ever but now it was just sex. We'd gone from closeness after I got back from seeing Pilot to a brief period of fun while we were away to plain old sex. What we did between brushing our teeth and going to sleep. The emotional payoff seemed to weaken every day.

I remembered dreaming of Alina and me again. Dead beside the dumpster. This time it was Damian who had killed us. His laughter echoing off the walls until he squatted down beside me. He grabbed my head roughly by my hair and pulled my face to his. His nose wrinkled as he smelled me.

"I've always hated that stink in you," he whispered then he spat in my face and dropped me. He stepped out of his blood soled shoes and walked away laughing.

I became aware that I was in Alina's hallway and it wasn't empty. There was a uniformed police officer standing where her door was, his back to me. I was down at one end. He was joined by another as the elevator opened in front of them. Two paramedics got out with their gear piled on a stretcher. I knew right away what had happened.

Hoping I was still dreaming I looked around for things out of place because dreams rarely got small details right but everything looked as it should. Damn, had Paul even noticed I was gone? A quick check of my phone for the date suggested we should still be in Edmonton, not Hope so calling him wouldn't make any sense.

"Excuse me?" I called out as I approached the officers. "That's my sister's apartment."

They turned. One stayed at the door and the other walked to meet me.

"Who's your sister?" he asked.

"Dr. Alina Creed … I'm Anna," I tried to walk past him but he stopped me.

"Do you have some ID?"

That was a stupid question but I opened the side pocket for my passport anyway.

"We're almost identical, can't you see the resemblance?"

He opened the passport and studied it then he looked at my face.

"No," he told me. "Wait here."

He took my passport into the apartment with him. I waited but not for long.

"I'm sorry," he said when he came out, handing me back my passport. "Your sister has been assaulted … she wants you. She needs to go to the hospital but she's refusing … can you try and talk her into going?"

I nodded. Knowing what happened and helping Alina through the minutes and possibly days after would be one of the hardest things we had been through together. I had seen the terror and heard her cries.

"Was it her boyfriend?" I asked keeping the wobble in my legs and out of my voice.

"Do you know him? She won't say who he is."

"Damian Howard," I told him. "American. Former military. Don't tell her I said anything."

"Thank you," he said and took my elbow leading me in.

Alina was on her couch where I dreamed she would be. A female officer sat near her and the two paramedics hovered but her arms were

271

tightly crossed and she wasn't cooperating.

"No James, I'm not going."

She was an emergency doctor. She would know them.

"Alina, please …"

Alina looked up at me and the female officer got up so I could sit with her.

"Anna?" She looked at my stomach.

"I'll tell you later … we're looking after you first." I opened my arms and she fell into me letting me gently hold her. I could feel Damian's child in her. I felt terrible. Part of my job was to let that happen. It was why I'd stopped demanding that Paul do something to help her but I didn't know until I dreamed of her last that this was how it would end.

"Sshhh," I whispered by her ear.

Alina struggled not to cry. No wonder the policeman couldn't tell how much alike we looked. Her face was swollen up so much already and I could feel lumps on her back from the blows. I cried quietly too.

"I'm here Alina … I'll take care of you," I looked up at the paramedic she had called James.

"I think her arm is fractured," he said. "It was all she would let me touch before she tried to send us out. But she's refusing transport. She knows better. She admits women who are only half as bruised as she is."

"No James," Alina said and I put my hand on the back of her head. Lumps there too. I blinked back tears while she couldn't see my face.

"Alina … what if we don't go to your hospital? I'll be with you the whole time. They already know someone hurt you and refusing care now is only hurting you more. The man who did this doesn't give a shit. He wants you in pain. Please?"

"I can take her to a different one," James said. "Alina … it'll stay quiet."

"No." Alina said again but I could tell she was ready to go. She was just too headstrong to back down now and just needed a little push.

"Alina," I said. "Remember when you snuck outside early Easter morning and picked up all the candy mom had hidden? Then you said you saw Kenny doing it? Remember how much trouble he got in?"

Alina didn't say anything. She knew where I was headed.

"If you don't go I'm telling Dad and he's going to make you fly home and come clean."

"I can't believe you're still holding that over me. I gave you half so you'd keep quiet," she hissed. I glanced up at James.

Thank you, he mouthed as he started clearing off the top of the gurney for her.

"And now I'm back to blackmail you with it in front of the police. You're going to let James look at you and then take you for a ride in the

272

pretty limo he brought all the way up here. These nice people have other folks to help tonight and now you're just being stubborn and holding them up."

"Fine," Alina said trying to sound angry. If going to the hospital had to be my fault that was fine with me.

I hid my bag in her room and got our wallets. The other paramedic asked her questions while James looked her over.

"You know you're going to x-ray Alina, any chance you could be pregnant?"

"No," she insisted.

"Alina …" I warned and she looked at me pleading then her eyes dropped.

"I am," she whispered.

James patted her knee and got her on the gurney. She acted tough sitting down but she couldn't even stand on her own. I locked up her apartment on the way out and pulled the blanket up so she could hide under it if she wanted. If any of her neighbours were around this time of night they could think I was her at least.

She was so embarrassed that she wound up with someone like Damian. I thought of Catherine. She believed he was a good catch at first too. But Damian didn't beat her to keep her alive. He beat her to kill her.

At the hospital they took her in before they would let me join her.

"I'm glad you showed up to talk her into going," it was James. "Anna is it?"

"Yes … Anna Richards. I can out stubborn her any day of the week," I told him. "How can a man do that much damage to a woman without breaking all her bones?"

James shook his head. "Practice."

I felt sick. "I hope I find him before the police do."

"If you do, call me … I want in on that," he was sincere.

"I will … thank you."

When they finally let me in they had made her comfortable. Her arm was wrapped up. They were going to hold off on the x-ray and treat her like it was fractured. Her doctor said she would be in a few days while they monitored the baby. Alina looked unhappy about that. There was nothing they could do if she lost it other than make sure she didn't lose too much blood.

"Anna … I'm going to ask them to take care of it while I'm here. I don't want any part of that man around me ever again. I'm so mad that he left it behind to keep hurting me."

I sat on the side of the bed and held her hand. Then I put it on my stomach. She looked away.

"I met someone last spring," I told her. "Another photographer

273

working the bike shows and rallies. We shared a hotel every chance we got until August. Nothing serious, no commitments … no promises. Then he called to tell me he couldn't see me any more. I didn't think it would bother me but it did. I'd fallen in love.

"A month later I found out about her. We're having a girl. I went after him to tell him. I loved her already and even if he could never see me again I would do the best I could for her all by myself." I laughed a bit. "Honestly I was more afraid of telling you that I'd gotten myself in trouble than of raising her alone.

"He's American, in the reserves. He was shipping out and thought that saying goodbye was the decent thing to do. Neither one of us expected anything long term but he didn't feel right just disappearing. I moved in. We got married. He's away for a while so I came to see you. I'm sorry I didn't call first … but you know I never do."

I got a little smile out of her. So I put her hand on her stomach.

"I know you loved your baby already when you suspected … and you did when you found out for sure."

She sighed. A little tear started to grow in the corner of her eye.

"I know you loved him all the way home to tell that animal. You were already set to give your little one everything he would ever need and more," I lowered my voice. "I know that you tried to protect him when that man hit you … I know you still love your baby. And he's yours now Alina … just yours. You're giving him your best already and everything that he's going to grow up to be will be because of you.

"You're not alone Alina … mom would be proud that we both have a chance to use everything she taught us."

"You're right Anna," she whispered. "I don't think I could have gone through with it."

"I know," I told her.

After a few hours they moved her upstairs. There were two beds in the room and the other was unoccupied so they let me stay with her. I watched her sleep for a long time. When I woke up I was in the bed and she was watching me from the chair. Her bruises were changing colour already and the swelling was going down. I knew that I had been asleep for a couple of days. Damn. I had no idea how to explain that to Alina or if I should even try. I'd obviously been admitted so she'd had the doctors here up to something.

"Anna?" she sighed with relief. "We couldn't wake you up. It's been two days."

"I know … can we go now?" I asked. I felt fine and wanted out.

"No," she said. "The neurologist is going to want to see you again. You have everyone stumped."

"Alina … I'll check in with my doctor when I get home. I promise. I was just sleeping."

274

I pushed myself up out of bed and started on the tape holding the tube to my hand.

She held my hands to stop me. She was mad. Disrespecting any doctor was disrespecting her. Just because I knew what was going on didn't mean that I could run out on her.

"Please," she said. "I'm worried about you."

And scared to go home, I thought.

"How long do I have to stay?" I asked.

"If they don't find anything wrong you can leave today. I know you don't like it here."

I gave in and lay back down.

"I'm starving," I told her.

She was right. There was nothing wrong so they let me out with a promise to see my doctor as soon as I could. We were able to get her in to her apartment without anyone seeing her and I got her tucked in bed. They had given her something for pain before we left the hospital and she had a prescription. She gave me her bank card and I went to fill it and get some groceries for us. She usually stuck to takeout as much as I used to so there wasn't much in her kitchen. As she slept I put everything of Damian's down the garbage chute to the dumpster in the basement. There was nothing of his that would identify him other than the sizes.

After we got in bed she whispered to me he had raped her. Held a gun on her and raped her. He bit her shoulder so badly they had to sew up the tears. The bad bruises on her back were from the gun. He hit her with it. It was what fractured her arm. Nobody would ever want her now with his bite marks in their face every time they got in bed with her. She hadn't told the police about the rape and made me swear I wouldn't. I knew it wouldn't change what she had ahead of her to recover so I promised.

I fed her and held her. Alina was so broken inside. The outside healed quickly like I had but inside her confidence was gone. She didn't go back to work. No plans to either. She wouldn't even leave her apartment and hid anxiously in the bedroom if I had to go out for anything we needed. I thought about giving her my gun when I was out but she was more likely to panic and shoot me so I kept quiet about it. Eventually I started getting groceries delivered.

I slept in her bed with her, one of us holding the other. Her nightmares woke me and mine woke her and sometimes when I couldn't get back to sleep I would sit at her table and wonder when I would finish what I had come here to learn or do and could go home.

Andre started to come to comfort me those nights I couldn't sleep. At first I just felt him in me, telling me to stay angry, to keep him close. We would get our chance. Me to get revenge on Damian for what he did to me and what he did to my sister. Andre wanted to get revenge on his Lieutenant for being weak and being a coward. But mostly because he just needed to.

The days became a week, then two.

The second time he came he sat at the table with me. His uniform was dirty and smelly. Mud was tangled in his curly blonde hair; his wire framed glasses were bent and cockeyed on his face, one eye looking sideways over the lens that was meant for it. I wasn't bothered by the deep jagged hole in his neck. It had stopped bleeding decades before and the stain it had made on his clothing was brown and almost indistinguishable from the mud that covered him.

We would talk for hours. About Alina, me, him. I told him I was scared. It just wasn't worth it. Damian had hurt my sister. Hurt her so badly. It was my job to let it happen. To ensure that their child survived. If fighting would cost me Paul then I didn't want to do it. Andre promised. He would make sure Paul stayed away. As long as I did what I was told Andre would take care of it.

He wasn't always a killer. He had been in love once before joining the army. She had written him. Pregnant by his brother. She didn't want him back. Killing became his drink. Every life he took erased another little piece of him and with it a little bit of the devastation he felt inside. She said she would save herself for his return but it hadn't taken her long to get in bed with someone else. He should have married her before he left but she would have done it to him anyways.

Andre wanted to die every moment since he got her letter. He would have cut his own wrists and bled to death at mail call but he believed that would be a sin. So he embraced his work, hoping that death would find him doing something more honourable than crying over a Dear John letter from a worthless slut back home. But Pilot had other plans. He wouldn't escape that pain until Pilot said so.

He didn't want me to be like him, he explained. He bore the guilt and remorse for the lives I had taken. He needed it. His little fix of dealing death to cope with the rejection he still felt. But more than anything he was ready for death himself. And peace. And when Pilot's task for him was done he would finally have it. His task was to use me to finish off Damian. I asked him if I was his puppet or he was mine. He laughed. Pilot was the puppet master. We were both bound to his strings. We would kill Damian together. He would look after Paul. And I would look after him.

So after three weeks of spending my days helping Alina relearn how to live and my nights helping Andre get closer to dying I put my head down on the table with exhaustion. Andre's rough hand rubbed my back; his calloused skin catching on the thin fabric of my shirt. He whispered that it would be over soon, that he loved me for what I was doing for him. He was the only one who would stick with me until the end. I fell asleep wondering if I had gone insane.

Chapter 51

I woke up alone in my own bed in my little basement suite. Night time. Dark. The only light came from the hall. The little rechargeable emergency light Alina had sent to me two years before. If it was on then the power was out. My arms ached from the death grip I had on my pack. I quickly went through it in the hall and found everything there. My phone wouldn't turn on; I had left the charger in the hotel and had been gone for three weeks.

Alina was dealing with the aftermath from Damian's attack alone now. She had been from the night it happened; the night I took the man from the mall. I started to shake inside knowing I couldn't talk to her. Couldn't let anyone know about her son. That was my fault too. She was on her own again.

I felt my way to the kitchen as my eyes filled with tears and panic started to build in my chest. Ray would have to call Paul. They could have been looking for me for weeks. I felt along the pegs above the counter by the door and took the one off the third hook. There was fresh snow on the ground and it froze my bare feet as I hurried up the black path and let myself in Bee's door.

Inside was just as dark as outside. No street lights. No numbers on her VCR. I crept as silently as I could through Bee's living room and past her closed bedroom door. Tears still moved down my face and I kept my breathing quiet as I passed through into the kitchen. Then cautiously around her table and chairs. I knew where everything was but I was still careful. If I kicked a chair I would wake her up and she would rain fire on me. I held my hands out before me for the door to the little hallway that branched off to her back porch, the bathroom and the stairs up to Ray and Denis.

The next thing I knew I slammed into the wall, my arm shoved painfully up my back. Cold metal pressed hard and twisted angrily just under my ear.

"Don't move asshole," someone breathed into my other ear, "or you'll break your own arm."

"D … Denis?" My voice shook with the sobs I had been holding and fear in response to his sudden move behind me.

As quick as he had grabbed me he let me go and put his arm around me.

"Oh, shit, Anna," he said, "I'm so sorry."

"Denis," I said again, "where's Paul?"

"Denis?" Ray's voice upstairs then I could hear him coming down.

I put my arms around Denis and held on, shamelessly crying now.

"It's Anna," he said.

"Kiddo?" Ray asked. He peeled me off Denis and held on to me. I could hear a snap as Denis put his gun away.

"Call Paul, my phone's dead and I've been gone for weeks."

"I'll get her downstairs," Ray said, "get your phone and meet me there."

"Okay."

I heard Denis go up and Ray and I went back through the house. Denis caught up to us before we got to my open door. Ray took me down to my room following Denis with a flashlight. I could hear the beeps as he dialled through the speaker.

"Yeah?" Paul had been woken up.

"John, it's Daniel," Denis said. "Rachel is here."

"Uh," he grunted. I could hear the phone on his whiskers as he rolled over. "She's here in bed with … Rachel?"

"I'm here," I said as I started crying again. "I woke up here."

"John," it was Ray, "can you get back right away?"

"Rach?" Paul said. He sounded wide awake now. "How did you get there?"

I was still crying.

"She says she woke up here … was gone for weeks … I don't know," Ray said for me.

"I'll be on the road in ten. Love you Rach … I'll call when I'm in the truck."

Denis stayed with me while Ray risked another trip past Bee's door for the first aid bag. He sat beside me on my bed holding me and let me sob all over his shoulder. I had settled down a bit by the time Ray returned.

"I want to give you something to help you sleep," Ray said. Even in the dark he would know where everything was in the bag.

"No Ray … I don't want to sleep more. I don't know where I'll wake up."

"Please Anna, you're falling apart."

"You know sometimes I just need to cry, if I needed sedation I'd be hysterical." I pushed the words out between heaving gasps for air, my bottom lip flapping on my teeth when I inhaled. I backed into the corner of my bed and wedged myself in between the headboard and the wall. Denis' phone rang and he went down the hall to take it.

Ray crossed his arms. I heard shuffling at the end of the room and in the light from the hall I could make out another man there, standing between the dressers. Light coming in along the door hinges caught a lens of his glasses and winked at me.

I won't let you go anywhere, Andre said, *we need to keep it together.*

I nodded in the dark.

Don't go soft on me, he sounded angry. *They'll sedate you ... keep you from getting revenge for Alina. They don't understand what you have ahead of you like I do.*

I sucked in air for a huge shaking sigh and tried to pull myself together. Ray was right. I hadn't slept well at Alina's and could use a rest especially if I was still seeing Andre, but not the kind of rest Ray wanted.

"No," I whispered to Ray.

The power came back on as Ray was getting what he would need out of the bag anyway. I looked to the end of the room and Andre was gone. I could still feel my chest heaving trying to cry.

The vial Ray had out didn't look like the morphine or the Gravol we had given Paul.

You're right, Andre said from somewhere. *They gave you something else at the hotel. They lied.*

"No," I said again firmly this time keeping most of the shaking out of my voice.

He watched me for a minute then put the things away. I pulled the blankets up over my mouth and concentrated on breathing into them. Andre was right. They would try and stop me.

"I want to be alone Ray," I whispered.

He was still sitting on the bed with me when I fell asleep shoved in my corner.

"I couldn't find her gun," Paul was saying, "or her wallet and passport, bunch of stuff."

I had tipped over against the head of the bed and worked my way down so my feet were closer to where they should be.

"In the bag ... she must have had it with her," Ray said.

"Weeks?"

"Yeah, she's bigger. But I won't check her until she's awake. The bruises are gone from her foot. I could see that last night so she was somewhere for a while."

Paul sighed.

"Denis thought we had an intruder ... he had her on the wall. He feels terrible."

"I know, he told me on the phone when I called back. Not his fault ... or hers. She would have done the same thing if he came in and she wasn't expecting him."

True, I thought.

"I'm going to grab a nap here with her. I've never heard her so upset. You did the right thing trying."

"She refused to let me give her anything and managed to calm herself down after a while. Even after she fell asleep her lungs kept gasping she'd been so worked up."

"Thanks for staying up with her ... you and Denis get some sleep too."

"Yeah," Ray yawned.

I felt the bed shift as Paul curled up behind me. His arm went around me and his hand rested on my stomach. I'd missed him so much. She was quiet now so after a few minutes I rolled over and tucked my head under his chin.

"Hey Sugar," he whispered.

"Hey," I said and slipped back under.

Chapter 52

Paul was still snoring when I went to the shower. He'd been woken in the middle of the night and had driven four hours to get back. He didn't seem to need any help catching up on what he'd missed. After I quietly got dressed I checked the kitchen for something to eat but we'd been gone for almost a month and Denis must have cleaned out anything perishable. There wasn't even milk for Paul's coffee and I didn't want soup and granola bars for breakfast. I left him a note and took my wallet and my keys for the Lincoln. I took my newspaper with me to the car and drove downtown.

He was drinking his coffee black at the table when I got back.

"Hi Paul, I got you milk," I said.

He came and took the groceries and put them on the counter then he wrapped his arms around me. Andre stood in the hall watching.

"Not out of my sight again," Paul said, "please?"

"Okay."

He let me go and started cooking eggs and bacon while I put milk

284

in his coffee and put the rest of the things away. I leaned on him by the stove while he worked and put in toast when everything else was almost ready.

"Alina?" he asked.

"Yes."

My eyes started to tear so I turned so he couldn't see. He briefly tightened his hold on me before getting down plates. We went to eat in bed.

"Are you going to sleep soon?"

"Probably," I shrugged. I didn't care. He'd go somewhere and I'd wake up alone again. I would be mad at him for not spending the next day or two glued to my bedside. He didn't want me out of his sight but it was okay for him to be out of mine. He'd be silently frustrated by having to wait so long to show me how much he'd missed me this time and I wasn't so sure I'd be receptive at all. All the nights sitting up at Alina's kitchen table had left me with pain on either side of my tail bone. "Do you want to talk about it?"

I shrugged again then I straightened up painfully and put my hand on my lower back.

"You lie down," Paul told me so I did while he took the dishes to the kitchen.

Ray joined him while he cleaned up.

"You doing okay?" he asked Paul.

"We're okay … she's really depressed. I think something happened with her sister while she was away."

"Is now a good time to check her?" Ray asked. "I'd like to before she goes down for a couple of days."

"Yeah," Paul said. "She's in bed. I think she's having some bad back pain now."

I heard Ray pat Paul on the back. They talked while Paul finished up the dishes and for some time after. The newspaper rustled. Ray hadn't been able to pinch it this morning since I'd gotten to it first.

"Come with me," he said. "We'll see if she wants to tell us about it."

Great.

Ray felt my stomach and measured it. Took my blood pressure. I wouldn't get up to fill his little bottle for him so he left it in the bathroom for me. I told him about the back pain. He said it was just my pelvis getting ready to have the baby. I should rest as much as I could and could expect it to get worse.

"Three months now … maybe twelve weeks left," he said. "How long were you gone?"

"Three weeks," I told him. I felt empty inside. Disconnected from all my feelings. It was hard to care enough about them now to cooperate much less actually want to reassure them. "Alina made me go to a walk-in for a check up a week ago. That doctor said the same thing."

"You were with Alina again?" Paul asked.

"He beat her Paul, the night I dreamed of her … the night I fought the man in the forest. We went to sleep in Hope and I found myself in her hallway. The police were there," I told them. "I had to blackmail her to get her in the ambulance. I asked James how a man could give her so many bruises without breaking everything. You know what he said? Practice. That bastard practiced on Catherine alright. He destroyed Alina."

"Who's James?" Paul asked.

"One of the paramedics. She's an emergency doctor … she knows them all. I think James is sweet on her." I wiped my eyes again.

"Turned out he broke her arm. He held a gun on her and raped her. Beat her with it. Bit her so badly they had to get a plastic surgeon to put her shoulder back together. Who's ever going to want to make love to her now with another man's teeth marks in his face?

"They kept her in a few days … the black sleep took me there. I woke up hospitalized, sharing a room with her. She had every specialist she could find get in on watching Anna sleep. She made me stay until they were sure nothing was wrong then they let me out.

"I took her home and fed her and held her. We did nothing for her Paul. Nothing." I was getting upset again. "I spent three weeks trying to put her back together and now that I'm back here she's going through the whole thing alone."

"I thought you were going to do something to help her," I yelled at Paul then I rolled over and turned my back to him. "You told me to do nothing … you would help."

"Get out." I ignored them until they left.

Paul wasn't around when I woke up but I wasn't alone. I could smell Andre's muddy uniform as he rubbed the small of my back.

Sshhh, he said. *They're in the kitchen.*

I nodded and waited. He sounded like he was going to be nicer now.

You want your child's father around when this is over?

I nodded again, more tears started. I was so tired of crying.

He's a good man, Andre said. *He loves you so completely, like you love him. But if you want to keep him alive he has to leave soon … we know that. I have a plan … don't be too easy to get along with. Make him work for it. You have to do what I say.*

"Okay," I told Andre but he was gone.

I spent a few minutes in the bathroom and went to join Paul and Ray at my table. They watched me come in and sit but they didn't say

286

anything. I wasn't as angry now and hoped to do a better job of keeping it under control. Part of me suspected they would stoop to involuntarily sedating me for my own good if I became too much of a problem.

"I'm sorry," I told them. "I hoped it was a bad dream I couldn't wake up from. I was so upset about her when I got back and had no idea how long you would have been looking for me. I felt terrible that I might have hurt you like that again.

"Anyways, sorry," I got up and started digging through the cupboards. Nothing. They were still eating at Bee's. I hadn't thought about her in a long time.

"Is Mrs. Desmond okay?"

"Better," Ray said. "Just an inhaler now … had to make her quit smoking."

I didn't envy them for having to be with her through that.

"Okay, let me know if I can help. I need some things. Can I go or do I need an escort?" I looked at Paul when I said it. He looked displeased at the little dig but he didn't say anything so I went back to my room and sat on the bed.

He's not letting you out alone, Andre muttered from the doorway. *He has too much at stake to risk losing track of you again.*

Bingo, I thought. Before I'd been back to see Alina I would have thought that Andre was being manipulative. Controlling. He was just stating the obvious. I felt emotionally shut off to keep the pain from what I had done to Alina away. I still desired Paul like always but it was a selfish need for gratification, not any need for bonding or strengthening our attachment.

I heard Ray leave and Paul followed me in. I realized my arms were crossed so I put them at my sides before he came through the door.

He didn't uncross his.

"I didn't hurt your sister, or send you there. I tried to pull in every favour I could. All I asked was that you look after our daughter." His voice rose as he worked himself up. As much as I had it coming I didn't want to hear it. He didn't know that I'd abandoned Alina and betrayed her, made sure she was left alone with Damian on the word of a stranger in a corn field. There was nothing he could say to me that would make me feel any worse.

"That was all I asked, but I have to spend most of my time getting you sewn up or finding you or wondering what the hell is going on in your head before I have to find you or sew you up again. The more I let myself love you the more it hurts.

"As soon as I think you're going to settle in to marriage you take off again and come back either hurt or pissed off or both."

He was yelling now. I lowered my eyes and wanted to cover my ears but I didn't move. His hands dropped into shaking fists at his sides but he didn't come any closer. Even Bee upstairs would be able to make out every word.

"I know my uncle did something to you. He changed you. I know you can't walk away from it. Do you have any idea how hard it is to love you so much when I hate the things you're doing? And more often than not now the hate is winning. Does any part of you even acknowledge that or care?"

"Yes," I whispered. Some part of me at least. I wasn't so sure I could find it right now. I listened to his deep breathing slow before I looked back up at him. His hands had relaxed but his face hadn't. I got up and stood in front of him, close, hoping that his stare would soften. He wouldn't budge.

Now who's working for it? In three minutes he's going to have you in bed giving him what he's supposed to be working for. It doesn't matter if you want it too. Make him Anna. He's not in here to leave you.

I realized that most of my ability to reason was wrapped up in a dirty dead man four feet behind me; standing by the foot of my bed. When Andre wasn't around all I had left was emotion. Sex and emotion. I would need him now to get through anything I needed sensitivity and eloquence for.

I took a couple of steps back and tuned Andre out. If it was a fight we were going to have then it might was well be a good one. Paul was getting madder after my weak attempt to redirect him so I let anger take me too.

"How many favours did you really have time to call in Paul? Just a few weeks after that you spent two months drunk on the floor. You didn't even come here to look for me. You didn't see if I was with my sister. You picked up a bottle, you beat up your best friend, and you quit."

His hands were back in fists. Mine were too. I'd be lucky to still have my voice after this.

"Or did I get the order wrong?" I taunted. "Maybe you quit first?"

I stepped closer.

"You know what I do when I find myself in a hole? I stop digging. My father taught me that when I was eight years old and you still do it. You dug yourself a hole so deep that you couldn't get out of it. I had to get you out. I froze on the side of the road. I found you. I brought you home. I seduced you in our own bedroom just to make you talk to me again."

He thought he'd get it off his chest, his speech Ray had helped him get ready then he'd get me in bed and could go on thinking that everything was fine. He wasn't expecting this.

"I didn't go looking to be what I am. I don't want it. But I'm fucking stuck with it. And being mad at me for it is as stupid as being mad at me for having skin. Every time I find myself in that hole I get out. I get pushed back in. I get out."

"Do you think I asked for any of this shit?" He yelled back.

"You did Paul, when you spent the night in my hotel room after using your grown up charm to get your virgin mate in the sack hours after you found her. Did you tamper with all the condoms Paul or just one? Did you want to be sure or did you want to gamble?"

"I …" he sputtered but I kept going.

"If you don't have the stomach for what I am then just say so. You can pretend that everything is perfect while I run around saving your family. And it is your family. I won't remember a thing. All I asked was that you help me protect my sister. I'll do whatever else was asked of me in return. I'm going to the wall for your family Paul. I just wanted her spared and you went on an epic bender instead."

Paul was furious. I paused again but he didn't have anything to say. I'd riled him up well past the point where he could put words together. Challenging his integrity was as close to crossing the line with him as I had ever been.

"Who's the grown up here now? You took your toys and left me in the sandbox and now you come in here on your high horse acting like you've been in here playing the whole time.

"Was it because it was a child's request to save someone less than a child? Are the regular people around here irrelevant now? Ray's sister wasn't. You took care of her. But then you weren't banging Alina, were you? Is that why my sister is disposable?"

I took the last step toward him and got right in to his face with mine. For now I was done saying what I could say to him within earshot of the others upstairs. I felt Andre's hand on my shoulder squeezing it. He knew how hard that should have been for me. Twisting what had happened into being a public and personal failing of Paul's. But it wasn't hard at all. Andre was showing me approval, not understanding. The cruelty I was dumping on Paul pumped something into my veins that I liked.

"If you think for one minute that my actions haven't had a thing to do with looking after our daughter I will continue to tear yours to pieces in front of our audience upstairs. How dare you question my love for her," I whispered. "Your actions don't hold up under close scrutiny any more than mine do. Raise your voice to me again and I'll keep going. Believe me, I'm just getting started."

Paul pulled in a shaking breath.

"I can't believe you would question me like that," he growled out between his teeth.

"Then promise me it isn't true." My face was inches from his, my belly pressed into him. He would cave soon, having me so close to him, listening to me breathe. "Promise me you did the best you could with what I left you with when I stole your bike and ran off. Tell me you would be just as upset if what happened to Alina happened to your sister, or your mother."

"You know it isn't true."

"I know a lot of things you won't tell me," I bellowed at him. "You want me to start at the top of the list or the bottom?"

I took a deep breath as I tried to come up with something but he flinched and put his fingers on my lips.

"Sshhh," he said, "please ... no more."

I leaned in a little closer and waited.

"I promise you Anna. I do the best I can for you every day. Nothing less. I'm sorry there were days when it wasn't enough."

I thought I'd feel worse than I did after humbling him into saying that.

Reassure him now Anna, Andre told me, *we have to play them like they think they're playing you.*

"I believe you Paul," I whispered. "Something's broken off inside me after seeing Alina. I feel raw ... emotional. My anger was misplaced. You're the first person I run to when I'm losing my battle with it because I'm safe with you but then it boils over."

"What do I say to you when sorry isn't enough any more?" I put my hands on his chest then I slid one up and held his face. Paul closed his eyes and pressed his cheek into my palm. From the corner of my eye I saw Andre disappear as he walked out of the room.

"I'll tell you if it comes to that," Paul said. He leaned forward and put his cheek on mine then I tilted my head a bit as he put his lips on my jaw. I could feel desire start to fill him so I put my other hand behind his neck and gave in.

My back was definitely worse. I was going to waddle and limp if I could move again.

"I think that's it for the pony rides," I told Paul as he helped me up. In spite of the pain I was in now I felt nearly normal.

"I guess I'll be going for more runs now," he laughed a bit so I patted the little belly he'd gotten eating all the restaurant food. "I know. I didn't think you would notice."

"Oh, I didn't," I said politely.

"Sure," he said.

"That works?"

"Sort of like the patch ... what works for you?"

A cigarette, Andre yelled from the hall.

"No ..." I answered him without thinking but suddenly I wanted one too.

"No?" Paul asked.

"No substitute for you ... but the back pain right now is somewhere between 'you're kidding' and 'no way'."

"Do you want me to give you something for it?"

"I still have what Ray gave me for my ribs ... I'll get a couple of those."

Paul gathered my clothes up for me so I could get dressed and found his.

"I'll take you out ... are you sure you can get in the truck or do you want to take the car?"

I gulped. "I'm not showing my face after that display. I made an ass of myself."

"Anna," Paul said softly, "I don't want you to be mad but they've had a friendly bet going as to when we'd have our first fight and who would win ... they keep having to change their bets because it's taken us so damn long."

"Jesus Paul, now I'm even more embarrassed."

"Car it is," he was laughing. Then he became serious. I was sitting on the edge of the bed and he knelt on the floor in front of me.

"Your words hurt me and mine hurt you. I'm not minimizing that at all. But there are no secrets between the men and I ... we're completely open with each other about our lives. Women, sex, anything. We're going to be together for too long ... there's really no point in pretending privacy."

I went ahead to the kitchen while Paul got cash and took a piece of paper and a thick marker. I wrote on it Anna 1 Paul 0 and tucked it in my coat. I thought back on our fight and now that the pleasure my mean words had given me was spent in bed I was starting to appreciate just how awful I had been. Just because he found the bet funny didn't mean I felt any better about what I had said. I knew he didn't either. If I didn't join in any ribbing from Denis and Ray would only escalate.

I figured that getting to the car would either make the back pain better or worse but I was wrong. It stayed the same. Ray and Denis were both watching from Bee's window when we got out front so when Paul got in to warm it up I held up my sign. Ray tapped Denis on the shoulder and held out his hand. Denis scowled and started digging around in his pocket. It was my Canadian money he would give to Ray. Then Denis held up his hand for me to wait so I did.

"I wanted to say sorry for how I greeted you the other night," Denis said when he got out to the car, then he smirked, "I know you could have hurt me."

"Damn right," I let myself smile back. "I didn't know my arm could do that ... can you show me that move some time?"

291

"Anyone who can take that hold without screaming like a little girl is allowed to learn it," he seemed relieved.

"I thought you had my back Paul," Denis said stuffing his hand in his empty pocket.

"What?" Paul said but Denis went back in the house laughing.

"I thought you knew me better," I called after him.

Chapter 53

Paul had volunteered for the first part of Andre's plan; cutting him off, but that wasn't going to make the rest of his plan any easier. He went missing a lot at night. I woke up alone or from the sounds of him letting himself out or back in. He'd gotten very good with the stubborn lock and could open it almost silently. I didn't ask or even let him know that I noticed and he didn't comment but I was certain that it was every night. He was tired too. Between the long daily jogs and being out for two or three hours when he thought I was out cold he was more and more drained every day.

Missing too were his public displays of affection for me. He would always return mine but I didn't feel his arm around me or his lips on the top of my head when I wasn't expecting it. It felt like the connection we had was suddenly gone. I still would have taken care of him without all the strenuous activity and offered more than once but he said no. Just a taste wasn't going to be enough Paul said. He'd ask for more, I wouldn't say no, then he would feel guilt and I would be in more pain. I told him that would be better than feeling like he didn't want me at all any more but he just put his hand on my stomach like he did every night now as he fell asleep and whispered of course he still wanted me.

Andre still followed me around. He praised me for getting my resolve back. He'd been worried at Alina's that I had lost it so he'd separated himself from me so that he could keep me on target. He said I was the kind of woman he wished he'd found. Respectable in that I'd saved myself for the man I would marry even if I hadn't held out until after the wedding. Sometimes he sat at the table with Paul and me, or in the back seat of the car. When Paul wasn't around we would talk. His plan for Paul. His plan for Damian. He told me he loved me and was grateful for what I was giving up to help him. I didn't feel like I had any choice. I knew he didn't either.

We drew names for gifts for Christmas. I pulled Denis' name and we weren't supposed to tell who we got. We also put a limit on the amount. It didn't make much sense to go overboard with things we would have to find room for in the truck. There was already all the extra clothing and winter gear we bought for our extended stay here.

Three days before Christmas Bee insisted that we all go to Mass on Christmas Eve. She had never missed it and didn't plan on starting now. I had taken her the past few years. Paul and I decided we would just wear what we had for out night out in Edmonton but I needed shoes that were more sensible than suicidal. Ray and Denis had nothing suitable so Paul stayed with Bee and I went shopping with them. I got my shoes first and waited while they were in the men's store.

I was cursing the hard bench out front of the store when Ray came out to check on me. Andre was on the bench, his arm around me. He'd been getting touchy with me lately, giving me the physical contact I so desperately missed from Paul. I craved it from Andre. Whether I tried with Paul or not made little difference to how much I got back. Andre's nose was by my eye and his lips brushed my cheek. They felt dry and almost powdery. I thought the dead soldier's breath would be vile but it was inoffensive as a pile of old cardboard.

It's okay to like it Anna, he whispered, *how is it any different than him going for a run to tire himself out ... you're not being unfaithful ... you're only just touching yourself ... what do you think he's doing when it gets to be too much for him ... he'd never hurt you by asking you to make love when you're in so much pain already.*

"Paul doesn't have a tie does he?" Ray interrupted.

I agreed; annoyed that I had to pull my mind out of Andre.

"I knew it. If Denis and I have to then he will too. What colours is he wearing?"

"Dark blue shirt, gray jacket," I told him. "Are you sure you have to do that to him?"

Ray laughed. "Don't be on his side about this ... it's Mass."

"Ray," I said as I put my hand on my chest, "I'm running out of antacid ... I'm just going to run down the mall to the drug store while I wait."

I didn't want to be bothered by him again.

"Okay. I gave my word to Paul I would keep an eye on you," he sighed. "Make it quick and come in and tell us when you get back. Promise you'll be good."

After the drug store I called Ray.

"I'm bending the rules on the gift exchange ... I'll be in the jewellery store."

I could hear him grumbling to Denis.

"Daniel is finished here ... he'll go with you."

"Okay bye," I hung up.

In the jewellery store I got Paul a nice waterproof watch. He had worn his good one here and the moisture from sweat and rain had gotten in. It still worked but the lens was half cloudy from the dampness inside. I'd put it in a bag of rice to try and dry it out but he kept taking it running. It was an expensive gift from his parents for his college graduation and would cost a lot to fix when it finally seized up. The one I got would be good to the bottom of the lake he was lapping twice.

"I don't think you even own a watch," Denis said on the way out.

I shrugged. "My father got me a couple but they always quit working. He figured I was careless but as careful as I was they just died. Even the windup ones. He gave up trying to get me to wear one after three. I think now it's that blue light. I'd never even owned any jewellery until I married Paul."

"We'll make a lady of you yet," Denis laughed.

"Good luck with that … I'll follow you in."

We walked back to meet Ray. Andre held my hand, whispering in my ear.

Christmas Eve Andre chose to follow Paul and me upstairs. Paul and I were both dressed up. I had passed on the rollers this time and wore the lighter makeup I'd bought the day after we met Keith and his family. I didn't want to go. I wanted to stay home with Andre but he said I had to. He said they were getting suspicious because I was so distracted and I couldn't get away later if I was shot up with God knows what and locked in my bedroom until I popped.

Paul was displaying a sudden inability to put on a tie.

"Do you want me to get Ray down here to do it for you?" I asked. We were running out of time.

"No, I'll just have to skip it."

Convenient, I thought.

"Come here," I sighed. My father had taught me as a kid and I hadn't forgotten. I always asked him to teach me whatever he was doing. I pulled Paul's collar up and did up the top button. That was half the challenge right there. After a little adjustment to the length I did a decent job.

"Damn, I didn't count on that," Paul laughed. He was standing close in the bathroom so I stretched my face up to his for a quick kiss. I got one but was disappointed that he didn't find the green dress as irresistible as he had in the hotel.

"Ray made me promise that if you weren't wearing it I would be. Sorry, you're not going without it. You know I'm on your side about it."

"It would look just as silly on you," he said.

I agreed and was glad I didn't have to find out exactly how silly. When we got upstairs Ray and Denis were both ready. The only other time I had seen the three of them dressed up was when the Colonel had come to Paul's. And that wasn't really dressed up.

"Paul, did you have to show her how to operate that?" Denis pointed at my dress, laughing.

Paul sniffed. "I thought it looked good on me."

I laughed, that got me off the hook then I noticed the look on Bee's face. I was standing to Paul's left and she was glaring off to his right.

"There's a dirty old piece of your line following you around Anna." She made a face. "It smells musty."

I followed her stare around Paul and saw Andre there. He yawned and picked absently at the hole in his neck. Then he winked at me.

"Stop doing that in my kitchen," she whispered quietly.

Andre dropped his hand and rolled his eyes. Bee watched him as he walked out of the kitchen toward the front door and disappeared. I kept staring to Paul's right. Paul was looking at her.

"Bee? What was that?" he asked.

"Anna sent it away."

Paul looked at me and I shrugged. Bee looked at me then the clock on the stove.

"It's time to go. I expect you all to behave," she said.

I suspected she meant that I keep Andre out of sight but she didn't know he got around of his own accord and even if I was alone with him it would be a waste of time to suggest he find something else to do.

Bee sat up front with Ray and I sat between Paul and Denis in the back. It was dark and past bed time. We had to park on the street a block away from the church since there was no way the massive Lincoln would fit into the overcrowded parking lot to even look for a place to moor it and it was just as crowded inside. We were able to all sit together in the back. I could see that Andre had taken a seat at the very end of one of the rows on the other side. Bee seemed to be ignoring him now, or maybe she didn't think she had any say so because this was someone else's house. I watched him though. When I held Paul's hand he glared at me so I took my first chance to let go and didn't take it again.

That night while Paul was out Andre stood in the doorway; arms crossed. He didn't say anything but I knew he was displeased with the attention I was still giving Paul.

Paul cheated on the gift exchange like I had and put some diamonds in my ears before I was out of bed. They were beautiful in the box and he brought in a mirror so I could see them on. The best part of getting them was having his hands on me helping me sit up even thought it hurt. Feeling his fingers on my ears and hearing him breathe so close as he took out the blue stones and pushed the posts of the new earrings through. Then carefully screwing the backs on. I was frustrated for him when he was finished but that brief intimacy stayed with me all day.

Paul was very happy with the watch I got him and promised to take his good one in for repair as soon as we got home. He made us breakfast and served me in bed then went through the manual for his watch learning all the settings. Not many things made him happier than getting a gadget with a book. By the time I felt up to getting out of bed he had the watch all set up the way he wanted it and was looking forward to taking it for his run the next day.

Ray had filled Bee's list of what she needed for Christmas dinner. Or what the boys would need as she hollered instructions from her bedroom and I interpreted from her couch. Mass had been tiring for both Bee and me. More so for her. I wasn't tired but being on my feet so much had left me with a lot of pain. I'd had to ask Paul for something stronger than the pills I had for my ribs just to get out of bed. I hated to give in to the medical bag but I wasn't blowing the same Christmas for him twice. I was feeling pretty good by the time I was upstairs.

As I expected Bee stayed in bed through the afternoon while Denis cooked. He had his idea how Christmas dinner should be and was able to work in all of Bee's ingredients and instructions so they both got their way. Bee made it to the table to eat and had to admit that it was better than what she and I usually put together. Ray ordered her to have a glass of wine with dinner and she enjoyed a few sips but nobody said anything when she didn't finish it. She'd become so tired and frail. I remembered the energy she still had when I met her and it was almost all gone now. Even the fork appeared too heavy for her hand.

She cheered up for exchanging presents after desert. Ray found her a very old copy of *Pride and Prejudice*, one of her favourites, that had an old inscription to someone named Beatrice from eighteen seventy-three. The coincidence thrilled her to no end as if it was meant to be hers. Ray had started reading to her on her bad days and she would read to him on her good ones. I thought they both looked forward to working their way through it.

Bee gave me an old wooden jewellery box that she'd had for many years. The trays and dividers inside were mahogany and most of the inlaid pearl was still intact. It had been a gift from an old suitor, including the ring inside with a ruby in a circle of little diamonds. The ring was worth many times more than our gift limit but she insisted that since it hadn't cost her anything more than a few stolen kisses she wasn't breaking the rules. It was a perfect fit on my right hand so I wore it the rest of the day. Since it was so old she made me promise I would get it checked before any of the stones fell out.

I got Denis some good cigars. Three of them he could share with Paul and Ray or have them himself. They came in their own wooden box with a top that slid open. He stuck his nose in it and inhaled, closing his eyes. He said the ones I'd brought back to Paul's were good but these were better. Ray had his eye on them so he carefully kept them out of his reach.

Denis got Paul a new electric shaver. Paul's had been slowly dying and harsh language had failed to keep it working reliably so he'd finally given up on it and switched to disposables which he found just as annoying. Denis said he was man enough to give one so Paul better be man enough to accept it. Paul laughed and said he was although I would be disappointed that the swear jar I'd put in the bathroom would probably never fill up with quarters now.

To complete the circle Paul had found Ray an old field trauma guide from World War One and the fold up leather case of surgeon's instruments that went with it. The book was in good shape and most of the instruments were still there. He knew Ray liked old books and medical things and that Ray didn't have anything like them. Ray said he'd read up and take the kit with him to try next time they shipped out.

Chapter 54

Early Boxing Day morning I was woken up by rough hands on me. I'd been dreaming about Paul. He promised me that he would find another way to deal with Damian. I cried with gratitude as his hands ran up my body, needing me like he hadn't in weeks. He'd just come in from wherever he went at night, his skin still cold from the winter as we took his clothes off together. He was breathing hard as his lips touched my neck.

Then suddenly he was squeezing too hard. One of his hands grabbed my hair and pulled me up sitting.

Traitorous bitch, the cardboard scented voice seethed in my ear. *Unfaithful cow. How could you turn on me with him? He's never going to help you. You'll be lucky if I do now.*

No I …, I tried.

But his other hand came up and pressed my mouth shut. I reached for Paul but he wasn't in the bed.

I leave you alone for a minute and your mind fills up with dirty thoughts.

I struggled to pull his hand off my mouth. My nose was plugged from the pregnancy and I couldn't breath.

Even in your dreams you cheat …

His grip on my mouth disappeared and my cheek lit up with hot pain; the sound of the slap exploding in my ear. I pulled my knees up as much as I could and tried to be invisible. To hold still. To keep him from getting any angrier.

I'll make you kill him … take your pretty knife and run it though his heart. He'll never come back if you're holding it when it happens. You have no idea how strong I've become.

I nodded and kept quiet. I'd been whimpering.

They'll blame you ... you'll have to kill Damian then or be stuck with him forever ... and me ... reminding you every day that Paul's death was your fault.

Please Andre, I begged.

What's it like to be so useless? So impotent? So pathetic? His voice softened. *You need me Anna, just for a while then you can have that again.*

Andre's grip on my hair loosened and his lips touched the stinging hand print on my face.

I'm sorry, he whispered. *We have to work together.*

Andre's lips found mine as his calloused fingers felt their way up under my t-shirt and he lay my head gently back on my pillow.

Want me Anna, he ordered.

And I did.

On New Year's Eve I came upstairs for a while to watch the big apple drop in New York at nine pm then Bee decided to call it a night. We had both recovered from Christmas Eve and New Year's wasn't such a big deal to her. I wanted to get downstairs to be alone with Andre for a while. Paul wouldn't be in for a couple of hours at least since he'd been talking about taking a taxi downtown with Denis and Ray for the annual street party.

As I saw Bee to her room she took my arm and stopped me.

"Did Denis remember to give you the message?" she asked.

"Which message?" I asked so Denis didn't get in trouble later for not passing it along.

"From that nice friend of yours with the motorcycle. Kent," she explained. "He came by to see you the day I got sick ... just before Ray had to go on the plane. Denis took him downstairs to talk and when they came back up Kent said to tell you hi. Denis said he would tell you and I shouldn't worry about remembering."

"Yes dear, he did," I smiled to her.

"I'm so glad. I forgot until now." She turned her cheek to me so I kissed her.

"You're sweet for remembering. I felt bad for missing his visit. I don't see him much anymore."

"He's gotten fat," Bee said bluntly. "His wife should mind her cooking."

"I'll whisper that in her ear," I told her. Bee didn't know that Kenny's wife had been gone for three years and he'd put on the weight since she left. She also didn't seem to know how many miles Ray and Denis had to run to avoid meeting the same fate at her table.

"Happy New Year Bee," I told her and gave her a hug.

That made perfect sense, I thought, as I pushed my feet into my

298

shoes and put on my coat. It explained why Paul wanted to keep an eye on me and why he was out at night. If Denis had taken Kenny downstairs the only reason would be to give him an envelope of cash for telling him that someone had been looking for me.

I found Ray, Denis, and Paul on a level spot between the garage and the house near my bathroom window. They had an outdoor fire pit and some lawn chairs and were drinking scotch and talking. Denis had a smoke and told me that since Paul and Ray had coughed up for good scotch he was going to share his Christmas cigars with them. I didn't bother to mention that the money that paid for everything came from a box in my junk room. It was the bargaining and the thought that counted.

They had a spare chair and I sat with them for a while but my childhood campfire luck had followed me into adulthood. It didn't matter where I sat the smoke blew into my eyes. They were excited to be going back and had to decide who would stay with Bee first but then Ray and Denis expected to take turns with her. I told them Happy New Year and went on to bed. Andre would be waiting to talk and I didn't want to get in trouble again for spending too much time with Paul.

Andre thought that Kenny coming back was a good thing. Something I could pretend to misunderstand later when the time came. Paul would see through it at first, until I crossed the line and set him off.

After about an hour in bed failing to sleep I went to the bathroom for a couple of the pills from Ray. They were still talking outside so I waited for someone to do something loud so I could crack open the window to listen. It didn't take long for Denis to cough. I'd already flipped up the lock so I slid the window open just half an inch or so and stood next to it.

"Are you sure?" Ray was saying. "She's not herself."

"Hasn't been for a while," Denis added.

There was silence for a bit as cigar smoke started to make its way in.

"This morning when I got in from watch I could hear her in the bedroom. The little noises she makes in the sack. I listened for a bit. Thought she was dreaming of me. I stopped sleeping with her after we got back from Hope. She's just in too much pain now. It's been a while so it's no surprise we're dreaming about it."

There was a pause so I peeked through the gap in the window and watched him lower his glass.

"Then she gasps. She says "Jesus Andre" and she gasps again."

I heard an "Oh shit" and an "I'm sorry Paul" but he kept talking.

"But then she yelps. She begs "I'm not thinking of Paul." She says "please, I wasn't" but then she's crying. "Don't bruise me," she cries. I stood in the hallway a long time after she stopped crying before I got in bed. But this morning there's a big bruise on her back. I didn't say anything. I don't think she even knew it was there."

I could barely reach the sore spot on my back.

"That wasn't the first time. She had a little bruise on her jaw on Boxing Day. Said she bumped into the bedroom door in the middle of the night. Then later at the table she's distracted so I asked her if she wants me to fix the door so it doesn't happen again. She said the house has settled and the bathroom door wants to be part way open. She just wasn't paying attention."

"Do you think Andre is becoming dominant?" Ray asked.

"I hope not," Paul said. "But I compare her mental state now to when we arrived in Hope and the Anna from before is gone."

"As long as she's not a danger we can overlook it," Denis said. "Pilot really messed her up."

"Yeah," Ray said.

Andre pinched the back of my arm. Hard.

You're being too careless. They need to suspect you're crazy, not know you are and not so soon.

I saw the tip of Paul's cigar light up in front of his face. He leaned forward and put another piece of wood on the top of their fire pit before he pushed it around with a stick.

"Yeah," Paul agreed then "that's not all of it though. I hear her whispering in the other room sometimes. At the table she keeps glancing at the other chair or behind me, over my head. She'll nod or smile when she thinks I'm not looking then the next minute she flinches like she's been yelled at and she's trying to hold back tears. She threw her plate at her front door yesterday and stormed off to the bedroom."

I deserved that.

Think what's been put on her, Paul," Ray said. "She believes she'll lose you, she's not going to make it. She told me before she went to Pilot that someone interferes so she probably doesn't know who. We know he's given her other things to do that she can't talk about so we have no idea how much more stress that's putting on her. But I agree with Denis. As long as she's only a danger to herself or to us we keep looking after her."

"She needs Andre," Paul said, "I know that. But I don't know if she's imagining him to try and feel strong or if he's really taking her over."

"Paul," Denis said, "nobody here is going to let her down. We'll stick with her as long as we have to. But if she's a problem you have to be sure before you put her down. It's your responsibility. Both to do it and to make sure it's the right thing."

"If you're not around we'll stand in for you for both if you choose us," Ray said. "Remember it's a kindness to her. If it's that bad she's

300

suffering. And it protects the family from the weakness of her failed upbringing."

"If you'll accept being my alternates I'd be grateful," Paul said. "I don't doubt that either one of you will make the right decision or fail to act. I don't care to live on without her. If we have to do it I won't be far behind. But that will be by my hand."

Chapter 55

The last time I dreamed of Alina and I dead at Paul's feet he kissed my lips softly and apologized for killing us then he gently put my head down into the pool of blood. He sat on the floor next to me, stroking my cheek with his fingers as he had when I was alive. I heard metal on something softer, echoing and rattling and I realized the metal was in his mouth. The gunshot was deafening. He twitched for what seemed like a very long time, gently bumping me, until he was still.

The alley faded and the ground lost its coldness. I became aware of a long line of lights leading off into the distance, then the fake gold decoration around them. I was upright, breathing, watching the policeman's uniformed back outside Alina's apartment door.

We'd been just a few days from returning to Paul's. According to the calendar we had left the compound the day before. I'd butted heads with Ray about returning to the doctor in Reno. The pregnancy was five weeks further along than it should be which Ray felt would easily be explained by a big baby since nobody would suspect time travel but there really wasn't anything they needed to test at the hospital that he wasn't already keeping an eye on. The other argument was whether we should jump back or drive. I didn't want to sit in the truck that long and Ray didn't want me going two days without food again sleeping off the trip. Either since the pregnancy was draining or because my jumps were becoming more complicated in terms of timing and extra passengers I had gone from sleeping eighteen hours to nearly two days. Paul insisted I use him again since he bounced back so much faster than I did but to me that felt like I was violating him even with his permission. Either way I had no intention of returning home with them.

I thought I'd only seen Alina again to learn about Andre but there I was back again that same awful night. I quickly checked for my passport and found it.

"Excuse me," I called to the policemen after James and the other paramedic took the gurney in. "That's my sister's apartment."

The same one approached as last time.

"Who's your sister?"

I told him then he disappeared with my passport again he let me in.

301

We took her to the hospital again. At her bedside I gave her the same talk about how she loved her baby boy after she said she was going to ask for an abortion. She changed her mind. After we were both discharged from the hospital she phoned in a prescription for codeine for me. She'd noticed my limp and the pain I was in and thought it was the least she could to. I picked it up when I got hers then instead of buying groceries I arranged to have them delivered so I wouldn't be on my feet any more than I had to. We got takeout, took our pain pills and went to sleep early watching the TV in her room.

When I woke up alone back in my own bed Andre was standing in the doorway.

It's time, Anna.

I knew it was. I hadn't taken anything out on Paul since my nasty outburst after my last trip to see Alina. He was still completely disinterested in me physically and I had lost interest in him but he was kind and helpful, making sure I had everything I needed when I was too sore to get around. I knew Paul thought I was crazy so I did my best to appear normal. To me though Paul was an intrusion. All I wanted was Andre.

Paul still went out at night. I knew why now but he didn't know that.

I pushed myself up out of bed. On the way to the kitchen I took the blanket I used when I slept on the couch and wrapped it around my shoulders. I turned off the stove fan light and sat at the table. Andre sat with me.

"How long was I gone, Andre?"

Just a few minutes.

I was angry about Alina all over again. I was in pain. And I thought that the broken heart I was walking into was going to do me in long before Damian would find me. I wanted Andre to numb me. To take me to bed one last time but now I had to be strong and get Paul out of my life for a while.

The numbers on the stove clock counted from half past two until a few minutes after three before I heard the lock quietly pop open. Paul's shape stepped in silently and he held the latch open as he closed the door and slowly turned it back into place once it was completely shut. Then he turned the little dial in the knob to lock it back up. He was nearly through the kitchen when I spoke.

"Had an itch Paul?" I asked. I was surprised by the coldness in my voice but I was sending him away for his own good and needed to use everything I had.

He froze.

"Anna? What are you doing up?"

"I'm asking about your itch you son of a bitch." I could feel my

302

voice trying to break.

"I …" he paused. "What itch?"

"I know I'm young and inexperienced Paul but I'm not stupid."

"What are you talking about Anna? You're none of those things."
But he sounded confused and I could taste his temper. Caution. He was
hiding something but not what I was accusing him of.

"Old habits?" I asked. Anger about Alina pulled on me making me
louder. "How long has it been going on? Since we got back? You've
been going missing at night for weeks."

"I … a while," he admitted. I'd just caught him sneaking in the
door. He couldn't deny it but he didn't like my challenge. I could hear
that. "How did you find out?"

He thought I was asking about their nightly patrols. I stood up and
stomped toward him until I was just a step away and bust into tears.
Angry, angry tears.

"You've been sleeping around you unfaithful bastard."

"What?" That blindsided him.

"Where did you meet her?" Between sobs I was yelling. Paul
didn't know if he should come closer or step back. "Running at the dam,
the lake? Is she just easy or did you use your charm on her? Were you
still thinking about her when you walked back through my door?"

"Anna … no," he sounded relieved. He thought I'd simply
misunderstood. That pissed me off more.

"Nothing like—" he said.

"Nothing else explains why you leave me alone so much!" I yelled
back.

"Anna I—" he tried.

"Was it in the back of my car?"

"I said I didn't—"

"Up against a God damn tree?"

"I didn't sleep around!" he bellowed back. Interrupting him had
pushed the right button.

"Bullshit, bullshit, bullshit!"

The pictures I had started making in my head of him with someone
else made me sick. I held my stomach and started rocking on my feet to
try and steady it. The heartburn was bad enough; if everything came up
it was going to hurt a lot.

"Go to your room!" Paul yelled. His arm was raised, pointing
down the hallway.

He would rather fight about his imaginary affair than admit he'd
been out on watch around my house. I lost the battle with my stomach
and went to lean over the sink. Paul didn't move until things started
coming up so I put my hand up like a stop sign to tell him to stay away.
He'd gone around my arm and tried to put a hand on my back. I pushed

it away. It felt like I was choking on puke; gasping to cry at the same time I was heaving. He didn't back off but he didn't try touching me again.

"You don't want it here anymore. You won't touch me. The only part of me you want now is the baby," I whispered. The yelling and vomiting had left my throat raw.

"No Anna," he said, keeping it short so he wouldn't get cut off.

"You couldn't wait? Or would you have done it anyway?" I held back tears again.

"I didn't."

"Am I that h … h … hideous now?" The sobs had started again. I focused again on Alina to get my anger back. Paul was softening since I got sick and I needed him angry again if I was going to get him to walk out.

"No."

I pulled the blanket up over my mouth. I could taste the bile and wanted to wash it back down with half a bottle of antacid but first thing was first.

"Are you just sticking around to protect your investment now?" I wasn't sure if I was getting my voice back or just forcing it out. Either way it hurt. "You know just what to say, don't you? To keep me loving you. To keep me thinking I'm all you want. Keep me needing you.

"It's just too easy for you to keep your hands off me now." I stuck an arm out of my blanket cocoon and wiped my eyes on my sleeve. "God damn cheating son of a bitch."

"I didn't Anna, you'll see that when you calm down."

"This isn't my fault!" I yelled. I thought of Alina. Of Damian leaving her as soon as he was sure he didn't have to get on top of her any more. "Why do I have to calm down? At least Damian wouldn't stick around to screw with my feelings when he didn't have to screw me any more to get a child."

That did it.

"You are a paranoid miserable bitch," he blew up at me. "There hasn't been anyone else since I found you. I haven't been looking. I haven't wanted to. I'm what you need now. That's how I look after you.

"Kenny came back the day you took off in Edmonton. He told Denis there were two men looking for you. Denis paid him and he left. He hasn't been back. We've been watching the house at night. Looking after you. You ungrateful … .ungrateful …" he struggled with what to call me.

"Is that what you were doing when I was throwing up the pictures in my head of you with someone else? Trying to come up with that pathetic excuse? You would have told me." I burst into fresh tears. "You promised. You wouldn't keep that from me."

"Of course I would keep it from you. Do you really think I would tell you? Make it even harder to look after you? So you could go get your hands all over Kenny again to find out where they went? So you could go get in another fight? You should have come to me about the one in the mall ... like you did about the ones at the pond."

He was breathing hard, just a step away. I'd only wounded him so far. I had to make it much worse. But then this was just the beginning.

"Is that what she is? Payback for Kenny? Go dig it in her to get a dig at me for that? I never would have crossed that line you bastard."

"There is no she!" he yelled. "Will you get that through your thick stubborn head?"

"Which betrayal is it Paul? Her or some bullshit about watching the house? Maybe it's both? Dropping the ball on all of us so you could go get your thing on?"

"I liked you better when you knew your place," he growled.

"Is that why you did it? I'm not delicate enough? Helpless enough? Childish enough?" I yelled back. The tears were drying up. There was just rage now. "I don't make you feel man enough? You had to go prove yourself with someone else?"

"Every inch of you is childish!" he was shaking now and took a few steps back. "You're arrogant, stubborn and mean. I can't stand who you're turning in to!"

I stepped into his face. My lips were pulled back from my teeth ready to snarl at him.

"Is that what you want?" I lowered my voice and hissed. "A nice normal mate like Marie? Sweet and gentle?"

He didn't look down at me.

"That's better than what I have to deal with now." Good. He was getting madder.

"Why don't you end this then Paul?" I yelled back. "Knock me around until we're not tied together any more ... go ask Keith for a shot with her? He said he wanted you backing him up."

"He'd refuse me for that."

"Really? You want me to do it?" I put my hands on his chest and pushed him toward the wall. He pushed back but he kept his hands down so I stepped to the table and picked up a chair. I wasn't trying to miss. The chair crashed into the wall where he'd been standing but he saw it coming and was in the living room before it left my hands. I picked up another one and threw it as he stepped back in to the kitchen but he backed up as it went tumbling down the hall. The twisting to throw put my lower back in a vice.

"God damn it Anna!"

I had another chair.

"You're a cheater and a liar Paul. Your word is dirt with me.

You're no partner at all." I felt half blind with anger; blamed him for every blow Damian laid on Alina.

"You know what you say when sorry isn't enough Anna?" My ears hurt he was so loud.

"Yeah Paul, get out of my house!"

We both stood shaking for a moment then he pulled his ring off and put it on the counter. My door slammed so hard behind him the house shook. I took a deep breath and started crying.

I turned the stove light on and took my necklace off. It hadn't been undone since he put it on me. I strung his ring on it and did it back up. It wouldn't come off again until he took the ring back. Even if that took forever.

In my room Andre held me while I cried.

It's not over yet Anna, you still have to show him you're insane to get him away from here.

When I could see again I got my bag and stuffed a handful of cash in the bottom. Then my knife, gun, bathroom things and a couple of changes of clothes. In my bottom desk drawer I had a few things handy for getting into cars. I took those too. I dressed and brushed my teeth, got my coat and boots on and opened my door.

Paul leaned against the door frame, one hand on either side. I stopped and crossed my arms and watched him.

"What just happened?" he asked after a couple of minutes.

I said nothing.

"Is this your big plan to keep me out of the way? Piss me off with some bullshit about an affair then throw me out? That's weak Anna. You can do better than that."

I tried to duck out under his arm but he lowered it to block my way and kept his hands on the frame. He was mad at me. Disappointed. In love. Hoping it was just a pregnant rant.

"I'm not going to stop loving you," he said. "You don't have to do this alone."

But I wasn't. He didn't get it. I'd promised our daughter I would do whatever it took to keep him away.

"I'm not leaving you … can I come in?" he asked. "Please?"

I took my pack off and put it on the floor beside the door then I stepped back out of the way. Paul sighed with relief and stepped in. He wouldn't leave. I was ready for that. As I packed I'd been focusing on my blue light and what I would do with it.

Paul put his coat over the back of one of the chairs still at the table and turned on the kitchen light. He looked at my bag.

"Are you really that ready to leave me tonight?"

I looked down and didn't answer, still focusing on the last thing I had to do to Paul. Both my body and my mind. He approached

306

cautiously. First he put his hands on my elbows. I thought about smacking them away and my arms tensed up but I didn't. When they relaxed he moved in closer and slipped his arms around behind me. I tightened mine across my ribs.

"You're so angry," he whispered as he smelled my hair. "That's not your shampoo … you've been with Alina again."

I pulled in a lung full of air and let it out in a shaky sigh.

"I thought so."

His hand came up behind my head and pulled it to his shoulder. I let him as his other hand rubbed my back. It had been so long. I was starved for Paul. Even in pain from throwing the chairs there was nothing I wanted more than one last night with him.

Anna … Andre warned.

I reached one arm around him then the other. Then I charged my right with just a bit of blue light and rested it on his back. He relaxed as I let the light explore the connections in his spinal cord. I was going to short circuit the ones to move his muscles. Not his heart and lungs. Just everything else. Just for fifteen minutes. I hoped what I was about to do wouldn't break our bond.

"I'm not sharing you Paul," I whispered. "I won't stand for you being with anyone else."

"There's nobody but you Anna," he whispered back.

"Bullshit," I said as the light entered him. He collapsed hard on the floor so I got down and made sure he was breathing.

"There never will be anyone but me. I'm going to make sure of it. I'm going to start with Marie. I'm going to kill her. Then I'm going to hunt down the others … as many as I can while I can still get them out of my way for good.

"She'll be dead before you can get there to stop me. I can dodge Patrick. He's good but his blind spots are a mile wide. She'll be in a pool of blood and I'll be on my way to number two before anyone even knows I've been there.

"All you men found was me and Marie. Your damn harem. All I have to do is get in a car and wish … get close enough to pick them up like a bad smell. In ten minutes I'll be within a block of Marie … in an hour I'll be slipping my knife into the next one. You won't know where to begin looking for me.

"Maybe I'll save Marie for last …" I said thoughtfully.

"Then it will just be us," I kissed his paralyzed lips, letting my tongue run along his lower one as I tasted his skin. "Mmm."

"You won't be tempted again."

I got up and quietly opened the door and tossed my bag behind the garage. Then I went back in and closed it again.

"Ray!" I screamed, "Help! Ray!"

I was suddenly terrified. I'd be on the run now. I'd attacked Paul and tears of guilt came quickly but I was past the point of no return. If he could move that would be it for me.

"Ray!" I cried and pulled the door open hard so it hit the wall. As I stepped out he was running past the garage with Denis close behind.

"It's Paul," I sobbed and pulled him in. Ray got down next to him.

"What happened?" he asked.

"I don't know," I was shaking, Denis holding on to me. "We were fighting, he … he'd gotten so mad, then he started rubbing his arm and he wasn't making sense … his legs gave out and he fell down."

"I … I … Paul," I cried.

"Denis, help me get him on his side."

Denis let me go and they rolled Paul over. Their backs were to the door, focused on him. I took a couple of deep breaths like I was trying to get it together then slipped out and opened the side gate. I hid behind the garage beside the fence and ducked down out of sight.

"He's breathing fine … get the big bag Denis."

Denis' boots ran up the gravel and a minute later came back.

"I don't know where the hell it is. You got your phone? He's stable but I might need an ambulance. Paul? Paul?"

Then after another minute I could hear Paul mumbling.

"He's moving," Ray said.

"Anna," Paul said.

"She was just here."

"Sit me up Ray," Paul said, "Anna's going after Marie … I think she attacked me. I just went limp. I could see and hear everything but I couldn't move.

"She's going to kill Marie; she says she won't share me. Keith told her how we get our second mates … he said he wanted me to ask for Marie. Anna said she's going to hunt them all down … you know if she kills them it's permanent.

"Get me on my feet."

There was shuffling and footsteps.

"Denis, stay here. Ray, you're taking me to the airport then go home. I'll warn Keith and get the first flight I can to Edmonton."

"I'm sorry Paul," Ray said. "I really hope we're wrong."

"I don't think we are … attacking me and threatening the others is taking it way too far for just getting me out of the way to protect me. If she wanted to go after him alone she would have just left."

Yeah, I thought, but you would try and track me down. Now you're committed to staying in Edmonton. Hopefully it will take you a long time to figure out my bluff.

It took a bit for Paul and Ray to leave. Paul was on the phone to Keith as he ran back in my door for a few things then they drove off in the truck. I closed my eyes to search for Denis. He was in the alley by the gate and I waited a long time for him to go back in the house. Then I waited more before I quietly slipped away.

"Come on Andre," I whispered as we neared the convenience store. "Let's get you a smoke."

About fucking time.

He'd had three before we found an unlocked car with sufficient cover. In a couple of minutes we were driving up to the highway. I jumped us to Redding, near the gas station we had filled up at on the way to Reno and drove around until I found an older RV covered in a tarp. I dumped the car several blocks away and walked back and broke in. It was stocked with a few things so I ate and curled up on the small bed inside to wait for Paul or Damian or Lord knew who else to find me.

Chapter 56

The last time I visited Alina was different from the others. It started the same. The hall, the ambulance, the neurologist. But this visit was missing Alina's talk of an abortion. She kept her good hand on her stomach in her hospital bed and seemed comforted by his small presence. Her wounds were just as bad and her nightmares would be just as horrible but the little light she carried with her gave her strength.

She let James and his brother come in on his day off to take out her blood covered sofa and bring in a new one she'd picked out online. She wouldn't leave her room while they were in the apartment but she called him the next day to thank him.

I was huge. The pregnancy was only a couple of weeks from being over and I pictured having to finish Damian off in Alina's little apartment. I spent my nights sitting on her new sofa when the heartburn was worse than the back ache and Alina's bed with her when the back ache was winning. She did as much for me as she could but her anguish filled whatever room she was in so I kept my needs as small as possible. I told her Paul would be back any day. I told her I was only thirty-four weeks so she didn't have to worry too much about him flying me home.

Andre stayed with us. He was quieter now. He could see the end coming; his and possibly mine. He would whisper to me to keep focused. It wouldn't be long. He said when the time came to let him work he would use everything we had together to finish Damian. He could rest and I could start down the long road to peace with Paul.

Andre didn't touch me any more. There was no need to distract me from Paul. I didn't miss the torment. The shame I felt from letting him treat me like that was only a taste of what Alina had gone though and more than enough for me to understand her humiliation and how much of her Damian had taken.

I realized after a week with Alina what the purpose of my disturbing and repetitive visits was. Damian's child had to grow up. And without giving her my speech over and over again he wouldn't. If I hadn't reminded her repeatedly how much she loved him she would have had the abortion. On my last night with her she curled up behind me, her fractured arm resting on my side. She confessed to me how much she loved her baby already; how she had from the moment she thought he could be there. How she had protected her stomach from every blow. It was a pretty good version of the talk I'd been giving her.

She thought people would think badly of her, loving that monster's son. I told her they wouldn't; she was brave and generous and her love was unconditional. There wasn't a better woman anywhere to be that child's mother than Alina. She sighed and kissed my back through my hair. I knew I could wake up somewhere else now that part of my task was finished and she would be ready for hers.

Alina lifted her arm off me so I could get the light and we sighed together as she put it back down. I fell asleep expecting to wake up in the back of whatever stolen car I had been in before I came here again but I woke up in my basement bed clutching my bag to my chest.

Andre stood in the doorway lit from behind by the light bulb in my stove fan down the hall in the kitchen. I pushed my pack off the bed and on to the floor and when I looked up again he was standing over me.

Rest now Anna, he said. *Your traveling is over. Our day is coming soon. The big man upstairs will take care of you until then. I'll be with you. I won't see you again until the time comes to go to work.*

He sat on the bed and lay down with me then he pushed himself back into my body and faded until we were one again.

Next thing I knew I heard the key in my door. It snapped open on the first try so it must be Denis. Mrs. Desmond hadn't been down here since the day in October when I brought Paul to her and she never got the hang of the fussy lock.

"Denis?" I called. "That you?"

The noises in the kitchen stopped.

"Denis?"

Then the sounds of a full grown bull charging down the hallway to my room.

"Anna?" he froze in the door when he saw me. I was sitting on the bed by then trying to stand but gave up.

"Hi Denis … how's things?"

"Good," he answered carefully. "You?"

"I got it back together now. What day is it?"

"February fifteenth."

"That all?" I muttered looking down at my swollen feet. The past week on Alina's expensive mattress had made a huge improvement in my back considering the previous two nights had been in the back of a stolen car.

"How long have you been hiding down here?"

"A few hours ... I think I'm here to stay. Is there anything to eat in the kitchen?"

Denis shook his head. I noticed his coat was undone and his right hand was inside it. He'd know what I'd done to Ray and knew I could take his gun in the blink of an eye.

"You know I couldn't hurt anyone."

"I'm not so sure," he replied. "You hurt Paul."

"Yeah ..." I couldn't deny that.

"I need you to tell me what happened."

I knew he did. He had to be sure I had Andre under control or he would have to do something to make sure I wasn't going to carry out my threat to kill all the women in the family.

"I ... I won't lose Paul over this. Pilot's task. We set it up. He had to want to leave me ... to stay away. He's the one who interferes. I don't know what will go wrong but he's safe where he is. As long as he thinks I'm after Marie he'll stay put in Edmonton ... it's his duty to take me out and he thinks that's where I'll go."

"Who's we, Anna?"

"Andre, me. He told me what to do to keep Paul away. Paul loves me so much ... it has to be like this. I feel my connection to him Denis ... all the time. I don't want to live a minute without it. I'll do whatever Pilot wants as long as there's a way to keep Paul alive. Even if I'm on the run from him forever that connection will be enough. I wouldn't hurt anyone other than Damian and his men. It's just not in me."

Denis sighed and thought for a few seconds then he took his hand out of his coat and came in and sat on the bed with me.

"Where is Andre now?"

"He's under control. I'll dust him off to help me take care of Damian then he can be at peace." I put my hand on my huge stomach. "It won't be long now."

Then I slowly reached for Denis' hand and took it. Put it on my stomach. There was a knee or something pressing and rolling. He held his breath while he felt it. His decision about me would be so much easier if I wasn't all full of Paul's baby.

"If Paul shows up he'll die. I'll die. I'll get back to Ray and he'll save her but it'll be too late for me. I can take him Denis ... she deserves both her parents. She didn't ask for any of this. If I use my energy to jump around now I won't have it to fight him. Look at me ... I'm going to need it. I'm not going anywhere."

311

Denis had a small smile on his face as he felt her knee slide by again. Then his hand jumped as she did her best to kick. He laughed.

"I don't think you're insane Anna," he said, "I think you're just in love."

"You can't breathe a word to him. You have to help me protect him. I can only hope that he'll forgive me when it's over."

My necklace was on top of my shirt and he picked Paul's ring up off my chest and held it for a moment. I still wore my rings and even if I could get them off my swollen finger I would keep them on.

"I suppose there's still hope," he said before he let it drop. "Do you want to come up and see Bee? She's been struggling with her health the past few days."

Denis waited for me to get dressed. Bee was glad to see me. She was disappointed in both of us for failing at marriage and said so in no uncertain terms. In her day that was shameful and she went at me until I couldn't be any more ashamed. I took it. I felt I deserved every word. Denis was silent. I didn't doubt that he agreed with her. She said the smell was gone, the smell that had been following me around. I agreed with that.

When we went back down Denis got me settled and plugged my phone in to charge by the bed.

"I'll be in and out checking on you so don't tackle me or anything," he grinned.

"Okay," I smiled back. "So is it just you looking after her?"

"Just Ray and me. He left last night after I got in. Paul won't call but he stays up to date. He knows he'll get the same speech from Bee that you just got. She doesn't know what happened between you and Paul, just that you split. Don't worry. I won't say a word," he said. "I don't like leaving you to finish Damian alone. But there has been so much I don't understand about you that I can't question it. There are bigger things at work here."

Then he laughed. "Like your stomach."

I let him put his hand on her for a while. His little sister.

"Denis … in my bag there's some codeine Alina prescribed me. Can you get me a couple and some water? Back is bad today."

He brought back a handful of bottles.

"These are all for the same date," he said.

"Every time I took her home from the hospital she phoned the prescription in for me. I couldn't tell her she'd done it the last time I was there. To her it was always the first time."

"I don't get it," Denis said. "You spent the last few weeks with your sister?"

"I …" I didn't really want to explain. "I kept finding myself there in the hallway outside her apartment the night Damian beat her and left.

312

Over and over. I would be stuck there for days; this last time was a week. Every time I had to convince her to get in the ambulance again … then the black sleep in the hospital. She would have all the specialists trying to figure it out. I would throw out all his things … deal with the blood covered couch. Try and put her back together as much as I could before I left."

"I guess that explains all the pills." He got a glass of water from the kitchen for me and helped me sit up to take a couple.

"Ray took Paul to the airport," Denis said. "Keith had Patrick and a couple of his boys on his way to guard Marie before they even left. I waited in the alley for you, didn't think you'd gone far but after a while I had to get in to check on Bee. I saw you run out the front."

I felt my lower lip tremble so I steadied it. I'd spent the last two months of mine either focusing on Alina, sleeping off my return trips, or looking for somewhere safe to hide out. When I didn't have those distractions I cried.

"I was hiding behind the garage, listening. I could sense you in the alley so I had to stay put until you were inside. I stole a car and jumped to Redding. I found an RV so I dumped the car a dozen blocks away and walked back to it and broke in. There were blankets, food. I stayed there a few days then I stole another car and moved on. When I wasn't with Alina I was either recovering from the return trip in the back of a stolen car or another RV or looking for another place to hide.

"When I left Alina last night I thought I'd just wake up in the car, but I found myself here."

"Didn't you take cash for a hotel?" Denis asked. He sounded disappointed with my living arrangements.

"I wasn't staying anywhere Paul could find me. I don't think I'll disappear again but if Paul comes I'll have to run."

"He won't know Anna, I promised," Denis said.

Chapter 57

Denis found me in my spare room. It had been two days and no Paul so I trusted that he kept quiet and understood why I'd asked him to lie for me. I was on the phone getting balances on my accounts not in my name and writing cheques to Anna to clean them out. I'd also made a list of all Anna's accounts for the lawyer. "I have to get to the bank today then to the lawyer," I told him.

"No," Denis stood in the door and crossed his arms.

"What?" I asked him.

"You're not filing for divorce," he insisted.

I stared back at him in disbelief.

313

"Jeez no Denis … I need a will. I want to make sure Paul and his family have no trouble getting my money if I … don't make it."

Denis looked at me suspiciously.

"I don't need a piece of paper to tell me just how badly I screwed things with him."

"Anna, I know someone," Denis sighed. "He's stubborn, selfish and sometimes too self-centered and arrogant. I've seen him be cold and ruthless. Brutal and hard. He's not afraid to be compassionate and loyal. Kind and devoted. He loves his wife without condition. He would walk to the end of the earth for her if someone even hinted that she would need it. But he expects loyalty and trust without question, most of all from her. He believes that his word is as good as gold and that he is always, always right. He doesn't take it well at all when he thinks someone believes otherwise.

"I know his wife too. She's cut out of the same cloth. They've met their match in each other. I've seen the conflict that's caused them. The passion."

I dropped my eyes as I tried to keep myself together. Denis came in and pulled the other chair up next to me and sat in it.

"This doesn't even make your top three and you've always worked it out," he said. "Forgiveness won't be far away when you decide to get your head out of your ass and ask for it. He has to be sure … he'll hear you out."

Denis squeezed me gently and stood up to leave.

"I have to get back upstairs but come say hi before you go out."

"Okay Denis, thanks."

In my heart I knew he was right.

Bee had a small list of things she needed. She didn't seem well. Tired and more confused than usual. Denis said she wouldn't eat much and it was an argument to get her out of bed every day and then another one to get her back in it. He said she knew her time was short. Ray just prescribed companionship and comfort for her now. She'd never been around this long before and being a frail old woman had lost the charm it once had. Denis said she was ready to go.

It didn't take long. Denis came in early the day after I signed all the final paperwork with the lawyer. Still dark. He didn't come in until after sunrise to bring me up for breakfast. Today I was already sitting up on the edge of my bed by the time he made it down the hall.

"Anna?" Denis whispered as he turned on the hall light and when he came to the room he saw that I was sitting up. He hesitated in the door for a second before he came in and sat with me on the bed.

"Anna," he said softly and put his arm around me, "she passed during the night. I checked on her at three and she was resting well but she's gone now. I'm sorry."

314

I took a deep breath and exhaled tears. Knowing it would come didn't make it any easier. It just told me which thoughts to avoid until I had to think them. I put my head on Denis' shoulder and cried. He didn't. For him it was an absence, not a good-bye.

"Am I being childish?" I asked him. My voice still shook.

"Yes," he laughed gently. "You are. I'd be worried if you weren't. Do you want to come upstairs? I don't know what to do here when someone dies."

I nodded. I didn't know either.

"Okay … get dressed. I'm going to swipe your coffee maker and take it upstairs. I need it. And I'm taking the coffee."

Denis had my coffee maker under one arm and a cigarette in his mouth when I left my suite. I didn't bother with a coat even though it was well below freezing. He ground it out in the gravel before we went in.

I waited in her living room for him while he went through to the kitchen and started a pot of coffee.

"You don't have to see her if you don't want to," he said when he came back into the living room.

"I do," I said but I wasn't so sure.

"I haven't called Ray yet … nothing he can do."

Denis had left her door shut part way and her table lamp on. He pushed it open the rest of the way and led me in.

Bee was on her back with her eyes closed. I would have thought she was just sleeping. I sat beside her on the bed and felt her cool hand, then her face. Her glasses were open on her table so I folded them up and put them in the case. Then I got her spare brush from her drawer and smoothed out what I could of her short grey hair. Denis watched me.

"That's better. It wouldn't do for anyone to see her looking scruffy."

I felt a little better that I had been able to do something for her but it still didn't feel like much. "She has a folder in her desk … she would never let me see it but she says it's there. We're supposed to open it now."

"Okay," Denis said but he didn't move.

"I guess I should call someone first. It's probably her will and where she wants to go. That sort of thing."

I put her arm under the blanket then I straightened the bed.

We looked up the number for the hospital. I thought of calling 911 but this wasn't an emergency and even at seven in the morning on a Friday they probably had real emergencies to deal with. They said they would send a policeman … a formality … and an ambulance. I thought the policeman was to make sure that there wasn't a trail of blood running from Bee to the axe out by the woodpile.

315

"Can you run down and get my Rachel ID for me? And you'll need your Daniel ID. I don't think they'll care to see it but just in case."

"Got it," he was back in a minute. We would have to be Rachel and Daniel since our names would go into any reports.

We sat at the table to wait. Denis was on his second cup and I got myself one.

"You want me to explain to Ray why you're off the wagon?"

"It's this or a smoke. Tell him I roughed you up."

He laughed. "Do you want the folder now?"

"I want to look after her first. Will you go back today?"

"Maybe … do you need me to stick around?"

"No," I rubbed my stomach, "one way or another I'll be back at the compound within the week anyway I think. If I get any bigger I won't fit out the door."

"Sure. I can stay if you change your mind."

Denis was on his third and putting on another pot when the police arrived. Satisfied that there was no suspicious trail of blood leading from the bedroom and that there was indeed a deceased person in the house he took our names for the file and left as the ambulance arrived. They were kind and respectful to her and gently took her away leaving me with instructions for whom to contact at the hospital to release her to whoever we were making arrangements with. It was getting complicated and I was having trouble keeping up. Denis seemed to have a handle on it.

Next we found her folder. There was a will done by the same lawyer I had seen and information about a place in New Brunswick where her parents were. Denis skipped through it and read her instructions to me. She wanted to be cremated and sent back home. First we called a funeral home that could look after her, then the one in New Brunswick. They would talk to the one here and keep us up to date.

The house felt so empty. Denis had arranged a flight for two days out but had to pay up front so I went downstairs to get him cash for the travel agent. As I counted out a mix of small and large bills something familiar tickled under my nose. I went cold. It was men … Damian's men. Close. Inside. I spun to face my kitchen and counted … three … four … damn, I was in trouble. Too many.

Then the door slammed and I heard shouting. Denis. I got to my dresser as fast as I could manage and took Damian's knife up the hall.

I quickly assessed the men in the living room; Denis and three still to go down. The one on the floor wasn't a threat. He was still. I noticed Denis was dripping blood from his hand but didn't have the luxury of looking very closely. He was loud and had their attention so Andre quickly slipped in front of the nearest one and opened his throat before spinning me out of the way of another.

316

My stomach started to cramp with the movement and as I came to a stop to take stock of the remaining men Denis pulled his knife from the one I had just avoided. There was far too much blood on Denis now to be explained by the wounds on the men on the floor. The last one went after Denis. I slashed deep into his back distracting him as Denis got him in the neck. At least that's what it looked like from where I was. I stuck him in the neck from behind and pulled him over by the handle of my knife.

It was all so fast. Just my breathing and the sound of Denis gasping. He started to collapse after the last of Damian's men hit the ground. Maybe it was all the blood on him that made him look so pale. I hoped desperately that it was but he was struggling to breath and even focus his eyes. I dropped my knife and got my arms around him, hoping to ease his fall to the floor but he was so much bigger than me and with my stomach cramping up I knew he was helping me down.

He leaned back on my couch, his hands on me; his knife on the floor beside us.

"Denis …" I said. I didn't know what to do. Andre never dealt with this.

"You're cut Anna," he said, "wrap those up tight … call Ray, he'll know what to do."

I had no idea I'd been hurt and he put his hand on my thigh and my upper arm to show me where.

"Damn," I said. "Denis, what do I do for you?" But he was already struggling to keep his head up so I wrapped my arms around it and held him close.

"It's okay Anna … I never liked this part but it's not so bad."

"No Denis …" I cradled his head in one arm and put my hand on his cheek.

"You're a good little fighter," he said. "See you on the other side."

Damian

Chapter 58

I sat a long time at Mrs. Desmond's table upstairs. The few things I packed before I ran out of the basement were in her bedroom. I had no plans to sleep there … or upstairs for that matter. I was waiting for Damian. As the sun went down I didn't fight it by flipping switches and let darkness fill the space around me.

The plate of cookies she'd covered in plastic wrap the night before sat in the exact center of the table where she left it. There was enough light from outside to sparkle on the folds as I swayed back and forth in my chair. My stomach kept cramping up since the fight. I wasn't sure how long it had been. I realized that even with the heat now off downstairs the smell would eventually give away what I had left behind. And I couldn't leave Denis down there with them like that. The others I didn't care about but Denis deserved far better.

I decided it was time to swallow my pride and call for help. Ray had been in touch with Denis every day so he was the only one I could find to reach out to now with Denis gone. Movement in the living room caught my eye making my heart race but it was just the shadows of the trees in the street light that came in her big front window. The rain had stopped but the strong wind was still breaking off small branches and scattering them on the ground. Low clouds seemed to boil down from above, lit by the city lights below.

It was too dark to see the keypad on the phone so I held it near the window and dialled Ray. It seemed to ring forever before he answered.

"Hey Denis … what's up?" he asked.

"Ray," I sighed. My stomach was cramping up again. "It's me."

There was silence for a few seconds. I was almost glad for it. I took a few deep breaths as I waited for the cramping to pass.

"Anna … .what do you want?"

I took a couple more breaths as the discomfort went away.

321

"I want Paul," I told him. I put my hand on his ring through my shirt; still dangling on the gold necklace he had given me for my birthday.

"You have a poor way of showing it. I can't believe what you said to him ... what you did."

"You know why it has to be like this Ray. At least the baby will have him ... if he interferes she won't have either of us."

I heard him sigh. "I don't know Anna."

"He has to want to be where he is now ... he loves me so much. I know I was in bad shape for a while ... Andre told me what to do. So he'd be out of danger. I'm ashamed of myself for what I did ... how I let Andre treat me ... but I couldn't see another way." I could feel my voice choking up so I covered my mouth with my hand to stifle the sobs that were starting.

"Anna? Are you still there?"

"Yes." I took a deep breath. I was getting confused. Starting to forget why I was calling him. "Something's happened Ray. I need Iverson ... help." I knew what I said wasn't making much sense.

"Let me talk to Denis."

I looked at the plate on the table. Cookies made by a dead old lady for the dead man in the basement.

"I think I pulled some muscles in my stomach in the fight Ray ... I keep cramping up."

"Anna ... did you hurt Denis?"

"No. He's downstairs. I'm so tired Ray, you know I wouldn't hurt anyone. Heartburn is so bad I have to try and sleep sitting up but then the back's worse. Where's Paul? I love him so much."

"Anna!" He shouted at me. "Get Denis!"

"I can't!" I shouted back ... then quieter. "I'm cramping up again." I took a few deep breaths. "You haven't seen me in a while ... I think it's almost over." I took a few more. "I'm as big as house ... lost a lot of time. It's been out of control."

"How often?" I knew I could count on Ray's medical training to kick in. He'd worry about how crazy I was later.

"I don't know ... I've just been sitting here in the dark. I don't know what to do. Can you get Iverson?"

"Anna ... why?"

"There are five dead men in the basement Ray ... I don't know what to do. I got my bloody clothes off but my leg won't stop oozing ... I think I got the cut on my arm under control." I was just wore a t-shirt and underwear. My thigh was wrapped up tightly with a torn up sheet but it wasn't keeping the blood in.

"Jesus Anna. Get Denis on the phone."

I reached my hand out and held it over the plate. I imagined I

322

could feel their warmth rising up to my palm. The hand next to my ear spoke.

"Anna?" I jumped; I forgot I was holding the phone.

"Ray?"

"Yes Ray," he said. "Put Denis on."

"He came down and got me this morning. Mrs. Desmond died during the night. Nothing we could do … so cool already. They sent an ambulance to pick her up … I was on the phone all morning … he helped me keep the arrangements straight."

"I'm so sorry," Ray said. "Have Denis bring you home, okay? We'll figure it out."

"He can't," I said. "I was in the spare room when I felt them in the kitchen … coming to the hall. He must have seen them follow me in. There was a lot of noise … he was shouting. I grabbed Damian's knife from my room but I'm so slow. Denis had finished one by the time I got there but he was bleeding. I got one quick but he was bleeding worse as he got another and we finished off the last one together but he fell on the floor.

"He didn't make it Ray," I sobbed, not doing a very good job of keeping it quiet.

"Oh damn it," Ray said.

"I don't know what to do."

"Please come back," he begged.

"No Ray …"

"I have to make a few calls … stay by the phone, okay? And watch the clock when you cramp up. You shouldn't be alone now if you're in labour."

"I tried Ray … I couldn't even drag Denis to the door. I don't know how I'm going to get him out of there. Mmm," I sighed as I started cramping up again.

"Anna, is it happening again?"

I kept breathing. "What?" I said between sighs. I needed some sleep … I was losing track of things.

"Your stomach cramping. Is it happening again?" he asked.

I started to panic. "How do you know about that Ray? Who's watching me?"

"You told me," he said.

I didn't remember doing that. "I didn't …" I said and hung up on him.

After I made it back to Mrs. Desmond's sofa the phone started ringing. I listened to it as I fell asleep, nibbling at my ears again once or twice.

Didn't they know what time it was? The damn phone was ringing

323

again. And ringing. Wasn't the courtesy if you didn't answer after four rings then you were sleeping or busy or something? It just wouldn't stop. I pushed myself up off the sofa and felt my way to the kitchen. The phone would probably go silent soon as got to it so I held my hand over it for a few more rings. It didn't stop.

"Yeah?" I said sleepily when I picked it up.

"Where have you been?" the voice said.

"Do you have any idea what time it is? People are sleeping."

"Wait—"

"Why don't you dial more carefully … wrong number ringing all damn night."

I hung up. All I wanted to do was get back to sleep so I sat at the table and put my head down on my crossed arms but the phone started ringing again.

"Yeah?" I said again.

"Anna don't hang up," Ray said quickly.

"Ray? Where are you?" I went to the window and looked out to the street. Everything looked okay but more men could be watching the house. I thought I could feel someone outside … watching me.

"Are you okay?" Ray asked.

"I think someone is watching the house," I whispered to him. I was too tired to focus enough to be sure but my skin crawled when I tried. "I don't see anyone … but there could be more."

"What about your leg?" he asked. "And your stomach … are you still cramping up?"

"Not since I woke up," I whispered. "I can't see my leg but the bandage I made is damp. I have to keep the lights off."

I looked down anyway. Lights wouldn't have made any difference. It was so high my stomach hid it.

"The Colonel wants you to get out of there. Take the car. Leave then call the police. He can't do anything across the border other than make sure Denis goes home to his family. Jump here … we'll keep you safe."

"I can't go yet … I'm not finished here." My stomach was starting to hurt. Not like the cramps earlier. It was hard and tightening as the pain grew. I started to try and breathe through it like Catherine remembered. She'd seen babies come. It seemed to help but Ray was talking again distracting me.

"Anna? Your stomach?" he asked.

"Ray …" I couldn't get a sentence out. At least I could talk through them before. After a dozen or so breaths the pain peaked and started to go away.

"I think that was the real thing," I breathed as it passed. "I'm running out of time."

"Call an ambulance. Please?" He begged. "If you won't come here go to the hospital."

"I'll come home when it's over ... one way or another. I have work to do."

I could hear him sigh. "Will you at least look at your leg for me? Go in Bee's room and pull the heavy curtains and close the door. The light won't get out. Take the phone with you."

"Okay," I gave in and took the cordless with me and did what he said. Then I took Damian's knife and tore up her top sheet for more bandages. I could see in the mirror that the old bandage was red and tacky blood stuck to my leg.

"Should I take the old bandage off?" I asked him. "It might have stopped but I don't want to make it start again."

"Do it gently ... I don't like to but I need to know how bad it is."

"'kay," I said and put the phone down. I was able to pick apart the knot that held it tight and slowly unwrapped it. I could see in the mirror over Bee's dresser that it oozed a bit as my leg moved when the last of the bandage came off but was better than it was before.

"It's about four inches long," I told him. "Most of it is closed but it's torn and open at the bottom. It's not really bleeding now ... well a bit if I move. I can't tell how deep it is."

"Can you wrap it back up tight? You need to get to a doctor."

"Yeah ... I can tie it back up. It's not as bad as you think ... it doesn't hurt at all. Have you heard from Paul? You can't tell him I'm here."

He hesitated. "Yes ... I know he'll come to you."

"So then what?" I yelled at him. "Once she's born am I fair game to have Damian's child? Another soldier for his army? What's Paul going to do to stop that? I like it here Ray ... neither one of them will have me if that's how things are going to go. Paul said it ... she's the only thing protecting me right now ... one way or another Damian can't have me.

"The baby will be here soon then there's nothing protecting me. From Paul or Damian. He won't listen, I went too far."

"You know it's not like that Anna. Please ... ask me to call him for you."

"Don't tell him ... you'll kill us both!" I flared at him. "I lost Bee and Denis today and I'm going to have to get through the fight of my life by tonight ... .you have to be silent. If you tell him anything then tell him I'm on the run. He can't come to me."

"I didn't," Ray said. "Come home or go to the hospital."

"Shit," I managed as my stomach tightened up painfully again. I held the phone away from my mouth so he couldn't hear the moans that were sneaking out as I tried to breath through it.

"Anna?" he was saying when I put the phone back to my ear.

"I'm here," I felt just fine when my stomach wasn't in knots.

"That was just over ten minutes … you need to get to the hospital." He hesitated then he quickly added. "Our babies can come quick."

He couldn't see me shaking my head. "Then get ready to catch … I'll come home when my job is done. If you talk to Paul tell him that. I'll give him his daughter and take whatever is coming to me."

"Please … don't do this. I'm not ready to lose you yet," his voice broke.

"I love you big brother. Thank you for everything. There's a letter with my lawyer for you that tells you where she is and what your task is when mine is finished. I left everything to Paul … if he doesn't make it then in trust to Ron and Camille and Joshua to raise her. I want you to help her grow up properly." I laughed a bit but I was choking up too. "I seem to have the quick and dirty job but yours won't matter if I fail. I'll see you soon Ray."

I hung up and turned the ringer off. Tears ran down my face for a few minutes then I got up and turned off the bedroom light and opened the door. I carefully checked outside all the windows again but nothing seemed out of place in the street or the yard even though I could still feel eyes on me. On my way to the bathroom my hand ran absently over my stomach. She pushed her foot into my palm … she was so tight for space she couldn't move without pushing on something.

"Sshhh," I whispered to her. "We'll go home soon … no matter what, you won't be alone." My hand dropped across my belly button and my fingertips traced over the bump it made in my shirt. My white t-shirt. I stopped, still tracing over and around it. The shirt in my dream. The shirt the woman in the mirror wore when I saw her in the hotel in Reno. I turned and started to Bee's room as another contraction began to take hold. My legs slowed and stopped as the pain grew and I held on to the back of a kitchen chair as I waited for it to pass.

When I got moving again I could see the face of the phone flashing as I walked past it. There was nothing Ray could do for me now other than get ready for my arrival. I could feel my temper focusing on him. Why the hell was he calling and not getting ready?

In Bee's room I could finally hear the rumble of the plane. At first it just sounded like part of the heavy wind outside but as it drowned the wind out I slammed the door and crouched down in the corner behind it. My bag was there so I grabbed it and held on. The only thing I would really need from it now was the knife. Still bloody from the fight.

The rumbling grew and the house shook. The roar of the screaming engines became deafening as it passed just overhead and the vibrating air in my ears tried to burst them. The only thing that told me I was screaming was the pain in my throat. The engine noise stopped as the house began to shake. Suddenly the bedroom door flew open and smashed into the wall next to me. Compared to the roar of the plane the sound of the explosion was devastating. Orange flames had smashed through the living room window and followed the door in. They spread over the mess I had left Bee's bed in after I raided it for bandages, they curled around the corner after me singeing the hair on my arms and the side of my face. Their heat seared whatever they couldn't reach. I held my breath until they disappeared and left behind only the quiet soft glow coming in from outside.

I sat for a minute deciding if my hearing was gone or if it was actually quiet. While I thought about it I got my shoes on. Broken glass from the living room had blown in all over everything. At least my back wasn't burnt like in my dream. If I'd been standing in the door when the flames flooded in I would have been washed in them like everything else.

When I stood up I tried to close the bedroom door to keep the heat out. It swung away from the wall a bit but its bottom corner hit the floor before it was a third of the way around. I shoved on it but it was stuck. The wall leaned into the room ... the door wasn't going anywhere so I put the pack on my back and stepped into the living room. My arm stung from the flames that had found me but not as bad as the burns would have.

The front door wouldn't open either; cock eyed as it was, orange light coming in around the edges. I gave up on it and went back into Bee's room to try my only other way out of the burning house. It was the only window low enough since it opened out onto her porch. Most of the glass was broken so I took one of the drawers from her night table and knocked as much glass as I could out then I stuffed her singed bed spread over the window frame to try and protect myself from the shards that I couldn't knock loose. It worked. Mostly.

My bike was still in Paul's garage, not where I dreamed it the last time and the huge old Lincoln stretched out covering nearly all the asphalt. I put my fingers on the trunk and ran them up over the roof and down along the hood. I looked back and forth up the street. Still nothing was out of place so I walked out to the road. Then I stopped, closed my eyes, and turned left to face Armageddon.

I was on the street in front of my house looking north, facing the flames. Another contraction came so I stood holding my stomach and breathing until it passed. The low clouds caught and shone the orange light from the fire. It covered everything I could see almost as I remembered it. The apple tree was truly beautiful, as was everything else the fire touched.

I laughed out loud in spite of the burning in my mouth and throat as I pulled the hot air in. It wasn't as bad as I remembered since I hadn't been gasping in flames this time as they filled Bee's room. Then I raised my arms and shouted at the sky.

"This is the last time!" I laughed hard. "The last time!"

I giggled, hoping Damian would find me here. It was perfect. Just perfect.

The entire north sky was bright and hot as the sun. I closed my eyes and the light shone through my lids. It filled me. Recharged me. I was excited to be reaching the end of my work. Andre was ready for his minute alone with his Lieutenant. Then he would be gone. One way or another it would be all over. I would circle that sun; slowly making my way to its center.

I sighed, waiting for my queue to start; the crack of the starter's pistol as half the flaming apple tree crashed to the ground next to me. The baby squirmed and kicked hard and her movements made me sway.

"Yes," I told her. "Soon baby. We'll see him soon." I could feel her need for her father. Her connection to him. Just as I had during my dream so long ago that sent me away for a week. I sighed and rubbed her through the skin of my stomach as I waited.

Ray asked me once if what I found with Pilot was worth the cost we paid to look for it. Up until now I'd been uncertain. Now I was sure. Peace was well worth the price I had to pay in this short lifetime of mine. Spending her long life mated to the son of the man who had spread so much pain would be terrible for her as long as a connection existed between him and Damian. With Damian gone from him there would be no father for him to be loyal to.

I breathed through another contraction, concentrating on the familiar pops and crackles of the fire around me. The tree would come down in moments so I held up my left hand like a gun pointed at it, two fingers extended and counted down through the last few seconds until it fell. I pulled my hand up a bit as the branch snapped imagining my pretend gun going off. Sparks flew up as the branch broke up when it landed so I laughed and walked down the alley to start my work.

Chapter 59

There was nobody. Nobody living that is. I thought because I'd only seen this place in a dream that it was only me and the dead. No injured, no firemen. Nobody but me. Maybe it was like the corn farm where I found Pilot. Private he called it.

As I circled the perimeter of the fire I found all the dead I'd seen for years; people killed in the explosion when the plane came down. A man in one home, a child in another. The child never would have been home alone but his surviving parents wouldn't be here. I looked after him now. Nothing was consumed by the fire; even though it moved and its heat could burn it too wasn't alive.

I was near my house completing my first circle; a half block closer to ground zero than I had been. Flames were getting smaller, not so hot. The dead were more damaged than they had been. Contractions still interrupted my progress but didn't seem to be any more frequent. Actually, I was too absorbed in my job to pay attention. They could very well be. I was moving quickly, enjoying myself. Taking satisfaction in doing this right … making sure they were all here.

I laughed again. My farewell tour.

Approaching one of the larger pieces of wreckage at the site something other than smoke tickled my nose. It was illusive; both everywhere and nowhere. I knew what I would find on the ground next to the piece of fuselage. Six seats, four bodies: two in the front three and two in the back. I approached them and noted three others on the ground as the tickle got stronger. When I concentrated it disappeared but when I ignored the feeling it crept back in.

I stopped when I got to the seats. I always had the impression that the two still buckled in front were traveling together. Their odd intimate embrace always made me feel that way. She was seated twisted around to face backward then she had fallen on him. He had just slumped toward her, between her and the seat, his face shoved deep into the front of her torn open blouse so all I could see was his ears, his arm casually around her. Both her shoes were missing and her painted toenails flickered with the nearby flames. His legs had always been covered by what was left of a woman's trench coat. I watched them for a minute trying to ignore whatever it was I was picking up.

BUTTON!

I flinched for a moment, overwhelmed by the volume, the deaths and the smell. Underneath the burning jet fuel there was the stench of burned flesh. It was all around me but here it was so familiar, so strong. A push of hot wind moved the charred coat and got my attention.

Oh dear, I thought. I knew this man, what I would find under the coat. Gently I took it in my hands and pulled it out of the way, instantly recognizing his injuries. Both legs gone, what was left of the right was longer than the left, blackened and torn. A bit of browned bone stuck out of the shorter left thigh.

BUTTON!

I looked at the longer leg and there was a button. He was wearing army pants, the thigh pocket buttoned shut. Judging by the bulge there was something in it.

"Sorry Rice," I said as I undid the button and pulled out a little leather notebook. It was maybe half the size of a paperback and about an inch thick. An elasticized string attached at the back was stretched around it keeping it shut. The initials embossed on the front told me what to do with it. S. I.

Sig Iverson.

I didn't think that Rice's family would know what to do with it when they got his effects so I put it in my bag for the Colonel. Then I put the coat back over his legs. It was burnt and had come apart in places but I was at least able to hide his injuries.

Chapter 60

I completed another half circle around the fire approaching the pair of bodies that always troubled me more than any of the others. The mother and her baby. He would be cradled in the only limb she had left but she would be looking at me, not at him. The torn end of her arm pointed accusingly at me like I'd brought death here. I would move him closer to her and tighten her other arm around him. Then I would turn her head to face him so she wouldn't worry where he was. There would be no resistance … the bones in her neck were broken.

They waited for me, concealed for now on the other side of a large piece of the plane. I couldn't tell what part it was. There would be no windows in the outer skin of the piece of wreckage. I knew that before I walked around to see them. For now all I could see were wires and insulation.

I took out a bottle of water. The first mouthful rinsed the dryness before I spat it out, the next I swallowed. I was still holding the bottle in my hand when I stepped around to face them but I froze as I processed what I saw.

Something was out of place. I started walking back, keeping them in sight. I tried to remember the man who was with them but I couldn't guess where he should be. I hadn't missed any of the dead and I couldn't picture him anywhere else. I tried to recall him from all the times I dreamed about being here and came up empty.

He was … undamaged. Unburned. He was on his back, head resting on the dead woman's stomach, his hands resting on his. His suit was nearly black in the orange light. I circled him slowly to see his face and as it came into view I recognized it. His narrow nose and thin lips. Eyes just a little too close together. He needed to get his head off her. It was so wrong. I had no idea why his men were obvious to me but he was transparent.

I quickly made sure that the handle of my knife was easily accessible through the opening in my bag then I put it on my shoulder, half on backwards so I could get at it quickly. He was maybe fifteen feet away. Too close for my comfort but too far away for Andre's liking.

"Welcome to my nightmare Damian," I said, Andre's eagerness for the knife trembling gently in my left arm.

"Anna ..." he said as the corners of his lips came up. "Nice place you have here."

"Indeed. I was worried I would go to all this trouble and nobody would show up," I laughed as I reached into my bag. "Did you come to dance or can I buy you a drink?"

He sat up and looked at me. Then he laughed. "It always makes me feel good to see my ex looking like shit."

It was true. My shirt was dirty and bloodstained, my leg bound with Bee's sheets. The cut on it had bled through down to my foot. My bare feet slid in my untied shoes. I didn't even have pants on.

"A drink it is," I said as I tossed the other bottle. He caught it and stood up. As he opened it I waved my hand at him to step away from the woman he'd been using as a pillow. He did and drank as he watched me rearrange her body.

"This is going to be too easy," he said.

"Yes," Andre agreed. "It is."

"Let's walk a bit ... I want to watch you weaken before I kill you."

I smiled over the back pain that ground my tailbone now with every step. "Yes ... we don't want to rush things." Andre and I agreed on that at least. "I always feel like she's blaming me for this. None of the others do ... but she does."

Damian lit two cigarettes and offered me one, holding it at arms length. I approached and took it before backing away. He waited to see which way I was going and followed me at a distance.

"So I heard a few days ago you made your way home," he said. He held his cigarette in his mouth letting it waggle when he spoke, keeping his hands free. His lips sealed around it and the tip brightened, then two lines of smoke lightly streamed from his nose.

"Those four shouldn't have had any trouble from that big idiot Martin and the old fossil you keep upstairs ... but then her phone lit up," he sighed. "If you need something done right ..."

I thought a moment then laughed as I exhaled.

"I'm always impressed how easily your men are swayed from duty," I told him. "Five grand a piece: barely a dent in my pocketbook."

His eyes narrowed as he laughed at me.

"But then your man you lost in Calgary was way off course when I found him. So easily distracted when they're not hanging off your apron."

"Bitch," Damian muttered as he lit himself another smoke. Didn't offer me one.

I kept to my route through the debris. Nothing else was out of place. Damian kept his distance, flanking me when there was room, falling behind when there wasn't. Arrogant ass. I could keep him talking until the baby fell out and we both missed our chance. The contractions kept coming. He discretely checked his watch with each one.

"So how is Alina?" I asked him. I knew already but I needed a fresh topic to keep his mouth running.

"I decided we needed some time apart," he said. "She wouldn't shut up about feelings and marriage. She needs some time alone ... to think about her place in the big picture. Like you did Catherine."

"You missed a few spots when you said good-bye," I told him but he ignored me.

I added revenge for putting his fists on my sister to the list of reasons he would die. Put it right at the top. He smiled, confident in his plan to tire me out.

"Marriage," he laughed. "Not how I roll. Catering to a woman. She needs even more discipline than a soldier. Your Richards will never lead. You've made him as weak as you are."

"If you were half the man my Richards is I would have died in the compound months ago," I told him.

"We disagree," he shrugged. He laughed as anger flashed on his face.

Yes, Andre thought. Andre was getting stronger in me. Demanding his shot. I would have to give in to him soon. Very soon.

Damian checked his watch again as I stopped. Coward, Andre and I thought. Waiting until labour had gone so far that I had maybe half a minute between contractions. I couldn't let it go that long. I was only managing thirty or so slow steps between the contractions now anyway. Time was getting short.

"Rex ... I think it's time for that dance I promised you," I told him. He could keep walking but if he walked away now he wouldn't get his chance if he left me behind. I was calling the ball here. Now.

He stopped and turned to me. I carefully took the knife out and dropped the bag on the ground. Andre was confident but I was scared I had let Damian drag this on too long. I breathed through another contraction. Small moans escaped past my lips every time I exhaled. My knees trembled as my resolve started to fail.

"Yes," Damian said, crushing yet another cigarette out under his foot. "There is no more pleasure in watching you pant your weak ass around in the dirt." He took off his side arm and tossed it aside. Then he drew his knife.

"Remember this Damian?" I said as I held mine up. Its delicate guard sparkled in the flames just as Catherine remembered.

"I'll be taking it back after I cut that bastard out of you with it," he laughed again.

Movement behind him caught my eye. At first I thought it was just the hot air distorting burning wreckage but as I kept my eyes on Damian I realized it was a man, taking a few silent steps closer to us. Maybe a survivor or another of his men. That figured. The coward would bring backup.

Damian looked down at his knife, running his fingertips along the edge of his blade, satisfying himself that it was sharp and deadly. I risked a quick glance at the man only a dozen feet behind him. My heart sunk; it was Paul. I couldn't read him like I couldn't read Damian. He put his finger to his lips and took another step and stopped, watching me.

No, I thought. No … you were supposed to stay away. You were supposed to let me do this.

Then Pilot's words came to me. *Perhaps she could send someone away*, he had said.

If you won't stay away Paul I'll send you away. I thought of our daughter waking up alone by the pond. I started to set my focus as pressure built in my hand. She would wake up with her father. Then I channelled the force of the next contraction into my hand. The blue glow that filled it fought the orange light in the air.

I took a couple of steps to the right circling Damian, Andre's fingers twitching on the handle of the knife, my fingers twitching with the blue arcs that circled around into the back of my hand. Damian glanced indifferently at my light show. Paul circled him in the same direction. Damn, I couldn't get a clean shot to him. The next contraction brought me to my knees. Damian laughed as I kept my eyes on him, still so pleased with himself like he'd had anything to do with me being in labour now. Paul took another step toward him, his hands out to me.

As I waited to stand up I decided I would move quickly to the side and discharge the energy in my hand past Damian into Paul, sending him away, but as I started to get back on my feet the baby kicked hard, triggering another massive contraction to roll right in on top of the one that was still fading.

NO!

I dropped back to my knees, then to all fours, keeping my head up as I panted. Damian took a few steps toward me, Paul matching behind. Damian's laughter sounding flat in the hot air. He was enjoying himself, taking his time.

NO!

Her connection to Paul fought me.

Your mistake, it said.

God, she was right. She told me they never found him and it was my fault. He had interfered but the screw up was completely mine. Maybe I needed my energy to jump fighting Damian alone … and with it almost gone by sending Paul away Damian had been able to fatally wound me before I killed him and got home.

Damian was still closing the gap to me as Paul closed the gap to him. I picked the knife back up and got up on my feet then I started walking backward as the two of them approached me. I wouldn't have long before the pain froze me again and hoped Andre could push me past it.

"Damian ... my love," I cooed to him. "How long has it been since you had me?"

A low growl started in the back of his throat. I knew Paul could hear me but I didn't break my eye contact with Damian. Paul would know what I was doing. Distracting him. Keeping him focused on me.

"More than two hundred years," I said as softly as I could without my voice being lost in the muted roar of the fire around us. "I can see the frustration in your face. The tension you think exists between us ... the attraction ... too bad it's one sided. But then you've always been a lousy lover ... no wonder you have to take it."

Andre held the knife loosely, patiently, he would only need a moment and he could wait a little longer. He'd waited seventy years already.

"You always were a shitty leader Rex ... you were then, you are now," Andre goaded him.

"Coward," we said together.

Rage filled Damian's face. His lips curling back to show his teeth. He would strike at me as soon as he got close enough expecting to sink it in deep right away. He was like a mugger on the street. Expecting fear and submission like he had seen from Catherine. Not resistance and attack. I held my arms out to my sides, appearing inexperienced and defenceless. He put his arms out like mine. Overconfident ass. He had no idea what was coming.

"Coward ... coward," I was singing to him but another contraction was starting so I stopped and took a step toward him as Paul finished closing the gap.

Another step and Paul had him from behind. Immobilized. Damian's face filled with surprise. He roared at Paul as he struggled. I whispered as I tried to blow through the contraction and forced myself to take my last two steps to him as the pain in my stomach grew and tried to freeze my legs. His head flew back into Paul's and they staggered back together a step. Blood burst from his cheek bone and I jumped from the sound from the impact.

Paul's grip slipped and Damian got an arm loose allowing him to turn on him. Paul quickly released his other arm as Damian pulled it free, before the knife in his hand could slash his arm on its way by.

They circled each other. Damian armed, Paul not. Damian getting closer and Paul backing up to stay out of his reach blinking to clear his watering eyes.

"I've won Richards," Damian taunted. "Surrender. I'll make it quick."

Paul didn't reply. He watched Damian closely as he kept glancing at me. Damn it Paul, I thought, pay attention. Look after yourself.

"She's soft ... so easy to hurt. But she'll take so much without complaint," he goaded. "I remember what it felt like, to have her want me. She's so trusting, loyal ... the look on her face as I put her in her place. Holding her down, making her submit, watching my fingers sink in to her throat."

"It was so satisfying when she finally started begging ... bleeding ... when I cut your stink from her. Made her watch."

Paul brought his hands up and took a half step forward. He wanted Damian, badly, but he held back.

"Yet again, your happy little family in a little dead heap at my feet."

Damian laughed as he made his move and when Paul committed to blocking he dodged the other way and swung the knife at his undefended side. Damian was fast with the overconfidence that being armed gave him. Paul was deliberate with caution. He only had his hands.

Without thinking I disappeared, reappearing almost on top of Damian as the contraction released me. Everything slowed down and I was distracted by the horrible feeling that what my daughter said was coming true anyway. Unavoidable. I had intended to appear with my knife already in his back but I was up against him, knocking the swing of his knife hand off course and away from Paul, slashing Damian's side.

Damian shouted with pain and turned on me, the greater threat slashing at my bound arm tearing the cloth open and digging in to my skin below. I lashed back catching the inside of his arm before I backed up a couple of steps hoping to lead him away but Damian backed away from both of us.

"You know how I know you're crazy, you stupid bitch?" he spat at me as he kept going.

Paul wouldn't look at me as he tried to get between Damian and I ... I kept moving to the left so he couldn't, my hand clutching my freshly cut left arm. I could feel the tingle of the blue light entering my body through the wound.

Damian's backward pace quickened as he moved his knife to his left hand, then he held up his right and filled it with blue light like mine. Little tendrils of blue lightning reached toward us as he sneered. I went right, passing behind Paul who was still going left, trying to stay between us.

Then Damian's hand appeared on fire, with blue lightning that seemed to drip from it to the ground. It hissed, a soft roar like a blow torch and as the breeze shifted toward me I could finally pick up

Damian's stink under my nose. I put my hand over my face to try and keep it out. Damian swung his hand in a slow circle, making the light follow in a bright rope trick. Paul looked over his left shoulder to make sure he knew where I was but I'd moved and as he took a step back and looked over his right Damian brought his hand up. He said something to Paul, too softly for me to make out as he snapped his light forward. I was looking at Paul's eyes as the blue fingers wrapped his body for a second then there was a soft pop as the air rushed in to the space he'd been in.

Paul was gone.

"God damn you!" I yelled as Damian backed away laughing. He gave me the finger as he disappeared into the wreckage. I sank to the ground, clutching my chest, watching the place where I'd last seen Paul. Trying to feel him. I could but it was so faint. Damian had done what I hadn't. Sent Paul away and there was nothing I could do to get him back now. My energy was intact … or maybe this was how things were supposed to turn out. Damian making Paul disappear and me pissing my energy away fighting him. Then my hands to my belly as the pain started again.

The least I could do now was make it home in better shape. I could survive. But not bound to the ground like this. As I rode the contraction I let my blue light explore it. I wanted to soften the pain, slow the labour. Not for long, maybe twenty minutes. Maybe half an hour. Just long enough to finish that son of a bitch. As the pain faded I let my light into me. Immediately my stomach softened and the pain disappeared. I could feel the baby still, she was okay and I carefully stood.

Damian's handgun was still on the ground nearby so I took it. It was loaded so I made sure the safety was on and put it in my pack with mine. I wasn't going to leave it for him to retrieve. I was certain that he'd want to finish me with something slow and personal anyway. Like I wanted to finish him.

I waited another minute as I checked my cut arm. The new wound was deeper than the one the remains of the bandage covered but it barely oozed. I took a deep breath. No pain, no tightness in my belly. Whatever I'd done was working. Paul was still connected to me, barely, but enough to know wherever he was he was alive. I tried to sense Damian but his smell disappeared with Paul. I felt completely alone here again. The way it was supposed to be but that meant I had to hunt him blind.

As I took a few steps toward the gap in the wreckage Damian had passed through there was a new sound. A distraught, choking scream, like the throat that made it wasn't working right. I paused and turned my head to try and make it out but the more clear it became the more I didn't

336

want to find out.

"Brandon …"

A woman's voice. More screaming, then again.

"Brandon …"

Then from another direction, a baby crying. My mind imagined what he had done. I tried to think although my own grief over losing Paul didn't want me to give a shit. They were dead, broken, jump started back to something like life by the man who saw me care about them. I'd looked after them for years, every time my dream brought me here. Never failed to make sure they were close.

I kept my pack over my shoulder, my knife in my hand. The opening still in front of me so the gun was easy to get to. Then I turned and hurried to the mother hoping Damian would think I'd be drawn to little Brandon. As I spotted her I felt a small contraction but nothing like the heavy labour I'd been carrying with me. I crouched down and watched her. She appeared to be alone, fighting to push herself up. There was no expression on her face but the screaming continued. I put my hands on my ears and looked around behind me to make sure that I was alone before I got up to go look for her baby.

As I got further from her I could make out his little cry again. It was the same wail, over and over. Like his mother's; three plain screams then a Brandon. They weren't alive; they were only doing what Damian made them do. Even though they were dead I had to put them back the way they were. What he had done to them was disgusting.

I circled around the middle of the debris trying to keep the same distance from the baby for a while before I approached. He was moving, his cries not coming from the same place twice. It only took a minute for him to stay put. I could barely hear his mother but Brandon's rhythmic wailing continued, no longer pacing me through the wreckage.

When I was closer I peered past a piece of the plane's tail section. Damian's back was to me, something cradled in his arms. My nose wrinkled as I glared at him then his hands dropped to his sides, the baby dangling from one of them by his ankle, the pace of his cries unbroken. Damian dropped him to the ground and turned slowly as I pulled back out of sight.

"I can smell that disgusting offspring inside you … couldn't resist coming for this one, could you?"

I heard him draw in a lung full of air past his nose.

"What makes you weak makes me strong," Damian laughed and I heard his foot drag on the ground. Brandon's cries became louder, like his head had turned toward me. "Yours will be even more fun to play with."

I could kill him here; take the baby to his mother. I took a step further back, waiting to see what he would do.

337

"Yes," Damian's voice, closer now, "I smell you there. Hiding like a child."

I backed away a few more steps, around the piece of tail. Brandon continued to sound off like a car alarm and Damian had gone silent. A quick glance over my shoulder to make sure he hadn't gone around then as I turned back his hand was on my throat, his other on my wrist controlling the knife.

"Stupid bitch," he worked his mouth for a moment. I tried to turn away knowing what was coming but he held me still. Spit hit me in the eye and down my cheek as I struggled. Another small contraction reminded me to hurry.

"Coward," I choked out at him as his grip on my neck tightened. I kept fighting him, distracting him as my free hand went in my pack and took his gun. "Chicken shit coward," I spat back as the safety came off.

I wanted nothing more than to fill him with metal from his own gun but I could feel Andre in me, angry that I would deny him his chance. Reminding me it had to be the knife. I pushed myself toward Damian and pressed his gun to his thigh as I pulled the trigger. His hands let me go as I put another round in almost the same place then I went past him as he fell sideways into the tail clutching his leg and swearing at me.

As soon as I was out of his reach I put the gun away and went to Brandon. Wiped the spit on my sleeve and got down to the ground to pick him up. When I looked back Damian was hobbling after me, one hand on his leg, the other held his knife. I couldn't imagine being on my feet after that. There was blood but not enough to worry about him losing it too quickly.

Quick as I could I started to the baby's mother led by her screams. I'd gotten some distance on Damian but he was still after me. I put my hand on the baby's chest and thought about quieting him. My hand filled with a bit of light and I let it find its way around inside him as I hurried. Just stop what Damian did, I thought and when the light stopped searching I let it into Brandon. He pulled in one last lung full of air and instead of crying he simply exhaled and was still again. I put my lips to his little head.

"I'm so sorry about the bad man," I whispered. "He'll pay for it."

As I took my last steps to the mother I prepared for quieting her. I tried to wrap her arm around him but she kept squirming, unaware that he was near. My hand went to her chest and as I watched Damian get closer my light explored, learning what he had done to her, until it was ready and I let it loose. She fell still and I put Brandon back in the crook of her arm and turned her head back to face him. I brushed her hair from her face and kissed his again. Then I stood as another small contraction came, stronger than the last few. Whatever I'd done to calm them was wearing off.

Damian was thirty feet away, still coming for me.

"You're going to be alive when I take him out of you … his screams will be real …" Damian's rage in every syllable.

I didn't reply as I stepped away from Brandon and his mother, leading Damian away with me, giving me time to decide on how to attack him before he forced me into reacting.

"That bitch Alina came home … so happy … imagine the surprise on her face after weeks of telling her how much I wanted it. She said, 'my sweet Damian … we're expecting.' My fucking Lord, she brought me flowers! I one punched her in the head, right on to her annoying little ass."

Damian laughed, his face contorting in pain every time he had to use his shot up leg. I'd seen the damage first hand, over and over. His horrible bragging couldn't upset me any more than I had been already the past couple of months.

"She didn't beg for me to stop until I was on top of her, sinking my teeth in. 'Is this how I filled you up?' I asked her, 'What's the matter, why don't you like it now?'"

The more he talked the more I wanted his end to last and last. I still had his gun. I could shoot him in the other leg, get him on the ground. Or I could paralyse him like I'd done to Paul. Keep him from hurting me as he felt everything. Another contraction came, longer and more painful than the last. I realized that I would have to do something soon.

I tucked my knife in the back of my underwear as I kept my distance from Damian, handle tilted to the left so I could grab it.

"Do you make the same noises she does when the pain is too much?" Damian asked me. "So much like the ones that came out when I made the earth move underneath her." His hand had moved to the front of his pants grabbing himself, excitement on his face when he wasn't wincing with pain.

I led him through the wreckage another half minute, getting more and more angry at him, before I paused and brought his gun up, aiming at his right knee. He was still thirty feet away, his right hand flashing with blue and going out, pressing it to the wounds on his leg. He'd used it all up on Paul and the woman and her baby.

"Shit, really? You almost missed from right on top of me! Stupid cow, you can't hit it from there."

I thought about it.

"You're right," I yelled back as I stopped and lifted the gun before I pulled the trigger and sunk a round deep into his right shoulder. Into the little soft spot just under the end of his collar bone.

"That's for biting my sister …" I whispered.

Then as he went down I shattered the knee of his good leg.

"Bitch!" he screamed back.

I went to him, slowing as my stomach tightened. Not enough to stop me but the next one would. That I was sure of. His knife was still in his right hand as he tried to push himself up so I aimed at it and squeezed the trigger. His two smallest fingers disappeared as well as a piece of his palm leaving him with the one good limb Brandon's poor mother had.

"Sweet, sweet irony," I breathed to myself against the train of angry bitches rolling from his mouth.

"Ready Andre?" I said out loud as I backhanded the butt of the gun that he'd hit my sister with hard into his face. Then I dropped on his one good limb. My knee sinking into the nerves inside his upper arm.

"Weak, impotent, coward," I whispered to him as he screamed at me.

I tossed the gun aside out of Damian's reach as Andre reached behind me for my knife. Pain was returning hard and fast to my stomach and if Damian pushed me off him I'd be in trouble. He'd still be stronger with one good arm than I would be frozen by a contraction.

Andre pressed the tip of the knife to Damian's chest, his left palm on the end of the handle, his right hand gripping it, fingers curled around under the delicate gold guard. He moaned through his teeth as his two fingered right came up and clutched my throat, digging in deeply, the pressure of his effort pushing his hot blood out and on to me. I felt it start to run down inside my torn shirt.

"You're the only man I've met whose worse than me," Andre said from my lips as he pushed me up on my knees and used my weight to force the blade in as I pressed my neck deeper into Damian's hand. My lips pulled back and my teeth ground together as the small vibrations of his body tearing inside were transmitted through the handle up into my palms. I watched Damian's eyes open wide and his body go stiff as the blade pushed up into his chest and into his heart. Damian's grip on me weakened, his fingers scrambling to keep their purchase. Andre turned it hard and quickly pulled it out then jammed it deeply into his left shoulder.

"Where did you send Paul?" I growled as I twisted the blade in him.

Damian was breathing hard as his blood soaked my shirt, bubbling from the hole in his chest.

"Don't know ... don't care ..." he grunted.

Andre's work was done and I could feel him start to fade from me.

"Didn't need you as much as I thought ..." I whispered.

Damian's struggles under me softened with the contraction and his hand fell from my throat. I put my right hand on his chest feeling him

340

fight to breathe as the flow of blood leaving his body slowed. I held a charge of blue energy in my palm and waited.

His pulse weakened as his damaged heart faltered. He looked up at me, the anger on his face replaced with a mocking smile.

"I'll see you again bitch," he managed with the last full lung of air he would draw in on his own. His breath started to hitch in his chest as his diaphragm tried to sustain him. I put my leg over him, straddling his body as I moved to his other side.

"Sshhh," I told him. "Sshhh. Let me help." I held Damian's nose shut and sealed my mouth over his then I blew and filled his lungs with my air as his heart stuttered. As it stopped I pushed the blue light into his chest, capturing the future end of his long life line where I had cut it before it could go free, holding on to it tightly.

I took my air back, filling my lungs with it, pulling the line into me. It found its way down in to my chest along with mine and the baby's. I held my breath, feeling it shift and move as it aligned itself with my own. I quickly thought which of my gifts I could tie down with it. Which would help the most. The family had plenty of fighters. Traveling only helped me. But reading the family would help everyone as we regained all that Damian had taken. I held that gift to Damian's line in my chest as it found its place and bound it self to me.

It was only then that I took my lips off his and pushed myself away.

"Your gift is mine now." I whispered to his empty body. I fell over as another contraction hit, landing on my side on a mat of scorched grass.

The next few contractions were agony, catching up on the work they'd missed when I stalled the labour. I dug my nails into the ground beneath me and screamed through them, in too much pain to breathe properly. I tried to relax in between, listening to the quiet sounds the flames made, the soft ticks the cooling metal made but they followed each other quickly. I knew I had to find the strength to get up on my feet. To try and walk out. I'd been in the wreckage for a couple of hours and nobody had come looking for survivors. It would be up to me to make it a few blocks. I hoped that help would be that close. Maybe I could get to my car, get it started, try to jump to Paul before the baby came … then get him home with me. I knew in my heart it wouldn't happen but maybe I could get to the hospital.

When I felt I had control of the contractions again I pushed myself up and got Damian's knife before I stood and walked around him for his gun. Both went in my pack then I held him down with my foot to pull out my knife but it came out easily, maybe because I'd been twisting it. I wiped most of his blood from the blade onto my sleeve before it went in to my bag. The Colonel said it was a gift but I still might have to return it. I had a cigarette at my lips and my lighter out as I breathed through another one.

As it passed I sparked the lighter to it.

"Andre? Why are you still here?" I yelled. If I wanted a cigarette it meant he wasn't gone. I pulled smoke deep into my lungs once. Then again. I was supposed to be free of him now. But I could still feel him.

"Andre?" I yelled again. "It's over … I want my head back!"

The tears that ran down my face now weren't dried instantly in the heat. I had another drag as I got my bearings. Home was a block and a half away, the fastest path would lead me past Brandon and his mother. I knew every bit of this place as well as I knew my own face.

After the pain had come and gone again I turned toward home and took a few steps, looking at Damian on the ground as I went around him to make sure I didn't trip. When I looked up I was facing a man. A vision of Paul, just ten feet away staring back at me.

"No … You're not here … He sent you away …" I said as I realized that sanity could still be a long way off.

The vision didn't move. My hands shook as I took another cigarette from my bag and lit it, only then realizing that I still had half of one in my hand. After a bit of indecision I kept the new one and let the old one drop to the ground. Andre was sick, sticking around to torment me now with hallucinations.

"You're not here … not here …" I breathed as it watched me through another contraction.

"Andre?" I yelled, sobbing, sending my anguish into the sky. "Is this because I didn't need you after all? He's gone … Damian sent him away. Take this from my sight!"

The vision stepped closer as I put the smoke to my lips again.

"Not here … not here …" I murmured as I exhaled.

When he got to me he took the cigarette and put it on the ground. He looked back at me. Angry. Pained. My mind putting everything I expected Paul to feel onto his face. His hand touched my cheek and went around behind my head. His fingers gently grasped my hair as his other rested on my huge stomach.

"I'm here," the vision whispered. "He sent me away, said I could come back when it was over … then I was with her at the pond. We talked a while … until I came back here and heard you screaming."

He let go of my hair and put his hand on my chest.

"Feel me here … I'm real," he said then his hand went back up to hold my head again.

I tried to put the cigarette to my mouth again but it was gone so I reached in my bag to get another.

"Here …" he said as he took my hand and put it on my chest.

Another contraction started to take hold and I put my hands on my stomach as my eyes rolled back and my lids closed, my head resting over on his arm. I could feel his fingers on my cheek but they were gone when the pain let go and I could open my eyes.

"It's a trick," I whispered, feeling my connection to Paul in my chest again. Hating Andre even more.

"No trick," he said as he leaned closer, putting his lips near mine for a few seconds before pulling back. I followed with my nose picking up the smell of sweet grass and wildflowers mixed with the scent of Paul.

"No trick," I whispered. He was really here. I wasn't sure what would have been easier. Ignoring the vision until I got away from this place or facing Paul and getting out of here together. Pain was still in his eyes, it hadn't let go one bit since I noticed him.

"Did you follow my screams to kill me Paul?" I asked. "You could have walked away."

He didn't answer. Anger replaced the pain in his eyes as his fingers worked their way further into my hair. Not painfully, but firmly enough to let me know that he was in control of whatever happened next. Whatever he was going to do I wanted him to get on with it. If we were going home we needed to hurry.

"She's coming soon ... take her Paul. I won't fight what I've got coming to me."

Paul frowned, his bottom lip pushing up into his top one then he pushed up my sleeve to see my makeshift dressing. He leaned to the side to look at my leg.

"Did he hurt you?" he asked while he looked at what I'd done to Damian.

I nodded.

"This is where you listen to me Anna," he said. He was dead serious and sounded like he didn't have an ounce of patience in his entire body.

I nodded in reply.

"I was on the phone with Ray when you called him ... he tied me in and I heard everything. And again when he got through to you later. I'm sorry about Bee and Denis. I'm sorry I wasn't there. That was how you wanted it. I know why you did what you did. You weren't yourself. I haven't seen the Anna I fell in love with in a long time. I thought about getting out of your life for good this time. Just one swing at you would free me. Ray told me why you did it but I didn't believe him until I heard you say it tonight. I was close ... Denis called me a week ago when you showed up at your place so I flew to Vancouver. Then when you called Ray tonight I came straight over. I was watching the house when the plane came down. I followed you; watching you with him until you got the knives out."

Another contraction had stopped, but I only nodded.

343

"I didn't know if you could do it or not … I stepped in anyway."

"I almost sent you away," I whispered. "I wouldn't have had the energy to fight alone if I had … she stopped me … he sent you where I was going to, used most of his to do it …"

"I told you to be quiet," he said. "Just nod … is it over now?"

I nodded.

As the pain returned again I felt something pop low inside me and water started to leak out down my legs. I looked into his eyes this time as I breathed and more came out.

"Paul," I managed as it faded. He didn't answer right away. I could see his mind working, deciding.

"I said be quiet. Where is Andre now?"

I could see Andre behind Paul as the pain returned again. His presence could only mean I was still crazy. There was nothing I could do about that now. I was breathing hard so I raised my right hand to point behind Paul but he grabbed my wrist and held it tightening his grip on my hair at the same time. I didn't blame him for being wary of that hand.

"I'm here, behind you Captain," Andre said, his words in my ears and not just in my mind. Paul's grip on me relaxed for a split second. He'd heard it too. Then he let go of my head and slowly turned. When he saw Andre he put himself between us, letting me go.

"I wanted to say goodbye. Pilot has freed me … I don't need her anymore."

I wanted to pick up my knife and stick it in Andre now. All the pain and manipulation. I could see it now for what it was. The woman who had left him for his brother had chosen wisely if that was the kind of lover Andre had always been.

"I think you're right about that Anna," he said.

"Andre," Paul whispered.

He nodded. Fire light made his bent glasses sparkle and turned his dirty uniform gold. His attention went to me as he spoke.

"You did need me Anna," he said with distaste. "You were so ready to give up at your sister's, just a frightened little child. Refusing to do your part unless you were certain you could still whisper dirty things to him in the dark when it was all over."

Andre made a face and leaned his head toward Paul. Paul stiffened with anger so I took his elbow and held it.

"I made you keep it together. You should be thanking me, not cursing me."

"Bastard," I breathed in pain, my arms still locked around Paul's.

"Pilot didn't tell you why Damian was incurable, did he?"

"No," I whispered.

Andre laughed.

344

"Pilot's father was incurably insane ... he fucked up his own brother to be the cure. Just like he did to you. He picked his weakest brother, just in case it went wrong. Damian failed, cursed forever with someone like me always whispering in his ear. Pilot got it right the second time, sending his other brother to do the job. Then he made you to deal with his mistake. Only a lunatic could sever the line from another.

"If we failed there wouldn't be another chance next time around. We'd be stuck with each other waiting for the cure."

"What I did to you," Andre said, "you brought on yourself."

I let go of Paul and took a step back as he took a step toward Andre. Andre didn't move. He knew what was coming. Paul's right hand stretched wide open then his fingers came together, pushing off each other until he was satisfied with their positions. He held his left up to guard as he swung his right up and around hard, connecting with Andre's jaw and throwing him back almost off his feet. There was the crack of bone and a puff of dust where Andre's face should have bled if his dried out skin could split.

"That's for putting your hands on my wife, asshole." Paul breathed.

Amen, I thought.

Paul kept his hands up ready to give Andre another but Andre only nodded to Paul. I knew what he was thinking. It was honourable to take the punch because he'd given attention to another man's property. Attention he thought would be acceptable if I was his. After a few seconds his body seemed lit by dull flames then I realized the flames were behind him growing brighter. He faded. When he was nearly gone he turned and walked away. After a few steps he disappeared completely as another contraction released me.

Paul still stood with his back to me as he spoke.

"Watching you tonight is the hardest thing I have ever done. What do you say when sorry isn't enough, Anna?"

"Forgive me Paul," I whispered. "Please forgive me."

He turned to me and held my face in his hands, putting his cheek on mine.

"Is he gone now?"

"Yes ..." I breathed in his ear. I could hear him breathing with me, gently.

"We do everything together from now on. Got it?"

I nodded and pulled out his ring from under my shirt. I held it in my fist for a moment then I opened my hand. He struggled with the clasp behind but couldn't get it, wincing as he tried. His hand was swelling, Andre's dust mixing with the blood from his cut knuckle. I opened the necklace to take his ring off it and pushed it back on his finger. Then I fastened it back up around my neck. As I did I felt the baby's line start to shift in my chest. We were running out of time.

I closed my eyes as he kissed me.

"I love you more than anything," I whispered.

"I didn't tell you to talk," he whispered back as he kissed me again.

"Paul," I said as I pulled away.

"I love you more than anything too," he said as he tried to pull me in again.

"Paul," I said. "My water broke and her line is loosening … we have to go."

"You're right … we've been here too long."

He took my bag and put it over his shoulder but we only got a few steps before labour stuck my feet to the ground. I leaned my head on his chest, turning my neck and rocking my forehead on him as he checked his watch. His other hand reached around and rubbed my back.

"A minute and a half," he said.

"Was that all?" He could have said forever and wouldn't have been far off. We didn't get far before another one started.

"Half a minute in between. I have to get you to the hospital now."

"No," I said when I could talk again. "Home … hospital will be swamped."

He gave me his phone and picked me up, my legs over his right forearm so he didn't have to grip my ribs with his broken hand.

"We'll never get there with you on foot," he said. "Call Ray."

We weren't far from my house. The phone should have worked but it said No Signal. Then Searching. Then No Signal. This was like at Pilot's. As we got closer to my house I could make out the sounds of the engines and blue and red lights. Voices. Bars lit up on the phone. The houses that had only been burning when I set off down the alley were almost gone. The orange had faded from the sky and the clouds had quieted. There were no stars, just a flat ceiling of dark gray from the city lights below.

"Where were they all this time?" Paul wondered.

"No," I shook my head during a break in the pain. "The question is where were we."

As we crossed the street half a block from my house a fireman approached us with a blanket, the first person I'd seen other than Paul and Damian in hours.

"My wife's in labour," Paul explained. "I'll take her myself … you folks have a lot on your hands."

He noticed the blood on me.

"Which house did you come from?" he asked as he put the blanket over me. It was cold now that we were away from the fading fire; Paul's body shielded me from the weak heat still radiating from the flames behind him.

"Back that way," Paul said tilting his head to the left as he kept walking.

"Anyone else hurt there?"

"No."

"Congratulations," he said and disappeared.

There wasn't much left of my house when we got to it.

"After the plane came down I pulled Denis out to the lawn ... out of the fire. The Colonel will take care of him. The house was going up fast."

I started to cry again.

"Sshhh," he said. "It's not goodbye."

I dialled Ray when the next contraction went away. By then Paul had put me in the car. I was surprised he still had his key. If he hadn't come back I would have had to break in and crack the ignition to get home. Other than some embers sizzling on the vinyl roof and some bubbles in the paint it looked okay. The wind pulling toward the fire had drawn the flames away from it.

"Paul?" Ray picked up right away. "What's going on?"

"Ray?" I said.

"Anna? What?"

Paul took the phone from me as I lost the ability to speak again.

"We're coming Ray," he said. He had started the Lincoln and was racing up to the highway. "Yes, it's over. She did it ... as soon as she can jump."

He was listening to Ray.

"Her water broke and she says she can feel the baby's line loosening."

Another pause.

"Minute and a half ... thirty second breaks," he listened. "Thanks Ray."

"He's ready ... we just have to get there."

I closed my eyes and concentrated. It was a good distraction from the pain I was in and I quickly focused on home. Paul didn't comment this time as he struggled to keep us on the road. He had taken a right onto the highway rather than waiting for the lights to go south. I could hear him sigh with relief when the gusts moved behind us.

"When I say so close your eyes and step on it," I told him.

"Me?" he asked.

"Yes ... I'm not moving," I waited until there was a straight stretch of highway in front of us. The pressure was getting strong.

"Anna," he whispered. "Use me to get us home."

I shook my head.

347

"Please," he insisted. "She'll need you more ... you'll be down for a couple of days. Me a lot less."

Paul reached his hand to me.

"Please," he said again. "Whatever you need is yours."

I took his hand and breathed through a strong one, feeling deep low pressure, wanting to push. When it passed I quickly checked my focus and felt Paul's energy in my hand. Just enough to recharge and get home, I thought, just enough. I didn't want to be without Paul again any longer than I had to.

We were pushed from behind again.

"Ready?" I asked.

"Yes."

I quickly checked my focus one last time and closed my eyes.

"Home," I said.

A moment later the car leaped.

Chapter 61

I leaned on the wooden shed by the gas barrels working through another contraction. The strong wind that whistled through the gap in the buildings stung my bare skin with hard bits of frozen snow. The sudden cold threw my concentration and I yelled in pain. Paul's calls to me stopped when he heard it and I felt his coat go over my shoulders as it passed.

"Sugar … we're here," he whispered as he scooped me up. The pressure I felt now wasn't letting up when my stomach relaxed.

"I have to push now …"

"Wait …" Paul said as he hurried trying not to slip.

"Now!"

"Breathe Anna … breathe," he kept repeating and I focused on his voice and did what he said.

"How's she doing?" I heard Ray say. I hadn't realized how much fear had gotten to me until I heard his voice and was sure I was home in one piece.

"She's pulled it together … she's okay now." Paul said as they kept walking. "Wants to push."

"Push Ray …"

"Okay Kiddo, let's get you inside."

"Now Ray …" I whispered as Paul started telling me to breathe again.

Ray got the door for Paul and they took me right down to the room at the end of the hall. The kitchen fell silent as we hurried past and Paul put me on the bed.

"Is that her blood on the shirt?" Ray asked.

"No," Paul said.

Ray gave Paul some scissors. "It's coming off then." He put a sheet over my legs and quickly started an IV then he put the stethoscope on my stomach and listened through a contraction.

"She's doing fine. Do you know if she's hurt anywhere else Paul? I don't see anything." Ray asked. I had a handful of Paul's shirt and couldn't talk.

"No," Paul said quietly. "I don't think so. She's been on her feet like this all night."

I felt her line had left me.

"Checking you Kiddo," Ray said but he put my leg back down almost as soon as he had it out of the way.

"She's right there ... no wonder you need to push." He said then he pulled over a small rolling table with a tray of instruments on it. "Do you know what to do Anna?"

"Catherine remembers," I said.

"Paul, get your arm behind her and help her curl up around the baby."

"Now?" Paul asked. He didn't sound very ready.

"Now," Ray said. "Unless you want to catch."

I was already grabbing my knees and filling my lungs. Paul got his arm under me and pushed me up. Ray counted, his elbow pushing on one of my feet. The cut was starting to hurt and I had a hard time getting that leg up.

"Good girl," Ray said. He quickly pulled on a paper gown to cover his clothes then he shook his head as he sat back down on the foot of the bed. "You cut things awful close ... one more like that ... when I tell you to breathe ... you breathe."

"Her line ... I can't feel it in me," I whispered. Paul put his hand on my stomach as I curled up around her again.

"She has it," he said.

I pushed twice before Ray told me to breathe. Stopping the push felt like I was trying to stop a train with my lungs. He was clearing her nose and mouth.

"My God," Paul laughed quietly. "There she is."

"One more little push Kiddo ..." Ray said.

I took a quick breath and nudged her out the rest of the way. Ray caught her and held her gently while he cleared her nose and mouth again and then he set her on my stomach.

"Paul ..." I said. Ray had a soft blanket and dried her off. Paul held my head in his arm as he watched then his hand reached to her and he brushed his fingertips on her cheek. Happiness and tears covering his face. He kissed my eyes.

"Thank you Anna ... I love you," he said.

"I love you too," I whispered as she started to howl. We could hear cheers from the kitchen. Ray had clamped her cord.

"Paul?" he said handing him the scissors. "Here … not my finger."

Paul cut and Ray took the scissors. She kept howling.

"I need to weigh her before you feed her Anna," he put her on a sling that he hung from a small scale. Then he measured her.

"Nine and a half pounds. Twenty four inches. Big girl," he said. Then he listened to her heart and lungs. She howled through the whole thing. Paul was near her at the table Ray had set up, looking back at me constantly as he tried to be in two places at once. Then he helped Ray put a little diaper on her and wrap her up before he brought her to me. Even for a big girl she looked so tiny in her father's arms.

"Can you turn on your side to feed her?" Ray asked. "Your leg is still bleeding. I can't leave it the way it is. I'll fix up your arm after."

I turned and settled her beside me.

"Impatient little thing," I said softy. "You hungry?"

We watched her for a while as Ray stitched up my leg.

"I was going to send you to her Paul … when I went to see her she told me I had to keep you away. She stopped me tonight because the mistake that killed us was mine. I used all my energy to do it so I didn't survive."

He was still looking at her, his nose on the back of her head.

"He sent you where I was going to … he had no idea how far and used almost all of his doing it."

Paul kissed the back of her head, then her fist which was still by her cheek.

"What else did she tell you?" he asked me.

I tried to remember, it had been so long ago.

"That she's mated to one of Damian's sons," I whispered. "This is the first life he'll remember too. But he's good, not like his father at all. She said I had to go get help because none of you knew what I was. She said to do whatever it took to keep you away tonight.

"She said that you would forgive me."

Paul nodded. "I do."

Then he smiled.

"I found myself at the pond, surrounded by a little metal fence, sitting on a bench. As my eyes focused there were two grave markers. Mine and yours."

He rubbed his eyes with his good hand.

"When I stood and turned I could see a woman lying in the grass. Long brown hair and a purple dress. I opened the gate, the noise woke her. She pushed herself up and reached for a spot in front of her where the grass had been pushed down. 'Mother' she said and started to cry. 'Sugar?' I said to her and she turned. It was your face … 'it's Dad.' I told her. She put her hand on her mouth like you do when you cry. I got to her before she could get up and held her for a while.

"She wanted to know where you went so I told her you were fighting Damian alone ... I would go back to you when it was over. She said if you failed she would at least have me ... if you succeeded we would all be together.

"I asked her what her name was but she just smiled and said that would be up to us. That we'd choose something different than what Ray chose for her."

I glanced over at Ray and he was smiling.

"Something caught my eye past her," Paul continued. "There was a man there, watching us. He looked so much like Damian. I asked if that was her baby's father, she turned and waved to him. He smiled back and started to walk over to us, but then I heard screaming, everything was dark. After a couple of minutes I realized I was back in the flames, the wreckage. You were still screaming. I followed the sound and found you after it stopped.

"I thought he had you but you were getting your knife out of him."

I nodded as Ray spoke.

"Everyone okay?" He had come over and was standing behind Paul.

I looked up at him. "Thank you Ray," I told him. "Thank you."

He leaned over Paul and kissed my cheek then he put his hand on Paul's back and patted him. Paul turned to him and Ray shook his hand gently.

"Thank you Ray," he said.

"It was my pleasure. I gave you something for pain ... you should have her on the other side for a while. And I need to see what's going on with your arm."

She wasn't happy to have to let go but settled down again once we rolled over and let go of me as she fell asleep. Paul helped me sit up and I rubbed her small back.

"Paul," I said quietly. "It's leaving me. Whatever he did to me is going."

"I know. I can almost see you changing."

I was relieved. Maybe we did have a chance.

"What about what Andre said about your father?"

Paul shrugged. "He never said a word."

"He knew, Paul. He could see Andre. Your father new exactly what Pilot did to me."

He never took his eyes off his daughter as she quietly rested on me.

"Are you going to phone your family?"

"Yes." He smiled then he was more serious. "We never talked

about names … I was thinking of your mother."

"Allison?" I said. "I like that … but not for her first name. If she was here she would appreciate it, but she isn't. I want to thank the woman who would have raised her in our place if things had gone wrong."

"My mother?" he asked.

"Yes," I said. "Camille. I want to thank her for raising her … even though she won't now. It doesn't change how much I appreciate that she would."

"Camille Allison Richards." He said then came over and kissed her little head again. "Happy Birthday."

I smiled at them then I yawned.

"Get some sleep now. You've been on your feet all night. You're fine in here as long as you want," he said.

I yawned and put her gently into Paul's arms then I fell asleep watching him watch her in the armchair.

Chapter 62

Camille was a week old when Colonel Iverson arrived unofficially, simply requesting her company for a couple of hours. He had a few small gifts for her and took turns with Paul, Ray, and I passing her back and forth at the table so nobody's food got cold holding her too long. After dinner he held her on the sofa in the common room for nearly an hour and a half. She was awake for most of it and quite content. I'd taken her once to feed her but otherwise he'd claimed her for the duration of his visit. Eventually though he passed her to Paul.

"Your daughter is delightful Paul," he said, "but I must apologize. I need to speak with Anna regarding a couple of things."

I knew exactly what. He had reports to complete about what happened to Denis and my involvement with eliminating Damian Howard. I would be happy to have all that behind me.

"I understand," I told him. "I have a couple of things for you Sig."

After excusing myself I made another trip down the road to the cabin we were staying in while the top floor was being renovated and dug my pack out of the bottom of the closet. Rice's notebook and the knife were still in it.

The Colonel waited in the hall for me. Paul stood nearby with Camille. He would know what the Colonel wanted and would find it hard not being with me. He knew more than anyone how hard that last day had been.

"Sig," I said quietly so Paul could hear but not the others still in the common room. "I've quit … omitting things from my husband."

He looked at Paul for a long moment, thinking.

"Congratulations Captain, I've just upgraded your security clearance to match your wife's."

Paul looked puzzled and I bit my lip to keep a straight face. This wasn't any type of military security clearance. It was family. He passed Camille to Ray and we went down the hall.

Paul and I sat on the bed and Sig pulled up a chair.

"What is said in here tonight won't be brought up again. Even amongst yourselves. Paul, you just listen. She doesn't know any more than what we say here today. Understand?"

We both nodded.

"What do you have for me Anna?" he asked.

First I pulled out a towel and unwrapped the knife. Still stained with Damian's blood.

"I think it should go back where it came from," I told him and glanced at Paul. He raised his eyebrows briefly but he didn't comment. Sig just nodded. I wrapped the knife back up and he put it on the chair beside him. Then I reached in my bag and pulled out the little notebook. The Colonel's face showed surprise. Surprise and relief.

"Where did you get this?" he asked, accepting it with both hands.

"I ..." then I paused.

"He'll answer to you if he breathes a word," he said.

I moved closer to Paul and took his hand. He'd be learning a lot about what I had been up to over the next while. A lot more than he ever suspected was going on.

"In the wreckage ... I picked up the same thing I picked up from you. And from Rice. Dodging me when I focused on it. Finding me when I tried to tune it out. I'd always been alone in that place in my dreams. Just me and the dead. Sensing I wasn't alone was unnerving. I hoped it was Damian ... labour was so far along."

I didn't look at Paul.

"I was able to follow what I was picking up to a bank of seats still attached to a piece of the plane. There were two people in the front three and two in the back three. Usually I just make sure they're the right four and move along but when I got close I heard it. Button. My mind flooded with the images I'd picked up from Rice the first time. It was him in one of the front seats. In the arms of a blonde woman. Were they traveling together?"

The Colonel shook his head.

"Always thought they were," I said. "There was a burnt overcoat covering his legs. When I took it off I saw his legs were gone. Like mine were ... like I told you about before. The smell ... I remembered it. His pants had pockets on the thighs. Buttoned shut. I pulled the book out and saw your initials on it so I took it because I didn't think his family would know what to do with it when they finally got his things back and I knew it's yours."

"Rice wasn't on that plane, Anna," the Colonel said. "His body wasn't in the wreckage. The only man I brought home was Denis."

I shrugged.

"I don't think we were in the real wreckage anyway. Nothing was ever consumed by the fire. Paul's cell phone had no signal ... even after what must have been a couple of hours in the wreckage I was the only living thing there until I ran into Damian. No rescue workers ... nobody but me. Like Pilot's corn field. Frozen somehow. Did you find Damian?"

"No," the Colonel said.

"Then he's resting in that eternally burning wreckage we were in."

"So Damian is dead?"

"Yes."

He nodded then he opened the little notebook and browsed through it for a while. Paul and I listened nervously down the hall for Camille. The tiny print gave way to blank pages only a third of the way through so he closed it and stretched the elastic string back around it before tucking it away into his inside pocket.

"What happened with Denis when Damian's men came?" he asked when he finally spoke.

Knowing the question was coming didn't make it any easier to answer. I was wiping my eyes before I even started talking and Paul tightened his hold on me.

"I was in my back room when I sensed them in the kitchen. I counted four and I knew I was in trouble. But then I heard Denis shouting ... must have seen them and he came down. I went to the other room for my knife but I was so slow. One of them was down but he was bleeding already ... dripping fast on the carpet. I took one and he got another but by then the blood was running from him. We both got the last one at the same time.

"His legs were failing and I tried to help him down but there was no way I could have gotten myself on the floor much less anyone else so really it was him making sure I landed softly. He showed me where I was hurt. He told me to tie them up tight and call Ray.

"His blood was pooling around my knees already. He couldn't hold his head up so I put my arms around it and held him to me. He said he never really liked the dying part but it wasn't too bad. I blamed myself for being so big and slow. If I was faster he would have been okay. I think he knew what I was feeling. He said I was a good little fighter. He'd see me on the other side. Then he was gone."

The Colonel got me a couple of tissues from the table beside the bed so I could wipe my eyes and gave me a minute. Paul pressed his face in my hair and ran his hand softly over my shoulder.

"No concern for himself?" he asked.

"He didn't hesitate to step in when I was in trouble. His last minute was spent making sure I would be okay. My wounds and my conscience."

"Do you know what I do for the family Anna?"

I shook my head.

"I'm a matchmaker of sorts. I don't put the names on the dance cards but I do decide who gets one. For the most part. I placed Rice here to observe Denis. To earn his first mate a man must prove himself worthy through his actions toward the mate of another. I had to remove Rice early because his projections bothered you. We know what they meant now but then they were assaulting you. By the time Rice was able to control them you and Denis were away so Rice took his book intending to try and find you. We never saw him again.

"Based on what is in Rice's book and what you have told me I have no doubt that a mate for Denis is long overdue. I don't have any say in who he would get and it will still be up to him to make it work with her."

He looked at Paul and me.

"Your son will have someone waiting for him on the other side."

Chapter 63

My father and Alina arrived the day Paul was at Arlington for the service for Denis. Paul's helicopter arrived about the same time I'd given up hope they would make it back that day. He apologized to my father for his deception at my house in the fall. My father found it strange that Paul would be sorry for something I had obviously put him up to.

After a quick reheated dinner Ray volunteered to show them to their cabins and the three of them left together, Ray carrying Alina's suitcase from the car. Paul and I watched them go from the window. First they dropped Alina off at her cabin then Ray took my father down to his.

"Paul," I sighed. "I ... did something when I broke his line from him. I don't know if it was bad ... it just came to me that I could and I did it. At least I think I did it."

"What did you do Anna?"

He didn't look happy with me.

"The piece of his line I cut off ... the part that goes into the future. The part he never touched. I took it ... I used it to bind one of Pilot's gifts to me so I could keep it. It became part of mine. It was selfish, I know. But I don't want to start over knowing nothing again. I kept my ability to read to help everyone rebuild."

"May I?" he asked as he put his right hand over my chest.

I nodded.

"I don't feel anything," I whispered.

His brow creased as he tested it.

"It's really secure," he said finally. "You did that yourself?"

"It felt more like it was doing it on its own."

He put his hand on my cheek. "I'm not disappointed. I've always wanted you as a partner in all the pieces of my life ... not just the pieces you could understand. You won't actually be grown up though until the next time around." Then he smiled at me. "So you still have to do what I tell you."

"Sure Paul," I smiled back.

We watched as Alina came out to wait on the road. I quickly turned off the living room light so they couldn't see us. Ray stopped when he got to her. They talked a while and I could see her toss her head back as she laughed.

"What happens to a son when the father's dies the real death before he's born," I asked Paul.

"I don't know," Paul answered. "Why?"

"I can feel her son connecting himself to Ray already. That's your sister Paul," I told him.

"My sister?"

"Yes. I killed her child's father. All I could read in him was you and Alina when she got here. Now he's becoming Ray's."

We watched as she put her hand on his cheek and he lowered his chin to touch his nose to hers. Then he took her hand and they started walking to Ray's cabin together.

"I'm sorry Paul. It was her I was protecting when I wouldn't talk. I had to abandon her to Damian, leave her to get pregnant. Make sure nobody interfered. I should have known he would have left her the way he did. I hated myself for it and took it out on you. I was scared the men wouldn't understand and might try to keep her from having Damian's child ... and he was Damian's until he died. How could I have chosen between her and anyone here? Gone after one of your men to protect that man's son. Or gone after you. She's my sister too."

Paul put his arms around me.

"I never would have guessed that's what you were going through," he said. "I can't be certain I would have understood."

"He has to grow up Paul. That tiny boy belongs to Camille ... their child will be important. I don't know how yet. I may never know. I just did my part."

He squeezed me tighter as they disappeared down the path to

Ray's cabin.

"We'll protect her and her son. She's Ray's mate now. He's been alone a long time waiting for her. "

"I've known who Alina really is since I saw Pilot."

Paul turned me to face him and tipped my chin up to kiss me.

"Can you tell me everything now Anna?" he whispered.

"Yes," I whispered back. "Now, or will you be my lover again first?"

"Lover."

… *turn the page* for a preview of
The Chronicles of Anna, Book 2

DEADLY DECEPTIONS

By Elizabeth Munro

I had no idea what time it was when a familiar presence in the hall got my attention and had my heart racing. One of Damian's men. Alone. Moving to my room. My panic had me wide awake and I read him quickly. Definitely Damian's but his loyalty was weak, soft. I didn't know what to make of it. My door opened and he quickly stepped in allowing a brief burst of dim light from the hall before he closed it behind him. He stopped at the end of the bed.

"Anna Richards?" he asked quietly.

I didn't say anything right away, I was running his line forward quickly in my head to find out what he was going to do. I saw him standing by the bed. He would give me something then he would leave. I relaxed. I could deal with that and was now very curious what one of Damian's men would want to give me that didn't involve the pointed end of a knife.

"I'm Anna," I answered.

"My name is Jack Roberts," the man said. "I apologize for the timing of my visit...I've wanted to speak with you privately for a couple of months and this is likely the only chance I'll get."

"You're Damian's ..." I said, still reading him.

"Yes," he sounded surprised. "How do you know?"

"His line ... close ... maybe his son." I compared Damian and Jack. He stood there. I didn't care about my manners; he had snuck into my hospital room in the middle of the night. "I don't know your mother. Your loyalty to him is not what I've felt before ... it's much softer, almost tenuous ... doesn't stink."

If this man's mother wasn't me or Alina then that made three mates for Damian.

"I don't know how you can tell that ... but you're right."

"You're not here to kill me." I stated. I wasn't in any shape to do anything about it other than scream for the unarmed nurse if he was.

"No Anna. I wanted to ask you to arrange a meeting for me with Captain Richards. Damian has been missing for months. No word, no body. Our group is big ... it's become difficult to control. There are three of us running it now in his absence and my men are faced with finding a way out or being destroyed. The other two left in charge with me are as volatile as he is. They know we're wavering. They're his sons too but they came along after insanity took him ... or the stink as you put it. I still remember Damian before it happened."

I thought a moment. If he wanted to separate himself from Damian's group it could make sense for him to reach out to Paul. In a strange sort of way.

"How can the Captain help?" I asked him.

"We want out. We're not looking to join you ... we just want to try and have a normal life ... the way things used to be. Our hope is that we can have an understanding to at least watch each others backs. The other two, Soros and Walker, are content to carry on hunting you. We think Damian is dead and they want to make as much trouble for you as they can. They won't move on you without his say so or without being convinced that they'll only see him again on the other side."

He didn't know exactly how dead Damian was. He wouldn't be regrouping with anyone anywhere.

"I know you don't trust me ... I'd like to offer you something to hopefully start building a dialogue between our groups. Walker is in Toronto ... Ray Jackson and his pregnant mate won't survive long if they return there. They've been watching her apartment for a while. He has someone in the hospital she works at. They can't go back. Soros' team is in Calgary ... they lost a man there a few months ago and have been trying to track him down. There are hints of another part of your group in hiding out that way. If they are there and you know of them be careful. Soros is watching and will follow you to them. He's a powerful reader, one of the best we have, and tenacious. He'll never be convinced they're not out there even if they really aren't.

"When they move on you, you won't stand a chance. Neither will we when our turn comes. Cooperation is a necessity."

We were both quiet for a while.

"I understand what you're asking Jack and appreciate the heads up." I told him. "I'll tell Paul what you told me. It's not my call ... I do get where you're coming from."

His conversation was draining me. Now that I was awake I was feeling overwhelmed with what had happened the day before and my interest in what he wanted had faded.

"That's the best I can hope for Anna," he said then he approached and gave me a piece of paper. "Leave a message at this number if you want to get in touch with me. Again, I'm so sorry to trouble you now."

Suddenly his head turned, looking back through the opposite wall. I turned my attention in the same direction and sensed Paul and Ray in the elevator. It must have been closer to morning than I thought.

"Your men are coming ... I have to go ..."

And with that he disappeared back out the door. I lost track of him in the stairwell.

It was only a couple of minutes before Paul came in.

"Hi Paul," I said as I pulled the string for the light above me when he opened the door.

"Hi Sugar," he came over and held me. "Ray's just checking over your chart from the night ... were you okay?"

"Yeah," I said softly. I didn't realize how much I'd missed him or how relieved I would be that he was with me and Jack wasn't.

"Whatever my chart says happened in the bathroom is way out of proportion." I had buzzed the nurse to help me get to the toilet because I was still dizzy even sitting but she took so long and I really had to go so I went on my own. I'd made it to the toilet but must have passed out. She found me leaning over against the wall.

"Okay," Paul said; not sure if he believed me or not. He sighed and kissed the top of my head.

"Paul, I had a visitor."

"Mm?"

I hesitated, knowing that Paul would be out the door and he wouldn't listen until he had failed to catch up to him. If Jack served with Damian then Paul would know who he was.

"Jack Roberts."

I felt Paul's arms stiffen around me. "Roberts ... when?"

"He was sorry to bother me here ... now ... just came to talk."

"When Anna?" he demanded. He let go of me and went to look out the window in the door.

"He ran out when he sensed you coming up the elevator." Paul was running down the hall to the stairs.

"Where is he off to in such a hurry?" Ray came in seconds after Paul went out.

"I had company. I think Paul's pretty pissed about it."

Ray came over to take my blood pressure. I didn't really see the point. The nurses had been waking me up constantly all night to check it and I didn't think it could change much if I was just lying down.

"Company," he said somewhat absently. His switch was set to

doctor at the moment. "Any trouble getting to the bathroom?"

"No, the getting there part went fine."

"So I heard." He squeezed my hand. "Otherwise how are you holding up?"

I sighed. "It was a long night ... can I go home today?"

"Yes, you're doing well. That plus a promise of a week of bed rest and two doctors next door is enough for me."

"Okay," I promised.

"Okay," he sighed. "Anna, you need to think about using proper birth control...you can't count on nursing."

"Why Ray? We decided not to be careful after Camille was born."

He thought a minute.

"If that's what you want then I want you to take a pregnancy test every month until your cycle gets going ... for dating and so we know to step up monitoring your health. Paul said you had cramping all morning. If we'd known you were pregnant you would have been here hours earlier."

He looked away as the hand near his face reached for a tissue then wiped his eyes.

"Come here," I told him and held my arms out. "Thank you Ray, I'm sorry you had to go through that."

He passed me a tissue after he let me go.

"I'm used to treating friends ... its part of what I do. It doesn't sink in until later." He shrugged. "It's just as hard to get through after whether they make it or not. If they don't I have the others to get through it with. I feel guilty even though I know I didn't hurt them and everything I did improved their chances. Sometimes nothing will ever be enough."

"Think about getting a hospital posting with Alina," I suggested. "Paul hasn't talked about resigning yet ... we need the military resources if there's going to be any more trouble from Damian's men, but when we're sure it's over."

"Yeah, I have. I'd go to Toronto if she asked but she wants to be near you which is fine. I already have privileges at this hospital and the one on Reno. Alina is a good doctor in spite of being so young. She won't have a problem getting on where ever she wants."

"If she's young what does that make me?"

"Kiddo," he smiled. "Where did Paul go again?"

"He went after Jack Roberts ... he was in my room."

"What? Roberts?"

"You just missed him," I told Ray. "He apologized for coming here...he needed to talk to me."

"Just talk?" Ray asked as Paul stormed in.

"God damn security Ray, where the hell were they?" Paul came straight over to the bed and took a few deep breaths to calm down. "Are you okay?"

"Yes Paul," I took his hand. "Jack's not a problem for us."

"Apparently not if we're on a first name basis." Paul said sarcastically, then, "I'm sorry. Even if he just wanted to talk that's dirty him coming here."

"I don't know Paul. He'd be in pieces if he went straight to you. Even alone."

Paul pulled up a chair next to Ray and sat down, putting his hand on my ankle through the thin blanket.

"You're right. How are you doing? I'm sorry I ran out."

"I'm okay ... Ray says I can go home today. You doing okay?"

Ray pulled Paul out of his seat and moved him to the one closer to me, then sat in the one by my feet.

"Better now," Paul said. "It's hard when there's something wrong I can't fix. I guess that's why I ran out after Roberts. At least I can do something about him."

DEADLY DECEPTIONS

… coming Spring 2012

Made in the USA
Charleston, SC
05 March 2012